MORAL INJURIES

About the author

Christie is professor of medical humanities at UEA and worked as an NHS nurse for over twenty years. She has written five previous books, including her first novel *Tiny Sunbirds Far Away*, which won the Costa First Novel Award, and memoir, *The Language of Kindness* which was a number one *Sunday Times* bestseller. Christie is a contributor to *The Times, Sunday Times, Guardian, Telegraph* and TEDx, and her work has been translated into twenty-three languages and adapted for theatre.

MORAL INJURIES

Christie Watson

WEIDENFELD & NICOLSON

First published in Great Britain in 2024 by Weidenfeld & Nicolson,
an imprint of The Orion Publishing Group Ltd
Carmelite House, 50 Victoria Embankment
London EC4Y 0DZ

An Hachette UK Company

1 3 5 7 9 10 8 6 4 2

A CIP catalogue record for this book is
available from the British Library.

ISBN (Hardback) 978 1 3996 1307 1
ISBN (Export Trade Paperback) 978 1 3996 1308 8
ISBN (eBook) 978 1 3996 1310 1
ISBN (Audio) 978 1 3996 1311 8

Typeset by Born Group
Printed and bound in Great Britain by Clays Ltd, Elcograf S.p.A.

www.weidenfeldandnicolson.co.uk
www.orionbooks.co.uk

For Daniel

'The individual suffering from moral distress need not be the one who has acted or failed to act; moral distress can be caused by witnessing moral transgressions by others. Moral injury can arise where sustained moral distress leads to impaired function or longer-term psychological harm. Moral injury can produce profound guilt and shame, and in some cases also a sense of betrayal, anger and profound 'moral disorientation'. It has also been linked to severe mental health issues'

Moral Distress and Moral Injury: Recognising and tackling it for UK doctors, British Medical Association

'Act with honesty and integrity.
65: You must make sure that your conduct justifies your patients' trust in you and the public's trust in the profession'

Good Medical Practice: The duties of a doctor registered with the GMC, General Medical Council

Prologue

The party was out of hand. Everyone was fucked. Everyone. I remember the air, thick with the smell of vomit and sweat. There was smashing, screaming, hysterical laughter, a thudding bass, a sticky floor. You can imagine it. The living room was packed, people dancing, a sofa covered in coats, coffee table full of empty beer bottles, pizza boxes, shot glasses. I had to move slowly, weaving, tiptoed, and I went past a couple really going at it, and someone I recognised from class was smoking a joint. He stretched his hand towards me and held my arm as I walked by, clinging on. I shook him off though, that was it, and stepped over more bodies, but he followed me into the bathroom. He was tall, gangly, a bit of a less good-looking Kurt Cobain.

He asked me for drugs. I told him I don't do drugs, but he laughed, and there were plenty of drugs there, I won't lie. A gold-framed mirror hung above the sink and I stared at my face as he kneeled and started chopping up and snorting off the toilet seat. My eyes looked different, which was weird. I'd put eyeliner on. That's it. When I turned around he was laughing and his nose was covered in powder. 'Enough to kill a horse.' It seemed funny. It didn't feel dangerous, or like anything was wrong. I mean I knew that enough drugs to kill a horse was a terrible idea, but it seemed normal, almost safe, warm. That's until there was knocking on the door. Really angry knocking. When we went out, people were fighting. That's when I knew for sure that something really bad would happen.

It turned into a big fight, immature, weird, almost like a school fight, and so we wanted to stay away from it. I saw an arm pulled back in slow motion, the rounded fist, then it sprung forward, arrow-like. I remember wailing and fists and splattering, chattering teeth. And screaming. It moved inside my skin and sat in my bones. Calcified. I wrote a poem about bones once. The pattern of bones, the honeycomb of our insides, like bees. It felt unreal, the whole situation, like I had stepped inside my own poem.

Another scream and then we ran upstairs. All three of us. And that's when it happened.

I looked at their faces at the bottom, full of shock. There was shouting for an ambulance.

Everyone scattered, and I remembered a box of insects my brother collected when we were little, tipping it onto the carpet, and the creatures scuttling to the edges, the dark, safe spaces. I walked towards danger, that's what people always said; to the point everyone is running from. But I couldn't look this time. Not at first. We ran down the stairs though and I could see straight away, he was hurt, badly. He was lying on his back, his head tipped back, mouth open. He was waxy like a beeswax candle. He was the colour of bone, chalk-white, grey-eyed, translucent-lipped, dead-looking.

He wasn't moving.

Everything was hazy then. It was like time stopped and there was a siren and screaming. I remember thinking: *Is he dead?*

There was a doctor there, wearing greens and working on him.

He wasn't breathing. I stared at the red rucksack open on the floor, its contents spilling out: cannulae, oropharyngeal airways, bags of fluid. Doctor things that I recognised. I know doctor things.

The doctor had the boy's head tipped back even further, and I tried to focus on the doctor's rucksack, kit, stuff, and she was looking down his body and counting out loud, *One; two; three; four . . .*

The waxy waney bone boy did not move. His chest did not rise. There was only blood. So much blood.

I heard whoosh, whoosh, whoosh and then someone was pulling me by the hand. Then I heard sirens. Blue flashes filled the room, and it was really weird but somehow in that moment, I had a clear thought, that we are bioluminescent, blue-glowed. Guess I was in shock. Or we were just out of it.

Then there was shouting.

Someone switched on all the bright wall lights.

'Wake up, snap out of it. Please. Please. Oh my God, oh my God. Fuck. He's fucking dead. Fuck.'

And it's like I was aware something was very, very wrong, but I couldn't move, my feet frozen to the spot. There is so much blood in life, isn't there?

Five; six; seven.

The doctor stopped counting, and her mouth was still moving, her eyes straight on me. The doctor. I hadn't even recognised her! I think it was shock.

Run.

And that's it, the truth. All of it. I did exactly what I was told. I ran, and ran and ran.

ONE

Olivia (2024)

Olivia looked at the patient's heart and thought of a rib-eye steak. It was too marbled with fatty tissue, the arteries thickened and stenosed, the red of the blood not quite red enough. She'd been doing this job a long time now. She could almost tell by the shade of red of a person's blood exactly how oxygenated they were, how likely to survive long term, the quality of that life. Olivia had once been dragged into a MAC store by her fifteen-year-old daughter, Freya, who insisted a £22 lipstick would enhance her look, and her life, and she'd stood in front of the red section, glaring at the different shades, giving them all a likely pH reading. Cardiothoracic surgeons never wore red lipstick.

'I'm assessing acid-base balance of red lipsticks,' she'd texted her husband, Dele. 'We need a holiday!'

This man's blood was Antique Velvet rather than Russian Red. He was in trouble. Olivia would fix him up and send him on his way, but she wasn't a magician. She couldn't undo years of bad choices, of processed foods, smoking, lack of exercise, and too much alcohol. God, she thought, she could use a drink herself. She stopped a moment, inhaled through the mask, smelling her own ketotic coffee breath. She hadn't eaten breakfast, which was a schoolboy error, and supper the night before had been boozy and late. She was trying to blot out the panic, Laura's face, her expression, the way she'd wrung her hands together, and mostly her words. *Life will never be the same for them again. Not quite.* Olivia had been anaesthetising herself with Dr Pinot all week since then, lest she wake wide-eyed thump-hearted, anxiety crashing through her system. Exhausted, anxious, hungover and hungry was not a good combination for any surgeon, a soup of risk factors. Still, she could do this operation with her eyes shut, and she often did. Dele said that during her sleep she moved her hands like a pianist.

The operating theatre was full and noisy, but Olivia liked it that way. She played music as soon as the patient was under: Beethoven symphonies, Prince, acid jazz, Little Simz, Philip Glass, all dependent on both her mood and how the operation was going. Silence was rare in this room, and it meant very bad things. If Olivia asked for the music to stop, everyone knew the patient would die, but this was a rare event, with her safe hands. Her hands were tiny. Her dad had always told her she'd either be a locksmith or a cardiothoracic surgeon. Her fingers were insured. Precious body parts and she cared for them as such, making sure to moisturise the skin, stretch them out, not overuse them by scrolling on Twitter. But of course her skin was permanently dry from so much washing, and arthritis an inevitability. She had started embroidery last year, which helped a little, after Anjali had given her a 'profanity embroidery' kit for her birthday which made her laugh and sent her into a rabbit hole of similar patterns, their downstairs loo now covered with expletives in delicate script. A quiet rage, Dele called it.

'Pressure's not ideal.' The anaesthetist was relatively junior, slightly arrogant, full of bravado, a younger Dele. He'd need a few knocks to calm down. He was nodding to the arterial pressure, the wave pattern flattening slightly, the numbers dipping. None of the alarms went off in theatre, it was too distracting and too frequent. They had them permanently silenced. Instead, they measured the weight of the air, the expressions in each other's eyes, the body language of the anaesthetist. Olivia was convinced that the air smelled different when things were about to go wrong, an outdoor smell, not entirely unpleasant. But Dele thought that was claptrap.

Olivia went into autopilot. Her body had developed muscle memory over the years performing the same operations, the same intricate movements time and again, dancing hands inside the patient's chest. The scrub nurse today was Frankie, a pale and thin, permanently tired man who was cheerful despite his dour appearance. He cracked quiet jokes as he passed her instruments, sometimes instruments she never even asked for, as though it was him operating and not her. He'd been working there a long time, and she trusted him, which as far as Olivia was concerned was the single most important factor in medicine. Trust. If her patients didn't trust her, or if she didn't trust her colleagues, or vice versa, then mistakes happened. Quick and precise fingers and sharp intellect were important, but transparency and integrity were the real skills of surgery.

'You're away with the fairies today.' Frankie handed her a scalpel and swabs. 'Need a break?'

Olivia shook her head, looked again at the pressures, dipping and flattening, like radio waves going out of signal. 'Let's get another six units and some fibrinogen. Is the FFP thawed?'

A nurse standing at the back of the theatre lifted her hand. In the other hand she was holding the fresh frozen plasma, and gently rocking it forward and back, like a newborn baby, to thaw it slowly without disrupting the properties. Olivia focused on the colour inside the pouch, an almost mustard yellow, the colour of mead that she and her best friends Anjali and Laura used to drink a million years ago at medical school; Anjali's parents used to send it up from Cornwall. She looked back down at her hands. They were not as steady as usual. She'd noticed that on the odd day: a slight tremor. It took all her energy and focus to keep them entirely still, and she stared at her fingertips until there wasn't even a fraction of movement. A millimetre of error could result in cardiac tamponade, piercing the outer layer of the heart until blood filled it and compressed the heart itself, causing cardiac arrest if not treated urgently. It was a serious complication of heart surgery, and there were others too. Infection, thrombolysis causing stroke, blood loss, arrhythmia, sudden death.

Olivia pushed her hands inside the man on the table in front of her. Covered in sheets and painted with chlorhexidine, he didn't look like a man anymore, rather a collection of parts. It was like looking inside a car engine, opening someone up. As she always told Dele, they were just mechanics or plumbers really. Coronary bypass surgery. Hours before, this patient had been propped up in A&E, grey, sweating, and with the most excruciating pain he'd ever experienced across his chest, as his fatty heart tried to squeeze the blood through an artery the diameter of a child's straw, thickened with plaque. Ten years ago, he'd be dead. In other parts of the world, he'd be dead. It didn't seem like he was a lucky man, sliced open and peeled back, his heart mechanically stopped so Olivia could fiddle around with it, all his circulating blood coming out of his body via vascaths in his neck, and around the bypass machine, a small fairground or waterpark of tubes and wires and large circular pads endlessly turning clockwise, perfusing his blood with the oxygen he was unable to himself, before going back into his body. He was lucky though, thought Olivia. They all were. The NHS might be underfunded and undervalued by the government, but it remained one of the best healthcare systems in the world.

It was helpful to think of this as a man, not, simply, a collection of parts. It drove her hands to be still and certain, her mind to be sharp. Olivia was quietly confident. No nonsense. She had never been a hothead like Dele, who once reportedly threw a surgical instrument in a fit of rage and had a disciplinary process thrown back at him. Freya had inherited Dele's fiery temper. Miles was most like Olivia.

Olivia thought of the handmade card she'd seen next to the patient's bed when she had visited him on the ward, a child's drawing of a sunshine on the front, and squiggly handwriting inside: *Get Well Soon Grandad*, and she allowed images to flick through her thoughts, of this man with a grandchild on his knee, digging carrots in an allotment, slow dancing with his wife in the kitchen. She imagined him having a booming loud voice. She pictured him on holiday, maybe on a Greek island, gazing out at the sea, deep in memories. She noticed the crappy tattoo on his forearm, faded puddle green that looked like it had been self-administered with a compass and ink – a prison tattoo perhaps. She allowed these thoughts to invade her head, until she was no longer looking at a fatty heart, and bad choices, but a life. A human life. Full of joy and pain, darkness and light, triumphs and regrets.

There was a sudden flashing from all the monitors and the anaesthetist stood up. Blood filled the cavity that Liv had created. A lot of blood. 'Fuck,' Frankie leaped towards her with suction, more swabs. A nurse positioned the light above their heads, another began pushing in blood, squeezing the bag.

Olivia was famous for being calm during storms. She knew what she was doing, and she understood that stress simply got in the way of a good job. But something was wrong with her. She felt outside her own body, her own heart hammering her ribcage, her mouth dry, eyes blurred.

She could not help thinking of life outside the operating theatre, the man's life in that moment, this man with an allotment and a wife he ate fish and chips on the beach with. And her life, the perfect life she had curated and worked so hard for, unravelling, opening, filling up with too much blood, a tear she had made in the artery. Squeezed. Compressed. Olivia, confident, capable Liv, who weathered the worst storms and was the safest, most trustworthy pair of hands, was losing it.

It was no surprise. Her head danced with danger. As hard as she tried to carry on, to minimise what had happened, what Laura had told her, the information was like a bomb, ticking away and about to explode at any moment. Or at least, this might be a dangerous fuse that could light a long-buried bomb. She couldn't tell Dele. She couldn't tell anyone.

Her fingers slipped and slid around, searching for the injury, all the while creating more trauma. Her mind raced with thoughts. He would die. He'd die and it was her fault. It was all her fault. She let him die. She was killing him. A murderer. A man dead because of her.

'Olivia.' Frankie grabbed her hands and nodded to the registrar opposite to take over. He was holding his hands in front of him as though being arrested, ready to assist, not quite prepared for this. 'Find the bleed.' Frankie pushed her slightly out of the way.

She stood, steeped in blood, and found herself unable to think, or pull herself together. She burned from her face to her feet, and felt sweat dampening her scrubs, the plastic of the inside of the theatre gown grabbing parts of her body. The room was buzzing and screeching but her head felt muffled, underwater. She heard a ticking inside her, and her hands shook. 'Liv!' Frankie was shouting. The registrar was frantically searching for the bleed, and someone had the internal defib paddles out, and she heard the noise of them firing up. They disappeared inside the patient like salad tongs.

'Stand clear!'

'He needs internal cardiac massage. Liv, we need you.' Frankie put his bloodied hand on her shoulder, nothing was sterile anymore. Nothing was safe now. 'Olivia.'

She heard her mother's voice inside her, *pull yourself together*. She shook her head a moment. This wasn't right. She was behaving like Laura. Overthinking. Steady, safe, competent Olivia was nothing like Laura. She needed to snap out of this. Calm everyone down. Avert danger. Olivia pushed away what Laura had told her. She took a large, powerful breath, and swooped towards her patient's open heart, plunged her hand inside and massaged in time with her internal ticking. It was hard to say where her arm ended, and she began to clear her mind and focus, focus, on saving this man's life. She had his heart in her hands. Literally. Liv willed it to start, and her head to snap into focus, but she wasn't even in the room, she was in front of a fire with Dele, and he was telling her that if you put one person's heart cells in a dish with a stranger's heart cells, they eventually begin to beat in time.

TWO

Olivia (1999)

She couldn't stop looking at the ring. A single carat in white gold. It contained all the possibilities of the universe. Everything felt glittery and shiny. The colours of the flowers, the smell of the sunshine, music sounded better, food tasted amazing. She was too young. Much too young, her parents suggested, at twenty-one, and this was not the right time to think of marriage – mid medical school. But Olivia had never been more certain of anything. They'd gone together to visit them, driven up to Winchester in Dele's beat-up MG convertible, roof down even on the motorway despite rain and cold wind, and Olivia's face was reddened by the elements, flushed and excited.

'Young women's complexions aren't what they once were,' her mother said, before kissing her near, but not on, her cheeks. Her mother smelled, as ever, of Chanel perfume and wet dog. She looked scruffy and immaculate at the same time, cashmere jumper and mud-covered trousers. She kissed Dele properly, Olivia noticed, on both cheeks, and then started making coffee.

Dele had handed her mum a bouquet of hydrangeas that Liv had told him were her favourites, but she barely acknowledged them. She put them on the kitchen sideboard, and while the coffee was brewing filled a large glass with water, put the flowers in and balanced them against the wall, before muttering that she'd 'sort them out later'.

Dele glanced at Olivia, half smiling. She'd warned him about her mum's standoffishness, her cold moods. She put it partly down to her mum having her later in life: she was forty when she'd got pregnant with Olivia, and never really had what she called 'young mum energy'. Her mum and dad had taken her, even as a toddler, to art galleries, and classical music concerts instead of to feed the ducks or the swing park. She'd be sixty-two next year, though looked a decade younger. 'It's not that she doesn't love us,' she'd said. 'But, like a lot of women her generation, she has a hard time expressing emotion.' Dele's mum was the total opposite. She'd met her only twice, in London and Lagos respectively, yet on both occasions been squeezed and kissed like a long-lost daughter. It was hard to imagine her sending Dele off to boarding school at such a young age. Parents were confusing.

'Where's Dad?' Olivia knew the answer. Her dad spent all his time in the office with the door closed, the room they'd been forbidden to enter as children. She imagined him in there, smoking a pipe, his small bowl of cough sweets, his photograph of her mum looking young and vibrant and happy.

Her mum didn't even answer. She often did that, ignored questions entirely and with no explanation. Olivia looked at her and held up her hand. 'We've got news.'

The diamond looked smaller somehow, and less sparkling as Olivia's mum examined it. 'Well, that's a shock,' she said. 'I was rather thinking you'd travel a bit, first.'

'I'm not becoming a nun and joining a convent,' laughed Olivia. But her mum flashed her a look, and the laughter stopped abruptly, as though her mum controlled Liv's vocal cords. She wasn't sure what she was expecting, perhaps concern, or delight, or questions about an unexpected pregnancy, but there was a moment of shock in her mum's eyes.

'Well, we had better get your father.' She left Dele and Olivia standing in the kitchen, and headed for the stairs, before shouting back, 'Set the table for breakfast, Olivia. This is big news. We'll need to digest breakfast first before digesting this bombshell.'

'Well, that went swimmingly.' Dele sat at the long farmhouse table, covered in coffee-cup marks and pen, and a lighter, sandpapered area that used to be a compass etching of a penis, which she had earned the belt for.

Olivia began opening cupboards. Her mum was forever moving things around, 'reconfiguring'. The cupboard above the microwave, which used to contain coffee mugs, was now filled with spices and jars. She lifted up a murky-looking jar. 'Out-of-date apricots.' She held it to the light, to show Dele. It was full of sediment and the apricots themselves were purple and rotten. 'She keeps things forever. Never, ever throws anything away, even when it's poisonous. She'd rather make herself ill than part with anything. *Best Before June 1982.*' She made a retching sound before replacing the jar.

Dele looked horrified. 'Will we be staying for lunch? Or should we stop at The Coach?'

Olivia laughed. 'Don't worry. No chance. And yes, let's have a good lunch somewhere later.'

The larder shelves that used to be full of tins now housed the antique cups her mum used for coffee, and there was a biscuit tin full of Garibaldis. She took out the tins, cups, biscuits and a tiny silver toast rack, then put some bread from the bread bin into the toaster. The toaster that was older than Olivia.

'Doubt thou the stars are fire. Doubt that the sun doth move,' Her dad had a booming voice, a bit like Dele's, and he liked shouting lines of poetry or quotes. He was a big man,

13

always stooping, as though he was worried his head might hit the ceiling, and clumsy. He knocked things over, and off shelves, and smashed so many glasses that her mum had threatened serving him only on children's melamine plates. He wore a house key around his neck on a string after the third time they'd had to change the locks, following a lost key. He hugged Olivia and turned to Dele. 'You know the rules, right? You ask the father first.' His voice was angry, but his eyes were twinkling. That he liked Dele so much had been a surprise to Olivia. When she'd first met Dele, a year before at the doctors' mess party, the night that Anjali christened the Doctors' Very Messy Party, she had loved him immediately. It was the flicking of a switch, before and after meeting Dele, there was no sudden build-up, instead a feeling of total certainty that they'd be together always. She had never believed in love at first sight – until it happened. There was a moment, a split second, when Laura and Dele were laughing at the bar and Olivia wondered if he'd ask Laura out instead of her. Laura was beautiful, of course, and Dele was strikingly handsome, but it was Olivia who had everything in common with Dele. Within mere seconds of talking, Dele and Liv shared a look of total recognition, as if they had lived a lifetime together already. Olivia had wondered how her dad would react to Dele's blackness; hers was the first mixed-race relationship in the family. But there were more similarities than differences between the pair: a privileged childhood, top schools, a love of cricket and romantic poetry, as well as more obscure subjects. When they discovered a mutual obsession with Korean horror films and had spoken animatedly about them all the way through supper, her mum had rolled her eyes and commented that they were like 'twins separated at birth'. They hardly ever talked medicine, though both sat cross-legged occasionally leafing through recent copies of *The Lancet*, a large tumbler of whisky in hand, nodding in time and agreement with certain articles.

Dele liked her dad. 'Doubt truth to be a liar,' he said, 'but never doubt I love.'

Olivia's dad beamed widely, and patted Dele on the back. 'Chip off the old block.'

Her dad was a surgeon too – ear, nose and throat. He scoffed at all but the most extreme cardiothoracic surgery: heart transplants or operations for congenital cardiac conditions. 'Try getting a carotid blowout under control,' he said. Once, as a teenager, Olivia was out shopping with her dad and a person rode past on a mobility scooter, with half their jaw missing. Her her dad nodded at them, leaned towards her and said, 'One of my patients,' adding, 'head and neck cancer is no joke. Don't smoke and don't drink.' After that, Olivia had been terrified throughout her entire teens to even have a puff of a cigarette.

Of course, her dad smoked (cigars, pipes) and drank alcohol. He had retired from medicine following a small stroke the year before, during which he drank Chianti and carried on with supper, famously announcing he'd 'drink his way through it', before her mother called an ambulance and sent their friends home, shell-shocked. 'Nothing a decent Chianti can't cure,' he told the paramedics.

'Stupid man.' Her mum had called Olivia, waking her up, and talked about her dad's stupidity and absurdity for at least ten minutes before mentioning that he was having a stroke and had been taken to the Royal Hampshire for thrombolysis. 'His face was drooped, his speech was slurred, he could barely move his left side,' she'd said. 'And still he was filling his glass up. Eventually he smashed the decanter and there was red wine all over Martha's handbag. Stupid man.' But Olivia could hear the total fear in her mum's voice. They had been married a lifetime. Her mother's entire life had been dedicated to propping up her father, she could see that. She was anchorless without him. He recovered entirely, thanks to the medical staff at the Royal Hampshire, who reminded Olivia why she wanted to work as an NHS doctor. The team had consistently cared for him as if he was their own father, and he was not an easy patient by any means.

'My little girl. Surely you are five years old, and we're making a den this weekend? Or playing *Star Wars*? You're not marriage age! It's preposterous.' He turned to Dele and patted him on the centre of his back.

Olivia noticed her dad glance at her stomach, his eyes no doubt trying to ascertain if there was a grandchild to find out about. 'Dad, we wanted to tell you and Mum first before anyone.'

Her mother had sloped in, and began busying herself with toast and marmalade, putting the butter dish out. Olivia watched her back, as she often had, the straightness of it, her shoulder blades digging slightly through her clothes like tiny wings. Her mum was as slight as her dad was big. She never dropped anything. She put everything on the table, and they sat down as she poured coffee into the antique cups. Olivia watched all of this, trying to see in her mother's small movements whether she was disappointed or happy. She was hard to read.

Olivia held her hand out for them to see the ring. It was a beautiful ring. Elegant, simple, classic. 'I'd have been happy with a Hula Hoop,' she said.

'Don't be so ridiculous.' Her mother began buttering toast but put a piece down and held Olivia's hand up, turning it side to side very slowly. 'Not platinum?' Her mum sat down and sipped her coffee. 'White gold will fade over time.'

'It won't.' Olivia looked at the ring, and pushed her hand into Dele's, before looking at her mum. 'It will change, but it won't fade. We checked with the jeweller.' Dele had wanted to give her his grandmother's ring, an enormous sapphire that jutted out far enough that when he tested it with gloves it ripped them every time. 'You'd never be able to wear it,' he'd said, 'not an appropriate ring for a budding cardiothoracic surgeon.'

'Will you give up medical school?' Her mum nibbled the edge of her toast.

Olivia looked confused. 'What do you mean?'

Her dad patted Dele on the back again. 'A son-in-law.'

'Well, with Dele's work there seems little point in you carrying on. Especially if you're planning a family. You can't possibly have two surgeons in the family. I can tell you that for free.'

Dele laughed out loud. 'Olivia is fully committed to medicine, as well as committed to me.' He lifted Liv's hand and kissed it. It was true that despite being only two years qualified as a doctor, he was working all hours day and night, with an on-call rota that was eye-watering. She imagined their schedules when she graduated, the precious little time they'd have together. But there was no question they'd make it work. It wasn't the fifties.

Olivia rolled her eyes. 'Of course I'm going to work. Times have moved on a bit. I could even work part time or job share if and when we have children. So could Dele.'

Dele made a sound, a small noise like he was clearing his throat. Her parents shared a look, the kind of look that parents shared, and children were outside of, no matter what age the grown-up child. There was a moment's quiet, then her mum stood up and began clearing the plates. Olivia closed her eyes a second, and behind her eyelids she was five years old and it was her grandpa's funeral. Everyone was wearing black and standing around eating small sandwiches and speaking in hushed voices or crying into tissues. Her mum wasn't standing still though. She was dry-eyed, weaving in and out of people, carrying a black sack, tidying and emptying rubbish into the bin bag. Liv opened her adult eyes.

'Lovely news,' her mum said. 'But I must get on.'

Olivia thought about her parents all the way home. She loved them, of course, and as she emerged from her teenage years, and life was less black and white, she tried to understand them too. But although her dad was an open book, her mum remained a puzzle that frustrated her. Dele had noticed Liv looking pensive, her face scrunched up in the expression she always adopted when replaying conversations with her mother, and he'd put his hand on her knee and left it there all the way back. 'You can't pick your family,' he said.

He was right, of course. Perhaps that was why Olivia invested and delighted so very much in her friendships. She had always had friends at school and at church but not best friends, until medical school.

She met Laura first, during orientation week, week one of medical school, in a lecture about fire safety. Olivia had watched Laura wide-eyed, studying the slides of different fires that had happened in hospitals, and the events that may have led up to them. She had put her hand up every time the trainer had asked a question, and stretched her arm high, and she'd reminded Olivia of a child desperate to have the right answers. Olivia couldn't take her eyes off her, the paleness of her skin, her thick red hair. She looked like she'd stepped straight out of a Renaissance painting. After the talk they'd gone to the campus café for a cup of tea, and Olivia bought them both flapjacks.

'I love your hair,' Liv said, as they waited.

Laura winced. 'Duracell battery.'

Olivia shook her head. 'More like Botticelli's Venus.'

'Come again?' She laughed, and looked down at a small dog near the counter. 'Toto, we're not in Kansas anymore . . .'

When Olivia handed the flapjack to Laura she had taken out her purse, despite Olivia saying don't worry about it, and given her the exact money.

The next day, they discovered they lived in the same first-year halls, a boiling hot corridor that had mice, and a sign on the shared kitchen fridge that said 'Stop Stealing Food Thief' and which always contained milk so out of date it resembled cottage cheese. They had both been standing in the kitchen, trying to work out which cupboard space was theirs, when they first heard it. Eee aw.

Laura frowned. Olivia flicked her head towards the door. It would be students messing around, making stupid noises. Some of the other people she had met seemed better suited to football hooliganism than medicine.

Eee aw. The noise again. 'Did you hear that?' Laura opened the kitchen door and they both walked into the corridor. Eee aw. Eee aw. 'It sounds like a donkey.'

A door opened a fraction and a head popped out, a small young woman with black-rimmed glasses wearing a messy bun with two biros pushed into it. 'Hsss. Hey you two, look lively.' She opened the door wider and ushered them both in. 'I'm Anjali,' she said. 'Nice to meet you.'

Eee aw.

'What is that?' There was a strong smell thick enough to make Laura cough. Olivia looked around the room. Anjali had clearly just arrived. There was an unpacked suitcase open on the bed, and nothing else bar a packet of roll-up tobacco on the side. But then she noticed the small bucket of fish. Olivia and Laura stood looking at the fish, both now covering their mouths with their hands. 'What is that?' Olivia repeated. Then the noise sounded again.

Anjali smiled. 'Oh yes, sprats,' she said as if it was a normal thing to keep a bucket of fish next to your bed. 'You have no idea how many it eats.' Anjali opened the wardrobe door.

A penguin. A real-life big shiny black penguin with a tuft of hair and a mustard yellow beak, stood blinking at the three of them. 'Eee aw,' it said, loudly. Anjali reached into the bucket and took a handful of sprats, threw them at the penguin and closed the wardrobe door. She leaned against it, breathless, and nodded at Olivia and Laura. 'Rag-week dare. I stole it but I didn't realise it was a jackass penguin. I mean who knew such a thing existed?'

There was a moment's silence in the room, and then Laura burst out laughing. She laughed so much she couldn't get her words out. Olivia began to laugh too, and then Anjali joined in. The three of them laughed and laughed with the jackass penguin eee-awing in the background. They laughed like – they all agreed afterwards – they never had in their lives.

And so it was that goody-two-shoes Laura and pious Olivia spent the first week in halls wrestling a jackass penguin, wrapping it up in the Egyptian cotton bedcover Olivia's mother had insisted she take to uni, and then carrying it in the dark through campus, like a scene from *E.T.*, all of them making donkey sounds to hide the truth. There was a moment as they left the halls of residence when Laura looked worried and stopped dead in her tracks. 'What if we get caught? I mean, I can't lose my place here. I can't.'

Anjali and Olivia looked at each other, a bit confused by Laura's slight overreaction, her desperation to be a doctor as if her life depended on it. But then Anjali laughed, and they walked on. 'I'll take the blame if we get caught,' she said.

Laura smiled broadly, so Olivia didn't comment that it was Anjali's fault anyway. They released Anjali's penguin back into the grounds at London Zoo, throwing it over a fence onto a bush as gently as possible, and watched it waddle into the night.

Olivia loved them both from that moment on, but Laura seemed to love their friendship the most. She'd had it tough, Laura, and she told them she never had friends at school, not a single one. She'd been badly bullied as a result of her beautiful red hair, which was baffling to Liv. She alluded to the trauma it must have caused her, chipping away at her self-esteem, the cruelty of children. Laura's hair wasn't just any red, but fiery, the perfect colour of a sunset, or autumn oak tree leaf. But Olivia suspected that it was Laura's intellect the mean girls were jealous of. She was whip-smart. The most academically able of all of them. But in any case, the bullying had clearly left internal scars and shadows and vulnerabilities. She was fiercely loyal as a result.

That first year of medical school they formed a solid trio, and by the second year were virtually inseparable, spending all their time when not at university glued together, weaving in and out of each other's rooms. They told each other their biggest secrets and darkest fears, and as well as laughing, did plenty of crying too – or at least Laura did. Her dad had received a transplant for liver failure and was recovering at home, but still seemed to have complication after complication, and needed frequent, last-minute visits. Olivia drove Laura to Dartford whenever Laura needed to go, frequently dropping everything. Laura would get teary on the journey, partly because of worry about her dad, but also because she'd never experienced a supportive friend. 'Liv, I'm so grateful. You have plans tonight. It's probably nothing, Mum was worried, but you know how she is . . .'

'Right, stop the tears. That's not helping anyone,' she said, as they sped towards Dartford in Olivia's once-silver VW Golf. 'Anyway, that's what friends are for. We're best friends, aren't we?'

By year four of medical school the three of them were like sisters, or better. They shared everything: gossip, food, clothes, make-up, anatomy notes, cadavers, secrets, fears, and hopes. They knew how excited Olivia was to be engaged, and how much she loved Dele. It was all so perfect.

'Did it go well?' Laura couldn't keep still; she was jigging with excitement. 'Was your mum pleased? My mum would be delighted. She's desperate to marry me off . . .' She tailed off, and her skin changed colour. Laura's neck reddened often, a mottled neck patch that spoke of slight embarrassment.

'She reacted as expected,' Olivia said. 'Brisk. Bit chippy. Said all the right words but ice cold as usual.' She sat in Laura's bed in between Laura and Anjali, all three of them wearing pyjamas and eating ice cream from tubs with a shared spoon. Laura's was the only room they ever congregated in. It was immaculate and smelled of cleaning products. She was surely the only medical student in the world who had fresh linen and a clean, organised desk. Olivia's room was chaos, clothing choices strewn everywhere and too much stuff. She had trouble throwing things away. Anjali's room was simply disgusting.

Anjali began singing, 'Ice, ice, baby.' Laura laughed. Olivia loved watching them both, how close they were to each other and to her.

'It's so, so exciting. We get to be bridesmaids. A hen weekend!' Laura had spoken of nothing but exams for so long, it felt like opening the window to hear her talk of Liv's wedding plans. She bought bridal magazines and sifted through them as if it was her getting married, not Liv. Anjali was less fussed. She lectured Olivia that marriage was an outdated social construct designed to keep women financially dependent on men, but once she'd ascertained that Olivia was happy, in love, and delighted to be marrying Dele, she warmed to the idea, and teased Liv wherever possible.

'Same dick for the rest of your life,' she said, scooping the ice cream. 'Surely that will get old.'

'Anj! Please. Be happy for me. I've had enough disapproval from Mum.'

'Of course I'm happy for you.' She smiled. 'Dele is great. You're great. You'll make great babies. Twins. Triplets maybe.'

'We could go hang-gliding.' Laura was animated; she was like a young child when she got excited. 'For the hen. Doesn't need to be drunken.'

'I can think of nothing worse than getting drunk with L-plates around my neck,' Liv replied. 'Except hang-gliding.'

They laughed.

'I'll be in charge of the hen.' Anjali looked serious then. Laura and Liv glanced at each other, their eyes widening. Liv knew that Anjali in charge of anything was a bad idea, but in charge of the hen night was out of the question. She loved Anjali, but her wildness scared them all. Laura hardly drank alcohol these days, preferring to study late into the evenings, but Anjali was still a party person. She had no handbrake at all and seemed to be getting worse with the arrival of Paul, who was taking a lot of drugs.

'A hen weekend organised by you would likely end in prison,' Olivia commented. They all laughed at the idea that someone would end up in prison because of Anjali's antics; it seemed both funny and ludicrous. Anjali was wild but she was also what Laura called 'pure of heart'. Laura leaned into that – the contradictory nature of life, despite her love of control and order – in a way that fascinated Olivia. She spoke evangelically about the NHS as if it was a higher power, despite the delays and cancellations. 'In the end,' she told them, 'the skill and dedication of the surgical team fixed my dad's body, the nurses gave him dignity. What a gift.' Her duality and ability to see good and bad in everything leaned her personality to medicine, more than all of them. Laura seemed to be a born doctor, able to hold both life and death in her hands at the same time, all the horror and hope that infiltrated hospitals. Olivia smiled, remembering Laura going through a Tarot phase shortly after they'd all met. *Tower card. Danger, crisis and destruction. But also liberation, change, and resisting tragedy.*

'I'll organise my own hen weekend. Maybe a cottage by the sea, some long walks, a cosy fire, some decent wine, and my best friends. That would be ideal.' Olivia's parents had a second home in the Cotswolds, another in France. She didn't like shouting about it, especially to Laura, but it would mean they didn't need to pay a penny. She hated that most weddings assumed wealth of all the guests. Expensive hen and stag weekends, the wedding itself in an obscure countryside place that required a hotel, a ridiculously expensive wedding list. Dele's friends were all from money. He was planning an entire stag week abroad. Olivia had to remind him that her friends were skint, mostly medical students, and would already be in debt for a decade. But really, it was Laura she was thinking of most.

'Fine. You win.' Anjali stretched. 'But don't make me wear peach.'

Olivia looked at her best friends. She had never felt so full of love as in that moment, wearing pyjamas, eating ice cream and planning a hen weekend. They had their entire lives ahead of them, lives that would be filled with friendship and laughter, brilliant careers that they'd worked so hard for. 'I love you both,' she said, sitting up, suddenly earnest and serious. 'I want you to know that. We'll be friends forever.'

Laura and Anjali looked at each other, then burst out laughing. 'You need to stop watching all those cheesy films,' said Anjali.

'I mean it,' said Olivia. 'I really mean it. Let's always be friends, no matter what.' She really meant it.

Anjali held up the ice cream. 'Cheers to that.'

THREE

Laura (1999)

Laura's mixed large, comprehensive school in Dartford was fairly typical of the times: disillusioned teachers, bin fires, not a great deal of learning, and even less inspiration. Nobody ventured into the library, but everyone went to the school disco, carrying smuggled-in lemonade bottles refilled with vodka. The teenagers were cruel, mostly, and ambitionless. They drew pictures of Laura rotund and spotty, and coloured her hair in with orange pen, writing 'Ginger Minge' underneath the drawing. They passed the picture around until it landed in Laura's lap, and she gulped back tears as everyone laughed. From that moment on she was nicknamed GM, and she had few friends. She ran home from school most days to avoid fights. The risk of violence was real. The girls in her class threatened daily to 'kick her head in'. She didn't tell her parents. Or teachers. Instead, she would cry quietly into her pillow, her dog, Smudge, on her lap.

The day of the accident Laura was in the shower. She heard a scream first, her mum's usually quiet voice, and came running out in a towel, dripping wet. Her dad was holding Smudge in a blanket, his body bloody and broken. 'He was run over,' her dad told her. 'But I expect he'll be OK. I'll take him to the vets.'

Smudge was not OK. The vet told her parents that Smudge's injuries were expensive to fix, and there were no guarantees that he'd survive the operation, so the kindest thing would be to let him go. She begged them to pay for the operation, to let him live. But they didn't have the money. He was suffering, they said. Laura held Smudge's head in her lap as the vet injected him and cried as his eyes slowly closed. It was enough to break a child. But instead, in Laura, it ignited something that hadn't been there before. She didn't cry. She thought of the meanness of girls at school, and Smudge dying, and her aloneness. That night, aged twelve, she announced to her parents that she would one day be a vet and she'd save lives, not end them. She felt better simply imagining it, that she might dedicate her life to helping animals and families like hers. It gave her a focus, a way to step outside herself; helping other girls like her was purpose that she'd never felt.

It was in the CT waiting room at City Hospital a year later that her ambitions evolved. Her dad was having the scan, and the waiting room was full of old people waiting for theirs. Laura, thirteen by then, sat with her dad's plastic bag full of puzzle books on her lap, and listened to her Walkman. Her mouth was dry, as it often was when she thought of her dad unwell; whenever she worried, he'd hug her and tell her he was as fit as a flea, and not to be daft, that he just needed an MOT, is all. And she believed him. She believed him again.

The alarms began to flash above the heavy swing door, and there was sudden movement, a few doctors running, a nurse pushing a red metal trolley towards the corridor where her dad was having his scan.

'Doughnut of death.' The woman to Laura's left leaned across her and started chatting with a man the other side of her, nodding to the CT scan sign. 'That's what they call it.'

Laura turned up her Walkman. But a tall woman wearing scrubs poked her head out of the door. 'Are you here with Vince?'

She heard her dad's name even above the music, and the alarms, and the now loud voices she heard echoing towards her. She ran towards the chaos. Her dad was lying in the centre of the room, making strange rasping noises, and his eyes were rolled back in his head. She stood unable to move, her feet stuck, then she rushed over and held his hand. 'Dad . . .' But he was far away. His face was tomato red, and his neck swollen. 'What's happening?' Laura's voice sounded small, like a younger child's, and nobody answered. Her dad couldn't breathe. She couldn't breathe.

A doctor moved towards them and injected something straight into the top of her dad's thigh, through the hospital gown. Laura closed her eyes and saw her dog, Smudge, close his, and she was gut-punched with terror. 'Hey, are you Vince's daughter?' The doctor had her hand on Laura's shoulder, and her voice was steady and calm.

Laura opened her eyes. Her dad was less red already. 'What's wrong with him?'

'Anaphylactic shock – he had a very bad reaction to the contrast dye.' Another doctor was opposite them, attaching a bag of fluid to her dad's drip, holding it in the air like a lamp. 'But he'll be totally fine.'

Laura let out the tears then, and sobbed, folding over onto her dad, whose breathing was slower and less noisy. The doctor placed her hand on Laura's back, and repeated, 'He'll be fine. I promise.' Laura had never in her life felt so safe.

Laura had worked long and hard to get to medical school, and she would not fail. She was the first in her family to attend university, and the first in her school to attend medical school. Most of her class dropped out at sixteen and those remaining scraped A levels, a few Cs, at best, and went on to apprenticeships. Laura had four As, the best results her school had ever seen, but only Laura could claim credit for it. She was single-minded and determined and now she'd arrived she would not waste this opportunity. Sleep was wasted time. Instead, she sat at her desk, organised and spotlessly clean, her textbooks full of Post-it notes and comments in the margins. She had a chalkboard and a pinboard above her desk displaying a grainy photograph of her and Smudge at Southend beach. She loved looking at that photo, or rather, imagining her dad behind the camera taking it. He was beaming that day and had forgotten to put sun cream on his nose. They'd eaten Big Feast ice creams, and Laura had made him laugh, telling him it was the best dinner she'd ever had.

She no longer ate ice creams, or much of anything. Food was fuel these days, and eaten in a rush, or as she re-read *Gray's Anatomy* or tried to memorise the *BNF*. She spent the weeks leading up to an exam drinking pots of coffee and taking caffeine tablets on top. Her eyelids twitched, but she needed to stay alert, absorb as much information as she could. Nothing was more important than this exam right now. She had to get an A, to maintain her average. Her last test score was not what she'd expected and came as a shock. A flicker of a thought ran through her head: what if I fail medical school? What then? She pictured, for a brief second, the look on her dad's face if she ever had to tell him she hadn't made it as a doctor. She pushed it out. She didn't even want to imagine it. This was her entire life. Her parents were proud of her. She had worked so hard to get here. During her school years she had missed every sleepover, every party, in order to study. She had no real friends back then anyway. But she'd sacrificed her childhood for this, for them.

She studied until her eyes blurred, and her head hurt. This stress was affecting her health. She hardly ate, didn't sleep, and could feel the weight dropping from her daily; noticed her dug-out eyes glaring at her in the mirror, the eczema that suddenly appeared on her elbows and wrists, which she subconsciously scratched until it was weeping, red and raw. Still, she continued, refusing anything that sounded relaxing or fun so she could cram more knowledge into her head. She sellotaped revision all over the shared bathroom until it resembled some sort of anatomy and physiology wallpaper, labelled diagrams of congenital cardiac conditions, Latin names of tropical diseases, lists of obstetric emergencies. Anjali complained that she'd like to take a shit in peace without thinking about fourth-year medical school exams, but Laura didn't want to waste a second, not even using the toilet. Her days had a rhythm. She woke at 5 a.m. and drank a pint of water before her 5K run, during which she remembered anatomical terms, sometimes speaking out loud, leaving dog walkers bemused as she passed them: 'Bones in the hand: metacarpal, trapezoid, pisiform, triquetral. Genetic disorders: gene mutation, single gene or polygenic disorders, chromosomal aberrations, structural or numerical chromosomal defects.' Medicine was a language, and she treated learning it as such. Repetition, repetition, repetition, until the unfamiliar terms felt less alien in her mouth. Until she dreamed in medicine.

It was still dark, freezing. She put on her fingerless gloves and extra socks, then her running gear, and earmuffs. Brockwell Common had been rife with crime and so was locked at dusk, but this morning despite the darkness it was unlocked, and she slid into the blue-black and ran towards City. She looked at the hospital in the distance, chanting her revision as she stared at it as though City Hospital was a shrine she was praying to.

She'd spent her entire life looking at the hospital, from the outside while on the train, and from the inside with her dad as he travelled back and forth, back and forth, for treatment and false starts – *We have an organ donor . . .* – only for her dad to have a fever, or the family of the donor to change their minds. Laura had a recurring nightmare as a teen of a hollow man chasing her, his bloodied liver in her hands.

City was a beast of a building, smoke always rising from the top, people scattered around the bottom, building work that was never-ending. The hospital changed shape so often it reminded her of the Lego she played with as a young girl, dismantling blocks, and rebuilding over and over. She couldn't see them from the park, but she knew a line of ambulances dotted the road outside, forever busy. Breathe. *Penicillin 125 to 500 mgs every six to eight hours.*

She was so engrossed in her mental revision that she almost didn't see Anjali walking towards her, holding a can of beer. She was dressed in a confusing way: an obviously expensive little black dress, silver boots, and an enormous, chequered coat with a Kermit the frog badge sewn onto the arm. Laura slowed down but kept her legs moving.

'All this early-morning running.' Anjali's voice was throaty with booze. 'You need to get a life, my friend.' She laughed and hugged Laura, the smell of sweat and cigarettes emitting from her.

'You know we have exams today? And it's nearly 6 a.m.?'

'I'll be fine and raring to go after a disco nap.'

'Your pupils are a size eight, Anj.' Anjali had the biggest, most gorgeous eyes that Laura had ever seen. Saucer-like even without drugs. She looked other-worldly.

Anjali laughed again. She started to dance as she walked along next to Laura. She was, even by her own admission, a terrible dancer, and looked out of place in a club let alone a park at dawn. She was all limbs and angles, famously clumsy, dropping every-thing. She would not, despite her ambitions, become a surgeon. That was clear to all of them. She'd taken up knitting in an attempt to improve her dexterity, but it hadn't worked. Instead, they all received uneven, scraggly, and mismatched scarves for birthdays. 'It was an epic night, that's all. I am dragging you out next time. All work and no play is not good for you.'

'Was Paul there?'

Anjali spun around. 'We're in love.'

'Yes. You may have mentioned it once or twice.' Laura thought of her own non-existent love life. The idea of meeting anyone seemed as remote as life on Mars. She barely had time to brush her teeth, let alone date. Anjali was a different story. She was in love with a different man every week. This one, though, seemed to be lasting a while. Laura worried he might be bad news for Anj. He was ten years older, and different to all their medical student friends. Anjali had met him at an illegal rave, which seemed like the sort of thing he should have grown out of by thirty-two. There was something off about him, a direct unblinking look he gave whenever Laura said anything. He gave her the creeps. 'The walk of shame seems to be becoming a regular thing with him?'

Anjali necked the beer. 'It's not a walk of shame, it's a proud march of a woman owning her own life. Anyway, he cooks for me.'

'City owns your life. Medicine does.' Laura looked up at the hospital building. She felt cold sweat drip down the centre of her back. A few sirens screeched around them, and there was faraway shouting, the familiar South London soundtrack.

'Speak for yourself. You're taking the wrong approach to all this, my workaholic friend. We won't get these years back, you know.'

Laura was fine with that. She didn't want them back. This was the painful part of the marathon to get her to the finish line. She owed it to her parents. Once she was a qualified doctor, she'd take her foot off the gas. She could relax then, knowing she'd done it. She'd made it. She was where she needed to be. But until then, there wasn't room for fun. There wasn't a backup plan. None. Her whole life had been for this, saving lives and helping people who needed help.

A squirrel jumped down from a tree and shimmied past them. A few people started appearing in the park. Runners, like her. 'Right. I need to get going.' She had to be on time. Laura needed to keep on track. She could not fail this exam. She would not fail. She hugged Anjali and began to jog on the spot. 'Get some sleep.' And she was off.

'You get some sleep,' Anjali shouted. 'Love you.'

The medical school smelled like home. The lecture theatres that were musty and mildewy and where everything echoed slightly, and the scratching of a biro on paper was amplified and sounded important. Even the dissection room, a place of death and dehumanisation, despite everyone's best efforts, was warm and welcoming to Laura. She felt it from day one, that sense of belonging, being part of something, a family perhaps. She loved the hospital, the smell of Hibiscrub and bleach and cheap lemon air freshener, even the bad smells that had others putting Vicks underneath their nostrils, she took it all in. The smells of life and death.

The culture shock for Laura always happened when she went to her real home. Her real family. Her fellow medical students were a mixed bunch, but although they were not all wealthy, Laura had never been around rich people before. Many of her new classmates had gone to private boarding schools, all

33

had been tutored to within an inch of their lives. They had financial help from parents with fees and living expenses, and skiing holidays and cars and trips to summer houses in France. Medicine was a new language to learn, and so was wealth. Even at twenty-one, some of her new friends seemed to know everything about wine, cars, and inheritance tax. They played squash.

Laura grew up in Dartford in a tight-knit community: the kids played kerbies and knock down ginger and water fights out front, but there was always an undercurrent of danger. From a very young age she knew to avoid Pete who was a paedophile, and Big Dave who was in and out of prison for ABH, and flat 65 which was a crack house, and the pub on the corner where the husband beat the shit out of his wife almost nightly. Once, when she was around ten, still in primary school, Laura phoned the police and told them about the pub. 'A man is trying to kill a woman,' she said. A police car turned up and she waited behind the bin storage, fully expecting to see the landlord come out, handcuffed. But the police just left, and it carried on, until one day the woman took a handful of pills and didn't wake up.

'Dad. You home?' She knew he would be. He was pretty much housebound these days. He slept in his chair all day, propped up so he could breathe easier, the TV on as he slept, endless aggressively cheerful game shows.

'That you, Laura?' His voice was yawning, broken into pieces, each word gained syllables: Th-at, you, Lau-au-ra. He'd just woken up.

He was sitting, as predicted, on the chair in the living room opposite the television. Next to him was a small table with a full ashtray, and a large transparent tablet dispenser with the days of the week clearly marked. She glanced over it, made sure Monday was already open. It was. 'You need to lock the front door, Dad. Anyone can come in! Where's Mum?' She kissed his head. He smelled of engine oil and mushrooms. She breathed him in.

'Gone to Jean's. Apparently they're off to a car boot in Grays, or something.'

'Oh dear.' Laura smiled. 'You'll end up with even more crap.' She gestured to the small glass ornaments that her mum collected and spent her life dusting. Hedgehogs and swans and Victorian women wearing pendulum skirts.

'Apparently,' her dad sat up, stretched a bit, 'she's a view to putting things away to get ahead of Christmas.'

'It's January.'

'Ah, you know what she's like.'

Laura walked into the kitchen and put the kettle on. Despite chintz everywhere, the kitchen was immaculate as ever, eerily so. She opened the treat cupboard, stocked as it always had been since she could remember, with different chocolate bars and crisps, a variety of biscuits. Next to the kettle were the teabags and fruit bowl, devoid of fruit bar one tragic apple. She thought of her friends' houses. Anjali's family home in Cornwall, full of books and piles of research and no television but Radio 4 playing everywhere, art all over the walls and a garden that was filled with flowers. And Olivia's. The time she invited her to the Cotswolds, their second home. The house was enormous and impressive, with a swimming pool, snooker table, even a baby grand piano, but the thing that surprised Laura most were the fruit bowls. Two. The first was full of fruits of all kinds she couldn't even identify: spiky, orange and red, angry-looking fruits. Then another bowl entirely full of Granny Smith apples. Olivia had seen her baffled expression and laughed. 'Oh, they don't even eat them, they're mainly aesthetic.'

She looked through the hatch at her dad. He was no longer yellow. His skin, post-transplant, had turned grey, ashen and dry. He was quite changed in all ways. He cried a lot these days. Sobbed for hours, holding a hanky to his face. He said it was the lack of drink that made him soft. He had nothing to dampen his emotions except Horlicks. Laura's mum couldn't handle it; she busied herself cleaning and cleaning, and organising things that didn't need organising and buying second-hand 'treasures': lace doilies, taxidermy mice, posters of landscapes, scratched records with interesting covers. Shopping and cleaning were the only things she talked about. She looked at her dad as if he was a stranger, and Laura overheard her tell her Aunt Jean that she was worried he'd somehow become someone else, via the new liver: 'He's not himself these days, does nothing but cry. That's not Vince at all.' It scared her that he felt everything so deeply. As her dad became full of more emotions, her mum lost hers, as though there was only room for one of them to fall apart at a time.

She stirred three sugars into her dad's tea and walked back out to him. 'How's your medical college? Have you nearly finished yet?'

'Got another year of uni. Then the training programme starts.'

'Jeez. It's never-ending.' Her dad slurped his tea. Made a smacking sound with his lips. 'My daughter. The doctor. Saving lives.' His eyes shone. He picked up her hand. 'Still not engaged? What's the fella waiting for.'

It wasn't a lie. She'd been telling them about Olivia's fiancé, Dele, who they'd all met at a doctors' mess party. It was serious between them, and Dele was lovely, and she'd simply been happy for her friend when she got engaged. Her mum had put two and two together and come up with five, as ever. 'Vince, she's got a boyfriend. I was beginning to lose hope.'

'He's not my boyfriend, Mum,' Laura had said, but her voice was lost in the excitement.

'He's a doctor too. Wait until Jean hears.'

After that it was just easier to let them think that she had a social life. She didn't want them to know that all she did around the clock was study or go for a run. She didn't want them to worry. They both had health issues, her dad post liver transplant had never quite been the same, and that her mum was diagnosed last year with multiple sclerosis seemed beyond a cruel joke. It was Laura's job to make them happy. And then make them proud. If a small white lie brought a smile to their faces, then how wrong could it be? She could save lives. She would. Starting with theirs.

She squeezed her dad's clammy hand tightly. 'No engagement ring. We're taking it slow. I'm only twenty-one, remember.'

His face glowed. 'Well don't leave it forever. I want grandchildren.'

FOUR

Anjali (2024)

Anjali had imagined that sex with another woman would be gentle and soft, less intense. She was wrong. She'd emerged after her first night with Donna a bit battered; she felt stretched and throbbing and electric. It was as if she could feel every cell in her body, her whole being fizzed, and her head was a kaleidoscope of colour. She realised that *la petite mort*, the French expression that likened post-orgasm sensation as something close to death, was wrong too. She had never felt so alive, so connected to another human in a spiritual sense, so connected to her own self, to the earth, the universe, and all things. 'Marry me,' she whispered. Donna laughed and hit her over the head with a pillow.

'You're a nutjob,' Donna giggled, and it was the nicest sound Anjali had ever heard. She looked at her freckles and tried to memorise the pattern of them, a constellation of stars on each cheek. She touched Donna's shoulder, traced her clavicle, slid her fingertips down the side of her ribs.

'Fine, don't marry me yet. But have dinner with me on Friday. That's the least you could do for discombobulating me like this.'

They'd met the week before after Donna moved down from Edinburgh where she'd been working in a hospice, to head up the new cancer centre at City. Anjali had taken a new role as

GP partner and had to have another induction to the trust, and they'd found themselves on a basic life support being updated by a man from St John Ambulance who treated them like idiots, while giving them stupid tips about chest compressions: 'Sing Lady Gaga, it will keep you in time.'

She'd been paired with Donna to run through a cardiac arrest, and they took turns pressing down on the plastic mannequin until he was satisfied they were delivering effective chest compressions to the right depth and in time. 'What a jobsworth,' Donna whispered. Anjali found she couldn't stop staring at her mouth, the way it twitched at the edges as though she would break into a smile at any moment.

Donna laughed again, then suddenly serious, rested her hand on Anjali's cheek. 'I can't do Friday, I'm afraid. Anyway, you were not part of my plan.'

'You have a plan? I admire planners . . . Saturday then.' They moved closer, shared the air between them, seesaw breathing, Anjali exhaling with Donna inhaling and vice versa until Anjali felt even more buzzy. 'Expired air is only 16 per cent oxygen,' she said. 'How long could we do this for, do you think?'

Donna kissed her hard. 'Fine. Saturday,' she said. 'But let's keep it casual.'

Things moved at what Anjali joked was lesbian speed; there was nothing casual about it. Within a few weeks they were staying over at each other's places, and Donna would meet Anjali after work at the GP practice, waiting in the car park with wildflowers and something home-cooked and ridiculously spicy. Anjali introduced Donna to her best friends – at a boozy, sunny picnic in Dulwich Park – and within moments all three were laughing and chatting as though they'd always known each other. It was easy.

Olivia and Laura were delighted for Anjali; after so many years of avoiding relationships since Paul, they seemed to revel in her happiness, bask in it, as though the glow of contentment emitted from Anjali was contagious. Of course, the three of them did not mention Paul. They never talked about Paul. They kept their word to each other, and themselves. He was gone, for good, and it was buried. It was so long ago.

Anjali had never been loved like this. It filled up a hole inside her. They were inseparable, besotted, and living together by month six. After only a year living together, they were talking adoption. Donna was her soulmate. Unexpectedly, and in her mid-forties, she had fallen in love like no love she'd ever known, a forever love, and they would become a family. *A family.*

Anjali linked her arm through Donna's, and they headed towards Herne Hill station. Donna listened to her music through her EarPods while Anjali made the regular Sunday morning call to her parents. Her mum had been talking to her the entire walk from Loughborough Junction, complaining about her dad's snoring, and the price of gas, before asking about Anjali's job. 'I stood on the picket line of the Royal Cornwall with the junior doctors. Told them all about my amazing daughter.'

Anjali laughed and Donna smiled at her, took an EarPod out. 'Mum,' mouthed Anj. 'Being an activist.'

She listened to her mum for another few minutes, describing how hot a day it was during the strike, and that she took some factor 50 sun cream for the junior doctors and a box of Calippo ice lollies to keep them going. Anjali pictured her mum in a high-vis jacket, telling everyone she could that her daughter was a doctor, and that was why she stood in solidarity with them all. She was so lucky to have the parents she had. They took such an interest in her life. Cornwall felt so far away, but they spoke on the phone every week and her parents visited Anjali and Donna every few months without fail, always bringing articles they'd cut out from the *Guardian* of NHS-related issues. Her parents would sit and chat healthcare politics with Donna until the late hours. They loved her as a daughter from the very start, could see how kind and steady and stable she was. Her mum had once whispered to Anjali that Donna was clearly her soulmate. Meant to be. 'This is the one,' she'd said. 'Donna is your person.'

'Send Donna my love. And the others. I expect you're on your way to Olivia's?'

'Nearly there. Have a great Sunday, Mum. Give Dad a big hug from me.'

Anjali put her phone away in her bumbag and squeezed Donna's arm tightly. The street food market was full of dogs and babies, many of them strapped to chests or in backpacks, making it nearly impossible to navigate the market without getting whacked in the face. 'Shall we get a hot dog?'

Donna widened her eyes. 'You never cease to amaze me. We are on the way to a roast dinner, *Olivia's* roast dinner, and you want to eat a hot dog?'

'Just a snack,' said Anjali. She paused at the queue and her stomach rumbled.

Donna laughed and leaned against her. 'You have many magical powers, but your endless appetite is surely the most developed of all.'

It was true, Anjali could always eat, and she had always been skinny. She checked her cholesterol once a month, knowing the demographic of patients she saw who were shocked as she told them that despite their body's healthy appearance on the outside, on the inside their arteries were getting clogged up, and it was essential they changed their diet or risk heart disease. So far, despite the volume of junk she ate in addition to Donna's organic vegetables, and her distinct lack of exercise, she was physically healthy.

They stopped at a stall selling vases depicting naked women. Donna picked one up and looked at the price, raising her eyebrows. 'You can't buy a doughnut in Herne Hill for less than a tenner.'

Anjali nodded at the vase. 'Do you think I have a magical vagina? There was an article about it in a magazine.'

Donna snorted. 'Fuck's sake, Anj. You need to stop reading crappy magazines.' But then she put the vase down, lifted Anjali's hand up to her mouth and kissed it hard. 'Absolutely. You have the magical powers of eating anything you want without gaining an ounce, which makes me hate you. But then you have a magical vagina, so that evens things out.'

They laughed and walked along in the winter sunshine, Anjali eating her hot dog, her mouth smothered in mustard and ketchup, Donna chatting about work, and plans for the cancer centre, and a new yoga class she was obsessed with. They walked on towards Dulwich as Donna asked about Anjali's parents and smiled upon hearing her mum's antics; she really did love them.

Olivia's house was set back from the road, one of those giant, beautiful buildings that people assumed were separated into flats, of which even those must cost millions. But it was all one house, bought on first sight, because Liv said she needed to be next to Dulwich Park and the Picture Gallery, as if nature and art were paid-for commodities. Olivia was old money. Anjali and Donna lived next to Loughborough Junction, the station end, where the alleyway was always full of human shit, and once she'd seen a pigeon and rat fighting over a chicken bone. Still, buying in London with a garden was not a privilege she'd ever imagined possible. But Liv's house was insane. It belonged in another century, where they'd arrive by horse-drawn carriages to attend a ball. That kind of house. A residence.

Donna reached a finger across and wiped the ketchup off Anjali's mouth. She kissed her cheek. 'I love the bones of you.'

Olivia answered the door, beaming as she always did, as though it had been years instead of weeks. Ever since medical school, they'd met regularly, and at least once every few months Olivia invited them for Sunday roast. 'Hi, Liv.'

'Anjali has a magical vagina, to let you know.' Donna took her coat off and laughed.

'Oh, thanks.' Anjali followed behind her and kissed Liv on each cheek.

Olivia winked. 'Well of course she has. That's not news. Come in, come in, you need to take me as you'll find me today. It's been chaos!'

Olivia had a cleaner who came twice weekly for six hours, yet despite this, the house was always messy. Muddy boots lined the hallways, and the teens dropped things everywhere: hockey sticks, rugby balls, hats, coats, violins, scarves; the skirting boards were lined with presumably unsuccessful mousetraps. The two Dalmatian dogs were out of control, and there was a parrot flying around the living room, what Liv called 'an ill-conceived birthday present for Miles'. There were piles of books and research papers everywhere and a large hostess trolley filled with carafes of thick red wine, and whisky, crystal tumblers, cocktail equipment, and an ice bucket.

Laura was sitting on a shabby sofa and drinking a cup of tea. She stood up, and hugged them both. 'Look at you two lovelies.' She was a bit tired; paler than usual. Anjali decided she'd call her in the week and check in properly. Find out what was happening in her life. She'd been so focused on adoption

43

she hadn't checked in with her friends. Laura yawned. 'Sorry. Crazy busy at the moment.'

'How is life at the coalface?' Donna asked.

Anjali put her hand on Laura's arm, gave it a squeeze. 'Don't overdo it, my workaholic friend.'

Laura shook Anjali off. She laughed. 'Work's just fine,' she said. 'Peachy. You know this week we were overstaffed, and resus was almost empty. The CQC rated us outstanding, and we had a huge private donation. They've given us all six-figure bonuses and an extra month's annual leave.' She swigged the tea. 'You?'

Anjali looked between them. 'Oh, I had dozens of thank-you cards from patients this week. Literally dozens. And half of them have acknowledged that their back pain is most likely emotional in origin and agreed to talking therapy. Oh, and the government has given the surgery four extra counsellors.'

Laura began to laugh, a fraction. But then she glanced at Olivia and there was a look between them, something Anjali was outside of. Donna didn't notice, she was busy avoiding looking up as the parrot flew around. She was terrified of birds.

'My favourite women.' Dele walked in wearing running gear. 'Don't hug me, I stink.'

'You always stink,' Anjali said, and hugged him anyway. 'What's new?'

'Ah, same old.' He hugged Donna and Laura and kissed Olivia on the cheek, then began mixing a martini. 'How's life on Hitch?' Dele smiled at Laura.

Donna kept glancing at the parrot, but joined in. 'Yes. Update please. We need to live vicariously through you. God, I miss being single sometimes . . .'

Anjali punched her arm, gently.

'I've deleted the app. I mean, sorry but who has time for all the admin, only to go for a three-course dinner and listen to hours of inane drivel from Ed who lives in Clapham and freelances as a web designer. I'd rather use Flame, frankly. It does what it says on the tin.'

That Laura was able to separate sex from emotion was a source of mystery to Anjali. She was never like that all those years ago at medical school. Still, she supposed, Laura worked too many hours these days to sustain a romantic relationship, didn't drink, smoke or take drugs, and needed an outlet from her life and work. 'You're the ultimate fuckboy, Laura, you know that?' Anjali laughed, but as she was laughing, she noticed Dele behind Laura, chugging his drink. The atmosphere was weird. Donna had turned away from the bird and was studying Laura.

'Hurry up and shower,' cut in Olivia. 'For God's sake, Dele. If you ruin my Yorkshires, I'll never forgive you.' She pulled him away and pushed him towards the stairs. 'Wash!'

Anjali laughed. 'I love that he's a consultant cardiothoracic surgeon and you have to remind him to wash.'

'He really couldn't boil an egg, that man.'

'Kids upstairs?' Anjali dumped her rucksack and headed upstairs, two at a time. The stairway was lined with photographs and paintings, large expensive oil paintings mixed up with children's watercolours from when they were younger. The house was four storeys, and Olivia's eldest, Miles's, bedroom took up almost the entire first floor. He had a gaming station, a king-size bed, a hutch with two guinea pigs, shelves devoid of books but full of the latest trainers, and a giant desk for studying that he used instead for playing cards – poker night with his friends, gambling for coins. Despite his astonishing privilege, Miles was a lovely kid. He was kind, smart, funny and beautifully odd.

'Hey, hey!' She knocked on the door and went in to find Miles and Freya, Olivia's two, and Rudy, Laura's son, all with games consoles. The three of them had grown up together and been thick as thieves from the off, which delighted everyone.

Miles turned around, put down his console and jumped up, hopped over to Anjali and picked her up in the air. 'My favourite godmother.' He twirled her around. He must be six foot three now at least, with a thick rugby neck and baritone voice.

'You shouldn't have favourites.' Anjali kissed his cheek. She liked that he never seemed awkward or embarrassed. Rudy, on the other hand, hardly looked at her. 'Playing anything interesting? Hi,' she waved. Neither Rudy nor Freya looked over. 'OK. Hello.'

'Just the usual.' Rudy's voice was a bit flat, and he continued gaming without looking around. They seemed a bit shifty. What was happening?

'Hi.' Freya half waved without ungluing her eyes from the screen.

Miles and Anjali shared a smile. 'I'll see you later,' she said. 'And leave you to it.'

Anjali closed the door, but Miles bounded out after her. He hugged her again, this time a hard hug, almost aggressive. He leaned to her ear as he did so. 'I need to come over soon,' he said. 'I need to tell you something.' As Anjali peeled herself away, she noticed something in his eyes that she hadn't picked up on in the bedroom. It was fear.

FIVE

Laura (2024)

Rudy had the expression of an abused animal on an RSPCA advert. Laura reassured him, repeating what Olivia had told her, that nobody was in trouble, but his forehead was criss-crossed with guilt and anxiety. Olivia was right. Nothing would happen. There was no need to panic. But Rudy seemed consumed with it all. She'd left for work very early but woken him up before leaving and made him poached eggs on toast that he hardly ate. Poor empathetic Rudy. This had shaken him to the core. She took out her phone and texted him as she walked: *Have a great day. Love you muchos.*

Olivia was as reassuring as ever. She had grabbed Laura in the kitchen on Sunday to help 'salvage the Yorkshires' and told her that nothing at all would happen, to stop worrying. Laura was about to explain how worried Rudy was when Donna burst in and looked confused, clearly aware she'd interrupted something. But Olivia, as ever, had calmed Laura down by then, and they all managed a lovely dinner and catch-up. They'd told Donna they were sharing work gossip.

Shaking her head free of the worry about Rudy, she went into work mode, like slipping on a familiar costume. She pushed open the heavy hospital doors that were meant to be automatic but never worked. The waiting area was full of people already, balancing on crutches, wheeling pushchairs containing overdressed babies who no doubt had fevers, a clearly homeless woman was pulling a trolley bag filled with plastic bags, her oedematous feet bursting through the gaps in her sandals, her flesh like sand dunes. A few doctors padded around in plastic clogs, drinking coffee from large recyclable cups; a group of nurses huddled together outside the gift shop. There were a lot of elderly people hanging around, holding printed-out appointment letters, looking lost. A man pushing an empty wheelchair walked past her, then a porter carrying a small oxygen cylinder and a box that said: *Urgent Bloods*. She weaved through it all, towards A&E, and the offices where the air ambulance staff took handover. She needed to focus. Work had always helped her do that. Work was a safe place. She knew exactly who she was. Here, she wasn't the mum of a teenager, or the daughter of sick mother, or the friend who had kept dark and dangerous secrets; she was Laura, air ambulance doctor for HEMS, the Helicopter Emergency Medical Service. This chaos, such as it was, was her sanctuary, her safe space. It always had been.

She *had* changed over the years, though. She was no longer idealistic, and was becoming increasingly superstitious. She walked through the department to Majors, tapped in the door code that someone had biroed onto the wall next to it, and pushed open the door. Majors was always busy. Patients spilled out into the corridor and there was constant noise, alarms and shouting, the smell of urine or bleach or NHS egg sandwiches. The central station was like a hive for medics, all on the phone, permanently harassed, their dark blue scrubs as crumpled as their faces, lanyards swung over their shoulders, pens stuck into ponytails. The countertop was covered in notes, half-empty coffee cups, an old tin of Quality Street containing only strawberry remnants. The ward administrator, a stern-faced woman named Nancy who was forever dieting, was sitting at the nurses' station. She was nicknamed Cerberus, the gatekeeper of the underworld, and only smiled once a year when organising the staff Secret Santa. 'Burning the candle at both ends?' she asked.

Laura realised she was yawning already. 'Oh, yes. Life's one long party . . .'

'Laugh a minute.' Nancy answered the phone and ignored the relative – a middle-aged man with a tracheostomy scar – standing anxiously waiting. Laura felt her body relax, and the worry about Rudy's state of mind evaporate, temporarily at least. Work was so familiar and so constant and so reassuring. She could count on her colleagues to knock her into herself again. Whatever went on outside these walls, this place was home. 'Just throw yourself into work,' Olivia had advised. 'Let's go for drinks with Anj. Stay busy. I'll do the same.' She had hugged Laura so hard it felt, for a moment at least, like everything would be OK. Olivia had that way about her, of always being reassuring. No wonder Dele always described Olivia as his rock.

A young man, pristine in freshly ironed scrubs, reached a hand out to her. 'Ravinder. I'm shadowing you today.'

Laura noticed the slight raise of Nancy's eyebrow. A secret code of old colleagues. A move that said, 'Rather you than me having a newbie follow you round.'

She looked at him, all eager and keen, a junior doctor and wanting to make a difference. His eyes were sparkling, and he couldn't stop grinning, and gesticulating with one arm. With the other hand he was holding a large Starbucks. 'Seems pretty quiet in here today . . .' he said.

Laura didn't have the heart to tell him that as soon as the red phone started, it wouldn't stop, and he was a brave man drinking that amount of fluid when there would be no chance to pee for hours. She liked busy. Distraction. Medicine was a language to learn. It was also a great place to hide.

'Don't say the Q word,' she said, and mouthed the word 'quiet', and he laughed as if she was joking. The phone rang like magic.

Zafara the HEMS nurse was scribbling the details, but Laura got more information from her face, which changed from hard to soft as she took the call. She placed the receiver down gently, looked at Laura. 'Woman and two kids. All with serious knife injuries. Paramedics en route but the mum needs airlifting.'

The room changed pace, sudden snapping on of aprons, backpacks, grabbing of gloves and various bits of kit. Rav stood in the middle, holding his giant Starbucks. 'Here we go,' he said.

She grabbed the coffee from his hand and chucked it into the sink. 'Let's go.' And then she was off, through the double doors, running a bit, and almost knocked over someone walking past. 'Donna! What are you doing here?' She was flustered.

Donna stepped backwards. 'I'm here to see a patient. First diagnosis and it's not good.'

Laura hardly ever bumped into Donna in A&E. She was always busy nursing in the cancer centre. But too many patients seemed to be getting late diagnoses these days, and arriving in extremis in A&E, often too late. Laura reached out to touch her arm, and give her a quick hug before running off, but Donna stepped back, again.

Donna folded her arms in front of her, and her expression changed. 'You OK? You seem a bit jumpy . . . I wanted to chat about you and Liv on Sunday. What's happening? Are you on a mission, or can we chat?'

Laura felt her face redden, the hotness creeping over her cheeks. Her hands were shaking. Donna looked at them, frowned.

Laura gulped air. She had to get away. 'Sorry, we're in a huge rush . . .' She turned as she ran. 'Sorry, sorry. Catch up later?'

Donna opened her mouth to speak. But Laura didn't wait. She turned and sped away without glancing back. She wanted to stop and find out exactly what Donna had overheard at Olivia's on Sunday, but there was no time. She ran up the stairs two at a time, the stairwell that echoed all the secrets of this place. She shook her head, focused. Woman and two kids, stabbing. The possibilities of what they'd find pounded her insides as she ran. A woman who had stabbed her own kids then turned the knife on herself? Not unheard of. But it was most likely a man, Laura thought. It was always most likely a man. Gemma was waiting at the top of the stairs, doors open, cold air thrown towards her. She heard the whir. There wasn't a single day on this job when she didn't remember the episode in *ER* where Robert Romano lost his arm. Laura, Olivia, and Anjali used to binge-watch every episode of *ER*, fully expecting their lives to follow suit. She pressed her own arms close to her sides and glanced back at Rav to make sure he was too. 'Crouch,' she said, and they ran side by side now towards the helicopter and clambered in, navigating the compact space and clicking seatbelts.

'Ravinder,' she said, glancing at the junior doctor's name badge. 'FY2.'

'Please. Rav,' he said, grinning. He was loving this, she could see. She tried to remember what she'd felt on her first call. But all she could think of was the colour of the sky, and how different it seemed in the air. Thicker, yellow and smoky. The colour her dad had turned all those years ago. She closed her eyes.

'Shall I lead this? I mean, if you're next to me it seems like a good opportunity.'

'Just stand back and take direction.' She smiled to herself, thinking back to her early medical years, and medical school, and her and Olivia and Anjali and how idealistic they all were. But as the helicopter drifted upwards into thick cloud, Laura felt her mind drifting back towards Rudy and the party that had traumatised him. *Another party.* She pushed the thoughts out of her head, snapped her eyes open, focused on Rav. She was getting tired of junior doctors on rotation. She knew it was her job to nurture and mentor and role model for junior colleagues, and plenty of her peers relished that part of their job. But Laura didn't want anyone holding her back. Lives were at stake. In her experience the newbies would spend a few elective weeks with the air ambulance, imagining themselves as future trauma surgeons, and they'd post selfies of themselves in uniform, mid-air, heroic, to Instagram – and then be gone to the next thing. She had to constantly try to remember her excitement when she first started, how pure she'd been, full of hope and devoid of cynicism. She had to remind herself how much she loved the job, even now, the difference she made. 'Just observe today, and if it's too much, wait in the helicopter.'

'It won't be too much.'

'If you feel sick, Juan has some anti-emetics. We used to dish them out in advance, but you know. Cutbacks.' She looked at the cockpit and Juan glanced back at her, half smiling, shaking his head. Colleagues became family in this job. They'd seen each other more than family anyway, and been through a divorce, cancer, and a house fire collectively.

'My friends call me Maverick,' said Rav. 'I wouldn't worry.'

'Well, Maverick,' Laura side-eyed Juan. 'Remember ALS, Advanced Life Support and ATLS, Advanced Trauma Life Support. Airway above everything except exsanguinating blood loss.'

'I did your ALS course last year. Must be fun to teach.'

'Well, it's a lot better than teaching paediatric resus, and APLS if you're vegetarian like me. We have to teach cricothyroidotomies on lambs' tracheas in the meat room. Carcasses everywhere for chest drains. Always three million degrees, no matter what time of year.' She looked out of the window as they hovered a while in the clouds, before climbing above Brockwell Common and higher until even Camberwell looked magical. There was a layer of mist clinging to the tree branches, cotton wool like, protective. Laura got her phone out and started texting.

I'll be home late. I really hope you are OK. Make sure you eat.

'Flame?' Rav nodded at her phone.

She laughed, after all. It felt good to laugh. To be at work and have normal banter with colleagues. *Everything would be OK.* 'It's my son, actually. I'm a single parent . . .'

Rav looked confused. 'How does that work?'

She didn't answer but looked out the window again and swallowed, her mouth tasted dry, a combination of cardboard-metal-dust.

'I didn't mean . . . Oh I'm sorry.'

'Don't worry about it. He's sixteen, Rudy. Best kid in the universe. Not that I'm biased.' She grinned, put her phone on silent, and zipped it into her bumbag, then opened the kitbag. 'Let's run fluid through now, do some math.' The helicopter hovered again, and slowly descended towards a park. 'Brace yourself, Maverick. I have a bad feeling about this one.'

A moment passed over his face, of doubt or fear. Laura leaned over and patted him firmly on the arm.

The patient had cut through a femoral artery with a bread knife. Large chunks of flesh ribboned about her. She had sliced herself up like a loaf of bread. In the centre of her groin a perfect arc of pillar-box red arterial blood fanned out like an elaborate water feature. The rest of her was the colour of chalk. There was chaos. A paramedic was performing two-fingered chest compressions on a baby, a rhythmic tiny crunch with each push.

Laura stood frozen for a moment, staring at the baby. Something welled up inside her throat, a blockage. She swallowed hard. Memories twisted around in the pit of her stomach, eels at the bottom of a river. A baby born much too soon. The midwife who brought her daughter in, wrapped in a pink knitted blanket, and put her into Laura's arms. The expression on Owen's face when he stared at the baby. He never looked at Laura the same way again after that. He sat night after night, a ghostly expression on his face, rocking back and forth. They tried to save the marriage, but nothing worked between them. Still, Laura's body grieved and took, but Owen was gone by the time she found out she was pregnant with Rudy. She was relieved.

'Laura!' Rav's voice had changed and was urgent. 'What do I do?'

She took Rav's gloved hand: 'Stick your finger there and don't let go.' She moved his ring finger towards the torn artery until he'd got the exact spot, and he was inside the hole. She went to the head end, where the woman was groaning, and began assessing her.

Every second mattered. Time had a funny presence during a crash call. It slowed down during the golden hour, the period they had where they might – or might not – stabilise someone, draw them away from death. But then later it would be a blur, a split-second-long memory, to store up in a secret room in her head: her doctor's graveyard.

Laura opened the kit and sat next to the patient. She had lost a lot of blood. There wasn't time to mess around trying to gain access. She took the EZ-IO drill out of the bag and checked for landmarks on the upper outer quadrant of the woman's shoulder, pressing her fingertips gently as though the woman's bony prominences were piano keys. She thought of the woman in anatomical terms now, not as a whole self but split into landmarks and chemical processes. It was better to think of her patients as a collection of parts than a whole human, with a life. *Palpate the greater tubercle of the proximal humerus.* And *look for signs of disseminated intravascular coagulation* sounded like difficult language, but it was easier to summon medical terms than to think of this woman as a mother, or glance at the baby, or imagine herself in this situation. Or worse, remember things. Imagine it was her baby. *Their baby.* Excess empathy in medicine could be dangerous for patient and clinician. But still, she noticed a small, pale blue blanket in her peripheral vision, smudged with dark red blood.

Rav looked up. He was pressing his body over the woman's leg and had stemmed the blood. He was saying something, but Laura zoned him out as she drilled into bone. The noise of the drill was replaced by a satisfying crunch. She took out a bone marrow sample, then began pushing in fluid via giant 50 ml syringes. She looked up, but too late. Ravi's eyes had disappeared into the back of his head, and he was keeling over on top of the patient. His hand fell away from the pressure and the artery began to spew blood. He fainted on top of her leg until both the patient and Rav were both painted red. Laura dropped the 50 ml syringe and felt for the artery, pushing her hand as quickly as possible, as hard as she could.

'Some help please!' she shouted. 'I need an arterial tourniquet.'

She managed to slide Rav off the woman and shove him away. He half opened his eyes, let out a massive sigh. 'Oh God.'

'Welcome back,' said Laura before pausing, then adding, 'Maverick.'

'Straight to theatres.' They manoeuvred the trolley through the hallway, the defibrillator pads attached to the patient already. Laura didn't want to have to try and resuscitate her in the lift. The lifts always broke down. There was a forever queue of people waiting outside, to stop at each floor. She used the porter lifts for emergencies like this, but even then, there was no guarantee they would not stop mid-floor, and they'd be stuck in a lift managing a cardiac arrest. All those Latin terms she memorised at medical school, and yet it was the practical details like this that were far more useful to her job: how to find the lift key. How many people died in the NHS due to broken lifts? But this time they were lucky. Theatres was on the first floor next to intensive care, and the team were waiting in the anaesthetic room.

Laura was covered in blood. She heard Rudy's voice whisper inside her, 'There was so much blood,' and shook it away. They moved the patient across on the transfer board and the emergency alarms began shrill ringing.

Peter turned all the alarms to silence in succession. First rule of anaesthetics, she often heard him say. He began to work, and Laura dropped back, breathing heavily. 'Thanks, hope to see you at the ethics meeting later,' he said. Laura nodded and stepped back. Her job was done. She had saved a life, most likely, or at least stabilised a patient long enough to have a chance at life. There was a feeling that filled her up as she washed her hands and forearms before waving at Peter and walking back out of the theatres.

Rav stood next to her, a look of awe on his face. 'You were incredible. What's an ethics meeting?'

'Ah, it was a team effort.' Laura smiled. 'Ethics meeting? You know, the grey areas between right and wrong. Basically, a room full of medical overthinkers.'

'Sounds intense.' Ravinder raised his eyebrows.

'It is! Which is probably why I love it . . . Right. See you tomorrow, 7 a.m.'

'You mean today,' said Rav, after pulling his phone out of his pocket and glancing at it. 'See you in literally five hours.' He was beaming with wonder.

Laura didn't have the excitement he did. The weighty questions that haunt doctors at the end of each day, follow them home, arrived in her head. Had she done all she could? Was there something she could have done better? Did she make all the right calls? She understood that the real trauma facing this family was not today, on the scene. She would not find out if the baby had made it, likely not even ask about the woman. It was a dangerous game to follow up patients after the initial phase, to see what had happened to them, if they'd lived or died or were still between spaces.

But there was another patient she needed to check on. She didn't want to. She had to be back at work in a matter of hours and needed to get home to see her mum, cook in advance for Rudy. It was acutely painful, and potentially dangerous too. But she had to know how sick he was, after one of those teenage parties where things can and do go catastrophically wrong. She understood that too well. The past felt so dangerously close. Laura walked the theatre corridors and headed towards the intensive care unit.

SIX

Anjali (1999)

You could hear a pin drop. The three of them stood side by side in the viewing area in the theatre eaves, all wearing scrubs, and masks and small net caps, and ill-fitting, borrowed clogs on their feet. 'Feels like the first day of big school,' Anjali whispered to Laura, who smiled with her eyes. Olivia ignored them both, she was concentrating so hard on the surgeons below. A heart–lung transplant. That they'd been allowed in to watch, their supervisor told them, was a miracle. Olivia had quietly begged, she was very persuasive, Anjali noticed, and somehow, they'd slipped on to what Anjali called 'the most exclusive guest list in London'. Laura, in typical Laura fashion, had gone to the ward to visit the patient, and find out about the person inside the body. But Anjali and Olivia just wanted flesh. Laura had returned to tell them he was an estate agent and played golf and had suffered with heart failure for many years, and wide-eyed, said she hoped this would give him a few more years with his family. Meanwhile, Anjali and Olivia were more interested in the ECG that their supervisor had shown them. 'Look at the left axis deviation!' Olivia said. 'That's the most impressively prolonged QT interval I've ever seen.'

The surgeon's hands danced below them, and the three friends watched as the hours fell away. Anjali's parents had taken her to the theatre a lot growing up, as well as to music concerts and art galleries. But this was the best show she'd ever seen. She'd struggled working out which field of medicine was right for her. Of all the possibilities, Anjali never felt like a natural fit in any particular speciality. There were gazillions of specialities, from dermatology to plastics, paediatrics to ophthalmology. Despite her previously talking about possibly becoming a surgeon, she had wondered if academic psychiatry might be an option, or pathology, or research, but watching this operation she understood Olivia's passion, her single-minded love of surgery. Anjali found her own hands moving in time with the surgeon's, and imagined how it must feel, to touch somebody's insides. There were video screens dotted around the room, and surgeons from around the world were watching, and learning technique. The lead surgeon was renowned for being the best heart transplant surgeon in the world. They were very lucky to be watching, the scrub nurse kept telling them. The patient was covered in drapes and painted copper with Betadine, and almost resembled a butchered animal, a carcass of sorts, emptied of humanity for the course of the operation as though during surgery a person's soul was given over to the surgeon as well as their body. It was a philosophical mind-fuck. Anjali was hooked.

'I'm definitely going to be a surgeon,' Anjali said. 'I know I said it before, but I really mean it now. No question.' They had stayed up all night watching the transplant, despite it being moving day the next day, and instead of feeling tired Anjali had never felt wider awake. 'I mean it.'

'Join the club.' Olivia had the window wide open. 'It was incredible, wasn't it?'

Laura was driving the van containing all their possessions. It smelled of vomit and the engine kept cutting out, but Laura had borrowed it for free from a cousin in Dartford. 'I'll stick to A&E. But it was amazing. I'm going to pop into intensive care to see him next week.'

Anjali laughed. 'He won't even know who you are. I mean can you imagine anyone else in that operating theatre getting to know the patient? Aside from the people who must, I mean.'

'It feels like the ethical thing to do. He consented to have medical students watch the operation, so it's morally right that we thank him.'

'She's right,' said Olivia. 'I'll come with you.' She leaned her head out of the window a bit.

Anjali laughed again. 'I'll bet you any money you are more interested in his scan results than his golfing stories.'

They arrived in Camberwell and slowly began unloading the van of boxes. The first thing Anjali unpacked was a framed certificate from the Butlin's Holiday Camp Make Us Laugh Talent Contest that she'd won aged five, with a joke about a frog. 'First place,' she said to Olivia, who suggested that the certificate would be better placed in Anjali's room than the living room. 'I'm proud of this.' Olivia rolled her eyes, but Laura smiled.

'We know.' Laura was unpacking a box that was carefully labelled like all her boxes. This one said: *kitchen equipment* and contained all the things that no student ever needed: a garlic press, a lemon squeezer, a handheld whisk. Laura spent rare days off trawling charity shops for unwanted goods.

'What's that?' Anjali held up a small Tupperware container full of metal.

'Oh, they're knives of different sorts.' Laura opened the box and pulled out what appeared to be an unusually thick butter knife. 'This is designed specifically for jam,' she said. 'What can I say? I like knives.'

'Clearly! What's the difference between a jam knife and an ordinary knife?' Olivia was busy sellotaping the ECG of the heart transplant patient to the back of the door. 'I still can't get over the QT interval. It's quite beautiful.'

'Case in point. Only you could see cardiac test results as art, Liv.' Anjali laughed.

Laura stood staring at it a long time, then wrote on a piece of paper and sellotaped that next to it:

In examining disease, we gain wisdom about anatomy and physiology and biology. In examining the person with disease, we gain wisdom about life. (Oliver Sacks)

The three of them shared a smile. They complimented each other, pulled each other up if they were out of line, their friendship making better versions of each of them. It felt extraordinarily precious. Anjali put up a framed photograph of herself holding the jackass penguin from the night they first met; both Anjali and the jackass penguin appeared to be smiling. They stood in front of the photograph a few seconds, arms linked, tired but full of happiness and excitement.

Laura continued pulling things, Mary Poppins-like, out of her carefully organised box. They spent the morning turning the magnolia blankness into something homely. By the time lunchtime arrived the walls were covered with Robbie Williams posters that Laura insisted were relevant, and Olivia's art and Anjali's elaborately framed abstract art. They decorated the ledge that spanned the top of the room with wine corks that they'd collected the first three years of medical school, each cork written on with biro to mark the occasion:

Laura 21 birthday
Olivia first argument with Dele
Anjali hair of the dog
The Venue night (Beatles tribute)

Anjali had loved the start of that night, their first proper night out, when she'd made them all eat an entire vodka jelly before leaving halls – despite Laura's protests – and queued outside the New Cross Venue for an hour, feeling the effects of the jelly slowly kick in until, by the time they were admitted, they were legless drunk, even Laura, who jumped onstage and high-fived the fake Paul McCartney. But then Anjali had woken in some random guy's bed, full of semen and self-loathing, and had to get the morning-after pill in A&E. Laura had waited with her, holding her hand, and given her salt and vinegar crisps. That evening, Olivia had come and sat on Anjali's bed and stroked her hair. 'You can't give consent when you're that drunk,' she'd whispered. Anjali had vomited all night into a saucepan. The following morning Laura and Olivia were both there either side of her, offering to report the random guy she'd slept with. Anjali had assured them she'd followed him home, not been taken, and aside from a thumping headache, she had zero regrets.

It was getting dark by the time the unpacking was finished and the three of them collapsed on the second-hand sofa, a box of wine between them, three mugs. Lack of money had moved them away from corks. 'Our first home,' Olivia said. 'The adventures we will have here.'

'Speaking of adventures' – Anjali glanced at her watch – 'I have clinical tomorrow. Care of the Elderly. Apparently, I'm to shadow the nurses to learn basic obs. Feels like a waste of time. I mean, one minute heart transplant, next minute wiping someone's arse.'

'At least it's useful, providing dignity.' Laura took a small sip of wine. 'I'm spending all day chasing blood results. Nothing works. It takes me all morning to log in to the computer.'

Olivia smiled at them both. 'It's so exciting. Imagine, in a year we'll be qualified doctors. One year!'

Anjali opened her eyes wide. 'Poor patients.' She laughed but was only half joking. She felt ill-prepared for any job in medicine. The high of watching the operation had long gone, and she found herself questioning surgery as a speciality. The training to follow was even more years than they'd done already, and there was little to no chance of a life outside. They were near the finish line. So near. And yet Anjali had the feeling that she was moving further from, not nearer to, what medicine meant. She could not imagine herself as a doctor in a year. She found it hard to imagine herself as a doctor at all. Still, it was too late to turn back and change her mind now. Much too late.

Care of the Elderly smelled so strongly of shit that Anjali had to swallow a mouthful of sick. This is not where she'd be working. She needed to work somewhere dynamic. She was a self-confessed adrenaline junkie, always had been. She remembered going to Thorpe Park as a young girl, and sneaking onto the scariest ride, despite being way underneath the height restrictions. It had a thick black bar that came over her head and clamped down, the thickness of a steering wheel, but Anjali was so small, and slight, that when the ride spun upside down, she had almost slipped out, and the teen boys sitting either side of her held her shoulders and screamed with the force of it all.

'You're shadowing me today. My name is Ivy.' A healthcare assistant with rheumy eyes who looked way past retirement age herself stood in front of Anjali. Anjali looked behind her at the ward round, a group of white-coated new doctors surrounding the consultant and nurse in charge, all peering into the bed at an elderly woman. The patient looked afraid and terribly small, as though the bed was swallowing her. Her skin matched the sheets: pale and thin, with unidentifiable faint stains on it.

'You can do the obs in bay five, then help with washes.' She pushed the machine in front of Anjali. 'Do you know how to use this?'

Anjali nodded. She'd used the Dynamap machine a million times already. It was the old-fashioned sphyg that was more challenging: this machine you simply wrapped around a patient's arm, pressed a button, then hey presto it gave both blood pressure and pulse readings, which Anjali had read were more accurate than the sphyg and stethoscope method that relied on human interpretation anyway.

'Off you go then.' Ivy waved her towards the bay where six beds contained six impossibly elderly women. She pushed the BP machine to the sink and put on an apron, washed her hands, and then made a start. Most of the women startled as she called their names, written on the whiteboards above their heads: Mrs Wilson; Mrs Grav; likes to be known as Petal. But when Anjali came to Mrs Bannister, she didn't rouse at all. There were hearing aids next to the bed. She gently tapped Mrs Bannister's shoulder, but there was no response.

Anjali leaned close to her ear and shouted, 'Mrs Bannister, I'm the medical student. I'm here to do the obs.' Still, no response. She looked around the bay at the impossibly elderly women, all either asleep with their heads tipped back, or awake simply staring at the wall. She had drawn the short straw for real. Laura was on clinical placement in A&E, and Olivia was on surgical rotation. Meanwhile, she was here, trying to wake up old people to do blood pressures, which was as difficult as pressing a button on a machine. She'd never imagined medicine as boring, but it often was. Medicine was far less about intellect and saving lives and being a hero, and much more about checking expiry dates of equipment and filling in unnecessary forms. Today medicine wasn't even about medicine; she was doing the job of a healthcare assistant, which Anjali believed anyone with a pulse could do. She sighed and wheeled the Dynamap towards Mrs Bannister, pulling her arm out from the covers. She didn't stir. She reminded Anj a bit of her grandmother, who had famously slept through a war. 'I'm going to do your blood pressure, Mrs Bannister.' She wound the cuff around Mrs Bannister's stick of an arm, pressed the button on the machine, and scribbled down 14 on the chart respiration box as she waited. 'First rule of medicine,' Dele had told the three of them, as they stressed about their clinical rotations. 'Everyone's resps are fourteen, don't waste a precious minute counting.'

Beep beep beep. The familiarly annoying failure alarm on the machine. Anjali sighed. She could see Ivy in the distance with her hands on her hips, staring at her. She smiled and waved. Kill 'em with kindness. 'Mrs Bannister, I'm so sorry but I'll need to do the blood pressure again, the machine's not working.'

'Bloody NHS,' the woman in the next bed suddenly perked up and started shouting. 'Bloody NHS!' Anjali made a shushing sound, but it seemed to only antagonise her. 'Fucking NHS. Fucking Tony Blair.' She started waving her arms around as Anjali wheeled the machine out of the bay.

'Causing a ruckus.' Ivy was checking dates on the crash trolley kit.

'Sorry. She seems pretty angry. And political. Also, the BP machine isn't working.'

Ivy held up a bag of saline. 'This reminds me of winning a goldfish at the fair one year,' she said.

Anjali stared.

'Well don't stand there: go to the ward next door and ask to borrow theirs. Late obs means late washes means late drugs rounds means critical incident form and I'll be late for bingo.' She turned back to the trolley and began aggressively ticking a list.

Borrowing equipment sounded straightforward but it never was. Anjali stood waiting for the nurse in charge to give her a receipt due to 'non-returning of ward items', and a half-an-hour window after which she'd 'personally come and find you'. Anjali had smiled sweetly and pushed the machine back to Mrs Bannister, who was still conked out. The woman in the next bed was asleep too – no doubt exhausted from the shouting.

It was not her day. She pressed the button twice, and triple-checked the cuff placement, and again, *beep beep beep.*

She gently unwrapped the cuff from Mrs Bannister's arm without waking her, and pushed the machine out of the bay area. Ivy had moved on from checking the crash trolley and was in a side room wiping down an empty bed. 'This one's not working either.' Anjali sighed. 'Nothing is working. I'll take it back and find the sphyg.'

Ivy stopped scrubbing and froze. 'Whose blood pressure were you trying to get?' She turned her head slowly towards the door.

'Mrs Bannister. She's got her hearing aids out, and she's asleep so I didn't disturb her at least but it's really annoying and, honestly, I don't think I'm actually learning—'

Ivy dropped the cloth, jumped from the bed, and ran, leaving Anjali standing open-mouthed, watching her move like an Olympic sprinter towards the bay. She walked quickly after her, still pushing the machine. 'What's happening?'

But Ivy was counting. She had Mrs Bannister's bed pulled out, and had tipped her already tipped-back head even further and was looking down the front of her chest:

'Eight, nine, ten.' She pulled the red alarm behind her, and everything began screeching. 'Cardiac arrest, bed five.'

Time slowed down. Anjali stood rooted to the ground as the crash team zigzagged past her, each person surrounding Mrs Bannister, Ivy at the heart of her, pushing down with her thick arms on Mrs Bannister's chest, the audible snapping of ribs as she did so. A doctor was trying to get a line into her foot, unsuccessfully, another attaching defib pads, only to pause the chest compressions and announce, *Asystole.*

Anjali looked at the flat line on the monitor, and at Ivy's face, and she knew at once there'd be no coming back from this, for Mrs Bannister, or for her.

Laura held her and rocked her as though she was a baby, as Anjali sobbed. 'She was fucking dead. Dead! I didn't realise. Do no harm! Do no harm!' she wailed. After what seemed like hours, she'd cried all the tears inside her, and was dry crying, every now and then taking a deep breath, and imagining Mrs Bannister's last. Had she died just before she got there? Had she died ten hours earlier? How could she be so stupid. How? Two blood pressure machines!

'It was the first epic mistake,' said Laura, 'of many, many more. That's all medicine is. Learning from mistakes. Trying not to accidentally kill someone.'

There was a beat. A short pause between them, then Anjali sighed. 'I'll surely get the sack. Surely! No wonder she had no blood pressure. She was fucking dead.'

Laura giggled then. 'I'm sorry, Anj, but you won't get the sack, I promise. Promise, promise. You didn't kill her, after all.'

Anjali sat up a bit and separated from Laura. They sparked with static. 'Oh, God, Laura. I wrote her respirations down: fourteen! Fourteen made-up breaths. I'm not cut out to be a doctor.'

Laura covered her mouth, and tried to cover her smile, with her hand. 'Everyone makes up resps. Just apologise, tell the truth, and hold your hands up. You'll be fine.'

'Sounds like terrible advice,' Anjali exhaled. But she listened to Laura. They were the same age, but Laura seemed a decade older, and much, much wiser. 'I mean, I wanted to be a surgeon yesterday and now I can't even recognise a dead person, let alone save them. I should give up and sell homemade earrings at the market . . .'

'Write a letter to the team, and to her family. A letter is always a good thing. I promise the more honest you are, the less trouble you'll be in.'

Anjali looked at Laura; honest, straight, hard-working Laura. She'd never have made numbers up on an observation chart. 'Think I'll give the letter a miss, but I'll 'fess up for sure. You're right. I didn't kill her. She just didn't have a blood pressure. Because she was dead.'

'She had a respiratory rate of fourteen, though,' Laura said, her eyes twinkling with the gallows humour they were so quickly developing.

'A miracle,' said Anjali. She hugged her friend. Laura made her feel better about everything. Even this. Steady, calm, wise, sensible Laura, who never made Anjali feel bad, even though she was so good.

Still, Anjali suddenly felt very small, and very lost. She cancelled a date with Paul, and he was cross about it, but all she wanted to do was go to bed. When she closed her eyes to sleep, she dreamed of Kos, the place her parents took her on holiday, to the Hippocrates Foundation, a neat building in beautiful countryside surrounded by neon pink bougainvillea and the thick smell of pine. Her dad had taken her into a room that was an old apothecary and was talking in a loud voice about the origins of aspirin, but Anjali stood reading the Hippocratic oath on the wall, *primum non nocere*. When he'd come out and found her, he patted her on the back, and said, 'You'd make a terrific doctor, daughter of mine.' She thought about how her dad had so wanted to study medicine as a boy, but instead he had to work three jobs before eventually getting to university to become a pharmacist. He never once complained. For a moment, Anjali half woke thinking she could hear her dad's voice, or the sound of the Latin, but it was totally silent, and in the dark all she could think of was Mrs Bannister. And regrets.

SEVEN

Laura (1999)

She didn't mean to cheat. She had been awake for three days, powered by coffee and anxiety, creeping out of the shadows of her bedroom only to refill her cup, or grab a piece of toast. Her head swirled with information. It throbbed at the temples, as if waiting to burst. Aneurism, she thought, *caused by athero-sclerosis, high blood pressure, occasionally wounds, infections.* She muttered to herself constantly, a strange thing, living not in the real world but inside the pages of her textbooks. She fell asleep briefly and woke with her face lying down on a book, the ink marking the side of her cheek, a tattoo of medical jargon that made Anjali laugh hysterically and Olivia adopt a look of concern before gently washing it off with a facecloth. 'It's not healthy, Laura. You need fresh air. Come for a walk?'

Laura shook her head and felt tears fill the back of her eyes. She wouldn't let them out. There was no time for crying. 'I can't remember everything. I know I'll fail. I know it.'

Olivia stroked her back gently. 'You are a straight A student. You never fail. Honestly, we're worried about you.'

Laura knew they were watching her. They did this, the three of them. When one of them was struggling – emotionally, physically, with work or relationships or family – the others banded round. She heard Olivia and Anjali whisper outside her room before knocking, to see if she wanted to take a walk or a drink or, once, to suggest a spa day, as though it was something all medical students did.

But Laura didn't want to leave her room, except to go to the library, and she carried on studying, long days and nights of cramming revision. The exams were always stressful but for some reason this felt worse than usual. She felt like she was letting everyone down – her parents, her best friends, herself. Insomnia was ever present and at four or five in the morning, the witching hour, Laura would look at the ceiling and imagine herself making mistakes, a future doctor with unsafe hands, unable to save lives, helpless. At dawn, when the first birds began chirping, she'd turn her lamp on and force her eyes to focus on textbooks. The harder she studied the more likely it was that she'd save lives. Her mum and dad's faces flashed in front of her like fireflies. She didn't want a life in Dartford with a trade, like her school peers. She wanted to run a million miles from home, and towards safety. Medicine, for Laura, was about saving people's lives, including her own.

She got herself dressed somehow and went to find her tutor. She'd ask for an extension. Better than failing. It was in her tutor's office that she saw the paper. It was sitting clearly and openly on the desk, Final Year MCQs Answer Sheet. Her brain flicked through various scenarios. Her tutor wasn't there. Nobody except Olivia knew she had gone to see her. There would be no way anyone would find out. She'd studied harder than anyone she knew. She understood it was wrong, but she knew in her bones that if she didn't take this chance, she would fail her course and fail her parents. She would never be a doctor. Never. But she couldn't do it. She looked at the test paper, right in front of her, the guaranteed chance that seemed to be offering itself up. She closed her fists. She pictured her tutor, a warm and homely sixty-year-old woman who wore bright red lipstick and colourful ponchos and called Laura her star pupil. She was not a cheat.

She closed the door behind her and was walking away, down the corridor back to halls when Olivia came running towards her. Olivia never ran. 'Laura, I've been trying to find you. Laura.' She stopped in front of her, taking large gulps of air.

'What's up? You look like you've run a marathon.'

Olivia stood, reached her hands out and held the sides of Laura's arms. 'It's your dad.'

Laura stood perfectly still. She felt outside her own skin looking down on them, two young women in the medical school she loved, getting stressed about the exam that afternoon. She hovered a while in the air outside her own body, everything in sharp, damning focus. Her dad.

'Did you hear me? Laura, you need to get to the hospital.' Olivia pulled her by the arm, and she felt her feet move one in front of the other, but they were completely numb, as if they belonged to another person, or she was wading through wet sand.

He was dead by the time she arrived at Ward 7, and there was a nurse sitting next to him, holding his hand, and talking to him like he was still alive. Laura stood at the end of the bed a while, Anjali and Olivia either side of her, like bookends. The nurse – Daphne – was Irish and kind, and ushered Laura over to take her place. 'Your mam is with your aunt. They'll be back any moment. I think they had to get some air.'

She moved Laura's hand towards her dad's. 'He's still warm,' she said, 'but he couldn't wait.' Laura saw Olivia glare at the nurse, ever protective, but she appreciated that honesty. She always wanted the truth. There was nothing more important, her dad had always said, than telling the truth.

'Oh, Laura.' Her mum had walked back in, her hand covering her eyes as though she couldn't bear to even look. Aunt Jean was holding her up. Laura stood and held her mum in a way she had never held anyone, pressing all the energy out of her, all the connection. They separated and Laura realised it was just them. Anjali and Olivia must have slipped away with Jean. She looked at her mum for the longest time, and then her dad, the small hospital bay area with the flimsy curtains around them like a cheap shawl. Above her dad's bed, a whiteboard: *Vince Byford. Nil by mouth.* Laura wondered if he had been thirsty when he died. If they'd done CPR, shocked him, performed chest compressions, and run through revisable causes of cardiac arrest. Her mind began the chanting: tamponade, hyperkalaemia, tension pneumothorax, but then her head stopped. Her go-to comfort blanket of intellectualisation and Latin terms and medical conditions fell from her brain, and instead she was left with one thought on repeat. She whispered it out to her mum: 'I hope he wasn't thirsty.'

She was sobbing then, leaning over her dad's chest, her ear flat against his hospital gown. Her mum fell the other side of him, and they cried holding hands across his body. They cried until his skin turned cold, and theirs did too, and the porters came with a special trolley.

'Rose Cottage?' they asked, which Laura knew was the place they called the mortuary lest they frighten other patients. They pushed open the curtain gently, wheeling a trolley that was deep and covered over with a sheet, or a shroud. How many people had made their final journey on that trolley, pushed by strangers through a hospital to the mortuary, nothing at all like a Rose Cottage.

Laura looked at her dad's face. It was changing shape already. He was gone. He had that look that all recently dead people had, of shrinking slightly. She kissed his forehead and whispered something only he could hear. Then she pulled her mum up to standing, and away from the bed.

Grief does funny things to a person. Some sit with it, heavy-weighted in their chests, others push it out violently, or are lost at sea a while, facing wave after wave of it crashing over them. Laura felt grief like danger, as though her dad being alive was a safety she didn't realise she needed until it was gone. Medicine no longer felt like a safe place either. The ground underneath her feet was moving. She felt dizzy all the time. Her skin was goosebumped even though it was warm in the church. Laura sat at the front, next to her mother who was quietly crying, her back straight, a white rolled-up tissue poking out of her sleeve. She leaned her arm against her mum's. They both looked straight ahead at the coffin. This was a place of death. She leaned back against the cold hard pew, and touched the wood in front of her, a Bible balanced next to the order of service. The stained-glass windows let in rainbows of dancing light and the pulpit at the front had a table next to it, upon which candles flickered. It was a hot day, and there were many people, dozens of relatives Laura didn't know well, aunts and uncles and second cousins once removed, all of whom asked her how she was holding up, as if she could be anything but distraught. The vicar had a warm smile, and direct gaze and spoke with a soft voice about her dad's joie de vivre, and his love of Everton Football Club before commenting, 'Nobody is perfect,' and the room bubbled with laughter. Her mum's arm pressed against Laura's, her skin clammy and sticky. She was wobbly, unsteady on her feet. Laura couldn't bear to answer her or imagine what the future might look like. One parent gone, another too fragile. Laura unable to save them.

Laura had no belief whatsoever in God. She looked across and behind her at Olivia and Dele; Olivia had her head bowed slightly. Laura watched her face, calm and accepting, and wondered what she was thinking. She noticed her mouth twitch a tiny bit at the corners. Perhaps she was praying, or talking to God? Olivia's faith had always seemed weird to Laura and Anjali. They'd discussed it over the years, her views that seemed to them at odds with medicine. That God created the earth and everything in it, and there was some grand plan for all of them. That all sins could be forgiven and washed away with confession. Laura had never asked Olivia about confession. But she knew that every Sunday morning she got up early, and went off to Mass, returning to their flat a little high as though she'd been out taking drugs with Anjali. Laura's eyes moved over Olivia's face and rested on Dele's. He glanced up at her. He lifted his hand and placed it over his heart.

It was at the wake, in an old man pub in Dartford, her dad's favourite, that Laura followed Dele into the men's toilet. The toilet stank of piss that had seeped into the carpet and been left, unwashed, for months on end. She gagged on the way in. But even that didn't stop her. She had no understanding of what drove her to follow him. This was totally out of character. She'd seen a zombie film once and watched as a teenage boy turned into a zombie, his body contorting and the uncontrollable animalistic lust course through his veins. Human flesh. She needed human flesh so hard, a desire she'd never felt, a raw, open-wounded ache deep inside her core. Laura had never felt longing like it. She was a prude; Anjali teased her almost Victorian attitude to sex. But grief and death enveloped her, and she had to erase the coldness of her dad's skin, the smell of dead bodies, with action and heat. The only antidote was this. Something had shifted inside her. She pushed Dele against the dirty graffitied wall and kissed him hard. It felt like coming up for air.

EIGHT

Anjali (2024)

Their social worker, Emma, was wearing mid-calf boots that looked as if they were cutting off the circulation in her legs, and smelled very strongly of Febreze. This was their third social worker in the space of six months. They kept going on stress leave. If medicine had problems with recruitment and retention, social work was on its knees. Still, it was hard to be sympathetic. Anjali had been furious with all the stop-starts of the assessment. 'I mean, there are what – six thousand kids waiting to be adopted? You'd think they'd get their act together.' A few times already, she'd suggested they give up. It caused a bit of conflict between them. Low-level bickering driven by the stress of the adoption process. It seemed to Anjali to be designed to be stressful. But Donna always talked her round.

'I'm sure growing up in Cornwall as a woman of colour must have been a challenge in some respects?' The social worker was fishing around for trauma. This was their home study, a gruelling part of the assessment that was described as 'getting to know you', but Anjali felt was more like 'digging around for your secrets'. At least in the NHS the staff were completely reflective of the diversity of patients they cared for. Not so with social workers, who seemed to Anjali to be predominantly white middle-class women permanently tilting their head to one side and gently nodding, as if they understood anything about the families they were assessing.

'I was incredibly lucky with my family, and my childhood was idyllic, really.' She was lucky. Donna was not. She had told her early on about the racism she experienced growing up in Stoke-on-Trent as the only mixed-race girl in school, with a single white mother who had got pregnant while at school, who was ill-equipped to help her even recognise racism. She talked about her time in emergency foster care when her mum simply couldn't cope. The reason she so wanted to adopt. 'To help a child like me. As well as build a family with you.' She was like that, Donna. Full of goodness. Despite her difficult childhood.

Anjali's childhood was the total opposite of Donna's. She had grown up in the suburbs of Truro, in a cul-de-sac of similar sixties block houses, all large with a driveway containing a sensible car. Mostly Volvos. Her mum was a physiotherapist, her dad a pharmacist, both worked ridiculous hours at the hospital but always made time, somehow, to be there when it mattered. She pictured them both at her first recorder recital, her mum waving frantically, her dad filming as though she was in the London Philharmonic instead of Grade Two recorder in a dusty church hall. 'We love you,' her mum shouted, standing up and clapping before they'd even finished. They were embarrassing, but really, she knew she had perfect parents, who always said, 'We love you no matter what.'

'They must have been very proud when you went to medical school?' Emma smiled, slightly sycophantic. The smile of someone who still believed doctors know everything and are inherently good. Someone who hadn't been through anything major yet. It surprised Anjali that people still perceived doctors as heroes or even gods when most of the medics she knew were complex, sometimes less than compassionate, a bit broken, jaded and did not have any answers. They punctuated the day with dark humour and dreamed of escaping the NHS and travelling off in a camper van to the Outer Hebrides. Doctors were ordinary people, some good some bad, most of them doing their best. If the NHS was a religion, it was a godless one.

Emma's face relaxed, almost melted into a wide smile. She wanted them to disclose any and all of their secrets. She'd already told Anjali and Donna that it didn't matter at all what their past looked like, nothing aside from a Schedule One offence was off limits. What did matter was honesty and reflection and resolution. 'If you aren't able to talk about difficult things from your past, how will you be able to support a young person to do that? Let's talk about previous partners. Significant relationships. As you know, we try and interview any previous partners from long-term relationships.'

Anjali needed to swallow but was worried it would be a gulp. She tried to keep her voice steady, her eyes focused. The back of her head swam with memories that she wanted to forget, and words she fought to keep inside her. *We did a terrible thing. I can't tell you about Paul.*

'The truth is,' said Donna, smiling at Emma, picking up Anjali's hand. 'Anjali hasn't had any proper relationships, which is totally baffling to me.'

The truth is more complicated. It always was. Anjali looked at her reflection, and splashed water on her face. She stared at her face a few minutes, the water turning into droplets rolling down her cheeks. She imagined the water as tears, the saltiness of crying, the feeling of release. But she hadn't cried in months. Years? The process of adoption was unearthing feelings she had buried, but not deep enough. She felt them inside her belly and throat, twisting around, and she started waking

at night, lying, and staring at the ceiling, or at Donna's beautiful face, twitching with dreams. Anjali imagined a baby there
with them, the smell of a soft head between theirs, the sound
of their child's cry. Her arms felt too empty, too light. She
splashed more water, and leaned towards the mirror, looking
straight into her own eyes. But she couldn't stare for long. She
glanced away and ran the hot tap until it was burning. She
held her breath and pushed her hand underneath it. Her skin
reddened immediately, and blistered a tiny bit, and the pain
was worse than she imagined. Anjali had a complex relationship with pain. She hated and relied on it at once. She took
gasps of air and held her other hand on the sink top to stop her
falling over, clenched her teeth together to stop her crying out,
closed her eyes, and counted.

One, two, three.

When she went back into the bedroom, the bedside light
was on and Donna was sitting up with her glasses balanced
on her nose, reading a book. 'You OK?' She folded the page
and closed it. 'You're being super weird.'

Anjali sat on the bed opposite her. She crossed her legs. 'I
need to tell you something.'

Donna frowned. She sat up. 'It's 2 a.m. Wait, is this something to do with Laura and Olivia at her Sunday lunch? I
heard them whispering . . .'

Anjali shook her head but found herself holding her breath
at the mention of her two best friends. What *were* they whispering about? Miles had been acting strangely too. Anjali's
skin goosebumped but she ignored it, exhaled slowly, steadied
herself. Focused on what she had to tell Donna. 'It's nothing
to do with Laura or Olivia.' Anjali felt that lie fall out of
her, but consoled herself with the thought that half-truth was
better than no truth. 'It won't wait. I'm sorry.' She took a

deep breath and wondered where to start. 'It was today, and Emma. I didn't tell the whole truth and I can't. But you need to know. I hate keeping things from you. I can't.' She closed her eyes and said one word. 'Paul.'

Donna reached out and picked up her hand. 'You've burned your hand. I'll get some Sudocrem . . .'

'Don't go anywhere, Donna. It's important. I need to tell you about Paul. It's just a tiny bit red anyway.'

'Paul who?'

Anjali opened her eyes and Paul wasn't in the room. She had thought he might be waiting behind her eyelids, or whispering in her ear: *You cunt,* but there was no Paul. Instead, Donna was open-faced and sitting in their bed, under the patchwork quilt she'd made herself at some sort of woo-woo craft club. She wore pyjamas with small pandas on them, and her hand on top of Anjali's was warm and safe.

'What is it?'

She told Donna about Paul in one go. What he did. The drugs, the violence and his time in prison.

Donna sat listening, her head moved slightly to one side, taking it all in without interrupting.

Anjali let the words tumble from her mouth. 'I'm so sorry. I'm so sorry I didn't tell you about him.'

Donna leaned forward and pulled Anjali towards her. She wrapped her arms around Anjali's back and sort of rocked her. 'I can't believe it.' She wiped Anjali's cheeks with the palm of her hand and kissed her wet eyelashes. 'It's a lot to take in . . . What a total scumbag.'

'I'm sorry I didn't tell you before.' Anjali sniffed. Her body was shaking. 'I should have told you. I think I felt such shame. It doesn't seem real, that time of my life. A dream. Or nightmare perhaps.'

Donna pulled her closer. 'You have nothing at all to be sorry for. Nothing. He got what he deserved . . .'

Anjali closed her eyes. She wanted to tell Donna the whole truth. But she couldn't. The three of them had made a pact long ago.

NINE

Olivia (2024)

A quiet catch-up in The Dog was never quiet. Olivia always laughed that they were stuck at twenty-one, having lived together at that age, but really, she loved that they hadn't changed all that much. At midlife with all the stresses of raising teens, and impossible jobs, nights out, the laughing and chatting as the trio felt like blowing the cobwebs away. They started off in a civilised manner. Chit-chat, hearing from Anjali and Donna about the adoption process, the strange ineffectiveness of social workers, and their plans to take a minibreak to Lisbon. Laura and Olivia shared a few glances early in the evening, but nothing Anjali would pick up on. They'd decided with all they had going on there was no need to worry them about Rudy and Freya's misadventures and the tragedy at the party. After all, it could open a can of worms for Anjali, and she did not need that, mid adoption assessment. It seemed clear to all of them that Anjali and Donna were destined to be excellent parents.

Donna was drinking Diet Coke and en route to a bank night shift. She kissed Anjali, who disappeared to the bathroom, then necked the rest of her drink. 'No rest for the wicked,' she said. She glanced at the door Anjali had gone through and suddenly turned to Laura and Olivia. 'Very quickly, I wanted to say thank you to you both. More when you're not on a crazy night out, but Anj told me about Paul yesterday. About how you looked after her during it all. Sounds hell . . .'

Laura whipped her head around, and stared at Olivia, who shook her head a fraction.

'Right then, you best get off.' Olivia swigged her wine and smiled as the bus pulled in across the road. She pointed. Donna ran towards it and looked backwards and waved before she boarded the bus. Olivia lifted her hand but turned her head and gave Laura a look, and whispered, 'It's fine. Totally fine. She'd have just told about her and Paul . . . don't mention anything.'

'But surely Anj must have told Donna about the party? What we did? Honestly, Liv, it all feels so close . . .'

Olivia gently touched Laura's arm. 'Don't worry. It is all fine. Totally fine. Let's forget it all and have a nice night.'

'I went to intensive care. I couldn't help myself. Joe Duggard – he's critical, Liv.' Her eyes filled up with tears.

Olivia squeezed her arm. 'Nobody has done anything wrong here. Don't visit again – it will cause problems for the kids. It has nothing to do with our past. And it'll make you anxious, unnecessarily. They're a fantastic team and he'll be fine, no doubt.'

Laura nodded and took a deep breath, exhaling with a whoosh.

Anjali returned with tequila shots, and they laughed as Laura shook her head vigorously, protesting that it was a school night. She was breathing easier already, Olivia could see. Relaxing again. She wore a pair of wide-leg jade green trousers, a tucked-in T-shirt, statement necklace, white trainers, and looked effortlessly cool, her hair still fiery red, now lightly speckled with grey, which somehow made her look more beautiful. Anjali looked ten years younger, slim, dressed like a stylist, with mismatched items that she threw together that somehow simply worked. Olivia always felt frumpy next to them, even more so than when they were younger. She shopped almost exclusively in Boden these days, which probably didn't help, and cracked up both Anjali and Laura. 'Tease me all you like,' she said, 'but you'll be borrowing my cardigan later. It's nippy out.'

Anjali snorted. 'Never change, Liv. I've got some fags.' She pulled out a packet from her rucksack, with a skull and cross-bones on the front and the words Deathly Cigarettes.

'Clue's in the name,' said Laura, shaking her head.

Olivia took one. 'I'll stand behind you, Loz. Freya might walk past.'

'Why are teenagers the fun police these days?' Anjali grinned. 'Though to be fair, I was waiting for Donna to go. Can't cope with the lecture.' She filled Olivia's glass with lukewarm white wine. Her mother would have a fit at what Liv drank these days. She'd done level three sommelier training simply to entertain her dad's doctor friends at elaborate dinner parties. The lives of doctors had changed.

'I got them last year in Mexico. They're mint; therefore they don't count.' Anjali and Olivia chain-smoked the pack, drinking, but even sober and waving smoke away from her with her arm, Laura wasn't at all left out. The three of them spent hours laughing, reminiscing. They never talked shop. It was the cardinal rule. They all understood the stressful lives they lived, and the difficulties of the careers they'd chosen. It was a secret code between them, an understanding that only came from embodied experience. Their careers were hard. Much harder than they'd ever foreseen. But much more meaningful too. When they got together they shook off the weight of meaning, and were simply three old friends having a laugh.

By nine Olivia was a bit drunk, and, despite working the following day, it seemed like a good idea to turn up, uninvited, to a friend of a friend of Anjali's party a forty-minute Uber away. Laura had groaned but gone along anyway.

As soon as they arrived, Olivia realised it was a mistake. They were clearly much older than Anjali's friends, who looked like they all attended art school and smoked too much weed. The flat was decorated in cheap furniture and there was a sign in the hallway that said: *Make Art Not War.* 'Blimey,' whispered Olivia on the way in. But Anjali and Laura didn't notice. They made their way to the kitchen and began talking to random people, and swaying to the music. Olivia stayed an hour or so. She chatted nonsense with Anjali and when a group of thirty-year-olds started dancing in the kitchen to Run DMC, she ordered an Uber back. 'That's enough fun for me,' she said. 'You coming or staying?'

Anjali looked over at Laura, who was flirting with a tall, bearded man, then back at Liv. 'I'll come with you.' She waved over. 'Laura, we're off. You all good?'

Laura stuck her thumb up. They were always leaving her at parties. She would likely stay out all night, hook up with that guy and then go for a ten-mile run in the morning. But it would do Laura some good. Olivia could sense she'd been unnerved by Donna earlier. She hoped Donna hadn't picked up on it.

Anjali curled into a ball in the back of the taxi and put her head on Olivia's lap. Olivia looked out at London, thinking about how lucky they all were. She hoped they'd be spontaneously heading to random kitchen parties together when they were eighty.

Dele waited up. She tried to sneak in quietly but dropped her bag, then bashed around until the dogs started barking. 'Sorry.' He stood up, brushing biscuit crumbs from his jumper. He'd have eaten the packet while watching documentaries. Dele had no interest in meeting up and going out drinking with his friends. Some men didn't seem to need that in the same way.

He spoke to his friends on the phone, brisk and businesslike, and they attended sporting events together, occasionally the opera or theatre. But there was no world where Dele would meet mates to simply mess around or go for a drink. He didn't understand the need for that at all. When Olivia, Laura and Anjali met up away from the pub, he was even more baffled. They'd made a pact a long time ago to every now and then attempt bizarre new experiences, and over the decades this had given them so much joy. Laura would text: *Life drawing class on 15th in Cambria, who's in?* and they'd have hysterics while doing something new. Over the years they'd tried welding, and Christmas wreath making, cold-water swimming, improvisation class. Anything silly or unusual or even ridiculous made them laugh and, in Laura's words, gave them life. 'These little adventures are the big ones, really,' she'd once said.

Dele leaned forward to kiss Olivia, and she ducked. 'I've been smoking, sorry. Gross, and immature, I know. I'll brush my teeth.'

He grabbed her anyway. 'It's disgusting but I can't resist you in any case.'

Olivia loved him so much it felt like her heart would burst from her mouth. After a while kissing, he simply stroked her face, looked into her eyes. 'How are they? The other musketeers?'

Olivia sat up. 'Oh, you know. Anjali and Donna are grinding it out with the adoption stuff. Laura is Laura.' She watched his eye twitch. 'Holier than thou, yet we left her at the party, hooking up with some stranger.'

Dele shrugged. 'You know Laura,' he said. His face didn't change a jot, but his pupils contracted. 'Well, I mean, Laura now. She wasn't always like that . . .'

Olivia continued, glancing away. 'I wish she wouldn't sleep around so much. Especially with random men she's just met.

She doesn't see that as harm, but of course that's far more damaging than alcohol and cigarettes. It's just a different kind of bad for you.'

'I fear that's not very modern of you.' Dele pulled her back towards him. He kissed her shoulder. 'But I'm glad you're not very modern.'

Olivia smiled. She was lucky. She and Dele were perfect for each other.

TEN

Laura (2024)

People assumed a mortuary would be the spookiest place in a hospital, but if ghosts existed, it would be here, in the shadows of the dimly lit ICU. Laura watched the faces of the staff, their expressions as they scanned the monitors and analysed the numbers. These nurses were mathematicians and magicians in equal measure. They worked between science and art in the spaces and gaps where concrete and abstract meet, and nothing quite makes sense. These were the people who witnessed all the horror of the world, and the occasional miracle too.

Laura needed a miracle. She looked at Joe Duggard in bed four, an eighteen-year-old and by far the sickest patient on the unit. She kept coming back to visit him, despite promising Liv she wouldn't, hoping to see signs of recovery, but he remained part human, part robot, kept alive by machinery. A tube from his nostril snaked down to the top of his lungs, inflating them via the ventilator – the settings of which, Laura could see, were maximal. There was no wriggle room here, he was requiring 100 per cent oxygen, and had pressures so high that lung trauma would be guaranteed, if he did indeed make it. If. A large fan of IV lines exploded from his jugular vein, measuring his central venous pressures (too high), and an arterial line measured his blood pressure (too low). Inotropes, the strongest of heart medications, pumped continuously into his femoral line from a stack of pumps on a drip stand; another containing blood, the red-packed cells ticking slowly into his system. A large chest drain contained blood, and a catheter dumped urine, and a vascath, another huge line, linked him to a haemofiltration machine, where enormous bags of jelly-like, straw-coloured fluid were pulled out of him, and clear fluid put back in: his kidneys weren't working.

It was the bolt that Laura found hardest to look at though.

A large bolt, the kind of thing you'd see in a hardware store, was drilled into Joe's skull, a thin wire from it leading towards a box with waves and numbers, measuring the pressure in his head. Laura could not take her eyes off it. Every time anything at all happened on the ICU – a bin closing, the lights going on, a nurse suctioning Joe's breathing tube – the number spiked into an enormous wave. Joe Duggard had fallen down a flight of stairs at a party and hit his head so hard at the bottom that he had a tsunami of brain damage. Freya and Rudy had witnessed the tragic accident. They could never unsee that.

She sat for a long time, watching the wave patterns inside Joc, willing them to flatten down, to decrease, to not spike. She thought of when her dad had taken her on holiday to the Isle of Man, and held her hand as they watched a storm. All the islanders had battened down the hatches and gone inside, staying well clear of the seafront. But her dad had screamed against the wind, almost knocking her over, and pulled her towards the promenade. She had never seen higher waves, an angrier sea. Boulders were being thrown over the side onto the road, one cracking the tarmac into two. She remembered feeling so afraid, terrified that they would die. But her dad just shouted and pointed at the giant waves. 'Everything is danger. Everything good in this world.'

Laura had a feeling, creeping around her insides. A sick feeling in her bones, like she was being watched. She heard footsteps behind her only to realise it was her own heart. Maybe it was the worry about Rudy being so traumatised by the accident? Or sadness for the poor boy Joe and his family? Or maybe, it was all simply opening a can of worms? There was a lot going on. Laura was brave, ambitious, calm in a crisis, and yet this was clearly unnerving her. She needed distraction from the thoughts swirling around inside her head. When she cared for patients or families going through stressful times, she always told them to rest as much as possible. It was a strange thing to be giving medical advice to her patients to prioritise rest, and then not taking it herself. But it was the last thing Laura wanted to do. Still, she had read an article that week about the percentage of smokers among healthcare workers. The highest numbers were found among nurses working on the lung cancer wards. If you stood close enough to a fire, perhaps it was inevitable to be drawn to the flame.

I'm not interested in a relationship. No-strings sex only.

Laura was straight up with men, but even then, they often didn't believe her. They'd come back with *Great!* And then suggest a restaurant, or attempt small talk, texting drivel accompanied by dozens of emojis. There was a time when she'd have liked that. A date with a nice man, and some chit-chat, the possibility of a relationship. There was a time when she'd have never even considered sex on a first date, let alone the kind of sex she increasingly fantasised about: anonymous, merely a physical act without any emotional intimacy. Grief was a turning point for her. After her dad died, sex became escape, release, the opposite of death. But finding men on board with that was not as easy as she'd imagined. Flame was better than Hitch, but it was the domain of late teenagers, not much older than Rudy, looking for much older women, which left Laura feeling nauseous. Hearted wanted to know her entire life story, as if that could predict chemistry, and Soulmates was the spiritual home for left-wing vegans who wanted to talk for hours and were terrible in bed. Laura had voted Labour all her life and abhorred Conservative politics, but everyone knew that Tories were better lovers, a fact that had cracked Anjali up when she'd told her. She'd laughed so hard she had to run to the toilet. *'I'm literally wetting myself . . .'*

She had been very clear with Mark that she simply wanted to have sex and not see him again. Everyone had to let off steam somehow. The job would kill you otherwise. Half of her colleagues smoked, drank. Took drugs. For her it was sex. A place to park her emotions, to forget about work, about her patients, about her past.

Laura liked that it didn't seem to faze Mark, her directness. Clearly, he was no stranger to this subculture of middle-aged hook-ups. He was American, only in town for a few nights, and suggested meeting at the Soho Hotel for a drink, then some no-strings sex if they felt like it. Perfect. Laura had no interest whatsoever in dating, or worse, a relationship. Laura agreed with Maslow: her hierarchy of needs placed sex next to food and breathing. She had no interest in love stories, in dates, or romance, but uncomplicated sex was therapeutic. Sex made her feel powerful, in the moment, present. And, for a short time at least, everything else vanished. She walked into the hotel and towards the bar, ignoring the voice inside her head that whispered, *It wasn't always that way.* She was good at ignoring that voice. Adrenaline overrode it. Perhaps that was why she was addicted to it.

He had a wide smile and good shoulders. American teeth. 'Drink?' He glanced at Laura's body.

She'd worn a white shirt and jeans, trainers. This wasn't a date. 'Sparkling water for me.'

They made small talk. He owned a company that sold electrical parts, and was looking to expand internationally. Laura told him she worked in PR. They finished their drinks quickly, and she followed him to the lift, and once inside, they simply stared at each other, unblinking. Laura pulled him towards her and pressed her body hard against his. Mark, who sold electrical parts, or whoever the hell he was. It didn't matter.

It was still light out when she left town and got the train home from Victoria. The gated community in Beckenham where she and Rudy – and now her mum – lived in a four-bedroom home next to a small canal, that felt something like sanctuary. It was a long way from Dartford, and a far cry from the days before Rudy had been born, when Laura and Owen had lived in a studio flat on Coldharbour Lane, the sound of vomiting and sirens and shouting wafting in through their windows all hours of the night, the carpet so old, tiny silverfish slithered across it, a shining reminder of poverty. She'd spent her whole life climbing out of poverty, raising Rudy to have every possible chance that she never did. She didn't want Rudy to suffer because she was a single parent. She didn't want him to suffer because Wendy came along with her meditation classes and smugness and slept with her husband. Still, what could Laura say about that? She deserved that pain.

Rudy did not though. Laura adored Rudy. She had always assumed the love of her life would be a romantic partner, *had been* a romantic partner. But when Rudy was born and she held him and studied his face, it was as if her heart had been ripped from her chest and placed in her hands. She had never known love like that. Total, unconditional, magical love. She studied his face and saw the face of her tiny daughter, born much too soon. 'Hello, you,' she'd said. She would do anything for that boy. She would not let the last few weeks ruin anything for him. She wouldn't. There was no need for his life to be ruined. She had willed her way out of trouble once, and if she had to, she would do it again.

Laura's mind flicked back to the party. She had stood in her HEMS uniform, Joe Duggard lying semi-conscious, Rudy and Freya standing over him. The other teens had been partying in the living room and heard the noise, the terrifying loud crack of something very wrong, and run out to find Joe Duggard bleeding from his head, and his nose, and his ear. By the time Laura arrived on scene most of the teenagers had run off or were huddled together in the living room in shock, crying. But Freya and Rudy simply stood open-mouthed above Joe, glued to the spot. Something instinctive had happened in Laura's belly, a memory-triggered response, before she even surveyed how bad his injuries were, and what had happened. *Run.* Later, at home, as Rudy and Freya had sat drinking hot chocolate and sobering up, they told her about the accident, and she consoled them both as they whimpered like much younger children. '*There was so much blood.*'

'Do we have to sit at the table?'

She hadn't noticed Rudy come in. He'd been staying out late since it happened, or hanging around with Freya and Miles, despite her saying it was not a good idea. They simply needed to concentrate on school, keep life as normal as possible. She kept telling him that it had been a shock, but in time he'd get over that shock and life would carry on. But she could see the worry on Rudy's face. When he was little and fell out of a tree or off a climbing frame, as young kids do, she would wince before he did, feel the graze, or once the broken bone, in the exact same spot. This now was no different, though it was worse. When he hurt, she hurt; she'd take away his pain in a heartbeat. She had to keep things normal. Upbeat.

'It's not good for your soul to eat in front of the telly,' Laura laughed. She would keep things cheerful and light. She kissed him as he came into the kitchen, dumped his bags, began running a glass of water from the fridge water dispenser. He was growing daily. 'Did you have a good sleepover at Freya's? I missed you. We get so little time together. I haven't seen you all week. Let's eat at the table and talk . . . Grandma is at Aunt Jean's tonight.'

Having her mum live with them was not what Laura had imagined. But Jean couldn't manage, and the idea of her mum going into a residential care home was out of the question. Her mum was such a wonderful woman who had given her life to caring for Laura's dad, loving him despite his difficulties. She had offered to move her mum in as soon as her multiple sclerosis became more difficult to manage, and a wheelchair necessary. The downstairs garden room became her mum's bedroom. It was tiring, having another person to look after. But Laura wouldn't have it any other way. Losing her dad had taught her that taking care of a sick relative is not a burden. It's a privilege.

Rudy held his hand up. 'I don't want to talk.' But he sat down at the table and began digging his thumbnail into the tabletop. He had a small patch of eczema on the inside of his wrist, she noticed. He hadn't had eczema since he was around ten years old. His body behaved as hers did. He'd inherited her minor malfunctions.

Laura began busying herself with dinner. 'Shall we watch a film after dinner?' She needed to distract him. It was a horrible thing to witness, but they'd get over it. Let it all blow over, and he'd be back on track. A levels, university and then following in her footsteps. She'd worked so hard to give him the chances that Olivia's kids had. Laura had been the first in her family to attend university, but she'd broken a curse of sorts, and she was dammed if Rudy's life would be less than perfect. Joe Duggard had fallen down the stairs. He'd slipped, drunk, and it was an accident. It was horrific to witness something like that, but they weren't responsible. She had automatically told them to run, to protect them from being in the wrong place at the wrong time, at the wrong teenage party where things can and do go wrong. She wanted to wrap Rudy up in cotton wool and protect him from all the darkness of life. That was her job. Every parent's job.

She looked at him, studied his face. Every day it seemed to change, from boy to man. She could clearly see already what kind of man he'd be. Handsome, capable, strong. But today his face looked tired. She noticed the puff around his eyes, the dullness of his skin. He hadn't slept. Rudy shrugged. His shoulders moved slowly, as if his body was independently depressed. He'd been crying. She hadn't heard him, but she could tell. She felt it in her heart, wore his emotions under her own. He was really affected by witnessing Joe's accident. 'Come on,' she said. 'Let's talk about this. There really is nothing to worry about, you know.'

'How's he doing?' Rudy's voice was quiet. 'The one who got injured.'

Laura turned around and looked out into darkness, the lights in the kitchen making it impossible to see the outside. Rudy and Freya did not know Joe Duggard very well. They didn't really know anyone at that party, except a friend from Rudy's taekwondo class, who'd invited them to *his* friend's party. 'He's stable,' she said. 'Same really. I checked in on

95

him in intensive care . . .' Her voice tailed off. She coughed. 'Main thing is that it was an accident.' Laura heard a tapping outside. Someone walking past. The security light flashed on. She went over to the window and closed the curtain tightly so there were no gaps. A split second and Laura could hear footsteps running on the cobbles outside. Was somebody outside their house? The skin on the back of Laura's neck turned cold. Was she imagining it?

'Mum.' Rudy's voice belonged to a younger version of him. He was breathing quickly. 'Mum, I need . . .'

He was crying, hard, afraid, and shaking. 'Mum. I need to tell the truth. Mum.' He bent over, sobbing, her almost grown-up son. 'We were there. At the top of the stairs . . .'

She walked back and kneeled next to Rudy and put her arm around him. 'It will be OK. I promise. It will all be OK. It was a horrible thing to see, that accident. Awful. You're not in trouble, I promise.'

Rudy stood and his voice changed to anger. 'It wasn't an accident.' He waved his arms and pointed. 'It wasn't an accident, Mum. Freya pushed him. She pushed him hard. Really hard, Mum. Freya pushed him downstairs.' He was crying and shouting, almost wailing. 'She shoved him on his chest. He was harassing her, and she was drunk. She got so angry. She was up in his face and shouting, and then she shoved him. He was standing at the top of the stairs, the wooden stairs with the metal table by the front door, and he just fell. He fell so fast, Mum, and even at the top we could hear the crack when his head hit the bottom. And we could see that he was really hurt. Straight away, we could see.' He flicked his arm again towards the window. 'There was so much blood, Mum. He looked like he was dead. We didn't know what to do. Freya was shaking. You told us to run.'

A flash of memory lit inside Laura's head. And another flash and another. She closed her eyes and saw Joe's face, but it melted and changed, and became the face of another young man, eyes open, staring at her but not moving. She heard a voice telling her to run. Olivia's voice.

ELEVEN

Laura (1999)

Medical student electives tell you everything about the character of the future doctor, Laura's supervisor insisted, when she'd told her she wanted to stay at City and work on the intensive care unit for a few weeks instead of travelling abroad. 'People go to developing countries or to exclusive US hospitals and there is no movement in between.' She'd touched Laura's arm. She had been incredibly supportive since her dad had died, checking in with her almost daily. 'I think it's wise to stay close to home. There will be a time for adventures.'

Laura was the only fourth-year medical student who was staying at home. Olivia and Anjali were off proving her supervisor's point. Olivia had gone to Mount Sinai in New York to work with Professor Irvine – the woman she considered the best cardiac surgeon in the world. Anjali was en route to Ecuador where she would stay with a tribe in the Amazon basin and provide basic healthcare, and where – she told Olivia and Laura – she fully intended to take ayahuasca. They were worried about leaving Laura and tried to get her to take time off. But although Laura was full of grief, she didn't want to take time off. If she took a few weeks away from the hospital she worried she might never go back.

Laura felt totally out of control, like she was no longer inside her own body. Her mind was playing tricks too. She saw and smelled and heard her dad on every ward. Men in their sixties, hard-lived men, crumpled and broken by life but still cracking jokes. She saw her dad's face on the gastro ward when she followed the barking consultant as part of a group of medical students wearing short white coats to reflect their inexperience. She heard her dad's raspy laugh when she followed the cardiac arrest team, only to find a false alarm, and a drunk man in the corridor. She smelled the mushroom and engine-oil smell of her dad's skin on the Care of the Elderly ward, and was rooted to the spot, eyes closed, trying to remember via the smell what it felt like to have her dad's arm around her shoulders. But she felt nothing on her skin, just numb, as though she didn't belong in her own body and her skin belonged to someone else. She didn't feel real, or human. When she opened her eyes, she didn't see her dad's face, just a sea of old women. All the men were dead by then.

Intensive care, where she opted to do her elective, was a space-ship cocoon, quiet and full of complex equipment. Laura had only ever been there once, and she'd liked the staff, found the cases interesting. It would be a good place to learn new skills, and so despite not being up to travelling abroad, she knew it would be valuable. Her supervisor had agreed and commented that it felt like a good idea to be in a place of control, when everything felt a bit out of control. Laura hadn't really under-stood what she meant. But she liked the idea of it. She felt lost. Drifting. Her mind flicking to images of her dad. Anxiety about her mum was keeping her up all night though she somehow didn't feel tired, just wired, too wide awake. She was glad the ICU was dimly lit, and aside from the near-constant alarms which the nurses seemed not to hear at all, the unit was quiet. Laura felt contained. Busy was good.

The patients in intensive care were all in medically induced comas, attached to life support machines that took over their multi-organ-failing bodies: haemofiltration for kidneys, ventilators for lungs. Laura would throw herself into learning the technology of ICU, the complicated formulae that were needed to calculate inotropes, the strong heart medications; she'd learn to interpret scans, X-rays, and analyse arterial blood gas results to work out if a person was too acid or too alkaline. She liked the idea of the goal of intensive care that is to maintain a patient's homeostasis, the state that humans can survive in, the pH numbers that need to remain at 7.35–7.45. Specific, measurable, cellular numbers, at the core of human bodies, of life and death. She didn't want to think philosophically or even holistically. She didn't want to imagine the person behind the disease, or search for meaning. She wanted anatomy, physiology, chemistry, the hard edges of medicine where everything was factual and solid and safe.

She spent the morning shadowing the registrar, a softly spoken man with an impressive moustache, and tried to absorb his teaching and the patients' diseases, and not think too deeply about her own problems. This was a place of tragedy, and even on her first day Laura felt she'd learned the most important lesson that intensive care taught: there is always someone worse off than you. She would get through this time of intense grief, and she wouldn't let it ruin her life, or anyone else's. She wouldn't let her grief ruin her friendship with Olivia. She knew what she had to do.

At the end of the day Laura swiped out of the unit and then walked through the theatres next door, scanning each room for signs of him. A few scrub nurses wafted past, their theatre gowns billowing around them like magician's cloaks. The thudding sound of the theatre clogs on the intensively polished floor was a reassuring soundtrack to Laura. She felt so disconnected from her own body, she imagined her heartbeat in time with the sound. Since the funeral she'd avoided Dele, and Dele avoided her. Grief had made her irrational; she could see that. Irrational was dangerous. She felt outside her own character, shocked by her own behaviour. Olivia was her best friend. They trusted each other. She trusted Laura. Nothing justified a betrayal of that nature. Not even losing her dad. Laura knew that. Laura couldn't avoid Dele anymore. She had to convince him to forgive her and forget it. She didn't ever want anything coming between his and Olivia's happiness, or their friendship.

She found him in the coffee room. Dele was wearing maroon scrubs and eating a sandwich. She stood in the doorway. 'Hello.' He stood and walked towards her, leaving his sandwich on the coffee table, nodding at a colleague on the way out. 'I wondered if I might see you. Liv said you were sticking around.' They walked down the theatre corridor. It was quiet. The elect-ives had all finished and majority of staff gone home. The operating department practitioners and scrub nurses were in various corners, checking equipment dates, autoclaving expiries. Much of the work in theatres was that of vigilance. Checking and checking. Laura had a friend who was a scrub nurse and had gone over for dinner once, to find the kitchen cupboards organised in such a way that her friend could only be a scrub nurse or a serial killer.

'Can we talk privately?' Laura nodded at the ODA, who was wiping a whiteboard clean. 'Do you have time?'

'There's an MI on the way, apparently. I'll need to scrub in but I imagine they're at least half an hour away. Let's go in here.' Dele opened a heavy door to an empty anaesthetic room, lined floor to ceiling with carefully labelled kit. 'How are you?' He sat on the trolley and Laura sat next to him. He smelled slightly of sweat.

She stared at the forest green anaesthetic bag, attached to the gas and air. She looked at Dele, expecting to feel awkward, but a flicker of something burned her insides, and the words she wanted to say tumbled out in a strange order. 'It was wrong. I mean, about grief and oh God, Olivia would never forgive me. Us.'

Dele shrugged. 'Don't worry about it. It was just a kiss, Laura.' He seemed totally calm. Laura knew his engagement to Olivia was unshakeable, and she'd been shocked when he kissed her back at her dad's funeral. But then he'd pulled away, semi-pushed her off, and whispered, 'This is wrong, Laura.' His words were certain, his voice kind, but Laura had noticed a look in his eyes then, something like yearning. Laura had always felt that Dele had a soft spot for her, loved her as a friend. Like a sister, she assumed. But there was something. A glance. A certain look he gave her before turning away, where his gaze seemed to travel inside her. There was a warmth coming from his skin as he hugged her.

She stared at the locked medicine cabinet, and Dele followed her eyes. 'My first day on the crash team was to theatres; the anaesthetist had overdosed on fentanyl . . .'

'Yikes. That's awful.'

'I know, right.' He looked at Laura. 'We are merchants of grief. Grief causes all sorts of madness.' He smiled, lowered his head slightly and looked at her. 'Don't beat yourself up.'

Laura exhaled and realised she'd been holding her breath. Dele put his arm around her and squeezed her shoulder a fraction. It was a friendly move, reassuring. But he let his arm drop quickly, suddenly flustered. He stepped back a few inches, but his hand remained in front of him, and hovered awkwardly between them.

She studied him. The skin on her shoulder where he had touched her was goosebumped. He looked down at his hand, then at Laura's face. The air between them changed shape. Before she knew what was happening, she had reached out to touch him, and he was pulling her towards him, and they were kissing and tugging at each other's scrubs, until they were half clothed, twisted and tangled as they pulled off scrub tops, and her hand was hot against his skin, or it was his skin that was hot? It was impossible to tell. Dele gazed at her, unblinking, while their bodies danced around them almost independently, without control.

She was fucking her best friend's boyfriend, her best friend's *fiancé* but she couldn't stop. Sensible, cautious, selfless Laura who was always doing the right thing. She couldn't stop. Wouldn't. She didn't care about anything at all, if someone came in and found them, if Olivia found out, she didn't care about any of it. She forgot all notions of why she had come to find him, to spell out how wrong they were, how it must never escalate. All she thought about in that moment was the warmth of him, the sound of her own heart beating and the safety of her bones. There was nothing else except the feeling of Dele inside her.

TWELVE

Olivia (2024)

Freya insisted her room was out of bounds, and Liv respected that, but after their cleaner, Pam, said she could no longer even get into Freya's room, she was left with no choice but to tidy up. She'd warned her a million times that if she didn't sort it out, she'd be forced to go in, personal space or not. Freya's room was painted sage green, the walls covered with photographs of her and her friends, and posters she'd collected over the years from art galleries. A large tapestry hung over her bed that had been left to her by Dele's family, his grandmother who had died when Freya Abidemi was born, her namesake. Aside from the curated walls, the entire rest of the room was a mess. It smelled bad enough that Liv coughed and opened the windows. Was it smoke? Vape? Weed? The smell was familiar, something sweet and sickly and musty, but she couldn't quite place it. There were crusted-over cereal bowls everywhere and make-up, half opened, all over the carpet, along with unidentifiable stains. Olivia remembered the time she'd come in and there were insects all over the floor, scattering under the bed and rug. Freya and Miles had been collecting woodlice, spiders, daddy-long-legs in a box and it had tipped over. She pictured them, aged five and seven, screaming and laughing, a mixture of terror and excitement. It all went by too soon.

Freya's schoolbooks were piled against the wall, and instead her desk was covered in clothes, many items with labels still attached, scrimpy, hoochy outfits that Olivia was forever telling Freya to change out of. Freya didn't listen. She said, 'My body, I'll dress how I like,' and while Liv respected young people's agency and body positivity, she couldn't help but panic when her daughter left the house, aged fifteen, looking twenty. Boys were easier. She picked up a plastic bag. It was full of wrappers, sweets mainly, and empty cans of Monster energy drink and Diet Coke. How hard was it to take rubbish to the bin? She could feel the anger in her throat. A hard knot that was twisting. She'd been a bit worried about Freya since Laura's revelation about the party. Of course, in the cold light of day it was easy to conceptualise. Nobody was in trouble, she had told Freya. All kids had some drama at some point. Olivia's own feelings of panic in the operating department were much more complex than the current situation. All current feelings were about long-buried other feelings, she suspected. And Freya seemed fine in herself, but perhaps Olivia had been subconsciously going easy on her – she hadn't insisted that she clean up before going out. She should have done. Her blood was boiling at the state of this room. Freya was old enough to understand how hard they worked. She'd just finished forty-eight hours on call and hardly slept or ate, and instead of sleeping she was having to pick up rubbish from Freya's room so Pam could get in it. It wasn't even that she needed order and tidiness, just not dirt, nothing rotting. It wasn't much to ask. Especially now. She'd watched a programme where a privileged British teenager was sent to live with a family in rural Cambodia, to learn discipline. She imagined Freya carrying water from a well, cooking on an open fire, sweeping the ground with a twig broom, no Wi-Fi, no TikTok or Instagram, no Deliveroo or Uber. It would do her good. When she'd mentioned to Dele that Freya could stay with his parents in Lagos to learn how to behave, he'd laughed and suggested she'd come back more spoiled than ever. 'She'd be waited on hand and foot, have staff doing everything for her, including her own driver, and be told she's the greatest princess the world has ever seen. The only thing she'd likely learn is how to play polo, or drink Moët. Rich Nigerians spoil their kids like no others; one of my friends flew his daughter via private jet to Italy, to get an ice cream . . .'

She looked under the bed, pulling out piles and piles of crap and throwing it into a bin bag. There were mouldy sandwiches, a pizza box with half-eaten slices covered in a layer of green. They'd get mice. She'd loved her children too hard. Given them too much affection, likely, as her therapist once suggested, overcompensating for her own experience of cold parenting. At least Miles appreciated her. He was the opposite of Freya in many ways. Tidy and helpful. Freya had a permanent scowl and everything Liv did seemed to irritate her. Mothers and daughters.

She looked at the photographs of younger Freya, fresh-faced, happy and wholesome. How she missed that version of her daughter. That version of herself as a mother when she was carefree, playful, and jolly. Olivia moved the desk clothes onto the bed and started piling everything on top. Pam would be able to clean the rest and Freya could sort it all out after school. On the way out, Liv glanced at the desk, on which there was a small ivory container with shells decorating the outside. She didn't recognise it. She opened the lid, expecting to find hair grips or lip gloss or small, folded-up notes that made no real sense. Her heart became hot. Inside the box was a small see-through packet, full of white powder. She stood for a moment, breathing. The back of her head felt separate from her body, pulled upwards, taut. She lost focus in her eyes, and everything was blurred a few seconds. Her feet turned numb. She picked up the packet and held it up to the light. Her fifteen-year-old daughter was taking cocaine. This was a lot of cocaine. She'd never done it, but Anjali had taken drugs all through medical school, so she'd been around it enough to know normal amounts. And this was a lot.

They waited for her together, Dele quiet and uncomfortable, insisting it must be some sort of mistake. 'She's not the sort,' he said. 'I don't accept it. Hogwash.' He and Freya had a special bond. They were similar characters, detached, funny, unusual. 'It's preposterous. She's fifteen, for God's sake. There's enough coke there to kill a horse. She's clearly been given it. I mean, where would she have got that sort of money anyway?'

Olivia looked at him. She opened her mouth to say, 'Who knows anything. Maybe she stole it. Or has an OnlyFans page.' Her expectations of Freya were increasingly dark. It had almost been no surprise when Laura had first told her Freya and Rudy had been at a party where a boy was seriously hurt. Miles had been home studying for an exam, so at least he wasn't there too. Laura had been calling all day today, but Olivia couldn't face talking to her. She'd said all she needed to.

Olivia had convinced Freya to keep quiet about the party, even to her dad. 'The less said the better.' Dele would dig around too much and want to speak to Laura. Olivia wanted to avoid that. But now drugs? She could not keep this from Dele. She'd paged him at work, ahead of work that evening, and they had a window, on Freya's return from school, where they'd get to the bottom of it. Miles was at Laura's for a sleepover, so the house was theirs. 'I feel nauseous.' Olivia sat next to Dele and thought about putting an arm around him but could see he wasn't in the mood for physical affection. His long legs were aggressively crossed in front of him. There was a time and a place, he always said, and Olivia guessed that confronting their daughter about a stash of cocaine was not the time.

The door. They heard the dropping of a heavy school bag, and the thud of DMs.

'Freya. Come here, please.'

There were a few seconds of quiet. Then they heard her run upstairs two at a time. Fast. Olivia stood up and walked to the bottom of the banisters. 'Freya. Get down here, right now.'

Dele didn't get up, he simply sat, heartbroken, holding the cocaine at arm's length, as if it might contaminate him.

Olivia didn't need to shout again. Freya walked down, slowly, her head scanning the scene. She was a smart kid, but Olivia could tell she wasn't trying to come up with anything. She saw panic and truth written on her skin. She smelled a lie a mile off. Trust, she always told the kids, was the single most important thing, their only defence against the dark arts. They were to tell the truth, always. They walked to the living room, and Freya sat on the sofa opposite. Olivia sat next to Dele. He held out the drugs.

Enough to kill a horse.

Freya cried softly, the number of tears disproportionate to the sound, squeaking like a caged animal. Her eyes puffed up, cheeks swollen, as they had since she'd been a baby, whenever she was extremely sad about something. She'd always been sensitive in a way that Olivia and Dele didn't understand but respected. They'd joked that of the two children, Freya would not be suitable for medicine, what with her anxiety about the destruction of warthog habitats in Kenya, leading them to have to boycott their favourite teabags, and her four-day sadness after watching *Marley & Me*. She was much more like Dele's family of thespians, arty and creative, a talented painter from a young age, obsessed with poetry. She also fainted often, which Olivia put down to squeamishness, but maybe it was drugs? She was skinny, dark-eyed and changeable, which Olivia assumed was simply teenage hormones, though had she missed a child taking drugs? How could she miss it? Everything flashed through her head. Maybe she was an addict? If someone as lovely as Anjali could end up with a drug habit, it was conceivable that it could happen to anyone. Even her daughter. Even at fifteen.

The drugs hung suspended in Dele's hand. 'Talk,' he said. His voice had hard edges.

Freya squirmed on the sofa, her body not knowing where to position itself. She wrung her hands together and curled up. 'It's not mine.'

Olivia felt herself breathe. There was probably an explanation. There must be. She was caught up in something and they'd help her through it, as a family, come out stronger. They always did. One thing her mother had given her, along with the less positive things, was stoicism. They were survivors. 'Freya, darling, you need to tell us who this belongs to.'

Freya looked up, a flicker of scorn on her face. Olivia waited. Dele crossed his legs. The parrot, Roger, started making a sound like a car alarm, like he always did when he sensed danger. Perceptive things, animals. 'It's not mine. I was looking after it.'

'You are telling me,' Dele's voice was louder, harder, 'that you are stupid enough to keep someone's drugs in our home? You want mum and me to lose our jobs? You want to go to prison?' He was shaking with rage. The room moved with it. Olivia reached over and touched his arm, but he shook it off.

Freya closed her eyes. Cried. Olivia felt like rushing to her, rocking her, telling her everything would be OK. But she knew this would not help, and likely enrage Dele further. She closed her eyes too. When she opened them, after what seemed like minutes, Freya was sitting up, taking gulps of air.

'Who do these drugs belong to? I will be phoning the police in precisely two minutes, so I suggest you start speaking.'

'They're Rudy's,' Freya whispered.

Dele's mouth dropped open. Olivia's head felt disconnected from the rest of her. It couldn't be true. She'd misheard. The drugs would be from a kid at school, all the mums chatted about how drugs were endemic in London, the fabric of teenagers' lives; cocaine was rife in the private schools, weed in the states. Maybe she'd been coerced, got in with a bad crowd. County lines, or similar horrors.

But Freya simply looked at the packet of cocaine and repeated herself. 'I promise. The coke is Rudy's.'

THIRTEEN

Anjali (2024)

The social workers had warned them of the intrusive nature of the ongoing home study, but Anjali wasn't expecting this level of questioning and probing into her past. 'I don't see why it has any relevance to anything,' she said. They were lying in bed, a tray of tea and marmalade on toast balanced between them. 'I mean sure, get references, but to speak to estranged family members and employers feels like spying.' She took a piece of toast and ate as she talked, which she knew irritated Donna. 'We've nearly done the nine-month home study. Then all those panels? Feels excessive, don't you think? I mean I understand talking about past traumas and childhood, when any child we adopt will have experienced trauma, but to ask for bank references? Ex-partners? Feels like we're being investigated by the police . . .'

Donna moved towards her, snuggling up. 'We've discussed it many times. Paul stays buried. There is no need to bring that up or we'll be talking about unresolved trauma for the next year. I want a baby, Anj. We do. Anyways it's only two panels now, the approval panel then the matching panel. Emma has spoken to everyone, taken all the references bar one, and she said she's certain we'll be approved. Certain. Chill. Get excited. And by the way, you're a disgusting eater. Did you always eat that way?'

Anjali was shovelling toast in her mouth while Donna talked. Donna had made the marmalade herself. That's what she was like. A marmalade maker. A homemaker in every sense. She even grew vegetables in a small raised bed in their garden, runner beans and carrots and kale. She somehow managed a full-time nursing job in oncology and still made time to grow things, make things. She crocheted and was in the community choir and one of the cold-water swimmers at the lido, and she never missed a birthday, anniversary, or event.

She was that sort of person. She would make such a good mum, Anjali knew it. But her? Anjali spent any rare spare time she had watching *Below Deck* or listening to podcasts about serial killers. Donna was full of goodness, but she felt inadequate. Still, maybe the two balanced each other out.

'We all ate quickly. I mean everyone working in the NHS, everyone learns to eat in seconds, right?'

'I don't know. I was on the slow eater table in primary school.'

'What's that?'

'You know, a separate table for slow eaters. Public humiliation from the age of five.' Donna laughed and took the remaining toast from her hand, put it on the tray and lowered the tray to the floor next to her before spooning Anjali and stroking her arm. 'I love you so much. A baby,' she whispered. 'It'll be worth it. Ours. He or she will be. Or they.'

Anjali rolled her eyes. 'Is a baby really ever yours, though? I mean, an adopted baby. Even a surrogate. I mean, who really is the surrogate?' They'd briefly discussed surrogacy after ruling out a sperm donor. Olivia had told Anjali they were barmy. 'You have two healthy uteruses. And you want to outsource? Head down to Wetherspoons on a Friday and pick a man. Actually, scrap that, go to the bar at Claridge's.' Laura had tutted and told Olivia she was classist and Anjali was choosing adoption for altruistic reasons. But the truth was, Anjali couldn't bear the thought that one of them might be more attached to a baby than the other. That love might be divided into shares, that they'd have totally different roles and experiences of motherhood. This was an adventure she wanted to experience with Donna exactly as Donna experienced it.

Donna smiled. Anjali could feel it through the back of her neck. Her smile travelled through air and skin and bones and blood. It reached inside you and filled up any gaps. 'We're not discussing this again. This is the way. We've talked about this. We're doing it. Really doing it. We are going to be parents. You agreed. You were excited. And you never get excited unless it's a new season of *Selling Sunset*. Which is beyond tragic, by the way.'

'Well, now I'm anxious. I like to keep up with the youth.'

'No young person watches TV anymore. Anxiety is part of it. We're doing it together though. Imagine your parents. How happy they will be.' Donna stopped talking a moment, and Anjali could feel no breath on her back. She was holding her breath, as she always did when speaking about family. It was easy to forget how lucky Anjali was. Easy to be insensitive.

'I'll ask Laura and Olivia, of course, about the last reference?'

Donna sat up. 'Don't ask Laura.' She frowned, picked up Anjali's hands in hers and kissed her fingers. 'I mean it. For me, don't ask Laura.'

Anjali shrugged. 'She's my best friend . . .'

Donna breathed out. 'I know and I love her, I really do. But something's off with her at the moment. I bumped into her ages ago at work. Pancreatic cancer diagnosed in A&E, I mean horrific . . .'

'That's sad,' said Anjali.

'Anyway, she ran past and she was odd. Her and Olivia were talking in the kitchen at Liv's and they seemed off. And then

at The Dog she seemed jumpy too. I don't know, it's probably nothing, but it's like she's hiding something.' She noticed
Anjali's expression. 'I don't know, maybe my sixth sense is off
. . . This adoption process is affecting all of us. You could ask
a work friend for the reference? They don't need to speak to
Stephen necessarily, just a colleague. Ask Bola. There's only
one reference missing then that's it, we've completed the home
study . . .'

Anjali nodded. She thought of Bola, the only other GP at
the practice who knew they were trying to adopt and had been
encouraging. *You'd be amazing parents. What a lucky child. Not
just one but two lovely, caring and spectacular mums? Fantastic.
Brilliant.*

'Laura's the most trustworthy person ever. But sure. And
that reminds me, Miles has been a bit weird recently. Said he
needed to talk to me a while back, but I've been so caught up
in this . . .'

Donna smiled. 'Let's have lovely Miles over soon. Probably
some teenage angst.'

Anjali turned around and rested the palm of her hand on
Donna's cheek. 'A baby,' she whispered. The air around them
smelled of plasticine and fresh rain.

The following day, and with Bola's reference, their home study
was completed. The approval panel was arranged immediately,
but of course it would be on the day they had been invited to a
wedding. Anjali hadn't expected to be invited but was touched,
nonetheless, and as important as the adoption panel was, she
would not be missing this. There was enough time between the
events to get across town, they'd decided. They'd both be there.
Anjali had no business attending the wedding of a patient; there
were professional boundaries with the job but every now and

then, doctors crossed them anyway, and with very good reason. Hannah Stewart was dying. She had been Anjali's patient for four years, since she was first diagnosed with colon cancer, before the metastases that littered a trail of tumours throughout her insides, before Hannah had received chemotherapy and radiotherapy, and later palliative radiotherapy then counselling and palliative care at the cancer centre. Donna always stayed in touch with her patients long after they left hospital. She spent her days off visiting people in their homes, or the local hospice, where she also worked extra agency shifts. She had been wedding-planning all weekend, made a wedding cake with three tiers and chocolate icing and sourced banners and balloons and ribbons and bunting to decorate Hannah's hospice room. Anjali watched Donna now, and the other nurses, rushing around Hannah's bed making final touches. Nursing was not about cure, Anjali thought. It was much more than that.

She took a chair over to Hannah and sat next to her. 'Well, this is exciting.'

Hannah smiled. She was in considerable pain, Anjali could tell from subtle clues – the tone of her voice, her slight wincing – but apparently had refused all painkillers. She wanted to be fully awake for this last, big moment. She looked beautiful as well as incredibly sick. Her hair was decorated with small white flowers, and she wore a creamy, silk wedding dress, and despite being bedbound, kitten heels.

'I'm glad you're here.' Hannah reached out her hand and Anjali took it and squeezed gently, before standing up and moving the chair away, making room for the oncologist who had wandered in, beaming.

He leaned over and spoke to Hannah softly as Anjali tiptoed to the back of the room. A nurse put some classical music on quietly, another opened the door and a few guests began to filter in, close relatives, and finally Hannah's own children, aged four and seven respectively. Anjali watched them climb carefully onto Hannah's bed and lean against her.

Dave arrived last. She had got to know him very well over the four years, both as her patient's fiancé, and as a patient in his own right, managing his inevitable depression and anxiety. Today, though, he did not look sad or afraid. He was a tall man, and proud. He beamed at Hannah as if she was the most beautiful woman he'd ever seen, and the hospital chaplain began the service.

Donna crept to the back of the room and stood with Anjali, and as they listened to the heartbreaking vows and watched the faces of Hannah and Dave and their children fill with love and with pain, she put her hand on the small of Anjali's back.

'It was the most incredible wedding we will ever attend. Hands down.' They had gone straight from the hospice as soon as the cake had been cut, and raced across London to the social services contact centre, eating cake on the way. 'That lovely, poor family. Isn't life beautiful – and terrible.'

Donna nodded. 'Really special. I'm glad we pulled it off.'

The waiting area of the centre was a bit like her clinic, uncomfortable chairs and well-read, tatty magazines in piles on small wooden tables. 'Wish we had time to digest it, but in many ways, it was a good distraction.' Anjali was nervous about today. Adoption approval panel was a terrifying ordeal, despite everyone's efforts to be friendly. The team who would decide their future, who had the power to make them a family, or not, were assembled in the next room, a group of social workers, doctors, adopters and other professionals, all discussing Anjali and Donna's fitness and ability to parent. They needed to be on their game, focus on answering the inevitable questions fired their way, but it was difficult after such an emotional morning. Anjali kept picturing Hannah and Dave, and the enormity of life and death, love and loss.

'We're ready for you.' Emma poked her head out from behind the door, smiling.

Anjali picked up Donna's hand. It was sweaty, despite Donna's calm exterior. They walked together into the room and sat down at the large square table, looking at all the faces in front of them. Emma sat beside Anjali.

'Welcome, welcome. Emma tells us you've rushed straight over from work and we wanted to thank you for making time for this today.' A man with thick-rimmed glasses introduced himself as Colin, and everyone went around the table giving their name and role, all of them smiling and nodding slightly, in a reassuring way. 'We have all read the home study that Emma has been working with you on, and now we have a few questions for you. Nothing to worry about. And I'm sure you'll have plenty of questions of your own. Then afterwards we will ask you to wait outside again and have a quick chat, then let you know our decision. All OK?'

Both Anjali and Donna nodded a bit too enthusiastically, Anjali thought. It was surreal. She wondered if her patients felt like this, a total handing over of control to strangers.

'So. First things first. Why is it that you'd like to adopt?'

Donna answered and Anjali listened. She discussed her desire to help, their ability, evidenced through their jobs, to deal with challenges. Their longing to become parents and have a child, and what they felt able to offer that child. 'We have so much love to give,' said Donna.

A woman with a severe haircut stopped writing and looked up. 'Do you think love is enough? Some of our children who need forever homes have had incredibly difficult starts in life.

Disrupted attachment patterns, all manner of trauma. They need extra special parenting.'

Anjali nodded. 'We appreciate that and we're ready for hard work. We've a great family network of family and friends and a good understanding of issues related to adoption and child development . . .' She tailed off. Donna was side-eyeing her. She sounded like she was interviewing for a corporate job.

'A patient of ours,' interrupted Donna, 'was married this morning. I know she won't mind me talking about it. She is dying of cancer. She possibly has a week left to live. Her family are facing the worst possible thing any of us can imagine.' She lifted up Anjali's hand and held it. 'But despite everything they are going through, it's love that is the glue holding them together. Love is not enough in any relationship. But it's the most important thing.'

The woman with the haircut smiled. There were mutterings around the room. They asked a few more questions, and Anjali and Donna asked some of their own.

'If we are successful, how soon before we could possibly be matched with a baby?'

'Is the matching panel a similar process?'

'What happens if we are matched but the birth family oppose the adoption?'

Finally, Emma stood, thanked them both, and ushered them out. She walked with them back to the waiting area. 'I'll be back as soon as I can. Won't be long.' She disappeared, leaving Anjali going over the answers, and wondering if she'd messed everything up.

'I came across a bit of a dick.' Anjali leaned her head on Donna's shoulder. 'But you were brilliant.'

Donna couldn't keep still. 'What do you think they're saying? I don't know why I brought Hannah into it. I mean, in my head I knew what I meant, but maybe I was being chippy? Defensive?'

They didn't wait long. Colin came out to the waiting area, Emma behind him. Anjali and Donna stood.

'I am pleased to say you are approved adopters.' He reached out his hand to shake theirs, but they were too busy bursting into tears and hugging each other to notice.

FOURTEEN

Olivia (2024)

Dele didn't seem sad at all, just angry. Angrier than she'd ever seen him. He was fist-clenched when they confronted Freya, and Olivia noticed that when she told them the coke was Rudy's, his knuckles became more and more prominent. She was adamant in a way that they had only seen once or twice in her life. She was telling the truth. Later, when they were alone in the kitchen, he'd told Olivia to phone Laura, and at the name Laura coming from Dele's mouth, a memory smarted, slapped Olivia hard across the face as though it was yesterday instead of decades before. Dele couldn't understand their dynamic, how she'd maintained their friendship, almost become protective of Laura, the person who'd betrayed her, who he'd betrayed her with. It baffled Dele that Olivia did not want to tell Laura she knew. She had Dele swear to her he'd never let on that he'd confessed. 'The only way I could ever deal with this,' Olivia had explained, 'is to pretend it never happened.'

Of course Dele *was* going to tell Laura everything. She understood that. But everything changed the night of the party. Everything. Olivia pointed out that if any of the events got back to the GMC, the General Medical Council, then surely all of their registrations as doctors would be at risk. Their reputations would be, at least. She had wanted him to completely

distance himself from Laura. To forget it ever happened. She
didn't want anyone to ever know about it. Olivia was ready to
say anything and do anything to keep Dele away from Laura
back then. But after the night of the party, Laura cut herself
off from Dele anyway.

'I forgave you and I forgave her,' she said. *Anyway – she was
grieving and not of sound mind, and you had no excuse whatsoever.*
But of course, it still hurt, and she never uttered the second
part. When it had happened all she could think of was her
mum's expression, her raised eyebrows, looking at the engagement ring, *it will fade over time.* She would prove her wrong.

People made mistakes. And they could be forgiven. But
history was repeating itself.

When she tried to convince Dele that they should *not* tell
Laura about the drugs, or tell the school, and definitely not
the police, he was confused. 'Why are you protecting Rudy? I
just don't get it, Liv. I mean why? She needs to know. You'd
want to know. She's his mother! I can't believe he would do
such a thing. If Freya had taken that, she could be dead . . .'

'I'll speak to Rudy,' she'd told Freya and Dele. 'Laura does
not need this right now. I mean it. Let's never talk about it
again.' She'd looked at Freya and made her voice ice-cold. 'I'll
deal with you later.'

Dele had finally agreed, after days of her pleading, to keep
the drugs secret, 'for the sake of Freya's future', he said. 'But
I'm so angry with Rudy. He better stay away from me, that's
for sure.' Dele still didn't understand why she wanted Laura to
be kept from the truth, from the pain. Why Olivia was always
protecting Laura and their friendship. Olivia suspected he
assumed it was her faith enabling her forgiveness. But everyone
knew that you keep your friends close, and your enemies even
closer. Surely everyone knew that.

'What hold has she got on you?' he asked. 'She doesn't even know that you know about what happened, about the affair . . .'

The word burned inside her. 'I told you to never speak of it,' Olivia said. 'It was a million years ago. Anyway, this is totally different. Honestly, she's close to the edge. She has so much going on and this will tip her over. Please, Dele. Please trust me.' She watched Dele pace up and down, angrier than she'd ever seen him. It should have been awful seeing Dele so cross, but it wasn't. There was something protective in it, something exclusively reserved for Freya. For their family. Something that Rudy – and Laura – were outside of.

'She'll lose her school place. Her future. She could end up convicted with a criminal record,' Dele said.

Olivia nodded, though she had been talking about Laura, while Dele had assumed she meant Freya. He conceded eventually, and they had agreed to bury the news – the crime, Dele said. The crime! Olivia would deal with Freya and Rudy direct, and this would never ever get out, or happen again.

They flushed the cocaine down the toilet and agreed to Just Get On With It. Stoicism, they were good at.

But Dele was unravelling a bit, Olivia could tell. Dele did not cry. He didn't cry, apparently, when his father died, or even when he arrived at boarding school, aged eight, holding so tightly onto his small square suitcase that his fingers formed blisters. He didn't cry the night he first met Olivia, when he knew with such a rush of certainty that she would one day be his wife that on the way home his knees buckled, and he fell down on the lawn. He didn't cry when he was kicked so hard in the shin during a rugby match that his calf opened up and the muscle slid out onto the pitch, wet and pale and flapping around like a fish out of water. He did not cry when their son was born.

Not even when Freya was born, and he called her his angel. He didn't cry as he begged Olivia for forgiveness when she found out about Laura all those years ago. He didn't even cry when Olivia told him what happened that night. What Laura did. The reason it needed to end immediately, even if he thought he loved her. He didn't cry when Olivia told him that anyone associated with Laura, should it all get out, would at best find their reputation irreparably damaged, and at worst be deemed unfit to practise medicine. She watched it sink into him, that possibility, the prospect of a life without his job. He could not.

Still, Olivia could see that Dele's mental health was deteriorating, despite his bravado. He was quieter, withdrawn, drinking more. She could see the cracks underneath his surface, the flashbacks that woke him at night, jolting suddenly and opening and closing his hands, as though he too was performing surgery. The edges of his tongue were serrated where he'd been grinding his teeth in his sleep. His jokes were getting more defensive, more offensive; they offered shallow and temporary protection from his pain, she knew it. He was so much like her father, increasingly so, that for perhaps the first time, Liv understood something new about her mother. She recognised the terror beneath. The job had taken away his mental health, eroded it over the years, chipped away at his soul. She pictured men returning from pointless wars, shell-shocked and unable to process the actions of their own hands. Moral injuries were the price of war. And they were the price of medicine.

They were lying in bed. Their bedroom was extremely colourful. House of Hackney floral wallpaper, thick velvet jade green curtains, elaborate lamps they'd found in Italy. The bedspread was covered in a quilt that had been made by Dele's grandmother, and the side tables she'd picked up in a flea market in Paris, along with the antique chandelier, and heavy wardrobes. Dele complained that the room gave him a headache it had so much going on, but Olivia knew he loved it really. There was a reading chair by the window, and he'd spend much of his time at home reading non-fiction, long legs crossed, a slipper hanging off the end of his toe. She'd wanted to create a house that was the opposite of a hospital. There was nothing whatsoever clinical about their home. It was filled with art and antiques and animals and children. Miles and Freya had friends in and out all the time. Their schools were a spit away and often they'd pop by at lunchtime with a group of hungry friends, red-faced and sweaty from sports and hormones. She had large Tupperware containers filled perman-ently with chicken, vegetables and potatoes, macaroni pies, lasagnes, anything stodgy with a high carbohydrate content. She'd stopped buying juice after Miles had a succession of fill-ings, and instead had large jugs of ice-cold cucumber water, to which once Freya et al had added a whole bottle of Grey Goose vodka and was subsequently grounded for a month. Freya had always tested boundaries. But nothing like this.

'I don't understand it. Why would she be so stupid? I could kill Rudy. I mean it.'

Olivia looked at his face and smiled. Dele had always looked at Rudy as if he was flesh and blood, and she liked seeing this other side of him. He was as handsome as when she'd first met him; more so, even, with flecks of salt and pepper in his hair, and a knowing expression in his eyes. Medicine had given him hard edges but there was a gentle softness in his centre that felt like a secret between them. When she saw his loyalty to Freya, it reinforced what she had always known. He belonged to her.

She reached across and placed her hand on his cheek. 'I love you,' she said.

He closed his eyes. Put his hand over hers and took a deep breath. When he opened his eyes, they were wet at the edges. 'Our little girl,' he whispered. 'Our baby girl. Drugs.' Finally, Dele began to cry.

But Olivia didn't cry. Instead, she thought about Rudy giving Freya drugs. She thought, as she often did, even now, about Laura and Dele, an image of them kissing lodged deep in her brain like a tumour, an astrocytoma that had tentacles which wrapped around everything until nothing was left.

FIFTEEN

Laura (2024)

If Laura was ever invited on *Mastermind*, stab wounds would be her specialist subject. She could tell by the exact location of a stab wound if it would kill or maim. In South London, any emergency doctor quickly gained expertise in the horrors of knife crime. Kids as young as ten would be sitting up talking one minute and on the edge of life the next, and it was only during the secondary survey they'd discover a slit the size of a coin over their liver or spleen or kidney, and the reason for sudden deterioration. Sneaky things, stab injuries. The physiology of a child meant they would compensate until cardiac arrest, maintain the blood pressure right to the end, and then collapse so fast it was breathtaking. Laura called these kids 'talk and die', the term medics gave those patients who had suffered head injuries with silent brain bleeds. *Like Joe Duggard.* Her soul ached for that poor boy, and his family; the chugging sound of the ventilator followed her around, like someone breathing on the back of her neck.

They arrived on scene to find a group of teens surrounding the patient, a young boy of around fifteen, sitting up, holding his side. He reminded Laura of Rudy, the expression in his eyes one of a much younger child. 'I'm Laura. Hi, Matthew.' She kneeled, assessing him as she went, before getting him on the trolley, strapping him in, despite his protests, and transferring him to the helicopter. His friends were joking around, unable to see the danger Laura knew was real. She wondered how many of them were carrying blades. She had retrieved kids who had been stabbed with every knife you could imagine, from machetes to scalpels. There were so many knives in Camberwell that the police had started an initiative, asking kids to hand in their knives and then having them melted down to build an entire gym from knives in the local park. It was meant to provide comfort, she suspected, to remind people good could come from bad and teens were handing over their weapons to the police. But Laura knew the truth. For every knife handed in to the police, there were ten not handed in. The only time stabbings diminished was during lockdown, when there was virtually no trauma and no knife crime, much to the team's surprise. 'Mandem are too frightened of the virus to be out swinging their knives around,' Juan had said.

'I don't feel so good.' Matthew tried to sit up. His numbers on the monitor remained stable, he was a little tachycardic but nothing extraordinary. But Laura could see the change in his colour, his face pale and eyes glazing.

She shouted to Juan. 'ETA?'

'Five mins max. All good back there?'

'We're fine.' She smiled at Matthew, but the alarms began to sound out at once, and his belly grew distended, swollen and shiny. Shiny abdomens were never a good sign. Unlike in films, Laura understood that people bleed to death on the inside, quietly and with only tiny clues. Doctors were detectives, really.

His eyes rolled back as he lost consciousness. Laura attached the defib pads to his chest, moved the portable defibrillator next to him, and stood above him with her fingers pressing into his neck. 'Juan, can you step on it? He's got a carotid output but only just. He's going to arrest.'

Nobody wanted to resuscitate mid-air. It wasn't safe. A few times they had to land the helicopter in a field en route to the hospital to try and stabilise the patient. But Laura could see City helipad out of the window. She squeezed a bag of fluid as quickly as she could into his cannula, put a non-rebreathe oxygen mask on Matthew's face and whacked it up. 'Come on, Matthew. Hang on in there.'

The Ethics Committee were the crème de la crème of hospital medicine. These were those doctors who were tasked with the most difficult of decisions, where the local medical teams were unable to reach a moral answer. They were a team of misfit doctors from various specialities, all of whom had a specific interest and vast experience in the grey, sticky areas of medicine. Laura had been part of the committee for a few years; like all the members, she'd always enjoyed figuring out the jigsaw puzzles of people's lives. They were a motley crew, woven together with their singular aim: to find the meaning in medicine, and in human lives. The doctors presented each case, with all the medical records and information, and discussed them in turn. The cases were from all areas of the hospital and covered all manner of complex decisions. A woman who was twenty-eight weeks pregnant and ventilated, the husband not wanting the C-section performed lest the baby didn't survive but the mother's chances of survival much improved if it was, a Jehovah's Witness refusing a blood transfusion despite a haemoglobin of 7, a child of thirteen with capacity and acute myeloid leukaemia refusing any more active treatment, and a man of ninety-two wanting it. Laura listened and discussed with her colleagues each in turn, gave her opinions based on her years of understanding trauma and emergency medicine. She was tired after the busy morning. Matthew had made it somehow, survived and was recovering on the children's ward, though with an ileostomy. She had contacted the charity Redthread, who came to see kids in hospital involved with knife crime, to prevent the retaliation they saw all too often, from one gang to another. She hadn't had lunch yet despite it being 5 p.m. She was about to excuse herself from the meeting, to grab a sandwich before ward round, but Rosa, an obstetrician and Professor of Medical Ethics who was permanently dressed in Lycra cycling clothes, held up a set of intensive care notes and nodded to Laura.

'This lad on intensive care is eighteen years old, and was brought in via you, Laura, with a significant head injury. He had neurosurgery and was bolted, and yet suffered catastrophic hypoxic ischaemic injury that is irrecoverable. Scans are here.' Rosa posted the scan images on the light board in front of them. They read scans like palm readers read palms, looking into an imagined future based on their perception. Intuition was a powerful, almost mystical force. Laura had worked with a nurse once who could walk on to a ward she'd never set foot on, and go immediately to the sickest patient based on a feeling in her gut. Medicine was never an exact science, despite what patients believed. But these scans were devastatingly clear. Joe had zero chance of recovery. Laura's skin became cold. She had no idea Joe Duggard would be presented at the Ethics Committee. The room began to spin. She pressed her hands into the chair, and her teeth together.

Laura felt two things simultaneously. Extreme sadness and pity for Joe's family. But also, a sense of enormous relief that it wasn't Rudy lying there. It could so easily have been. A terrifying truth.

'He's stable, no? It's early days?' Laura sat up and tried to keep her voice even.

Rosa shook her head. 'He made some respiratory effort a few days ago, but the scans are clear. I think we need to recommend withdrawal of treatment.'

'What's the story?' Peter stood up to look at the scan. He was eating a Fruit Corner yoghurt. He put his spoon down. 'That's nasty.'

Laura kept her voice level and professional. 'He was at a party, fell downstairs and smashed his head on the side of the table. His GCS was 4 on scene . . . It was pretty horrid.'

'So tragic.' Rosa shook her head. 'One minute here, the next somewhere else. What a tragedy.'

'So – we're all in agreement with the ICU team? They wouldn't normally even raise it with us, but the hospital legal team want any potential withdrawal of ventilation discussed at Ethics Committee. Too many high-profile cases . . . But this is cut and dried, a continuing vegetative state, and that is only going one way. We're simply prolonging this lad's suffering at this stage. Poor family.'

Everyone nodded but Laura. The world stopped. The room blurred. All she heard was Rudy crying and telling her the truth. That Freya had pushed him. Freya had pushed Joe Duggard and he hit his head so hard on the table at the bottom of the stairs that he had irrecoverable brain damage. Freya hadn't intended any of this to happen, but even so, Laura knew that there would be consequences. There *should* be consequences. Laura had held on to the fact that he might recover. Perhaps he'd recover and with memory loss and it would all be a bit vague but put down to a tragic accident. Joe would turn a corner and get better. That's what she'd told herself, even though deep down she knew it wasn't true. She knew everything Rosa was saying was the truth. It was futile. He had no chance of survival. He was suffering and they needed to let him die. But then what? Freya pushed him. She caused the injury that seriously hurt him; even unintentionally, the outcome remained. The injury that would kill him.

'Let's recommend discussion with the family about withdrawal of treatment, and if still relevant, we can review again next week after Amir is back.' Rosa closed the notes and took a new set out. 'Right, this one is a bit less black and white. End stage lung cancer, and the surgeon wants to perform a pneumonectomy . . . Bit trigger happy.'

Laura could barely hear Rosa by then. She leaned forwards as the room spun in front of her, taking large bites of air. An image landed inside her head, of Freya, with blood on her hands, but the image came into focus, gained clarity and hard outlines and it wasn't Freya at all. It was Laura.

She couldn't breathe. 'Feel faint,' she whispered. Her colleagues rushed around her, laying her flat, raising her legs, and she tried to slow-breathe out, but her head was far away, and their voices were far away, muffled, except one word she heard over and over inside her, the word like a bolt in her brain: *run*.

Olivia was with a patient when she found her, performing an echocardiogram in a totally dark room. It was unusual for doctors to return to the hospital they'd trained at, and a testament to City that both Olivia and Laura had been drawn back. Of course, Anjali had followed them; although not practising hospital medicine, she was near enough to City that they sometimes met in the canteen, the three of them, sitting on exactly the same table they had sat at during medical school all those years ago. The table may not have changed much, or even the hospital, but she had, thought Laura. She'd become far less naive and optimistic. Anjali had perhaps changed the most. Yet Olivia was as steady and sure and capable as she always had been.

Laura opened the curtains a fraction and watched Olivia. She even looked the same. A slight frown of concentration, long neck, bobbed brown hair. Aside from the laughter lines around her eyes and a few extra pounds, she could have been Olivia at twenty-one. She was glued to the monitor, her hand with the probe moving over the patient's chest as she stared at the screen. The sound of the whooshing blood matched the stress noise in Laura's head. The colours on the screen were bright blue and bright red, the patterns of abstract art that only experts like Olivia understood. She clicked the keyboard a few times, leaned forward, recorded a whoosh and a triangle-shaped area of blue, then lifted the probe from the patient and spun around in one movement. 'The valve is working beautifully,' she said. She stood and flicked on the lights. Laura stepped back, hidden from their view but peering through the curtain she watched the patient's face, his relief.

'Thank you, doctor.' He was a bit teary, but Olivia laughed.

'Just a valve replacement,' she said. 'Like changing a washer on the washing machine.'

The patient sat up. He was properly crying now. Olivia stopped laughing and sat next to him, lifted his hand. 'You'll be fine, Bill. But I don't want to see you again, OK? Lay off the fry-ups.'

Bill smiled, wiped his face of tears, and looked at Olivia as she stood up. 'You've saved my life.'

Laura watched a few moments, then slipped away and walked quickly off the ward. She could barely breathe. Her chest hurt; her ribs felt bruised. A line of sweat dripped down her back. She had been calling and calling Olivia but had almost been relieved when there was no response. She had to tell her, but it would cause her so much pain. Olivia adored Freya as much as Laura adored Rudy. They were equally protective of their children, fierce advocates. Laura found it hard to even imagine Olivia's face when she found out Freya was in trouble. Thinking of Olivia hurting filled Laura with hurt too. She was like a sister to her. But she had to tell her the truth.

SIXTEEN

Anjali (1999)

Being with Paul made Anjali feel completely seen in a way she'd never experienced. She wasn't a medical student, or young woman with a brilliant brain, or perfect child with perfect parents, she was Anj, a bit rock 'n' roll, and carefree. She liked his confidence, the way he made her feel like the single most important thing in the universe, his intense and direct eye contact. Anjali didn't realise, at first, that he was dealing drugs. She never questioned his car, the rent on his apartment, his collection of expensive watches and trainers, and designer clothes. Surely, property developers earned a great deal more than doctors? It seemed obvious once she knew, though. There was scant evidence of much property developing. She spent a day walking around and thinking about it. Could she or should she date a drug dealer? She came to the conclusion that anyone who had taken drugs, including her, was complicit in supply chains and illegality, and the people who sold drugs were no worse than those who took them. She decided to turn a blind eye to that part of his life, and even briefly wondered, on some level, if she found it exciting. She'd always been careful with money. Her parents had saved every penny they had to fund university courses and Anjali's future wedding. But Paul burned through money as if it grew on trees, buying her expensive gifts, paying for everything.

They would go to fancy restaurants and fancy bars and snort fat lines of coke in the bathrooms, before going home and talking until dawn, before making love and smoking weed and making love again. It was utterly hedonistic and felt somehow magical. Of course, the daytimes were not so easy, and Anjali, for the first time ever, began to lose her concentration. She found herself at the City Tavern, necking a shot of tequila at lunchtime to get through afternoon lectures. During clinical placements, she could smell the alcohol leaving her skin, and spent a small fortune on heavily perfumed moisturiser to try and disguise the smell. Heavily scented people were always hiding something.

'This is the longest journey in the universe.' Paul was driving, wearing sunglasses and a checked shirt that was ironed so well it had sharp lines on the outsides of the arms.

'Cornwall is far. I brought snacks, though.' Anjali opened the glove compartment of Paul's car where she had stuffed bags of crisps and chocolate bars.

'I have no idea how you stay so skinny,' Paul said. 'Or don't have diabetes.'

They listened to music and chatted for hours, stopping at a service station for bathroom and coffee breaks. Paul was more cheerful than usual. He had pushed to meet Anjali's parents, said it was the right thing to do, and Anjali had avoided it for a few months but relented when her mum also asked to meet him. 'We'll stay in a hotel,' she said.

'Nonsense,' her mum had replied. 'Stay here. This is home and we want to get to know Paul.'

They weaved through the impossibly narrow streets, stopping and reversing occasionally for other cars, then a flock of sheep, then a man on a horse and cart shouting, 'Any old iron.' Paul raised his eyebrows and gave Anjali a perplexed expression. 'Jesus, it's like stepping back in time.'

After a six-hour drive they pulled into Anjali's road, and parked up. Paul had a boot full of gifts for her parents, flowers for her mum and her favourite perfume, which she only wore on special occasions to make it last, and a handmade chess set for her dad. Anjali told him it was excessive, and her parents weren't expecting gifts at all, but Paul had insisted. He liked playing chess on a handmade set that Anjali had commented her dad would love when they'd first met. Paul had a replica set made especially for her dad, which Anjali said was way too much, but she'd imagined her dad's face, and how much he would adore that gift.

Her parents opened the door, beaming, and padded out of the house in their slippers. They hugged Anjali in turn and then hugged Paul too. They went inside chatting continuously, and sat in the living room, while Anjali's mum poured tea.

'It's wonderful to meet you both.' Paul bit into a piece of cake. Her mum would have been cooking all day. Possibly the day before too. 'This is delicious.'

Anjali watched her mum and dad glance at each other with shining eyes. They were happy.

It was a few weeks later when the student nurses invited Anjali to City Tavern after work, a particularly grim day on a stroke ward. Anjali thought nothing of going without Paul. She didn't think to call him and tell him that she was out, or who with. He liked her being with him all the time, described them as inseparable, but it was nice to go out with work friends as well as with Paul, especially after the day she'd had. It turned into a heavy night and Anjali woke feeling sick. She'd been blackout drunk before, but not like this. She woke up disorientated, uneasy in her body. Something was very wrong. Her ears were ringing, and her head burning. A split second of wondering if she'd been drugged flashed behind her eyes, then she remembered pre-blackout, her insisting on shots, too many shots. She remembered vomiting in a taxi, into her hands, cupped hands full of sick that she threw out the window. It came spraying back onto the glass with the wind, chunks of her dinner, and the taxi had stopped, and the driver told her to get out. Them. There was someone with her. She knew him. Dean. He was in the final year above her but needed to retake an exam and they'd sat together and laughed like old friends. She'd grabbed his arm, it felt familiar and sturdy, and he'd held her hair as she puked again, roadside. He'd asked if she was OK. Really OK. Then nothing. Not a thing. Blackness.

She woke in her room, a full ashtray balanced on her chest of drawers, the smell of stale smoke hitting the back of her throat. She lifted her head slowly, the rest of the room coming into focus. Piles of medical textbooks and battered novels were strewn across the carpet, an old pizza box, sweet wrappers everywhere. A salad bowl was the other side of her, presumably in case she vomited in the night.

She had to get up for uni, but she couldn't move. Her stomach was churning with acid and her head was churning with confusion. She closed her eyes again, drifted back to sleep.

'I'm worried about you.' Laura was standing in front of her bed, holding a steaming cup of coffee.

Anjali opened one eye slowly, then the other, yawned. 'What time is it?'

'It's noon. You've missed cardiac physiology. You're becoming a vampire, out all night, sleeping all day.'

'Nobody gives a shit about cardiac physiology except cardiac physiologists.' Anjali sat up, reached for the coffee that Laura was pushing at her. It was strong, gritty with the cheap NHS-style granules they'd all grown accustomed to.

'Honestly, Anj, I'm really worried.' She sat on the bed and Anjali watched her scan the mess of the room and turn her nose up slightly. 'Olivia is too.'

'I'm OK. Honest, guv. I'll have this, shower, then be back in class before anyone misses me. Oh God, it's not Rogers, is it?'

Laura shook her head. Her hair was perfectly blow-dried, which Anjali always found amusing, as though she was going for afternoon tea at The Ritz instead of a draughty lecture theatre with a Pot Noodle. 'It's the skills centre.'

Anjali groaned and covered her face with her pillow.

'Paul's been calling,' Laura said. 'Four times. I told him you were sleeping, but he sounded stressed out.'

Anjali lowered the pillow, put the cup down on the bedside table and swung her legs out of bed. 'Why didn't you tell me?' She pushed past Laura and towards the house phone, which was permanently on the landing. Perhaps she should have called him last night? Was he worried about her?

Laura followed her out and leaned against the door frame as she dialled Paul's number. 'This isn't healthy, Anjali.'

When she woke up again, Paul was there, holding a McDonald's bag. 'Haute cuisine,' he said. 'Sausage & Egg McMuffin. Breakfast of champions.'

Anjali rolled over and groaned.

He stroked her arm gently. 'How do you feel?'

She propped herself up onto her elbows and rubbed her eyes. 'I've felt better. How did you get in?'

He smiled. 'Sounds like a good night then. Laura said you weren't going in this morning.' He paused, put the McDonald's bag down, and straddled her, hugging her then kissing the tip of her nose. He sat up on top of her and held Anjali's wrists in his, then he stopped smiling.

'Paul, I feel sick. Get off.' She twisted beneath him a fraction.

Paul didn't move. He stared at her, his face moving closer to hers. 'Who were you with?'

Anjali looked away, squirmed, and tried to push him off.

He laughed and rolled off her. 'I'd love you anyway. My little raver. So. Who were you with last night?'

She sat up and reached for the McDonald's bag. 'Just a bunch of reprobates. Nursing students mostly.' She opened the bag. Something about Paul's expression prevented her from telling the whole truth, despite it being innocent. That she took a taxi home with Dean. There was nothing in it. She was blackout drunk and he was her friend getting her safely home. But she was beginning to think Paul had a jealous streak, he was so protective, and there was no point upsetting him. Paul was quiet. Too quiet. Anjali always knew when he was annoyed. She was never quite clear why though. His moods would increasingly change from one moment to the next, from boisterous and full of enthusiasm to dark and moody within minutes. But still, weirdly, it made her feel more than loved; she was cherished.

Paul looked around at her room. 'I don't know how you live like this, Anj. You really are the messiest person alive.'

'I know, I know. I'll clean it today. You're the best, bringing me a McDonald's.' She bit into the muffin. 'I know you hate it.'

Paul leaned back against the headboard and looked around the room. 'I'd do anything for you. You know that.' He touched her cheek with his thumb. 'Where were you?'

Anjali searched his voice for clues. The tone of it. The spaces between words. The pitch. Every syllable gave her information about his feelings. He *was* angry. 'Oh, I had a few drinks with some of the nursing students. They're party animals, you'd love them.' She kept her voice even and steady. Had she made plans to see him? Her mind scrambled around. No, he'd just expected her there. Always, he'd said, I want you with me always.

Paul pressed his thumb harder against her cheek and his fingers the other side of her face, until he was squeezing her cheeks, painfully. He moved his face close to hers, and squeezed her face even harder. The room became darker, the air around her felt thicker somehow, and blurry. 'You cunt,' he whispered.

Anjali didn't *feel* like an abused woman. This wasn't domestic violence. Paul liked her extroversion and going out and partying, and that didn't fit with the stereotype in Anjali's head of a woman who was kept beaten behind closed doors. Paul gave her drugs and encouraged her wildness. He'd show her off as his future surgeon and buy her revealing dresses and tell everyone how proud he was of her. Theirs was a passionate love story; she was insanely in love with Paul, and he with her. It felt so exciting and life-affirming to be with him. Of course he was angry when she got blackout drunk. Who wouldn't be?

But his moods became increasingly unstable; he started wanting to know where she was all the time. He sat outside waiting for Anjali after her clinical placements. He phoned her dozens of times a day. And before Anjali knew it, she felt torn in two, a space she could not share with anyone, not even Laura and Olivia.

The hitting came first, then the strangling. They had a lecture about forensic medicine, where the pathologist taught them fatal strangulation timelines:

7 seconds loss of consciousness
15 seconds bladder incontinence
2–3 minutes cell death
4–5 minutes brain death

Anjali sat motionless, listening, caught between fear and love.
A double agent.

SEVENTEEN

Anjali (2024)

It was going to be busy, she could tell by the car park, the queue of people already outside the practice, some of them leaning against the wall to stay upright, a few who looked like they should be in hospital. She walked past them quickly, avoiding eye contact, especially with Mrs Hart who'd not stop talking once she started, and was near impossible to disentangle yourself from. She ducked into the reception, already filling up with the smell of cheap coffee and perfume and feet, a few of her colleagues firing up computers, the phones constantly ringing.

'The BMI machine is busted again.' Mo was fairly new, replacing Sue, who'd stomped out mid working day a few months ago after yet another abusive patient, saying she'd rather work in Tesco. 'Guy coming out at eleven to fix it, but we need a new machine.' He had a cigarette tucked behind his ear. Anjali smiled. She liked him. She walked past and gestured to her ear, and he raised his hand and his eyes, clearly an oversight, and whipped the cigarette out and tucked it into his pocket, before winking thanks at her. 'I owe you a Double Decker,' he said, quietly.

Her room was next to the waiting area; she'd drawn the short straw with that as her patients sat on plastic, spaced-out chairs, staring at her door, and despite the confidential nature of her job, she was sure some conversations could be overheard outside. She had a fairly comfortable office chair in front of her desk, on which sat a large computer that frequently froze, a phone that didn't work, a buzzer that flashed aggressively, and a small, framed photograph of her, Olivia and Laura at medical school, holding up their certificates at graduation, their faces full of pride and possibility. Anjali remembered that day, the three of them holding hands and whispering, 'We did it.' They made a vow then and there to move forwards, to forget the past, and to live their lives. Olivia and Laura seemed to manage it. Their careers shot ahead of Anjali's. They both got married and had babies, while Anjali spent so many years making sense of what she'd been through. She'd given up on children but loved theirs as her own. Especially Miles. Anjali remembered the day he was christened, how she took her role as godmother so seriously, and wrote him a list of promises: *I will guide you and support your parents. I'll love you no matter what but will be there to advise you on right from wrong.*

The rest of the room was clinical, wipe-clean, and functional: a sink with boxes of gloves about it, a giant roll of plastic aprons, a small trolley containing blood bottles and the blood sugar machine that they'd all had to take a half-day training for, as though it was a space shuttle, and tourniquets and tongue depressors and an SaO_2 machine. There was a noticeboard on the back of the wall, next to fire safety, with information about talking therapy, sexually transmitted diseases, baby clinic, wellness rooms, emergency out-of-hours psychiatric helplines. A new defibrillator was stuck near the window. The trolley behind the curtain was broken and too high so patients had to climb up on it no matter their state, and Anjali had bought a bright blue toddler step from IKEA, which was sturdy and wipeable. A light above the trolley meant for examining rashes or cervixes or unexplained bruising was movable, but sprang back to starting position, often smacking her in the face.

Anjali hadn't intended to become a GP. She'd loved hospital medicine, the teamwork and camaraderie and fast-paced nature of it. But after suffering depression and anxiety, as well as migraines and irritable bowel syndrome, and being helped so much by her own family doctor, Anjali conceded that general practice felt like a good home. She hadn't imagined that the job of a GP would be one less like medicine and more like business manager. She spent her life dealing with budgets and complaints and HR. Some days, most days, it wasn't at all what she'd expected being a doctor meant. Still, there was at least the odd day she felt like she was doing some good.

'Ben Walsh?' She looked down the corridor at the waiting area, full already. A woman stood up and followed her back into clinic, pushing a buggy.

'Are you Mum?' Anjali ushered the woman in, and she sat on the plastic chair, lifting the hood of the pushchair.

She nodded and began unstrapping the baby. 'This is Ben.'

It only took Anjali one look at him to know he'd need to be seen in A&E. He was pale, floppy and grey, and every time he took a breath a small dip formed at the base of his throat; his nostrils were flaring. She took her stethoscope and listened to his chest. 'Right. It sounds like he's got a chest infection, but because of how he is breathing I think we need to get him seen in hospital, so I think it's wise we call an ambulance.' She dialled 999 and handed over: *six-month-old infant suspected sepsis, Sats are only picking up 89 . . .*

By the time Anjali put the phone down, Ben's mum was crying, and Ben was gurgling and making normal baby noises, kicking his legs. Anjali leaned over and touched his mum's arm. 'He seems to be coping very well, but it's best to be safe and he needs a bit of oxygen. The ambulance is the quickest way to get it.'

Ben's mum nodded, sniffed and dried her eyes.

'Can I ask you some questions while we're waiting?' Anjali began tapping on the computer while keeping one eye on Ben's chest, to monitor his respiratory rate and recession, the amount he was working to suck air in. He seemed slightly better. 'When did he last have a wet nappy? Any milk? Has he turned blue at any point? Any shaking?'

Anjali kept them in her clinic room until the paramedic arrived and whisked them off. She waved them out of the car park and exhaled. Babies got sick very quickly, and Anjali did not like the look of Ben's breathing at all.

The afternoon whizzed by. In the space of a few hours, Anjali had dealt with suspected cancer, worsening dementia, athero-sclerosis, heart failure, a viral infection, back pain, COPD, asthma, psoriasis and high blood pressure. A woman with no heating shivered and cried as Anjali listened helplessly, and a man with diabetes and a poorly managed diet told her he had no money for food. Anjali found herself prescribing fuel tokens, and foodbank vouchers, as well as talking therapy, even anti-depressants, because there was no cure she could offer for 'desperation' or 'existential suffering' or 'hopelessness'.

She managed to eat a quick sandwich between patients, and was about to call the next in when the phone rang, which was unusual during clinic time; the reception team knew how busy she was. She picked up and held the receiver to her ear with her shoulder as she tapped on the computer, scrolling the appointment list, half listening.

'Anjali, it's Emma.' The phone line was crackly.

There was a moment or two before Anjali could place the voice. A relative, no doubt, making a complaint, or informing her of a bereavement. 'Emma?'

'Emma George. From Lambeth Children and Families team. I tried to call Donna, but she's tied up at work.'

'Is everything OK?' Anjali swallowed; her throat suddenly dry. Why was the social worker calling? Getting hold of a social worker was mission impossible, and they never called unannounced. It felt like ages since they'd been approved as adopters, despite it only being a matter of days. This was surely the worst part. Knowing they were greenlit to take a baby yet having to wait for social workers to match them with one.

Emma laughed. The phone crackled. 'Everything is better than OK,' she said. 'I have news. There's a child. She's two and a bit. A little girl.'

Anjali pressed the phone so hard against her ear, it echoed like the inside of a seashell. She heard everything and nothing all at once. 'A girl,' she said. 'A little girl.' There was a small cry from the waiting room, and Anjali's heart swelled double in her chest.

EIGHTEEN

Laura (2024)

Camberwell had changed so much in two decades that Laura barely recognised it. Peckham felt more familiar, despite the rooftop bars and organic wines, but Church Street in Camberwell was another country. 'Remember when the only food we could feasibly get in this area was one-pound chicken.' Olivia had suggested they meet at a new Kurdish place that served hibiscus negronis that she'd read about in the *Dulwich Diverter*. Laura, unlike Anjali and Olivia, was still not that interested in food. She ate a healthy diet of mainly protein and vegetables, tofu and steamed broccoli, or an omelette with green beans, and every now and then the occasional carbohydrate fest. She couldn't remember the last negroni she'd drunk. These days she tried to avoid drinking anything but water. She'd even cut out caffeine. But this place felt like the right setting to tell Olivia the worst news. Olivia seemed to have been avoiding Laura recently. Maybe she was imagining it, but she'd answered her phone even less than usual, and cancelled Rudy going for a sleepover that weekend. She was probably just busy. They all were.

'I really need to see you,' Laura had said. 'I'll meet you after work. We can try that place, sounds good. Hibiscus negronis.'

'Really?' Olivia sounded surprised. Laura rarely suggested dinner on a school night, let alone cocktails. She loved it on the rare occasions when she talked Laura into drinking with her. 'Shall we call Anj?'

'Can we do just us this time?' Laura paused. 'We need to talk about the kids. I've been trying to get hold of you.'

Olivia bristled, Laura could feel cold through the telephone and into her ear. Olivia was more like her mother than she ever dared to admit, Laura thought. Once a matter was closed, she liked it forgotten about, and she'd been adamant they forget the situation and get on with life. Olivia's voice was slightly different. Was she hiding something? Had Freya told her already? But Olivia returned to her deadpan tone quickly, as she insisted they throw themselves into work and move on. Only, of course, they really couldn't. Joe Duggard was fighting for his life on intensive care. The Ethics Committee were going to recommend withdrawal of treatment. This was not going away. *Not this time.*

She looked around the pretty restaurant, brick-walled and candlelit, small wooden tables full of colourful plates, the hum of laughter and chatter. The clientele was typically South London. They were a young, bohemian crowd, wore scruffy, baggy jeans and plush velvet, colourful jackets and dirty trainers. Everyone looked twenty and wore heavy eye make-up, regardless of gender. A waiter smiled and winked at Laura looking around as he walked past, but Laura didn't smile. She thought of the twenty-year-old students who could afford to drink hibiscus negronis and wear clothes that looked like they had been retrieved from a skip, the money and confidence that took. The privilege.

'Are we starter-ing? I skipped breakfast and lunch, so my vote is yes . . .' Olivia held up the menu, and Laura poured some tap water into thick blue glasses. The waiter swung back, and they ordered; he memorised the food that Laura felt certain they would never eat, but let Olivia choose nonetheless: jasmine rice with apricots, Baharat fries, Kurdish pickles, shish, lamb for her, aubergine for Laura. She ordered four cocktails to 'save the waiter going back and forth'. She was drinking too much. Olivia had always been obsessed with wine, appreciating it in a way that Laura didn't understand. But over the years, she'd sipped less, and glugged more, and instead of asking for a sommelier in a restaurant and questioning what particular grape would work with what dish, Olivia would simply glance at a wine list, then hit a mark with her index finger, and order vast quantities of mid-range dry white wine.

'I need to talk to you about the party.' Laura leaned close. The small wooden tables were sufficiently cosy and the restaurant buzzy enough that she felt certain nobody was listening.

Olivia flashed a look at her, eyes open wide, and for a split second Laura wondered if she understood what party she was talking about. 'Are you referring to Donna knowing about Paul? Because I spoke to Anjali, and she really didn't tell her anything that isn't public record . . .' She looked up and noticed Laura shaking her head. Then she bristled again. 'Ah. Rudy and Freya and their party. Present day. Gotcha. Let sleeping dogs lie. I mean, look, Laura, it was a terrible accident, that's all. Bury it.' But Olivia's eyes didn't meet hers. She was more worried than her words let on, or she was thinking of the past. Was she hiding something?

The waiter lowered the four cocktails onto the table from a silver tray and disappeared. Laura took a tiny sip of hers. 'We reviewed Joe Duggard in the ethics meeting. They want to withdraw treatment. He has profuse ischaemia and they're reluctant to do brain stem testing as it might be inconclusive and, regardless of any signs of life, he's in a persistent vegetative state.'

'Laura,' Olivia reached her hand out and put it over Laura's own, which she realised was trembling. 'You're waffling. I'm banning work chat. What is it? Really?' Olivia's eyes were open wider again, and Laura could see the frown between them deepen.

Laura took a deep breath, and she began talking. She told Liv that Joe Duggard was on the edge of life, and his parents wanted the suffering to end. The team wanted the suffering to end. They were going to discontinue his life support, turn off the breathing machine, and let him die. There would be no recovery for that poor boy, but maybe an end to his suffering was the best possible outcome.

Olivia listened and drank, then sat back as the plates arrived. The food lay untouched between them, and Laura thought of her mum and Aunt Jean attending Weight Watchers' meetings, then buying fish and chips and leaving it there on the table to 'test their will' before the weigh-in, only to eat the lot on their return. Laura sniffed. Her throat felt scratchy, as if the words were too sharp, cutting her on the way out.

'It's tragic,' said Olivia. 'But this is our job. Separate what happened from this. The life support should be withdrawn. Poor family . . .' She nibbled on a samosa. 'We've got this far. I understand how this would cause anxiety, but raking up the past is not going to help anyone, least of all this patient.'

Laura wiped her face on a napkin. 'You don't understand. Olivia, it wasn't an accident. There are implications. I mean . . .'

Liv was momentarily silent, then she swallowed and put a samosa down on the plate, tilted her head to one side. The restaurant hum carried on in the background but the air around them was quiet, as if air could hold its breath.

'If he dies,' Laura gasped. 'Well, a tragic accident would become *manslaughter*. I've researched it. Involuntary manslaughter. Olivia, I don't know where to start.'

'What do you mean? You said Rudy and Freya were there, that's all – where Joe fell down the stairs? He fell and cracked his head on the table, that's the truth . . .'

Laura looked straight at Olivia. She watched her face change with understanding, embodying the terrible knowledge that Laura had been carrying around a few days. The room was spinning. 'Rudy told me. It wasn't an accident. Joe Duggard was pushed. He was pushed down the stairs and onto a table where he landed on the back of his head. It caused a skull fracture, as we know, and a catastrophic intraventricular bleed, which led to diffuse, irreparable damage.'

'I don't believe it.' Olivia leaned forward, took a gulp of air. She looked at Laura with shocked, yet kind eyes, anger, and pity all at once. 'Rudy would not push anyone downstairs. Never.'

Laura felt the terrible truth burn as it left her body. 'It wasn't Rudy. It was Freya. Olivia, Freya pushed him.'

Laura woke to the security light in the garden. She looked at her phone, slipped it into her pyjama pocket, swung her legs out of bed and padded to the Juliet balcony, peering out through the blinds. The back garden was a strip of manicured grass that Anjali had said reminded her of a Brazilian bikini wax. Either side were raised flower beds, filled with the most colourful plants, foxgloves, forget-me-nots, begonias and at the top end, a large lavender bush and herbs that Laura threw into roast dinners or summer drinks: rosemary, sage, handfuls of mint. It was not long ago that Rudy would help, water the garden every day when Laura was working, pick out any weeds, tidy up. Not long ago. Since telling her the truth about the party he'd been withdrawn, hardly coming out of his bedroom. He was avoiding her, it was clear, ashamed and afraid, feelings Laura was all too familiar with, and had never wanted to pass on. A legacy of anxiety.

The floodlit garden was empty, the light probably triggered by a fox or a rat; she'd once seen a rat the size of a cat run across the garden, and when she'd phoned the council they'd cited the river as a reason for rats, as opposed to their shoddy, two-weekly rubbish collection. Laura's shed in the back was painted a cheerful blue, and from it came a sudden thud so loud she saw the shed door shake from the window. Somebody was out there. Somebody was in her shed. She jumped back from the window. Think. Think, Laura, it's what you're trained to do. Deal with crises. With emergencies. Think on your feet.

The security light went off, and everything was plunged into midnight. Laura took her phone and dialled the number for the security at the gate, as she walked towards Rudy's room. She peered in as it rang. Rudy was fast asleep in that teen-boy way, his feet hanging over the edge of the bed, head tipped back. The room smelled musty as though the windows were permanently closed. He was safe.

'Hi, hi, it's Laura from number 14.' She closed the door and crept away, breathing hard. 'Someone's in my garden . . .'

In the time it took security to walk across the path, Laura had also called the police. The security light flashed back on, and she stood, now by the back door, rooted to the spot, hardly breathing. The security guard, and the police, both, had said to stay inside with the door locked. 'Do not move,' they said, 'we'll be there soon.' But Laura found her hand moving towards the door handle, and unlocking the Chubb bolt, almost involuntarily. Her body was full of fear, her autonomic nervous system had kicked in, flight or fight, that rush of adrenaline that she was so used to at work, the fine line between danger and excitement so often blurred for emergency doctors. She couldn't stop. Her legs were jelly, her breathing fast enough she saw spots and flashes in front of her eyes, and yet she couldn't stop. She walked towards the shed, and the cheerful, flower-filled garden suddenly felt threatening. Too bright, like the mortuary. The security light made the grass seem luminous, unreal, and clinical. The shed door was slightly ajar and banging back and forth in the breeze. She stood still, ears pricked up, and listened hard. She thought she could hear breathing, a low groaning, a rumble, but these noises could be coming from her own body. Her entire arm was shaking when she reached out her hand. She pushed the shed door, gently at first, then threw it open, the light streaming into the dark wooden corners.

NINETEEN

Anjali (2024)

Anjali paced up and down in the kitchen. Where was Donna? She tried to keep busy, put the radio on, started tidying, but every ten seconds she went to the living room and looked out into the darkness. Of all the days Donna would be late! She was bursting with excitement. She literally couldn't wait to tell her. Emma had sent across a Child Permanence Report and a single photograph of Khadija. Anjali kept staring at the photo and couldn't stop grinning. A girl. Of course, it was early days, and this was simply a discussion about a potential match, and there were many hoops to go through, but it felt perfect. It was real. They would be parents. A family. Mums. They'd raise a little girl, and be tied together, the three of them, forever. Her parents would be so happy. All those stressful long months of the adoption process. The intrusive questions, and the soul searching. It all vanished. All Anjali could think about was Khadija. Where was Donna? She paced and looked, then went to the spare bedroom that they'd already painted light grey, after Donna insisted that it be gender neutral whatever happened.

That's what she was like, Donna. Thoughtful, progressive, inclusive. Khadija would be so lucky to have her as a mum. Any child would. Anjali didn't feel deserving, but she knew that Donna was. Between them they'd make a good team. A solid base. A family. She was going to be a mum. It was sinking in. Anjali attempted to make fish pie, but she'd overcooked it and the white fish was chewy. It didn't matter. This was a celebration dinner, no matter how badly cooked. She lit some candles and opened a bottle of decent wine. She waited. After an hour, Anjali ate a small plate of fish pie and covered the rest, putting it in the fridge. She blew out the candles.

She tried to focus on the news of their potential match, but the hours passed without any news from Donna. Anjali began to panic. Her heart thumped inside her, her lips became dry. Had something happened to Donna? Anjali spent her life waiting for bad things to happen. Anjali was a worrier by nature, and this was unusual. Donna always called her if she was going to be late. She paced up and down and went from total joy to total fear in the space of a few hours. Had Donna had an accident? She called and called again. No answer. Donna's phone was never off. She was about to call the hospital when the front door opened.

'You're so late.' Donna walked in wearing gym kit, long after the gym would have closed.

Anjali hovered in the hallway while Donna took off her trainers.

'I went for a long, long run.' She was breathless and sweaty. She was shaking a tiny bit too, Anjali noticed.

'It's nearly midnight. I've been calling and calling. Donna, where have you been really? No chance you were out running.'

Donna took a deep breath. 'I don't need this now, Anj. I just want to go to sleep.' She started running up the stairs, two at a time.

Something flipped and then burned in Anjali's head. It was bad enough that Donna had not answered her calls, and she'd had to sit until it got dark, watch the dinner get ruined. But it was clear Donna was lying to her. She'd been so full of excitement, desperate to tell Donna the news, and instead she felt her insides fill with acid. She ran upstairs after Donna, who was in the bedroom peeling her gym kit off.

'I needed to talk to you. I was here waiting all night and you didn't answer me, and it was an urgent thing.' Anjali was shouting. She never shouted.

Donna glanced up, clearly surprised, but then carried on undressing. 'Calm down. It's no big deal, Anjali.' She walked into the bathroom and turned on the shower.

Anjali followed her in. She was boiling hot with anger now, all thoughts of adoption disappeared. The only time Anjali's mum had ever hit her was when she was three years old and ran into the road to chase a ball, right in front of a van. The van screeched to a halt, and Anjali's mum pulled her by the arm to the kerb and smacked her so hard it left a handprint on Anjali's thigh. Her mum spent weeks apologising. She said the anger that stemmed from fear was uncontrollable.

Anjali opened the shower door and switched it off, leaving Donna standing there covered in shampoo. 'You've ruined everything!' she shouted. 'Where have you been? You're fucking lying, I can tell.' She was screaming and crying.

Donna reached for a towel and stepped out of the shower. Anjali imagined for a split second that she was going to slap her. Donna's arm pulled back, and her expression hardened. But Donna pulled Anjali towards her and held her tightly. 'Stop this,' she said. 'Stop shouting. This is not you.'

They slid onto the bathroom floor, a tangle of wetness and shower gel and tears.

Donna wiped Anjali's tears with the palm of her hand. 'What's this about, Anj? This isn't you.'

'I'm sorry,' Anjali whispered. 'I don't know.'

*

The next morning, the calm after the storm, they brought coffee and bagels to the park, and sat on the grass verge opposite the small paddling pool. The swing park was full of parents and toddlers, and in the paddling pool children of all ages splashed around, giggling and laughing. 'Try not to stare, people will think we're child snatchers.' Donna ate her bagel, smothered in cream cheese, and managed to get a bit on her nose.

After the argument they had dried off and put their dressing gowns on, and gone downstairs. Anjali kept apologising and Donna kept forgiving her. 'Guess what, Anj. You're not perfect. And nor am I.'

Anjali explained her fear that something had happened to Donna, and her excitement about the matching. She showed her a photograph of Khadija, and the burned fish pie. Donna studied the photograph for the longest time. She read her Child Permanence Report and cried some more. 'She's not a baby though,' she said. 'Already two. A toddler!'

'That doesn't matter, does it? I mean, she's had a rough start in life, a few foster care moves, but there's nothing in the CPR that gave me alarm bells.'

Donna had glanced at the document on the computer, and at Anjali. 'It's just so sad though, that a child as young as her doesn't have a forever family. Look at her face.'

'She does now,' said Anjali. 'I waited and waited for you. I didn't want to tell you on the phone. This is an in-person convo.'

'She looks a bit like you,' said Donna.

Anjali studied Khadija's photo. She did. A cheeky grin, and unkempt hair. Her heart was so full it felt like it was pressing on her chest wall.

The fight was a distant memory already. Anjali laughed and wiped the cream cheese off Donna's nose with a tissue. She looked around the park, and the children playing in front of them. 'Look how cute they all are. Surely we'll be here every day with Khadija. Can you imagine, pushing a swing, or helping her down a slide.'

'You're going to be so overprotective; I know it.'

Anjali smiled. She leaned into Donna's arm. The air around them smelled of newly mowed grass and warm sunshine. Everything was golden again. Anjali had never felt so happy, yet even then, remained self-doubting. 'What if there's another family who are better?'

Donna laughed. 'You're such an idiot. Who could love a child more than we will? Honestly, it will be OK. But also, perhaps we shouldn't get this carried away so early. We have to go through the whole matching process, and panel, before she comes home. Then it's fostering a while before official adoption.'

'You're right. But also, I feel she's ours. It's weird. I know it.'

'Well then, let's get carried away. For one day, at least.' Donna lifted her cappuccino towards Anjali's. Then they leaned back onto the grass, and watched all the families walking past, listening to the sounds of the children laughing.

TWENTY

Olivia (2024)

Olivia liked outpatient work. It made a change from surgery and was usually gentler. She could sit down, which in itself felt like a luxury. Surgery had given her varicose veins. Clinic was getting busier every week though. The waiting area was stuffed full of people sitting on unmovable chairs, or leaning against the walls, or queuing up to check in with the reception team, holding their appointment letters aggressively in front of them. Olivia made her way through, trying to avoid eye contact with anyone. Eye contact meant questions, and questions cost time. Complaints came thick and fast, over waiting times, or clinical errors, or cancelled operations. Doctors were becoming spin doctors in this political climate, whether they liked it or not. *'We've no intensive care bed for you post op, and that puts you at great risk if we go ahead with surgery. No, it won't affect your heart function at all if we postpone the operation again . . .'* It was a truth of sorts, but she never told the whole truth. The whole truth was that there were beds in intensive care, but no nurses to care for the patients in those beds. She could be the best cardiac surgeon in the world, and her hospital have the best technology, but without nurses nobody gets an operation. It seemed pretty obvious to Olivia. And of course waiting for an op affected heart function.

Once in her clinic room, she closed the door and stood in the darkness a few moments, just breathing, before flicking on the strip light and opening the blinds. She tried to squash down the feeling of nausea she'd had since meeting Laura at the restaurant. Since she'd found out that Freya had pushed Joe. Freya. It seemed impossible to believe, and even thinking of it threatened to overwhelm Olivia, but she mustn't let it. Though how? It was bad enough to imagine Freya taking drugs. That episode was enough to deal with. Even worrying that Freya had simply been at the party, wrong place, wrong time, was a headache. But this? Olivia needed clarity in order to help Freya. To protect her from this mess. Her job relied on her aptitude for problem-solving. She was good at this. She simply needed to breathe. Think. Her mind kept skipping to Freya's face, the fear in her eyes, how Olivia had missed that fear. They had talked about the party on just two occasions, during which Olivia had told Freya it would all be all right, and that sometimes teenage parties go wrong, badly wrong, and it was a horrible accident, that was all. Freya had not mentioned pushing Joe, not once. She let Olivia believe a lie. That young man Joe had not slipped or fallen downstairs and hit his head. Freya pushed him, and he might die. Freya. Small, skinny, frail Freya. Olivia felt so dizzy she had to hold the desk just to prevent herself from fainting. She felt her eyes fill with tears and forced them back inside her. She couldn't break down. She had to be strong. Olivia had to solve this for Freya. If the truth got out . . . She thought of a clotting cascade, a physiological process of forming blood clots. The process is protective, as it stops people bleeding after injury. But it can go very wrong, and if it does cause blood clots in the wrong place, that leads to disability or death. A tiny event can trigger a chain reaction. Of course, this wasn't a tiny event.

But if it got out it would trigger a cascade of truth, crashing down after it. Irreparable damage.

At first, Olivia hadn't believed Laura. And even after she was convinced that was what *had* happened to Joe Duggard, that Freya *had* pushed him, causing the fall that caused the injury *that might cause his death*, she would not accept that Freya could be in any trouble whatsoever. It was an accident, after all. She may have meant to push him, but she certainly didn't mean to push him down the stairs. She didn't mean to injure him, only to get him away from her. They'd googled, and then Olivia asked a school friend who ended up at Harvard law, and Laura was right. The friend told her about unlawful act manslaughter – involuntary manslaughter in the UK – where a charge is attached to the kind of injury that results in death, even when completely accidental. 'If a person dies after being pushed or punched, it usually ends in a custodial sentence,' he'd said. 'Regardless of the circumstances.'

But if the police have shown no sign of suspecting that anyone pushed him, Olivia thought, why would that change if he died? It *would* mean that Freya and Rudy, having heard, which they inevitably would, that Joe had died, would have to stay quiet forever or there would be a police investigation. They were full of ideals and optimism and misguided righteousness. She couldn't risk it. The news would spread like wildfire in school, no matter how she tried to hide it. Currently they felt very bad because Joe Duggard was in hospital. But not bad enough to hand themselves in to the police or some such stupidity. Olivia had to think. Think. How could she fix this? This terrible event was the first domino, and it must not fall.

The bleep buzzed loudly and shook in her pocket. Olivia took it out and looked at the banner headline as she tried to decipher the muffled train announcer-type sound. *Fast bleeping cardiothoracic surgeon. Fast bleeping cardiothoracic surgeon. Please call A&E urgently.*

Olivia picked up the phone. There was an emergency. A real one. A woman, dying, right now, unless Olivia could get there in time. There was nobody else in the hospital skilled and experienced enough to handle this. Olivia was it. Her heart was hammering as though her chest was a tree and there was a woodpecker inside her. Hearts spoke a language all of their own. Everything vanished. Adrenaline replaced anxiety and she had no room in her head for anything except surgery.

She ran. A surgeon running meant things were very bad indeed. Her shoes squeaked with each step on the too-shiny hospital floors. She was running at the speed of supraventricular tachycardia, SVT. Freya cleared from her mind. Everything cleared. All she could think of was the speed at which hearts contracted, the way the chambers moved in synch or out, and how cardiac tissue felt in her hands. She thought of the waiting patient. An aortic dissection. A woman, thirty-eight weeks pregnant, with a tear in her most major blood vessel, full up with a baby, and full up with blood. Her chances of survival were almost nil. The baby's chances of survival were almost nil. Olivia was their only hope. She pushed the heavy doors to theatre open and rushed into the changing rooms, peeling off her clothes and climbing into scrubs, and clogs. She drank some water, but not too much. Enough to avoid serious dehydration but not enough to need to pee every five minutes. She nipped into the toilet, and hovered over the toilet seat, a trick Anjali had taught her in a nightclub. *You've broken the seal now; you'll be peeing every ten minutes. If you squat over the loo rather than sit on the seat, your bladder will empty completely . . .* Olivia needed her bladder to empty completely. This surgery would last twelve or fourteen hours.

The obstetrician, a man named Bilal who looked sixty but was in fact thirty, was pulling the baby out of the woman as Olivia walked briskly into theatres, holding her freshly scrubbed hands out in front of her as though being arrested. 'Fuck me, she's full of blood. Not a moment too soon.' He shook the upside-down, grey baby as he spoke and handed it to a nurse to run to the resuscitaire, already glowing warm orange in the corner.

'Don't close up,' said Olivia, peering into the woman's thick-edged uterus. 'I need to see what I'm doing, so the more she's hollowed out the better.'

Olivia got to work and zoned out, focusing on what she needed to do, and not what was happening around her. There was much activity around the baby, but she couldn't think of that now. But then there was a cry, and Olivia felt it in her breasts, relief mixed with something deep and profound and long ago. She had one window to save this woman's life. To give that baby, should she survive, a mother. In this moment it was life and death, and Olivia was God. Still, she prayed to her God too, for her surgeon's hands to do their job. She painted chlorhexidine over the woman's sternum and held the saw. 'What is her name?' she asked.

'Does it matter?' the anaesthetist gestured to the body on the table, opened up at the abdomen like an unzipped bag. It was true she didn't look human. None of us do during surgery. We become meat on a slab. Surgeons all used to be butchers, Olivia once told her dad, as he was carving a chicken. 'We still are, my dearest!' he replied.

'It matters.' Olivia glanced up at the scrub nurse, Barbara, who had been in the job so long she had Olympic-sized calf muscles and permanently starfished hands.

'Her name is Bluebell. Bluebell Forbes.'

'Bluebell,' said Olivia. She began to cut through her skin, which was as easy with a sharp scalpel as cutting non-refrigerated butter with a butter knife. The skin separated into two open curtains. Cracking this woman's chest took considerably more effort, and Olivia could feel her biceps tense up. She was fairly out of shape these days, unable to get to the gym, but she had the arms of Michelle Obama, thanks to the job. She pressed down heavily, sawed through the patient's bone, and each layer of her like the earth's crust until she got to the molten centre, the barely throbbing, blood-filled heart.

Bluebell's aorta was swollen, split open and bleeding. The fresh, impossible red of the blood inside us never ceased to amaze Olivia. She worked quickly with clamps and the graft and stitching everything together. Olivia studied the landscape in front of her. She'd had friends at school who were fascinated by the ocean, learned to dive among shipwrecks or in coral reefs, and described the other-worldliness, or those who were obsessed with the stars and planets, the infinite universe, the night sky an entire new world to explore. But it was inside people's bodies that Olivia thought was the most beautiful place of all. Our internal landscapes, each unique and designed so carefully, the colours and beats inside us, all the breathtaking patterns. There was disease here, a tear in the wrong place, the most dangerous of places, the blood escaping areas it should stay within, filling up areas it should not. Olivia looked at the flesh and blood and bone of Bluebell and thought about how connected we all are in our fragility, our vulnerability to accidents and illnesses and diseases, and small things like tiny tears that if they happened in the wrong place could prove deadly. 'How precious and precarious this life,' she said.

'Amen,' said Barbara. 'What music today?'

'I think this is a job for Chopin, don't you?'

Barbara laughed, 'I only listen to Elvis. But whatever floats your boat, doc.'

The music filled the room as quickly as the blood filled Bluebell's abdomen. A split second and Olivia recognised it as Chopin's Piano Concerto No.1 in E Minor. She remembered what Dele had told her: 'Chopin said it was a romance, calm and melancholic, giving the impression of someone looking gently towards a spot that calls to mind a thousand happy memories.' Dele was a man full of random facts. He remembered everything.

Olivia found the tear. Despite the biggest fear of all, the worry that every parent knows contains all the darkness of the world, that Freya might be in serious trouble, Olivia was no longer 'Mum'. She was surgeon. She was the best cardio-thoracic surgeon in the country. Her hands were the safest of hands. Today, she would save a life. Surgery was meditation. It was prayer. She zoomed in to the moment, the second, the task at her fingertips, and her hands played piano inside another human and, even splashed up to her neck in blood, could think of nothing but bluebells. She was inside another human, and for a short while, surgeon and patient were one being. What greater privilege was there than that?

When she got home, Dele had run her a bath and lit her favourite candles. He ushered her in, and a few minutes later came into the bathroom with a glass of wine. He sat on the edge of the bath, kissed her shoulder. 'What's all this in aid of?' Olivia frowned. Dele was not the sort of man who ran her a bath after work.

He drank a sip of her wine. 'I wanted to thank you,' he said. 'The Freya drugs thing. My reaction was nuclear. As ever, you're the voice of reason, Liv. You always know what to do, even in the worst possible situations.'

She swallowed. The cocaine was nothing compared to Freya pushing Joe down the stairs. She had to keep that from Dele above all things. Olivia sat up a bit, causing the water to slosh around. He'd put so many bubbles in the bath they were almost up to her chin. 'I haven't seen you cry like that for years. Or ever.'

Dele folded over. He sighed. 'It was all a bit much. I've been feeling out of sorts anyway, and then that.' His face filled up with tears again.

Dele was struggling. That was clear. The job was breaking him. He'd had a string of complaints about waiting times, and at least five of his team were off sick. The hours were unsustainable. He could do with a sabbatical, but he'd never take one. She thought about suggesting talking therapy to help him cope with the demands of life, of being a doctor in the NHS, then imagined his reaction. In a strange way she didn't mind it either, Dele's mental health being less than tip-top. It was a terrible thing to admit, but it reminded her of when the children were small and had chickenpox. Of course she felt sorry for them, itching and being under the weather, but she loved them snuggling up to her, putting calamine lotion on them, cooking them soup. She liked being needed. There was no way she'd add to his pain and tell him about the party. And in any case, she couldn't risk it. Truth led to other truths.

Dele stroked her back. 'I love you, Liv,' he said. 'You're my rock.'

TWENTY-ONE

Anjali (2024)

Anjali couldn't stop thinking about Khadija. She was consumed. Her head and heart and gut were full up, and she felt slightly stoned, a vessel of wonder and awe. Every five minutes she took her phone out of her pocket and stared at the single photograph that Emma had shared with them, along with Khadija's CRP, the official history of her life that led to her needing adoption. Donna had read it and re-read it and cried as Anjali held her; they were both in love already. 'It's the saddest thing I've ever read,' Donna said. 'She's two and a half years old and has been through more than any of us experience in a lifetime already.' They had wanted a baby. Everyone wanted a baby. The age range they agreed to was up to two years, but Emma had sent Khadija's details across. Anjali took one look at the photo of Khadija laughing in a sandpit and something moved inside her body, like furniture was being rearranged inside her. She studied her eyes, her grin, her grazed knees and her jelly shoes, worn on the wrong feet.

'She's ours,' Anjali kept announcing. She'd never felt more certain of anything in her life.

Donna laughed. 'Look at her smile. Khadija, Khadija,' she said, repeating her name like a song.

The wait for a social worker to get back to them was always excruciating but this wait, now Anjali had seen the child she knew was theirs, was painful. She left five messages at the office for Emma to call her, and two emails.

Hi, Emma, it's Anj again. I'm sorry to bug you but we really do love Khadija's CPR and wanted to know if you've shared our home study and had a response from Khadija's social workers yet? We think we might all be a good fit. Call us.

Anjali had no idea how she'd get through the week. She sat down, checked her phone, took a second to look at the photo of Khadija, and texted Donna.

Her jelly shoes. On the wrong feet. She has blue paint on her hands too. LOVE.

She then put her phone away and turned the computer on, scanning the list for the day. Tried to concentrate on work. Too many patients. The patients were too sick; most of them, mentally. She would be here until 8 p.m. at least, and still be late with phone appointments. Like all days, today could bring anything through the door: ear infection; self-harm; atrial fibrillation; drug abuse; vaginal prolapse, chronic obstructive pulmonary disease; cancer; sepsis; back pain; chlamydia; depression, depression, depression. Everyone, regardless of condition, illness, or disease, would be in pain. Anjali knew by then, a GP's job is to treat pain, some of it physical, but by no means all. Had OxyContin been available to prescribe as readily in the UK as it had been in the US, her entire practice would have been wiped out.

'Don't get sick, and don't get old.' Mrs Franklin was folded in half, her spine crumpled. She sat opposite Anjali holding her walking stick in front of her like a talisman. Anjali liked this woman. She was sharp-eyed and wise and had that no-nonsense stoicism of the very elderly, which would likely die out with their generation. Anjali had known her ten years, during which time she'd survived her husband, her son, and two bouts of ovarian cancer. Each year folded her a little more though, and her osteoarthritis left her in constant pain, and the earth was pulling her back towards it. 'Die young, if you can. Suddenly. Best thing. You look happy today. There's a glint in your eye.'

'I'll do my best,' Anjali nodded. 'You're right. I am happy. It's kind of you to notice. What can I do for you?' Anjali didn't glance at the clock on her computer. She was so time restricted, but it was important the patients felt they had enough of her. It was false economy to rush people. Often it took until the last minute of the appointment for people to declare what was really wrong: *I haven't slept in four weeks . . . not a wink*, or, *I really don't want to live anymore*, or, *There's blood in my poo . . .* It was frightening, coming to the GP and telling a relative stranger the darkest of problems. Nowhere was more vulnerable, more human, than the space between family doctor and patient. It wasn't celebrated in the way of much medicine. It wasn't bombastic, or shouty, or glamorous, her job, yet GPs saved more lives than neurosurgeons, and that was a fact.

But Mrs Franklin didn't ask Anjali about pain medication, or talk about depression, or grief, or pain. 'I watched that Davina McCall documentary and wondered if it's too late for HRT patches.'

Anjali smiled. Mrs Franklin was ninety-four years old. Davina McCall had a lot to answer for. She was about to launch into the futile nature of HRT in preventing osteoporosis after it was as severe as Mrs Franklin's, or at her age, but then she noticed something in her expression, a kind of hopefulness that there might be a straightforward answer to ageing. Fuck it. 'I'll start you on a low dose of gel,' she said. 'Let's see if it makes you feel better.' She half smiled and looked at Mrs Franklin's mischievous expression. 'How's your libido?'

Mrs Franklin smiled back in a conspiratorial way, then laughed out loud. 'I'll be like GI Jane next time you see me,' she said. She shuffled a while, trying to get her coat back on, and pressed down on her walking stick to stand, wobbling a few moments.

'Let me help you.' Anjali walked alongside her and put her arm around her. She thought of her own mum, who'd just turned seventy-five. Things would start going wrong. She'd start losing people that she loved. Anjali needed to be there for her, much more than she had been. She often felt like a terrible daughter, caught up in her work and her life and the adoption. But Khadija would give her mum the most joy, she knew that. Her parents had been wanting grandchildren since Paul. They'd cleared a spare room, and the last car they bought was a people carrier. She imagined sharing the photograph of Khadija with her mum. The expression on her mum's face.

The rest of the day rushed past: a rash on a baby's nose (impetigo); a leg injury (torn Achilles tendon); blood in urine (UTI); blood in stool (needs investigating); severe right-sided migraine and blurred vision (A&E); suicidal ideation (talking therapy – wait list); a smoker's cough that was getting worse (cancer – most likely); extreme thirst and frequent urination (diabetes); six women with menopausal symptoms (thank you, Davina); fifteen-year-old hearing voices (first presentation psychosis – schizophrenia?); Edith (nothing wrong with her but comes in every week for a chat); baby with asthma (poor housing / mould); numbness in legs (flare-up, multiple sclerosis); syncope (cardiac arrhythmia); a man with an ingrowing toenail; a teen with gender dysphoria; a couple wanting IVF on the NHS (no chance); a Ukrainian refugee suffering with malnourishment (refer to foodbank); a woman whose husband was dying (heartbreaking conversation) . . .

'Anj, there's a young man waiting for you.' The voice belonged to a new receptionist, a compassionate Scottish woman with a significant underbite. Anjali looked out of the window into the car park, to see Miles, Olivia's son, leaning against the wall, listening to his music. His head nodded with the beat. She looked at her godson, his wholesome youthful skinny good looks, like an Abercrombie & Fitch advert. He'd been wanting to come and see her for a while, but it was virtually impossible with his after-school schedule: hockey, drama, coding, basketball. Olivia was the original tiger mother in many ways. Anjali had been a bit worried about him, given that he had seemed afraid, but she'd told herself it was probably nothing. Teenage somethings often were. She smiled, logged out of the computer, threw her shoes off and trainers on, then switched off the lights. She stood in the darkness of her clinic room a while, breathing in the smell of the antiseptic wipes that lingered on long after being used. Everything smelled good, even that. She was going to be a mum. She and Donna would be a family.

Donna was home when they arrived, cooking beef bourguignon as though everyone ate like that on a Wednesday. 'I was going to make an omelette,' said Anjali, dropping her keys onto the table and kissing her. She wore an apron over her clothes, and her hair was wet.

'We need to feed you up. You get thinner and thinner!' She smiled at Miles. She always loved seeing him. 'This is a lovely surprise. Almost as if you could smell the meat from home.'

He laughed. Like all teenage boys these days he was obsessed with protein. It was true he looked skinny. Behind his laugh Anjali could tell he was worried. She'd known this boy since the day he was born, been the first to hold him, as Dele was knee-deep in a stage one Norwood procedure when Olivia had gone into labour. She'd rushed to the hospital and told Liv she'd call Dele and get him out, but Olivia had insisted she didn't. 'Hypoplastic left heart is no joking matter,' she'd said, without any further explanation. 'You can be my birth partner.' Anjali had been a bit surprised she hadn't asked Laura, but delighted, nonetheless. Olivia refused pain relief and made sounds during labour that were animalistic. She groaned and groaned then pushed until tiny red blood vessels burst in her eyeballs. It astonished and terrified Anjali in equal measure. Anjali held Miles in her arms, all sticky with some of Liv's insides still covering him, and kissed him anyway, kissed and kissed him. Perhaps that was why she had such a special bond with him compared to the others. Still, no matter how much she wanted to, she couldn't mention Khadija yet. Emma had told them both that, until they were officially matched, having gone through the various stages, they were best not sharing details of any children they were considering, no matter how certain they might feel. Anjali was good at keeping secrets, but Khadija's name threatened to burst from her mouth. Donna must have felt the same; she kept smiling ear to ear. Miles was young enough, and clearly had his own things going on, to not notice a thing. Teenagers were good at that.

Donna poured some wine for the three of them and served large plates of the beef bourguignon, and they lit some candles, and sat chatting about all things. She liked watching them both, imagining Donna as a mum one day. She pictured Khadija in DMs instead of jelly shoes, sullen and skinny, but still with an oddball laugh and smiling eyes. It was easy to imagine, despite not having even met her yet. Anjali trusted it. That certainty felt like a safe space. Meant to be. Fate. She focused on Donna, who spoke to Miles as though he was an adult, took a real interest in his life, and listened properly. Miles revelled in that space, telling Donna about his rugby tournament and latest crush.

Anjali began clearing the plates and turned to Miles. 'You wash, I dry.' They didn't believe in dishwashers. Another weird eccentricity that she and Donna shared, the idea that there was something therapeutic about washing plates. They shared so many quirks. Perhaps that was why it felt like such a good match. Khadija was already quirky, that was obvious.

Miles was quiet for a bit, then he turned to Anjali and looked at Donna; his face changed shape. 'Aunty Anj, Aunty Donna,' he whispered. 'I need to tell you something.'

She hung up the tea towel, and they sat down again. It was clear that this wasn't a catch-up visit. Despite the chit-chat and the meal, she could sense in the way Miles sat, too upright, that all was not well. She needed to concentrate. Maybe it was girl trouble? Miles often told Anjali things he didn't want to share with Olivia: the time a condom split, the ketamine incident, once, when a friend disclosed sexual assault. Who'd be a teenager these days? Any days? 'Shoot. We're here.' She reached for his hand, but he moved his away as if hers was hot. He looked sheepish. Donna slung her arm around his back.

'It's Rudy and Freya . . . And you can't tell anyone about it. Not this.'

Anjali shrugged. 'You know I can't promise that, Miles. Not if someone is in serious trouble.'

'I mean it. This time, I can't tell you unless you swear not to tell.' He looked suddenly much younger than his seventeen years. She saw his baby face inside him, bursting out. He was still a young child, though these days in a man's body.

Anjali sat up in her chair. She waited. The silence filled the room full of possibilities. Had Rudy and Freya taken drugs?

Were they bullying Miles? Freya and Rudy had done that every few years, ganged up a bit on him.

'There was a party,' Miles started. 'Just some kid everyone vaguely knew from Ruskin College. This boy, Joe Duggard. No one really likes him. He's a misogynist . . . obsessed with Andrew Tate. But he fell down the stairs.' Miles sniffed. 'He was seriously hurt.' He was sobbing now. Snot running down his face.

Anjali took a bite of air. She was in her kitchen with Miles, but she was also at a party with Paul. Someone was hurt. Seriously hurt. A young man. Her head filled up with cotton wool and felt as if it was floating away from her body. Memories lit up in parts of her brain, and she could picture an MRI scan, areas of bright colour indicating activity.

Anjali saw Olivia and Laura. She saw Laura, out of control, grieving for her dad, totally out of character. She was unhinged, dancing in jerky movements, gurning, throwing drugs around like sweets. Then there was chaos. An ambulance. Paramedics. Doctors. A lad, seriously hurt, not breathing. Olivia pulled Anjali to a dark corner. Anjali could hear Olivia's voice whisper to her, *It wasn't you. I saw Laura give him the drugs. It was Laura.*

Anjali shook her head, and the kitchen that Donna spent so much time making homely was full of blood and death and sirens. What Olivia had said was not making sense. A memory pushed up into her consciousness, a seed trying to grow. Anjali and the boy who was hurt. Confusion. Olivia's certain words. Anjali telling her that wasn't right, and Olivia squeezing Anjali's arm so hard. *I am right. I saw her.*

'That's horrible,' Anjali said, finally. Miles looked up, sniffed. 'Why didn't you guys say anything?' She placed the palms of her hands on the table top and pressed them down hard, trying to push away the memory of another party.

Donna glanced at her. 'What a horrible thing,' she said. 'I'll bet Freya and Rudy are really shaken up. Is he OK now? Joe?'

Miles shook his head. He was ghostly pale. 'He's in intensive care. Mum and Aunty Laura told them not to talk about it at all. Not to tell anyone they were there.'

Donna flicked her head towards him. 'He's in ICU? At City?'

Anjali frowned. 'That's weird. Probably didn't want us to worry.'

Donna watched them, and she leaned forward with her hand resting on her chin. She looked confused.

When it was time for Miles to go, he sniffed and wiped his nose on his sleeve. 'I needed to tell someone. I know Aunty Laura told Rudy to keep it a secret, but it was such a big accident. I needed to talk about it. Can you check if Joe is doing OK?'

They both nodded. He hugged Anjali then Donna, and then put his earbuds in before disappearing.

Donna closed the door then turned to Anjali. 'What the fuck is going on? Why would Laura say that? Why? What the hell is happening here? I knew something was off, I just knew it. She's hiding something. I overheard her, I mean, her and Rudy . . .'

Anjali shrugged. 'When? What do you mean? It's probably nothing – maybe she's worried they'll get in trouble? Don't stress about it, I'll talk to her.'

Donna sighed and walked out.

That night when Anjali climbed into bed next to her, Donna was already asleep. Anjali closed her eyes and searched and searched for Khadija's grinning face, but she couldn't find it. All she could see was darkness.

TWENTY-TWO

Anjali (1999)

999 Nights at The Ministry of Sound in Elephant and Castle were designed for anyone wearing uniform to let their hair down in a safe environment. Of course, the fact that a nightclub was filled to the brim with police officers, medical and nursing students, paramedics and firefighters meant drugs. A lot of drugs. Teeth crunched together, sinewy young men and women jerking everywhere to dance music. The toilet was entered two by two like a cocaine Noah's Ark. Toilets were flushed, the sound of chopping, then snorting, a pair came out as another went in. Anjali and Paul were in the women's. He'd slid his hand down her bra as she separated the white powder into two fat lines and took an already rolled-up tenner from her purse. She had to be careful about that. Her banknotes all curled up independently and during lunches at the hospital canteen they'd spring out, tubular, telling her secrets to the cashier who looked at her with disapproving, knowing eyes, before scanning her chicken salad sandwich. Once, a man who was clearly a heroin addict, grey, skinny, scratching his arms and with pinpoint pupils, looked at the rolled-up banknote she handed over to pay for a bag of crisps and gave her an understanding, wise glance. She was not proud.

'Your turn,' she slipped away from Paul and gestured to the coke as if it was a banquet of oysters on a champagne bar instead of gritty cocaine on the lid of a piss-stinking toilet seat. 'You go first.'

Paul grinned. She looked at his eyelashes. Studied them. They were perfectly hazel and curled over. His eyes were extra shiny. He leaned down, taking the rolled-up tenner, and stuck it up his nostril. 'Always right side,' he said. 'There's an anatomical reason for that – bet they didn't teach you that in medical school.' They *didn't* teach her that in medical school. In fact, she wasn't learning much of anything in medical school, as her attendance was so poor. The late nights were easy at first, a few full-fat Cokes and an energy drink and she was good to go. But a sustained bender pretty much since she'd met Paul had left her limping through each morning, one painful step at a time. She knew she was out of control. She went out with a group of first-year medical students, drank until she could barely stand, and started saying they should all 'get to a fucking cashpoint' to take out cash for drugs. They looked horrified. One of them said she had twelve pounds to last the rest of the month. Anjali felt like double shit then. She had no idea why she was out of control, but she felt it, unable to stop.

Paul kept sniffing long after it seemed possible for a human being to continue. She leaned across him and took her line, making sure she dabbed her finger into the remnants and swished it around her gums, toilet seat or not. The numbness was pleasant. Anjali liked feeling nothing where something was supposed to be.

He kissed her then. Hard enough to clank teeth. He pulled her to him, and pinched the top of her arms as if she was Play-Doh and he was moulding her into a shape. Her body lost all motor skills when he touched her. She'd looked after a boy once who had muscular dystrophy, and whose muscles were wasting away one by one. He was floppy and jerky in seesaw motion and described himself as 'a human ragdoll'. She felt the same. Owned, possessed, and completely cared for, in Paul's total control. Her body lit up when he held her. Everything looked golden, even the piss-stinking toilet. It was only the next morning that she noticed the fingertip bruises, the pattern of his grip.

He held her tightly. There were moments when Anjali felt so held, so understood and loved by Paul that it was impossible to imagine they were not destined for each other. Often these times were wordless; he'd stare at her after they made love, look so intensely into her eyes it felt like he was reaching inside her. Their chests pressed together, she couldn't quite tell if it was his heartbeat she could feel or her own. It was all-consuming, loving him. She felt like a teenager, daydreaming constantly about his face, his smell, the way he moved, how he made her feel so needed, so adored. 'I can't live without you,' he whispered. 'I can't and I don't want to. If you ever leave me, I'll die. I mean it.' She believed him. Of course, he wasn't perfect. He lashed out at her every now and then, he said, because she was the closest to him. He told her he would get therapy, get help. Because he never wanted to hurt her again. Ever. He'd grown up in violence. Nobody was perfect. She'd hit him back once, given him a black eye, and he hadn't even mentioned it. When he was angry his face changed colour. It was redder, and less shiny. She'd accused him of lying. It was probably her fault for doing that.

'I know that night you said you were out with the student nurses you weren't. You're gaslighting me, and I fucking know it.'

His voice was loud, and that felt like comfort. When he lowered his voice to a whisper, Anjali felt her body tense up. But he suddenly took a swing at her, smacking her jaw so hard bells rang inside it and there was a crunching sound and it felt at an odd angle, her teeth not coming together. She should run. Run back home and let him calm down. But she didn't run. Instead, before she knew what her own arm was doing, it retaliated and her fist met his eye and cracked.

The next day they were both swollen and bruised, and they laughed. 'We're a couple of hotheads,' one of them said. Anjali couldn't quite remember which one.

Anjali knew things were better, and this was destiny. She would sit in lectures and daydream about him, the all-consuming passionate nature of their romance. She looked around at the other medical students that were nothing like her. She felt more like an artist than a scientist, and every now and then wondered if she had ever wanted to be a doctor, after all, or had simply been swept along with expectation. But whose expectation? Her parents had never pushed her, not in the way of some of her peers who had been hot-housed for medicine since before they'd been born. Her mum would have been happy whatever she did. But when she'd naturally excelled at school, her teachers had steered her towards the idea that she was good at remembering facts, and would likely secure a place at medical school, she'd felt bigger somehow, surer, in love with the *idea* of being a doctor. The reality wasn't what she'd thought it would be. She hated the smell of hospitals, and all the endless studying, and after being the most able in her secondary school, here she was a small fish in a big pond. Nothing special. Paul made her feel remarkable.

'There are seventy-eight organs in the human body. But only five needed for survival. Though even those lines are becoming ethically blurry. Anjali. Are you with us? Are any of your seventy-eight organs in the room?'

Everyone laughed and Anjali watched Olivia across the room mouth, 'Wake up.' Laura hadn't turned up that day, which was unlike Laura. She'd muttered something about a family thing but was vague. She was increasingly vague these days, Anjali realised. She hadn't been paying attention, so wrapped up was she in Paul. This was the first time that Anjali had been in love, and the first time she understood. She'd had friends at school who mooned over boys, spent hours writing their name in notepads or applying make-up, starving themselves of everything except perceived passion. She'd never understood it, how consuming it would be to fall in love for the first time. Yet now she could think of nothing else. They'd read *Romeo and Juliet* for GCSE drama, and despite ending up with an A*, Anjali had spent two years scoffing that Juliet was an idiot, and Shakespeare total nonsense. The irony that now she finally got it, her grades were suffering.

Clinical placements constituted most of the fourth year and were easier than studying, but still, she was distracted. Gynaecology seemed like a place where distracted medical students could be absorbed, but it was the opposite of that. This was a room full of women with fibroids or uterine cancers, or post-abortion, or with polycystic ovaries, or heavy menstrual bleeding, or endometriosis, or uterine prolapse, or vaginal atrophy, or cervical cancers. A young woman in bed five had undergone a radical vulvectomy for vulval cancer, and in the next bed another young woman was booked in for reversal of female genital mutilation. Their vulvas looked identical, which made Anjali dizzy.

'Penny for them?' The consultant was a serious woman with a facial tic and joyless eyes. 'Are we in there? Anyone home?'

It seemed to Anjali that ward rounds were designed solely to make a fool out of medical students and make the more senior doctors feel better about themselves. The patient in the bed in front of them was post-hysterectomy. She was middle-aged, obese, a bit broken. She wore slippers that reminded Anjali of her mum's: the warm, fluffy kind, yet toes were exposed, which seemed pretty pointless. 'Sorry, I'm a bit tired.' Anjali kept her voice monotone and slippersoft. She imagined flying so far under the radar this consultant would leave her alone. She needed a coffee. Or ten.

'Mrs Brenton here had her operation two days ago and has been experiencing pyrexia, tachycardia and increased respiratory rate. So. Thoughts.' The consultant stepped backwards. She winked at Mrs Benton. The patient and doctor were both clearly set on making the medical students work hard.

Mrs Benton started coughing, a raspy thick guttural cough. She leaned forward and spat a glob of khaki phlegm into a small plastic cup, then waved it at the medical students. 'Green,' she said.

This job was disgusting. Laura and Olivia seemed to get offered placements that involved high stakes: neurosurgery, paediatric emergency department, plastics. Meanwhile, Anjali had a lot of green-phlegm placements. Still, even then she wasn't doing so well. She searched the insides of her head for medical answers, but her brain was blank. She'd killed off a few brain cells the night before, for sure. She opened her mouth, hoping that a potential diagnosis would spill out, but her mouth fish-gaped, empty. A flashback to the toilets in the club, and the cocaine, and the dancing then drinking shots at the bar, the love-making at home which carried on until dawn. It was a miracle she was awake at all. Still, she could collapse later, take a bath maybe then eat a plate of chips and gravy in bed.

The consultant sighed. 'Anyone else, then?' A bunch of eager hands went up.

'Post-op infection.' A voice behind her confidently boomed out the correct answer and it echoed inside her. Of course it was post-op infection. So obvious. 'Maybe a pneumonia too. Mrs Benton would benefit from physio.'

The doctor nodded and Mrs Benton nodded too, as if she was happy about having a post-op infection. 'And the treatment?'

'Broad-spectrum antibiotic, consider fluids.' Anjali's voice was croaky and her mouth dry enough that her lips cracked a fraction. She looked at the other students around her, all fresh-faced and wide-eyed.

Later, the consultant from ward round found Anjali in the sluice, tipping out a bedpan that a nurse had handed her as though that's all she was good for. 'Not sure about the patient,' she said, handing Anjali a Lucozade, 'but you look like you need some fluids.'

Anjali took the Lucozade, despite wearing gloves that were likely splashed with urine, and held it tightly. 'I'm sorry.'

'Look, we've all been young. But remember why you're here.'

She couldn't remember why she was here. Anjali felt lost. Dissociated. A bit numb. Medicine made no sense to her now, and instead of learning she felt like she was tumbling, unlearning, running backwards. She phoned her mum. It was almost 10 p.m. by then, and her mum would be asleep already, or propped up in bed reading. But she needed to hear her voice. 'Mum.'

'Anjali? What's wrong?' Her mum's voice was fully awake at the sound of Anjali's. Late-evening calls were rare. Any calls were rare these days. Anjali wanted to talk to her mum, to tell her how, since she'd fallen in love with Paul, she had fallen out of love with medicine, but both facts felt terrifying. Since meeting him a few months before, they had not spoken of anything else since. 'He's a grown-up,' her mum had said. 'A real man. Is he kind? He seems kind.'

'Nothing's wrong. I wanted to say hello. I'm sorry, I didn't realise it's so late.' She closed her eyes and imagined her parents.

Her dad would be trying to get the phone off her mum, her mum swatting him away. Theirs was a forever marriage. They went to bed every evening by 10 p.m. and lay side by side in their pyjamas, reading novels and sometimes reading sections aloud to each other.

'Oh, that's good. I've been worrying about you working too hard. I'll send up a care package. You need soup. How's Paul? Everything OK?'

Anjali gulped. She heard the subtext. Her mum didn't want to hear that there was anything wrong. 'He's good. Sends love.' Her voice sounded tiny.

'Oh, that's great. Such a polite young man, and he's clearly besotted. You deserve it. When I met Dad he was much the same, pestering me until I agreed to go to the cinema with him . . .' Her mum carried on talking but Anjali moved the phone away from her ear.

A car headlight at the window and beeping. She wasn't expecting Paul, but he often turned up late, unannounced. She was desperate for sleep but still, excitement swelled around in her belly. Or maybe it was danger. She held the receiver close and whispered. 'I've got to go, Mum, I'm working nights. I only wanted to say hello.' The beeping again. She watched Paul get out of the car and look straight at the house, at her window. He was drunk. She could tell, even though he was in semi-darkness. Something about his posture was off, a slight curve to the right. Anjali couldn't think of any differential diagnoses of patients. On the ward, her brain had been empty of medical information she'd taken years to carefully learn. But in that moment her mind filled up. *Why is he angry? What has he taken? What have I done? How can I calm him down?*

TWENTY-THREE
Olivia (1999)

The dress shop was in Knightsbridge, and by appointment only. Olivia, Anjali, and Laura sat drinking champagne and listening to her mother tut or say the word 'ghastly', until 'at last' the poor girl working there brought out the simple dress that had her mother sit even more upright and nod: 'Farrow & Ball Slipper Satin.' Laura looked confused and Anjali's eyes danced with mischief. Olivia tried on the dress, which was too small and would not do up at the back. The sales assistant produced some sort of back extension which she slid into the dress, reassuring Liv that alterations were possible. When her mum saw the amount of back flesh Liv had on show, despite the extension contraption, she turned to Laura and asked her how she managed to stay so slim. 'Built like a shire horse,' her mother had once joked about Liv. 'Sturdy.' Anjali and Laura carried on drinking champagne and commenting on how beautiful Olivia was. But that day – despite the comments from her mother – she looked in the mirror and glowed from within. She stood facing them all on a small podium in the dress and Anjali gasped and Laura cried. Laura cried for a long time and had to go to the bathroom and splash water on her face. 'You're so beautiful, Liv,' she said. 'Inside and out.'

Lovely Laura. She always made Olivia feel better, even when being jabbed by her mum's snide remarks.

*

Olivia was beaming and desperate to tell Dele all about it, but when she leaned over to kiss him, she was taken aback. Dele smelled different. His skin smelled different. A softer, sweeter smell, like the vine of a tomato. She recognised the smell immediately. Her dad had been growing tomatoes for years, each year yielding a larger crop. His mum complained that he talked to the tomatoes as if they were small children: 'Well done. Look how you've grown.' Last time she'd visited, her dad had stuck his fingers in front of Olivia's nose. 'Best smell in the world. I defy any perfumier to come up with a more attractive scent.' Her mother rolled her eyes and muttered something about the dangers of romantic men. Olivia breathed it all in. Dele smelled of romance.

There was a puppy dog look in his eyes that suggested guilt. He'd bought her flowers. 'They're beautiful,' she said to Dele, 'I love lilies.' But she couldn't help frowning. He smelled different. He'd bought her flowers. This wasn't Dele.

He handed them over, lowered his eyes to the flowers, and he stared intently at them. A snake of a thought wrapped around her trachea. Could Dele ever cheat on her? Would he? She pushed the idea away, but it kept flying back at her. He smelled different. Was acting strangely. Buying her gifts. He was being obscure with information, and a bit cagey. *He smelled of tomatoes.* She prayed that she was wrong. She kneeled down every evening and laced her hands together hard enough her knuckles turned white.

Guilt was an emotion Olivia knew by heart. It crept around, guilt, in the shadows, low to the ground, moving in slow and measured ways. She'd heard the priest say that guilt would eat you from the inside like a worm at the core of the apple, and turn everything rotten. But to her it felt more ninja-like than that. Less natural. Guilt was an emotional terrorist, not a parasite. It wanted to hurt you in the worst ways possible, to blow you up. Olivia knew that the only way to deal with guilt was to name it and give it no room to hide. She had to confront Dele, and his guilty expression, and his tomato vine smell.

Dele lived in a flat in the hospital where junior doctors were given basic rooms in exchange for two years of their lives. It was scruffy yet functional with a threadbare sofa, large fridge with a different shelf for all residents, a corkboard on the wall of social events they never had time to attend and phone numbers for occupational health out-of-hours service in case of needle-stick injuries. He often worked hundred-hour weeks, and would collapse in a heap after twenty-four, sometimes even longer, days, only to have to wake to the alarm after a few short hours. Olivia got used to waiting for him in his bedroom, also functional yet soulless. Upon his bedside table balanced a novel or two, some poetry always and two alarm clocks lest he sleep through the first. The desk was covered in medical papers, and letters from Nigeria that Dele kept bundled up in cloth, the fabric of which he said was specific to his family, like a signature. 'At weddings we all wear the same thing, so people know we are the same family,' he'd told her. 'At our wedding we'll all wear the same patterned Ankara cloth, including your mum.' Then he laughed at Olivia's horrified expression, imagining asking her mum to don something bright and patterned in the interest of cultural norms. Her mum was a spring, she forever reminded them, and had tried to get Olivia to 'have her colours done', because 'sallow skin is usually fixable' according to a woman she knew from church who had something called a 'colour wheel' and could tell by holding this thing to your face whether you needed to wear deep maroons or acid turquoise. 'I suspect you're a winter,' she'd told Olivia once, 'in spring clothing.'

She waited on his bed, curled up in semi-darkness, for him to get back from theatres, where his colleague said he was assisting in an ablation, an operation that purposefully burned the inside of a person's heart to disrupt the damaged electrical system. It was a quick operation, and straightforward, but could mean the difference between a person having a stroke, and becoming severely disabled, or not. Sometimes the smallest surgeries made the biggest difference, Olivia was learning. The quietest of actions could change the course of history. A whisper. She smelled the jacket hanging on the back of Dele's door. There was a whiff of something familiar, barely perceptible, but it was not Olivia's, that was for sure. Her heart lurched.

She waited and waited, and eventually must have fallen asleep. 'Liv, what are you doing here? I thought you were at your mum's until next week?' Dele was kneeling next to her, stroking her face. 'You OK? God, I missed you. New York is far . . .' He was wearing dark navy scrubs, half folded over his biceps, and she could see his small patch of chest hair at the V-neck.

She sat up and stretched her legs out, yawning. 'Hey, what time is it?'

'It's 3 a.m. Shuffle over.' He kicked off his clogs, and climbed beside her, and spooned her. 'I'm absolutely shattered, but I have to say this is a wonderful surprise. You're like a present, a perfect gift waiting in my bed . . .' Olivia imagined unwrapping a present of secrets and lies and betrayal. She started to feel guilty herself, for thinking Dele capable of sleeping around. He was a bit of a lothario in his younger years, she knew because he'd told her. He was transparent like that. Telling her the truth. Surely he wouldn't do such a thing as have an affair? But the thoughts and feelings and her gut wouldn't let up. She had to know.

Dele started kissing her back, between her shoulder blades, pulling her vest down at first and then lifting it over her head and unfastening her bra in one movement. It was near impossible not to melt into him, even then with all that was going on in her head. Her body became molten when he touched her, completely pliable in his hands, as though she was his puppet. But even from behind her, Olivia could smell the difference on his skin. It was the familiar smell again. Tomatoes – it must be. Something that she deep down recognised. A smell of home, somehow. She flipped over and pulled her vest back on. 'I need to talk to you.'

He was momentarily completely still. Stunned. Then he smiled and stroked her cheek with his thumb. 'Talk dirty to me or lose me forever.' He laughed.

'I mean it, Dele. I need to talk to you. It's important.' She sat up and switched on the bedside lamp that they'd bought together in IKEA, the day they had an argument in the gardening section, then got cheap hotdogs and meatballs and laughed that an argument in IKEA is a rite of passage. 'It's really important.' She hadn't realised that she was crying until he pulled her towards him, and under his arm, a wing above her. Olivia's face rested on his chest. She could hear his heartbeat. Steady, normal rhythm, a rate of around 70.

'Hey now, what's wrong?' He rocked her slightly and said, 'Shhh.'

A few moments and sniffs later and she pulled away. 'Are you seeing someone else?' She looked at Dele's face. Studied it. She tried to take in every slight movement, right down to his pupil reactions. They stayed the same, size five, and his eyes didn't blink. MI5 intelligence officers are trained to detect lying, but if you really want to know if someone is telling the truth, ask a doctor. Olivia was an expert bullshit detector. She understood involuntary autonomic responses and pupillary reactions. Dele's mouth opened to say something, but then closed quickly. He took in a big breath.

Olivia felt her heart beating irregularly. It skipped a QRS complex. She understood this to be impossible, that an emotion could cause an arrhythmia. But she also knew that hearts were full of mystery. Doctors and scientists did not understand any more than artists or priests. Perhaps they weren't meant to.

'I'm so sorry,' Dele said. His voice was clear and true. He made a noise as if he was being strangled. 'I'm sorry, Liv. I'm so, so sorry. It was just one time. It didn't mean anything . . .'

They were lying down, but still Olivia felt as though she was falling. She closed her eyes, then snapped them open and stared at him.

'We didn't mean it to happen. It should never have happened. Olivia, you need to forgive me. Us.' Dele sat up, swinging his long legs over the side of the bed. His head dropped down into his hands. His long fingers reached his forehead. 'Liv, we fucked up.'

'We?' Olivia sat up but moved away from Dele. Drew her legs up to her knees. Pressed them into her chest.

'Laura wanted to tell you . . .' Dele glanced at Olivia then stopped talking. He closed his mouth and frowned. 'You didn't know.'

'How could I have?' Olivia's head pounded and cracked, the whooshing travelling through her entire body until every cell burned. Laura.

Laura. Laura. Laura.

Everything became blurred. Her chest hurt. It felt as if someone had shot into her sternum. She somehow sat up straighter and turned to Dele. 'Laura.' Her best friend. The person she loved the most. The friend she would have forever. Dele had been fucking her best friend in the world. And worse, Laura had been fucking Dele. She leaned her hand on the mattress. Everything was spinning. 'Laura,' she repeated.

Dele dropped his head into his hands, then lifted it and looked at Olivia. 'I'm so sorry, Liv. It just happened. We got engaged so quickly, I mean, Laura was there that first night, and then she sort of vanished and then at the funeral . . .'

'Wait,' Olivia made her face hard. Her insides icy. 'At the *funeral*? That was *weeks* ago . . . Do you *love* her?'

The room was silent. Olivia felt sick in her mouth before she could stop it, and retched, falling in front of the bin next to Dele's desk. She vomited and retched, vomited, and retched some more, then took large breaths, sitting on the floor, facing Dele. Olivia waited for him to deny it, to say it was a terrible mistake, that he was a man, and Laura had been there while Olivia was in New York, and he was weak and would pay penance for the rest of his life, and marry Olivia and they would somehow, somehow, put this behind them. But Dele didn't answer at all.

TWENTY-FOUR

Laura (1999)

Laura knew pain. Her childhood was spent living with the terrible knowledge that her dad would die. He was diagnosed with liver failure when she was eleven years old, but he'd turned the colour of straw long before then. She knew he drank. He drank more than everyone else on the estate, many of them heavy drinkers. But her dad was different. He poured whisky onto his cornflakes and laughed as if it was funny. The day he was put on the transplant list her mum and dad had come home from the hospital shell-shocked, quiet but snappy. They had eaten bread and cheese for dinner before making hushed phone calls. Laura sat on the stairs landing after bedtime, her legs dangling between the bars, and listened to the late-night conversations.

Her dad spoke in a tired voice. 'Seems unfair that someone will die so I can live when I have caused this problem myself. Best to give the liver to someone deserving. This is the end of the road, love.'

'There's nobody more deserving than you.' Her mum's voice was thick with tears. It made the landing and banisters feel wobbly. 'You had nowhere to put your pain is all.'

Laura crept back into bed and pulled her covers over her head. She lay in the darkness trying to make sense of things. Her dad was in pain? He'd put his pain into whisky and that had given him different pain? Was he deserving? Who was giving him a liver? Would her beloved dad *die*?

Laura went to the local library after school the next day, and the next, looking for answers to questions she didn't quite understand. She sat in the musty-smelling medical textbook section, balancing heavy books on her grass-stained knees, trying to make sense of statistics around survival of transplant surgery, and psychodynamic theories about addiction. By the time she was thirteen Laura understood that her dad would never see her get married or have a baby of her own. He might see her become a doctor though. The idea of that was a thread that held her teenage years together. A steel rod inside her that was really holding nothing but air.

Still, her dad knew she was going to be a doctor, perhaps that was enough. She'd let him imagine that she was getting married too. She heard her dad's words inside her head. 'Our Laura got herself a fella. A doctor himself. Be giving us grand-babies very soon.'

Her dad imagined that Laura would get married and have babies. She'd let him think that. For a moment, a stupid moment, she'd imagined it too. She'd let him believe it was her and Dele together, not Dele and Olivia. A white lie.

It was wrong. She knew it was wrong. But when Dele kissed her, when he'd fucked her, and touched her, and looked at her the way he did, everything evaporated. Their surroundings in the operating department anaesthetic room disappeared, along with any idea that what they were doing was wrong. Laura had always looked backwards, and forwards, and never stood still. Until then. For the first time in her life, she was in the moment, completely in the present. It felt, for a hot second, that nothing else mattered. There was something about what she felt with

Dele that felt like a glimpse behind an important curtain. Laura remembered letting her parents think Dele was hers. Long ago. Had she wanted him to be hers?

In the cold light of day, she returned to feeling pain. Grief felt raw, spike-edged and dangerous again. It had clearly caused a particular kind of madness. Her head felt like it had been removed, her skull opened and her brain taken out by a surgeon's hands. There were fingers inside her. Prodding and changing the patten of her, fiddling with her thoughts and impulses and personality. She thought of the gastrointestinal surgery she'd assisted in as part of her surgical rotation last year, and the second-year medical students who'd been brought into theatre and encouraged to practise a pelvic examination on the anaesthetised woman, without her consent. 'She'll never know,' the male surgeon had barked, as they stood one by one, inserting gloved hands inside her. 'How else will you learn?' Laura stayed silent. It felt wrong, but it happened all the time, so it must be normal.

Who was she? Laura was mad with grief, and out of character, she knew that. She kept remembering that her dad had put all his pain into whisky, and how she had wondered why he would do that, exchange one pain for a bigger one, a new pain that would cause so much damage. But that was before she put her own pain into Dele.

How could she? Olivia was her best friend in the world and all Laura could think of was Liv. She looked in the mirror the morning after it happened, the sex, her eyes hooded and haunted, her skin pale. Laura was skinny. Since the funeral she no longer ate much. Her skin hung off her like a loose-fitting apron, and her collarbones jutted out like tiny cliffs. Laura had imagined the kiss at the wake was a one-off, a madness never to be repeated or spoken of. No harm done. A disaster averted. She had gone to find Dele to tell him so, and made a bad situation much, much worse. She hated herself. She was the kind of woman that she hated. A cheat. A liar. Laura looked straight at her eyes, her bones, the shadows inside her, and imagined Olivia's pain. Pain wider than the sky. She did not know what to do.

Should she tell Olivia?

She could explain and tell her it was a terrible, terrible mistake and would never happen again. Olivia would surely forgive Dele. She may never speak to Laura again, and that would shatter Laura's heart. But she deserved that. Or should she not say a word? Cut off her feelings for Dele and bury them. Protect Olivia from ever knowing the truth. Her mind swirled with questions and worry. She ignored Dele's phone calls. Olivia and Anjali would be back in a few days, and she needed to get her head straight. Dele called her a few times a day, she knew it was him by waiting until the phone stopped ringing, and then pressing 1471 to see which number had dialled. He pushed a note through the door. *I'm sorry. It wasn't your fault. Let's talk about this?*

Olivia and Anjali returned from electives buzzy and full of excitement. She hugged them both, listened a while to their stories, and made them tea, before disappearing back to bed. They were both back to clinical work almost immediately, much to Laura's relief. She was avoiding Liv, as well as Dele. She still didn't know what to do. Should she tell Olivia this terrible thing that had happened while she was away? Her arms and legs were heavy. She kept thinking of her dad, her mum, Dele, Olivia. Everything hurt. Her body was full up with grief and with shame.

A week had gone by since they'd returned and Laura had kept busy and distant. Olivia hadn't seemed to notice. She had gone to stay a few days with her mum and was now back with

Dele. Anjali was working or seeing Paul. Laura imagined they assumed her quietness was about her dad. Anjali kept giving her little hugs, which only made her feel more terrible. Despite hating herself, she kept thinking of Dele. Replaying what had happened. She did not want to imagine him lying in bed with Olivia. She hated herself.

Laura hadn't intended on going to the City Tavern, but she craved distraction. She didn't want to listen to the voice inside her that whispered *Dele*. And an even deeper voice that whispered *love*. It was a stupid mistake. A bad one. Dele belonged to Olivia.

Laura walked through the vaults, the smell of mould and mice. There were a few nursing students, and she recognised a porter, but the place was nearly empty, except Anjali's Paul was there, propping up the bar.

'Laura! Don't see you in here much . . .' He kissed her on both cheeks. 'I'm waiting for Anjali to go to that party later. Assume you're being dragged there too? Let's get a beer?'

She looked at him. He was the kind of person who asked many questions without waiting for the answer. Laura wasn't sure what Anjali saw in him, but she was besotted. In any case, who was Laura to be a judge of character now? 'OK, sure. But I'm thinking a shot. I'm not sure about a party . . .'

Paul raised his eyebrows then shrugged and grinned.

They sat at a small wobbly wooden table in the corner and drank tequila shots and warm Foster's. Paul described his latest building project, a total refurb of an office building. 'How's life treating you?' Paul's voice was smooth and quiet, and he gave unblinking eye contact that made Laura feel uneasy.

'Pretty awful, actually.' She smiled. 'Hence the drinking.' She was a bit slurry already. Her brain was getting quieter. She drank gulps of the beer.

'Hmm. Anjali said you didn't go for an elective. I wish she hadn't. God, I've missed her. I was tempted to get a flight to Brazil! Listen, Laura, I'm so sorry about your dad. Anyways, I don't know how you do it. Saving lives. Minimum wage. You all deserve medals; I keep telling Anjali.'

Laura felt tears at the back of her eyes. 'Not all of us,' she said, and looked away. The certainty she'd felt earlier gave way quickly to horror. Her and Anjali and Olivia were the best of friends. Friends forever. She'd ruined everything. She had become the kind of woman she hated. A woman who was evil to other women. To her best friends. She gulped the beer. She had to tell Olivia. It was the right thing to do.

'Easy there.' He frowned. 'Are you OK, Laura?'

She forced a smile. 'I'll be OK. I just needed an Anjali hug, you know?'

'Oh, I know.' Paul's eyes sparked when Laura said Anjali's name. He wasn't so bad, after all. 'Anjali has a gazillion stories from the Amazon. Expect you've heard most of them this week? Anyways, come to the party with us later? Be fun . . .'

Laura downed the rest of her beer. 'Is Olivia going?'

Paul shrugged. 'I think she's gone back to her mum's . . . not sure, to be honest.'

Laura closed her eyes. She had to tell Olivia. She had to do it before bumping into Dele. He was on call that weekend, she'd checked the rota in theatres. She had spent a week ignoring his phone calls and notes, and, on the whole, avoiding Olivia. She couldn't live with this lie, no matter the consequences, and Dele would surely talk her out of it. She'd take the entire blame. It was her fault. It was grief. It would never, ever happen again. Olivia would forgive Dele, and she'd forgive Laura. She'd keep the secret a day longer and tell Olivia the truth tomorrow morning. The decision was made. She wanted this day gone. Obliterated. She wanted to sign out. To feel something other than horror. Even temporarily. Laura rarely drank, and she certainly never took drugs. But she looked at Paul. 'Maybe I'll come along. Do you have any drugs?'

Paul recoiled in mock horror. 'Who are you and what have you done with my friend Laura?' But then he smiled. 'I've always got drugs. I'll definitely sort you out.'

TWENTY-FIVE

Laura (2024)

'The parents don't want to see him suffer.' Peter bit into his sandwich, egg by the smell of it, and spoke with his mouth full. 'They're in full agreement. In this political climate, that says everything. I'm not entirely sure why it's been raised again at committee? I thought we agreed last week?'

Laura stayed quiet. The staffroom was extra hot that day, as the radiators had broken on full heat and despite Works 1544 written on the whiteboard there was no sign of anyone coming to fix it. None of the windows opened more than an inch – 'Lest we jump,' she'd told Ravinder, and he'd laughed.

Rosa read out parts of the neurosurgical report and tutted. 'The scans are pretty impressive. An absolute lack of any reactivity, and the areas of injury in both the grey and white matter, numerous bundles of damaged myelinated axons.'

Laura remembered these clusters of words and phrases, despite neurosurgery not being her speciality. Most of the terms used in neurosurgery were alien to all of them. Medicine was a language with many different accents. Some dialects that were hard to understand, even for doctors.

'Extensive grey matter discoloration,' Rosa continued, reading the report out loud, 'indicative of neuronal death.'

Joe had extensive white matter damage *and* grey matter

damage caused by a lack of oxygen to his brain following a huge bleed. A slow-ticking time bomb. Laura listened to the team discuss his care with another secret medical language. She thought of how beautiful the words sounded, despite their meaning.

Rosa mumbled on, reading the report and holding Joe's scan up for them to look at. Most of the Ethics Committee had no clue what they were looking at, all being from different specialities, but they all understood one thing. Joe would not recover from this injury.

Of course, like all medics, Laura had witnessed the occasional person who survived against the odds. She remembered caring for a woman after a road traffic accident once, whose blood results were incompatible with life; her pH, the acid level of her blood, was outside the framework it needed to be for human life to exist: it was below 6.8. She made a full recovery, and now had the blood result printout framed on her bathroom wall. Another patient, a two-year-old child, drowned in a grandparents' pond. The hypoxic ischaemia – lack of oxygen causing swelling then injury – was not unlike Joe's. The scans showed a toddler who would not make it. Yet that child was now eleven and starting secondary school. It had been winter when he'd drowned, and the shock of the cold was protective for brains. 'Always drown in winter,' Laura had told Olivia.

Olivia. Laura's mind ran back to their conversation. Olivia's voice had a tone to it, a softness, that felt safe. It whispered in her ear, even when Olivia was not there. Like a conscience, of sorts. *The King's Ear*, thought Laura, dismissing that thought immediately. Still, she remembered Liv's every word, clear as if she was speaking in the moment: 'You need to convince them to do brain stem testing. That Joe Duggard has a chance. Muddy the waters.'

Laura closed her eyes and pictured Joe in ICU, the Frankensteinesque bolt snaking out of his head. Her stomach lurched and filled with acid bile. She wished Anjali was with them. Anjali cracked jokes at the worst possible moments. She searched her head for what Anjali might say. *Well, he won't be running the London Marathon next year, but still, he has a chance.* It was clear that Joe was not brain stem dead, but also clear it was cruel to keep him alive. Beyond cruel. The kind of cruelty only doctors understood. A place where no consciousness existed other than inside nightmares, fuelled by the pain, and the medication to try and limit it. People who did not believe that hell existed had never met a person who should have died but was kept alive by an over-zealous medical team. It was torture.

But despite all this knowledge of extreme suffering and the nature of decision-making in medical ethics, despite her reservations about what Olivia was suggesting, despite all of this, Laura found herself opening her mouth and letting Olivia's words come through her. She pushed the words out one by one, imagining Freya standing in a courtroom, the word *manslaughter* ringing inside her. 'I disagree here. We should do brain stem testing and, assuming he's not brain stem dead, we should watch and wait a few more days at least.'

There was silence in the staffroom. Laura watched a bead of sweat travel down the face of her colleague, Sam. The atmosphere reminded her of the Westerns that her dad used to watch, and they were in the scene in the deserted town in the deserted bar before the fight began. Her dad did an impression of John Wayne every time a Western film came on the television. He stood, and limped, and balanced an unlit cigarette on his bottom lip, before saying, 'Well, looky here . . .' and laughed until he had a coughing fit.

'You're kidding, right?' Peter popped the last of his sandwich into his mouth and pressed it into the side of his cheek like a hamster as he spoke.

Laura shook her head. The room became hotter. 'I've spoken to the team in ICU, and I don't think it's yet time for the word futile.' She blinked, robotic. The words came through her but not from her. They sounded rehearsed – they *were* rehearsed.

'His family want to let him go,' Peter's voice was coloured with anger. 'This isn't about whether he's brain stem dead or not, he's in a vegetative state and withdrawal is the only option.' He was protective of young adults, teenage boys particularly. His own son had died by suicide three years ago. Since then, Peter seemed to be at work twenty-four seven. 'In whose interest is it to keep him alive? The parents don't want it, and the patient is suffering. It doesn't even warrant an ethical discussion.'

'But we don't know that with 100 per cent certainty,' said Laura. 'All this is assumption. I think it's clinically appropriate to undertake the tests in this case.'

Peter stood. 'Are you feeling OK?'

He checked his bleep and walked out of the staffroom, frantically shaking his head.

Laura looked at the others. 'We need a consensus, right?' The team looked back at her, confused. This was entirely out of character. That was why, Laura knew, they would trust it. Laura was *always* level-headed and sensible, as well as bright. Her colleagues often looked to her for answers to difficult questions. There was no going back. She felt like a Russian doll, a story in a story in a story. On the outside, Joe Duggard and whether he lived or died. Then Freya, Rudy, whether Freya's life was completely destroyed or not, for one stupid teenage party. And in her centre, always in her core, were Olivia and Anjali, the three of them, and another party that they'd buried deep inside.

*

The intensive care unit was experiencing what the nurses termed a Bad Day At The Office. The patient in bedspace four was weaving in and out of cardiac arrest every hour or so, and none of the staff had left the unit for pee breaks, let alone to eat or drink. The air buzzed with alarms, and nurses and doctors wearing placenta-coloured scrubs danced in and out of each patient's bed area, fiddling with ventilator settings, or monitors, piggy-backing inotropes, the heart medicine that was strong enough that you couldn't simply change one syringe for another, you had to reduce one down in tiny increments as you increased the replacement.

'It's a swingers' club today!' The consultant, Stanley, walked past Laura nodding at all the berserk arterial blood pressure alarms. 'There are not enough bedside nurses, so inotrope crossover time has become fun.' He was sweating. Tiny pinprick beads pockmarked his forehead. He looked at another patient monitor that was flashing and beeping; the woman's blood pressure was way too high: 210/190. 'It will be a miracle if nobody has a fucking stroke,' he said, rushing over and reducing the syringe driver that was double pumping heart drugs into her, giving her the eye-watering blood pressure.

Joe's blood pressure was not swinging. Laura pulled a plastic chair up next to his bed, and the thin, crappy curtain around slightly. She looked at the waves on the monitor, the patterns inside him, steady and regular, too steady. Looking at his numbers felt like being in a house where a toddler was quiet. The absence of chaos meant something was very wrong. It was a cocoon of calm in Joe's bedspace. The machinery chugged and whooshed rhythmically, and Laura watched the rise and fall of his chest. He had one of those almost pigeon chests of adolescent boys, too thin despite, no doubt, an extraordinary amount of food. Rudy had a similar chest. They grew an inch overnight around this age. Rudy's feet had long hung over the edge of the bed, and he'd persuaded her to get him an extra-long bed despite the certainty he'd be off to university soon enough.

She blinked tears back in her head, made her stomach tight.

Joe would not be going to university. He would not be going anywhere. She thought of Miles telling them that Joe was a misogynist, one of those boys who treated girls terribly. Laura had known boys like that at school. Remembered the entitlement. The thought of what Joe could become made the room spin, but she breathed in time with his ventilator and everything stopped moving. Still, like Rudy, he was at the age where he was forming his identity, and his future self was in a state of fluidity. But there would be no chance for him to redeem himself now. He'd never get the chance to grow, or to change, or to look back at his younger self with regret. He would not walk again, or talk, or laugh, or smile, or eat, or sit up, or use the toilet. He would, at best, be frozen in time, his needs taken care of by strangers and his family. His family would likely fall apart under the strain of it. Divorce rates in those caring for severely disabled or ventilated children were sky-high. His family would suffer, even if Joe was comatose, and unaware. Laura knew all of this. She knew what was right. What medicine should and should not do was much more important than what medicine could and could not do. This was a truth through the ages, and yet now, as technology overtook philosophical thinking about that technology, it was being forgotten. 'We can keep pretty much anyone alive these days,' she had discussed with Anjali, 'but should we?'

'Oh, hello there.' A woman slid the curtain back and stood in front of Laura, a confused frown cutting her forehead in two. 'Sorry, do I know you?'

Laura stood and extended her hand. 'I'm Laura. One of the doctors who has been reviewing Joe's case. Thought I'd come pay a visit and say hi.' It was unethical for the Ethics Committee members to meet families. Already a line she was crossing. A giant step forward and more *no going back*.

'I'm Sandra.' Joe's mum wore a large yellow raincoat with a small goose embroidered on the arm, and bright pink lipstick. She looked exhausted; her eyes were sunken so far that her eyelids were invisible, and yet she'd clearly had her nails painted and put some make-up on, a sign, perhaps, of some sort of extreme resilience. Joe's family were going through the worst possible time imaginable. Facing a situation that no human being should ever have to face. The loss of a child. It was against the natural order of things. Grief echoed off the walls in here.

Laura studied Sandra a moment. Sandra was too busy watching Joe to notice. 'They are taking his breathing tube out soon,' she said. 'I talked to that other doctor, the tall one. And he told me that, if Joe was his son, he wouldn't want him to suffer.' Her face was completely dry, which was far worse than seeing tears. 'I don't want him in pain.'

Laura pressed her teeth together until she heard a cracking sound in her mouth. She thought of Rudy, and Freya, and most of all Olivia. When you have been friends a lifetime, you see the person then and now at once, like all parents who look at their adult child and see the baby they were. She saw Olivia, the dreadful night of the other party, all those years ago. She carried with her Olivia's concerned expression, her protective words. She saw Olivia and Anjali pulling Laura away.

Enough drugs to kill a horse.

She remembered herself in that moment. Sobering up with a thump. Olivia telling her to run. 'Someone is dead. You need to run.'

Run. Run. Run.

She remembered the weeks and months afterwards, Olivia stroking her hair and telling her that it would be OK, and how scared they all were, how frightened Anjali was, the terror in her eyes. How unafraid Liv was. Steady, certain Liv who told Laura she did a *very* bad thing, but that bad thing could forever be forgotten if she simply told one lie. A good lie. It was a lie to save Anjali. *Do the right thing now*, Olivia had said. *And this will all go away.* Olivia told her how Paul had been violent to Anjali. Multiple times. He'd beaten her up. Laura's skin became so cold she could not feel her body.

She owed Olivia her entire life.

Laura felt sick whenever she remembered what Olivia did for her that terrible night when Olivia had gone to the party, and literally saved Laura.

Laura felt even more sick when she thought of what she'd done to Olivia, how she had never had the chance to tell Olivia the truth, and how the cheating with Dele remained inside her, a toxic secret. She was the worst friend in the world, and lived with that all these years, despite Olivia not knowing. But now, here, Laura had a chance to put things right. She could help Olivia. Maybe her guilt demons would finally be laid to rest. She owed Olivia. She thought of Liv's face when she'd told her that if Joe died, and it was investigated, there was a possibility that Freya might be charged with manslaughter. A remote possibility, she'd added, but by then Olivia's face had changed colour. She could help Freya avoid trouble. She had to.

Laura put her hand on top of Sandra's and squeezed a fraction. 'I've looked at all of Joe's notes and his scan results. I think we should talk.' She watched as something lit up inside Sandra's face that made her skin glow. Hope.

TWENTY-SIX

Olivia (2024)

Olivia sat opposite Freya. She'd chosen a café that was, aptly perhaps, being run by prisoners or ex-prisoners, not for that fact but simply because Gail's always had a queue around the block, and she didn't want anyone overhearing them. The queue for Gail's had never shortened, not even during lockdown. There was forever a line of Sweaty-Betty-wearing yummy mummies and bearded Camper-shoe-wearing men, talking, mostly, about how wonderful their children were. These were the people, Liv could only assume, who had run advertising agencies, or been hedge fund managers, and were now full-time parenting, competition-less, so had to put that pent-up ambition into the kids, gym, even cafés.

Freya sipped coffee. She was in a black coffee phase despite, clearly from the expression on her face, finding it bitter.

Olivia felt like she was falling. The ground shifted beneath her, and she watched her daughter, hardly different than when she was a baby, wide-eyed and perfect. She'd always been more protective of Freya. Perhaps because she was a girl, or maybe due to her being the youngest. From the moment she was born, Olivia had worried about her. These times she was growing into. Drugs. Social media. Pressure to look a certain way, to grow up too quickly. She'd purposefully tried to parent her the opposite of how she was parented by her own mother. Freya was loved unconditionally, and she knew it. A child could never be loved too much. That's what she'd believed. It was impossible to imagine Freya pushing someone downstairs. Impossible to imagine her child taking cocaine. Those were incidents that were facilitated by Rudy, she was sure of it. It must have been Rudy. He was probably jealous. Jealous of their home, their privilege, of two loving parents who showered Freya with love and attention. That was it. Jealousy. *Jealousy*. A dangerous emotion.

Freya put her cup down. Open-mouthed she leaned back in her chair. 'Mum, you're scaring me. What is it?'

'You tell me, Freya. I'm all ears . . .'

Freya's eyes widened with understanding. 'You *know*. Laura told you.'

'I wish you'd told me. It's hardly something you can keep secret.'

'It was an accident,' said Freya. 'I mean, I pushed him a bit, but I didn't push him hard at all. Honestly, Mum, it was a total accident.' She gulped. 'Does anyone else know? Wait, does Dad know?' A tiny green vein in her neck pulsed too quickly.

'Are you telling me,' Olivia leaned forward, spoke in whispers, 'that you pushed someone down the stairs?'

It was clear from Freya's expression, as well as her words, that she had no idea how much trouble she was in, or how sick Joe Duggard was. 'He was disgusting,' she said, 'spreading lies about me . . .'

'What lies?' Olivia watched Freya's face break for a moment, and even during this, her heart cracked for her. She wanted to scoop her up and keep her away from all the horrors of teenage life but she couldn't. Not now.

'He lies about all girls. He basically put his hand up my skirt. Rudy saw him. I think Rudy would have pushed him if I hadn't. But honestly, it was an accident. Does Dad know?'

Olivia poured some Earl Grey into a china cup and a thousand memories flashed inside her. Boys and men, overstepping the mark. Freya surely did what any girl would do. *Should* do. Part of her thought that they should simply ignore it all. After all, only Rudy and Freya knew the truth and it sounded like Joe Duggard deserved to be pushed. Surely that was an act of self-defence? Even if he died, the police might not investigate at all. It would almost be a perfect murder. But she couldn't do that. She had to take control of the situation. It was too risky, relying on teenagers to keep a secret forever. Relying on a system that was broken. Olivia had to fix this, so that even if the worst happened, and the truth came out, Freya's life would not be ruined.

'He might die,' she said.

Freya's mouth fell open. Her baby. Her youngest. She had to protect her, but first Olivia needed Freya to understand how serious this was.

They were both silent a moment. Olivia looked across the café at a mother getting exasperated with a toddler who was refusing to put his coat on. She was red-faced and seething with anger. Liv remembered it so well, the years that she thought at the time were the difficult years, how she was almost wishing them away and wanting the kids to grow up a bit and become easier. Nobody warns you about the teenage years. Nobody. It's a parental secret that the hardest time of all is not the babyhood, it's the teens. The most gut-wrenching, stomach-churning, anxiety-ridden phase of life is if and when you find yourself parenting a teenager. Imagining a boy putting his hand up your daughter's skirt? Unthinkable.

'I thought he was OK,' Freya said. She was staring straight at Olivia. 'He went into hospital, and you said he was stable. You said.' She was blinking hard, but still her eyes were filling up with tears.

'I was trying to reassure you before I had all the facts. Anyway, he was stable. Is stable.'

'Then what's the problem?' Her hands were shaking.

'Why didn't you tell me?' Olivia tried to make her voice detached. She was not Mum. She was speaking as a guidance counsellor, and she needed to be very clear with her. Everything was at stake. Their entire future. 'Freya, this is so serious. Why didn't you tell me, darling? I understand why you did what you did. I get it. But you should have told me. The consequences . . .' Freya's future floated in the air. 'Joe's stable. But he sustained a serious head injury. When you pushed him, Freya, you pushed him down the stairs. A lot of stairs. He hit his head on the table at the bottom, then the wooden floor, and had a bleed in his brain. A life-threatening injury. Do you know what that means?'

Freya picked up a serviette and dabbed her eyes. Suddenly she seemed a lot younger. Smaller. Bug-eyed.

'It's a serious injury,' Olivia whispered, but nobody in the café paid them any attention. They were in a bubble. An anxiety booth. The world moved around them, but they were almost oblivious in the intensity of their words.

'He might die?' Freya couldn't dab the tears now. They fell in splashes onto the table. Freya scrunched the serviette up into a much smaller one, then rubbed her eyes until she resembled a rabbit that had been used for cosmetic testing. She was beginning to breathe more heavily, which Olivia knew would mean a panic attack. She'd had a few before, resulting in hours of hysteria. She reached over and put her hand on top of Freya's. She took a breath. She knew what she had to do. She'd do anything to protect the ones she loved. Anything. She'd walk through fire for Freya.

'If Joe Duggard dies,' Olivia said, 'whoever caused it might face a manslaughter charge. Even if it was accidental. I'm sorry, Frey, but we need to talk about this. Make a plan.'

The shock was palpable. The table rattled a fraction.

'This isn't happening, this isn't happening, it isn't . . .' Freya rocked front to back.

'If Joe survives, I doubt much will happen. The police don't even know you were there.'

'So, nothing will happen?'

Olivia's thoughts flicked to what her doctor brain knew. She visualised Joe Duggard on a permanent ventilator, breathing through a tube the diameter of a straw, thick yellow sputum needing to be suctioned up it every few minutes. She took a gulp of air. 'Not to you. No. Not if the truth stays secret forever.'

Freya closed her eyes. Her eyelid twitched. 'Thank God. We won't tell. Nobody saw me push him. Nobody. Rudy won't ever tell . . .' She looked confused a tiny bit. A flicker of something. 'But he might die?'

'What is it?' Olivia glared at her. 'You need to tell me the whole truth now. Honestly, Freya, I suggest you tell me everything . . .'

'It's just Miles.'

Olivia shut her eyes. When she opened them, Freya was shaking her head.

'He might die,' she said. 'He might die?' She shook her head slightly, as if trying to concentrate. 'Miles doesn't know. Nothing like that. It's just he knows we were there that night. He was asking about it. What if Miles says anything?'

Olivia breathed. 'That's OK. I'll tell him not to.' She picked up Freya's hands. Freya looked at her with perfect trust. They were co-conspirators now. 'But I am worried. Because if Joe dies, that could be a different story. Even if it stays a secret, the police will investigate further. Surely, other kids saw you there that night. Eventually they'll want to interview you. It becomes more legally complicated. There's a law that means even accidental death can lead to a conviction of manslaughter.'

Liv watched Freya's face expand and puff out.

'What should I do?'

'You have two choices. Tell the truth and you might be arrested, whether Joe dies or not.' Olivia waited to see her expression. Freya was clearly afraid, her eyelid was twitching again. The café around them melted into background noise.

'Or? What are the other options?' She was breathing quickly now.

Olivia looked at a dead-eyed waiter serving smashed avocado to a woman across the café. He had a tattoo on his neck and the posture of sadness. She looked back at Freya, who seemed more concerned about getting caught than the news a person could die because of her actions. She was counting on that level of self-absorption. 'The second option is that you blame someone else.' The sentence formed in the air between them, heavy and with hard edges. *Blame someone else.* 'Or even better,' Liv was whispering now, 'let someone else take the blame.' She closed her eyes and let the word blame swell up inside her until it joined shame and guilt and all three words echoed and echoed and echoed.

'But who else? It was only us two there. He fell. That's what everyone will think. We made a pact, me and Rudy, to say that.'

'I know. Rudy broke your pact. He broke your trust and told Laura. Freya, darling, I know this is hard, but you need to say Rudy pushed Joe,' Olivia said. She kissed Freya's hands. 'Or better still, get Rudy to confess it himself.' She had déjà vu so badly she had to put Freya's hands down and press her hands onto her thighs to steady herself. She opened her eyes and Freya was staring at her, horrified. 'Rudy gave you a ton of drugs. Enough for a long prison sentence for possession with intent to supply. Laura doesn't know that. You could use that fact to encourage him to protect you . . .'

Freya was shaking her head. 'Who would do that? Who? How could you even think it?'

Olivia felt upside down a moment. Inside out. 'Well then.' Her voice took on jagged edges, and she sounded so cold and like her mum that a universe inside her cracked open. 'You'd better hope that Joe Duggard survives. Or that you and Rudy can keep a secret forever.'

Laura's house was hideous, Olivia had always thought so. A Barratt-built toy town house in a suburb, decorated with art that was mass produced and in immaculate frames, paintings of abstract scenes chosen for their ability to blend with existing colour schemes rather than the artist's ability to paint. Even the doorbell annoyed her. A jingle that sounded like an ice-cream van, meant to be ironic but actually annoying.

'Hey, hi.' Laura answered the door, wearing her running gear and with her red hair piled on top of her head in a messy bun. She looked skinnier than ever. Somehow more beautiful, Olivia thought. Even now.

She walked in, taking her shoes off quickly, then hugged Laura, who smelled of lime. 'I spoke to Freya,' she said. 'Did you speak to the family?'

'Let's sit down.' They moved apart and walked through the hallway, past the glitzy mirror and fake antique chandelier, which made Olivia wince when she first saw it, and caused an argument between her and Dele. *You're such a snob*, he'd said, despite his polo playing.

The living room was immaculate, all muted greys and Jo Malone candles, the source of the lime smell on Laura's clothes. They sat on the sofa opposite each other, Laura's legs curled beneath her. 'It was horrific.' She hadn't slept, Olivia could tell. Her face was like it used to be at medical school after she'd revised all night: serious and worried and slightly crumpled up. 'His mum, Sandra . . . well, I think giving that woman hope is possibly the cruellest thing I've ever done.'

'How can hope be cruel?'

'We both know that's a silly question.' Laura uncurled her legs. 'I mean, we both know that.'

'Remember when we started out?' Olivia closed her eyes a moment and felt the warmth of the memory fill her.

'I remember. Idealistic, naive and full of hope. Conscious optimism.'

Olivia sat up. 'What are we going to do about Anjali? They've been matched at last. A toddler. I think the matching panel is in a few weeks. We can't lay this burden on her now. I don't think she can know that Freya,' Olivia paused, 'and Rudy – are in trouble. It will derail her and their adoption process. Throw up all the shit that she's buried . . .'

'We can't tell her.' Laura shook her head. 'But now Donna knows about Paul's existence, it all just feels too close. Even more secrets? More lies? It feels like the past is here right now, and we're reliving everything that happened with Paul. Imagine what it will do to her and Anjali if the whole truth gets out? What I did.'

'What we all did,' said Olivia. 'We all did. And we fixed it then, we can fix it now. There's no need for lives to be ruined because of one stupid mistake.'

Laura nodded, but anxiety slid down her face. Olivia dug into her handbag and found a tissue. She passed it over. 'No tears. That's not you, Loz. Absolutely no tears. This will be OK. We can fix this. We are good at fixing things.'

Laura took the tissue and wiped her eyes. 'I'm getting senti-mental in my old age.' A cloud of sadness and anxiety was so palpable around her, the air itself looked a different colour.

'Honestly, I think I'm losing my mind. I keep imagining I'm being followed.' She paused. 'I swear I feel like I'm being watched. I heard footsteps behind me last week. I thought there was someone in my shed, but the police arrived and found nothing. I'm losing it.'

'It's your imagination. The stress. The job.'

Laura blew her nose. 'How's Dele doing?'

Olivia pushed sick from her mouth into her throat and made her voice lighter. She felt her head pound when Laura asked about Dele. It had to come across as natural and breezy, her answer, but as ever it felt like someone had stabbed her in the sternum. 'He's doing well. Been working too hard, but we're looking forward to Zanzibar . . .'

Laura looked at Olivia as if she could see inside her. 'Lovely. We all need a break, that's all. I'm very sure I'm imagining worst-case scenarios. Maybe I'll take Rudy away in half term. Mother–son seaside time. He'll hate it but secretly love it.'

Olivia turned away, her eye snagging on the photo of Rudy in a small pseudo-antique frame next to the grotesquely large television. She focused on him giving Freya drugs. He was clearly a bad influence. She knew Laura loved him so much and would do anything to protect him. But Laura trusted Olivia entirely. She would believe that it was Rudy's fault that Joe Duggard was seriously hurt. Olivia was good at fixing things. A beat inside her. A flicker of memory. Laura and Dele and the look that passed between them that nearly threatened Olivia's whole life. Her eyes hurt. 'Apparently, it wasn't clear it was Freya who pushed Joe,' she said.

Laura uncrossed her legs. She frowned.

'She says it was Rudy who pushed him. Then he slipped and fell down the stairs. They heard the crack when he hit the floor, but she said he also hit his head on the table at the bottom.'

Laura's mouth dropped open, then she snapped it closed. 'No way. Absolutely no way my son pushed him. No chance.'

Liv reached out and put her hand on Laura's. 'Rudy pushed him. If Joe Duggard dies, there's a tiny chance, but still a chance, that Rudy might be charged with manslaughter. I'm so sorry.'

Laura was moon-pale at the best of times but the colour drained so far from her face that her freckles disappeared. 'No way was that Rudy.' Laura leaned into Olivia and lowered her head onto Liv's shoulder.

Olivia held her tightly, protectively. She breathed in the lime smell of her friend and wondered how it was possible to love and hate at once.

'What's that?' Laura lifted her head from Liv's chest and stood. An outline was at the window, which was slightly open. Then, a voice. 'Hello?'

Donna? Laura looked at Olivia who jumped up and walked to the hallway. The last thing they needed was Donna here. Donna would tell Anjali about the party, *this party* and the waters would muddy beyond belief.

She opened the door and Donna was there in cycling gear, propping up a bike. 'Olivia! That's a nice surprise . . .' She hugged her and Laura rushed into the hallway behind them.

Olivia looked at Laura's reflection in the mirror. She glared at her.

'Did you overhear us?' Laura blurted out before Olivia could think.

Donna stepped back, leaned her bike against the wall, and smiled, widely. 'I was tapping on the window. You didn't hear the doorbell?'

Laura looked slightly confused. Olivia smiled back at Donna. 'Yes we did. We were just knee-deep in work chat . . .' She waited to see if Donna reacted and assess what she had heard. Donna's face was unmoving, and her expression hard to read. She'd probably heard nothing at all. And even if she had, she was too naive to connect any dots.

TWENTY-SEVEN

Anjali (2024)

'Anj, get out here, Anj.' Hammering on the wall and shouting.

Anjali smiled at the man sitting on the chair opposite her, a seventy-four-year-old with high blood pressure. 'I'll just pop out,' she said. He shrugged.

It was chaos outside the clinic room. Screaming and shouting. A woman was standing with her iPhone trying to film the scene. Bola had produced a screen from somewhere and fashioned it around the downstairs toilets to block it from view. One of the receptionists was running with the AED, a small defibrillator. One of her shoes fell off as she ran.

'What's the story?' Anjali pushed past the waiting-room staff and patients and the curtain to find Bola leaning over a woman on the floor. She kneeled opposite and took everything in at once. The woman was the colour of pigeon shit. She was stick-insect thin. She smelled of sweat that had dried, then been covered up with cheap deodorant. She had a needle sticking out of her arm, a shoelace homemade tourniquet above it. 'Fuck. We have any naloxone?'

Bola stood. 'I'll look. Get an ambulance.' She ran back towards the reception, shouting for an ambulance.

Anjali leaned down and tipped the woman's head back, studying her chest for any signs of life. She counted, ten – no signs of life – and started pressing down on the woman's chest, two per second, her arms locked, fingers laced together, pulled away from her sternum. Even with good technique, she could feel ribs cracking underneath her, the sound of walking on gravel. She looked down at the woman as she pressed hard on her chest. A drug user. An addict. Vilified and disregarded by society. Imagine how desperate she must be to do drugs in a GP clinic toilet? She looked at her face. Her half-open glazed-over eyes. Pinpoint pupils. All she saw was pain.

The paramedics arrived within a few minutes, and she was given Narcan, the drug that reverses the effects of opiates like heroin. The drug that they should have had stocked in their drug cupboard, since they started running addiction clinics, but Bola couldn't find. Still, it didn't work. Anjali had administered it before, to a man collapsed in the car park, and despite being unconscious and barely breathing, as soon as she pushed the needle into his thigh muscle, he sat bolt upright, fists clenched, swearing and shouting. This woman was already dead by the time they found her, so it was unlikely to ever work, but they tried anyway. She was unmoving, a scrap of a person, the needle still dangling from her arm. 'Leave that there,' the paramedic said, indicating the tourniquet. He took the needle out and carefully dropped it into a neon yellow sharps bin. The GP clinic had been mostly cleared of patients by then, but a row of them hovered around the corner, waiting or gossiping. Anjali noticed them filming the paramedics as they lifted this Jane Doe onto a stretcher and out to the ambulance, carrying her carefully as if she was alive.

Donna wasn't home when she got there. Anjali stood in the hallway, dropped her shoes and coat and bag on the floor, and walked to the kitchen. Her head was all over the place. Seeing that woman dead, trying to help her, had unlocked something in her own memory. Maybe the visit from Miles triggered it too, describing Freya and Rudy's party: history repeating itself. Donna had been in total shock after Miles left, and they talked about nothing else the next day. She'd initially wanted to go straight over to Olivia's or Laura's and have it out – ask what the hell was going on. But they'd decided between them that with the adoption imminent the less they knew about anything shady the better. There would be a reason that her friends had not told them Freya and Rudy were in trouble, Anjali had told Donna. 'Keeping us stress free to focus on Khadija,' she'd said. But Anjali had a lurking feeling in her legs and arms, a heaviness, and Donna was planning to visit Joe Duggard in any case, as promised. Who knows what she'd find out? It felt like the past and present were colliding somehow. Two parties and danger separated by time. Anjali felt it inside her brain, an itch she couldn't quite get to, from another teenage party ending in tragedy, the night when the medical student, Dean, died. The night their whole lives turned upside down. Anjali had broken her leg falling out of a tree when she was ten years old. She'd had a cast for eight weeks and been driven mad with itching underneath it. Her grandmother gave her a knitting needle, and she pushed it into the tight space between skin and plaster and felt both pain and relief at the same time. Her head was full of itching. Flashes of the dead woman's face lit up in front of her and mixed with flashes of Dean. Both of them, glazed eyes half open, staring blankly at Anjali.

Anjali slid down to the floor of the kitchen and leaned against the cabinet. Her heart was suddenly in her ears and all she could hear was a whoosh. A knitting needle prodded inside her brain. A memory just in reach. Olivia's voice. Another dead person. Drugs. Laura. Olivia's voice again.

Her head felt dull then full, and something inside her flicked, like a switch, from darkness to floodlights. A panic attack. She hadn't had one in years. *Not since Paul.* But here she was, in the kitchen, unable to breathe. Her chest thumped and hurt, and she couldn't breathe. *Breathe.*

But instead, all she could picture was herself, Olivia and Laura at age twenty-one, and the awful night of *that* party. She could see it all, a film in her head, and hear it too in surround sound. *One. Two. Three.* She heard Olivia's voice telling Laura to run. She heard Paul shouting. The police arriving and chaos, Paul in handcuffs, swearing, his face red and swollen, his anger. She heard Olivia's voice, calm through it all, *I'll fix all of this.*

Olivia was waiting on a bench when Anjali got to the park, holding two coffees. She shook off her headphones and stood up, kissing Anj on the cheek. 'This one is mine' – she looked at the cups – 'breakfast tea. Here's your oat flat white with an extra shot. Because you're a wanker.'

Anjali took the coffee and sipped it. 'Extra hot too. You know me so well.'

They strolled off, arms hooked together. Dulwich Park was busy with dogs and people, all walking, cycling, a few rollerbladers. 'It always strikes me,' said Anjali, 'how a person becomes their landscape. The parks say everything. Ruskin is full of spiky plants, and also the place of interesting haircuts. Art crowd. Brockwell is what my mum would have called "all fur coat and no knickers". Pretty, but a constant smell of weed. Like the people who hang out there.'

Liv laughed. 'You're so right. What about here?'

'Dulwich. Hmmm.' Anjali looked around. 'It's the most manicured, best kept, smartest.'

Olivia leaned into her. 'And? Go on? I love your philo-sophical ramblings.'

'Dulwich Park is almost too green, too pruned. Everyone in Dulwich Park looks botoxed. A bit fake.'

'You are right!' Olivia nudged Anjali and pointed at a dog walking past, a large labradoodle with a cartoon face. 'Even the dogs.'

They walked a while, and caught up on work, and Anjali told Liv about the adoption. 'We've matching panel next week. All being well, we get to meet Khadija after that. Don't tell anyone, OK? I don't want to jinx anything.'

Olivia pretended to zip her mouth. Then unzipped it. 'Anjali, I am so delighted for you both. You will be such amazing mums. I mean, look how much the kids adore you, especially Miles.'

'Speaking of Miles,' Anjali said, 'he came to see us. He told us, Olivia, about the party.'

A look swept over Olivia's face. A brief, split-second expres-sion that Anjali had never seen her wear. 'Oh.'

'What's happening? He said there's a patient on ICU and there was a party and Rudy and Freya were there, but you guys told them to keep it secret? What's going on?'

Olivia unhooked her arm from Anjali and finished her coffee. She sighed, then told her all about Joe Duggard, and how he fell downstairs, and Rudy and Freya were there. 'It's a white lie. To protect them. Joe Duggard, that patient in ICU, is bolted, oscillated and on the filter. Not looking good.'

'Jeez. Come on, Liv, they shouldn't lie. It was an accident, but lying will get them in serious trouble. Why do it? Tell them not to lie, or I will. I mean it, Olivia. I kept thinking about us, ever since Miles told me . . . It's weird, but I'm sort of remembering things about that night Dean died. Only it doesn't make sense. I can picture you telling me that Laura gave Dean the drugs, but I can also remember giving Dean drugs. I'm sure I did.'

'This is exactly what I wanted to avoid.' Olivia's tone changed, and she sounded brisk and businesslike.

Anjali shook her head. 'I'll be telling them not to lie.'

Olivia stopped walking. She looked at Anjali as if trying to decide something, then spoke in a very low, angry voice. 'I need you to keep out of this. I'm protecting Freya, and that's what all good mothers do.' She leaned forward. Anjali watched the vein in her neck throb. She'd never seen Olivia's vein throbbing before. 'When you're a mother you'll understand. If . . .'

'What are you saying?' Anjali was shaking. She'd never seen Olivia like this.

'I'm saying,' said Olivia, 'if you get involved then the truth might have to come out about you.' She paused. 'I told a white lie before, all those years ago, after the party, and it saved your life.'

Anjali closed her eyes, and the entire park around her seemed to spin. When she opened her eyes, Olivia was walking away, straight-backed, striding off with her head held high.

TWENTY-EIGHT

Laura (2024)

As soon as Olivia had left the house, she'd got on to Dazzled, and was hooking up with some guy within three hours. She couldn't take in what Olivia had told her. She'd purposely searched for kink, not her usual thing, but some dark part of her brain had been activated by the idea of loss of control, and she needed exactly that, to be controlled. She hungered to be held, for someone else to be in charge of her, to switch off her brain. She needed darkness, perhaps even violence, to contain her. They met at his flat in Beckenham, a bit too close to home, but Laura wanted to be back before Rudy finished school and her mum returned from the day centre. She needed to forget all this for a few hours. This was better than crying. It cleared her head, not muddied it. She had to think. Stop falling apart. Snap out of this weakness.

Jack was fit. His flat was clean. He offered Laura a drink, which she declined, and led her to his bedroom.

On his bed were various ropes and paddles and instruments of torture. It looked a lot like an operating table. 'Safe word?' he asked.

Laura just stared.

*

Crush injuries were the worst. The heavy object held a person together, and they could be breathing, talking, and conscious, the damage unapparent. But as soon as the heavy object is lifted from a person's skeleton, they fall apart, with nothing holding them together. That night was an extra shift, covering for yet another colleague on stress leave. Laura checked her phone mid-air. Seven missed calls from Anjali. That was unusual, but not unheard of. Anjali could be impatient, and it would likely be a dinner invite or some exciting adoption news. She couldn't speak to her. Anjali would hear the worry in Laura's voice, no doubt. Everything felt like it was unravelling, as if Joe Duggard was a thread that had been pulled, that ensured everything else fell apart. The afternoon of kinky sex with a stranger went some way to relieveing Laura of worry. She had studied the emerging bruises when she'd got home, and the soreness gave her some kind of perverted comfort. But it was short-lived. When Rudy came in, she could see how afraid he was, and it filled her again with worry. He was adamant, though, that it was Freya who pushed Joe Duggard. Not that it really mattered in the end. It didn't change what Laura would have to do.

The helicopter landed in a large, nearly empty car park. A bumpy landing. They were all tired. It was an industrial estate, like the kind her mum and dad used to drag her to at weekends, to look at furniture they would never buy, discuss interest-free credit options only to be told their credit score wasn't at the level needed. Her mum would squeeze her dad's arm, and say, 'I think ours is comfier anyway,' and never mention the fact that Dad hadn't worked for nearly a decade, or that the sofa was lumpy and covered in stains that, despite her best scrubbing, were beyond removal. Her mum was so full of goodness it radiated out of her, like a sunbeam. She always told Laura that she didn't have much to give, but was glad she'd given Laura her values: *hard work, kindness, and honesty.* She was managing well but had MS relapses more frequently now. Her mum talked of Laura's dad every single day, despite the decades since he had gone. Time seemed to provide no solace at all. Laura was glad she could support her mum in practical ways, at least, and make sure they were all financially secure. She could work. Keep busy. Distract herself. *Throw yourself into sex with strangers,* a voice inside Laura whispered. She knew she was reckless. It was a strange compulsion. But she needed some kind of release valve for her life. Or, she knew, it would blow up.

Laura's head filled with echoes. She somehow tied her hair into a low ponytail, plonked on a hard hat, grabbed what she needed, and ran out past the empty buildings, towards the danger. At least she could work hard too. It was something. She knew who she was at work. Laura, the doctor.

The drama was in a meat-packing warehouse. The smell of dead bodies and blood. A group of dirty-aproned men stood outside the entrance, smoking, ashen white. They spoke in whispers and stood aside, heads bowed, as Laura ran past them. A strange sort of respect.

'He's breathing. Normal respiratory rate.' The paramedic had arrived on scene first and was lying next to the patient on the ground. A giant industrial fridge (the kind that Boris Johnson had hidden in) had half fallen on top of him, crushing his abdomen, pelvis and right leg. He had an oxygen mask on but even beneath that Laura could see he was fully alert, slightly frowning, and frightened but with no real understanding of what would likely come. The Advanced Life Support standards had changed and these days a severe crush injury causing crush syndrome was treated quickly by removing the heavy object. But Laura knew that taking that fridge away from this man meant he'd be dead in seconds. There was no chance for him.

Not in these circumstances. Very few things in this game were certain. But of this, Laura was sure.

'Fire brigade en route, and they'll get this thing off you.' The paramedic chatted in a bright and breezy voice to the man, but his eyes were dark and ominous to Laura. They both understood. 'Anyone we can call meanwhile?'

The patient reached out his arm, wincing, and slightly pulled down his oxygen mask. 'I'm an idiot,' he said. 'I saw it fall. My wife. My wife's at work, a teacher, she'll be in class.'

Laura kneeled next to him and took out her portable gas machine from her kitbag. 'What school?' she asked.

'Peartree Primary.'

She nodded to the paramedic, who was already standing, brushing himself of dust, and taking out his phone. She had never met this man before, but trust was everything. She had to trust that the paramedic understood the priority here was not to get the fridge off, it was to get this man's wife here before they did that. She had to trust that he understood that the patient would be dead as soon as his compressed torso filled with air, for it would fill with blood too, and there was no surgeon in the world who'd be able to fix it, and he'd lose consciousness in seconds. They had to work fast. Her job was sometimes about saving lives, and occasionally, it was about something even more important than that. It was saving the lives of an entire family network, by giving them a memory and a single moment to say goodbye.

'Right then, I'm going to sit with you while we wait for the fire brigade to get this beast off. So, we might as well get acquainted. I'm Laura.'

The rest of the team dispersed and whispered around the edges of the room, busied themselves with phone calls and paperwork, and Laura sat alone with the patient, chatting, as casually as she could keep her voice given the circumstances. She learned his name was Ryan and he was working at the warehouse for extra cash as his wife had just had a baby. 'Saving for Christmas,' he said, before replacing the misty non-rebreathe oxygen mask.

Laura smiled. She tried to remove the sadness from her face lest his last moments were filled with terror. Poker face. A doctor's poker face was unreadable. All those things she learned in medical school, the pharmacology, anatomy and physiology, cell biology, chemistry, and yet it was the skills she learned on the job that were the heart of medicine. The ethics of this situation, for example, should be taught to medical students instead of learning obscure diseases. You could look up obscure diseases, but you really had to think hard to manage these desperate times. This man would die as soon as the fridge was lifted. The medical standard instructed to remove the crush object regardless. The General Medical Council, the regulator of all doctors, expected doctors to follow NICE guidance in their clinical practice. But the people who wrote the guidance were writing it from air-conditioned offices, coffee in hand. They were not sitting on a meat-packing warehouse floor, with a man about to die. The real-world situations that Laura faced sometimes didn't fit any rule book. She lived in the grey, in-between spaces. Medicine was about best, evidence-based practice, but it was art as well as science, and creativity was as much a part of her job as cell biology. Occasionally, all good doctors had to break the rules. Or at least step outside the lines to protect their patients. Should they lift the fridge anyway before his wife arrived? Should she tell him the reality of his situation so that he would get to say goodbye, and risk his final moments being in total anguish? Should she let him think he would survive?

There are no easy answers in medicine. None.

Ryan made a gasping sound and put the oxygen back over his face.

It snapped Laura back into the warehouse, into the situation.

Ryan held his breath a few moments and looked at her as if he was deciding something. 'Can you call my wife,' he said. He looked down at the fridge and moved his head towards the side where he looked at the people on the peripheries of the warehouse, paramedics, and some fire brigade arriving. She didn't need to call. A woman was suddenly running in, wearing a red coat. She slid, almost falling, but kept running, and dropped by their side.

She sat next to Ryan's head and leaned down and kissed him. 'Will he need to go to hospital when they get this thing off? The man who phoned said a fridge had fallen on you, but I didn't expect this massive one. God, Ryan, you must be in agony. What if you've broken your legs? Wait, is this your way of getting out of night-feed duties?' She laughed. Ryan laughed. They had literally no clue what was to come. None of us do.

Laura stood up and walked away. 'Give them a moment,' she said to the fire brigade personnel, hovering at the edges in high-vis jackets, like streetlights. 'Let's not tell them, just get on with it.' Sometimes, she thought, the truth was unhelpful. Every now and then, the most ethical thing to do was to lie.

TWENTY-NINE

Olivia (1999)

It was her mother who was the most devout of them all. She would dress immaculately in a skirt suit, and hat and gloves, and march her off every Sunday morning. Olivia's father often worked, on call weekends he said, though Olivia had been with him to work at the weekend before, and she knew mostly they chatted, and ate fairy cakes he brought the nurses on a large tray. But her mother never missed service. Olivia would sit next to her and fiddle and fidget, breathing in the wood polish and slight mildew as the priest spoke in a booming voice of forgiveness and sin and the weakness of humans. Sometimes she would watch her mum, staring at the stained-glass window, or eyes closed, quietly praying. She'd watch her disappear into the confession box and be there for ages, while Olivia played peek-a-boo with the baby who was round-faced and always smiling, and sat in front of her every week, his fat arms reaching out to grasp Liv's hair.

'Why do we have to go to church every Sunday?' Olivia walked beside her mum, heavy-footed, trying to get her T-bar Clarks shoes to make the same sound as Mother's stilettos. They thudded instead.

'Church gives you roots,' she said. 'So when life blows you too hard, you don't fall over.'

Olivia's mother leaned against the fence in any case, wearing a Balfour rain jacket, jodhpurs and khaki wellies. Her hair was tied up in a Hermès scarf that Liv knew cost more than most people's rent. Her mouth was pursed closed enough that the tiny giveaway papercut wrinkles appeared; her mother smoked a cigarette every evening at the bottom of the garden. Just one. She said it was hardly a vice, and anyway, she didn't want to live to be a hundred. 'Hurry up, Olivia, there's a pie in the Aga and Rupert is popping around this afternoon at two, something about Celia I expect, causing them all a headache.'

Olivia picked up her pace. She always felt ungainly next to her mum, as though she was waddling rather than walking. 'Mum, I wanted to talk to you . . .' The words came out before she could stop them and they hung mid-air between them, almost changing the grey-green light, making it darker. Olivia rarely talked to her mum about important matters, at least not anything of consequence. She was terrified of her reactions, her curt put-downs, and ability to make Liv feel fourteen years old again. But she didn't know where else to go. Not with this. 'I really need to talk.' The words again. Each one firing now, and tears behind them. Olivia stood sniffing and sobbing in front of her mother, neither of them really knowing how to respond.

'There, there.' Her mother patted the outside of Liv's left arm. 'Oh darling, what is it?' She reached her hand up to Liv's face and it hovered there, almost wiping Olivia's tears away, but not quite.

Olivia took a giant breath. She looked out across the country-side, the mist clinging to the ground, the dogs darting around. A large oak tree stood thick-trunked in the middle of the field, its leaves turning yellow gold and rust. Almost the colour of Laura's hair. The air was cold, wind blowing strands of her own mousy hair, whipping them in front of her eyes every so often. Olivia glanced at the tree, moved her legs hip-width apart, and pressed her feet to the ground, as if about to lift something very heavy. 'Dele and Laura have been having an affair.'

She told her mum everything. They sat in the kitchen at the table and ignored the pie on top of the Aga, and ignored Mother's friend Rupert knocking at the door, and the dogs whining to be let out. Her mum listened, leaned across the table, and put Olivia's hands in hers. 'He confessed . . .'

'So, it was one time?'

'Yes, according to Dele. Laura doesn't know that he confessed. She's in the dark, that I know.'

'Well, one time isn't much to write home about. A one-off is more a misdemeanour than an affair . . .' Her mum noticed Liv's expression and closed her mouth. She took a breath. Shook her head. 'I'm sorry, darling. Of course if you feel it's an affair then that's what it is. After all, seeing comes from the heart, not the eyes . . .' Her mother's expression changed, her nose turned up as if she could smell something bad. She often spoke in abstract ways, not quite making sense, contradicting Liv's concrete thinking. Her dad told her a long time ago that if they hadn't got married so young, her mother would have likely gone to medical school too. She was smart enough. Smarter than him. Liv imagined her as a doctor. She wondered what kind of doctor she'd have been. Maybe in private practice, working with the ridiculously rich, those Saudi families who flew over by private jet for treatment. Or rich Nigerian politicians who, Dele had told her, were corrupt enough to embezzle billions and leave the country without basic healthcare, while jetting off to the UK for an ingrowing toenail.

Olivia told her mum that there were no retinal ganglion cells in a person's heart, only cardiac cells. 'Cardiomyocytes, mural cells, ECs, myeloid and lymphoid immune cells.'

'It's not really funny,' her mother said. 'Is it?'

Liv didn't want to cry, but tears popped out anyway. 'He swears it was once, but I smelled Laura's perfume on the coat he had hanging on the back of his door. The perfume that only Laura ever wears, L'Air du Temps, a nasty sickly-sweet smell that she bought because it was on special offer at Superdrug. He said he was wearing the coat that day and hadn't washed it but, oh I don't know what to believe.'

Her mum's face scrunched into a smaller one. 'Revolting. Who on earth buys perfume in Superdrug? It sounds cut and dried. He made an error of judgement. Men being men, and all. I think you need to assume he's being honest now. They are honest when they're found out.'

'These were the two people I love most in the entire world . . . Friends, I mean, and they love me back. I can't believe that they'd betray me in this, the worst possible way. That Laura would.'

Her mother cocked her head to the side as Liv talked and talked. She was listening harder than Olivia had ever seen her listen. She blinked exactly every six seconds, a slowly controlled metronome.

'When I was on elective, I knew something was up. I just knew it. For weeks he'd been listening to music that was not opera or Beethoven or early chamber music. Jazz. The fucking Fugees. And his voice was a fraction higher, lifted up.' She stopped there, before she blurted out that when she climbed into his bed and he woke her up kissing her, he tasted different, of apples and ginger, sharp, a taste that stayed inside Olivia's mouth long after she'd brushed her teeth. A constant reminder that felt as if, every time she swallowed, she was swallowing Laura's and Dele's relationship, filling up her insides with it until it became part of who she was.

Her mother eventually lifted her head and released Olivia's hands and sat upright. Liv waited for her to suggest that she let it go, or that she must be mistaken, how she needed to forgive – after all they were Catholic and their faith was built on forgiveness.

'Do you believe it is over?'

Olivia closed her eyes. 'I told Dele not to say anything to Laura. He agreed. I said the only way I could ever live with it, was if we acted like it had never happened. Forgotten. Not spoken of. He said it was one time and it was over, and he didn't want us to lose our friendship. He begged for forgiveness. Begged.' She paused. 'But I also asked him if he loved her.'

Her mum stood bolt upright. 'And?'

'He didn't respond.'

The dog howled at the sound of the doorbell. Olivia was about to get up to answer it, but her mother stopped her. She put her hand on Olivia's and squeezed tightly. Her hand was small and bony, a broken-winged bird. Olivia wondered again if her mother might advise grace and charity. For all her icy coldness she was woven together with Catholicism. But she didn't suggest any of that. Instead, she simply leaned forward, looked Olivia straight in the eyes and whispered, 'Sabotage is underrated.'

THIRTY

Laura (1999)

Laura had never tried drugs before. She'd avoided smoking weed with the group of medical students who'd offered spliffs between them; she had avoided doing a line of cocaine with Anjali, who insisted it was medicinal; she'd avoided the ecstasy tablets that she saw her nurse friends take, before watching their pupils dilating so wide that their irises almost melted away. Laura had grown up around drugs, and she could see nothing glamorous or fun about it. The kids on her estate sold everything from hash to heroin, jumping on their BMX bikes and zooming from dealer to buyer. She grew up with them and watched as they fell off the earth one by one, becoming addicts themselves, or ending up in prison. Friends she went to primary school with had died from overdoses or long-term drug abuse or were queuing up at foodbanks, homeless, jumpy, scratching and covered in sores. These were her peers. Not the medical students who had the money to buy a gram of cocaine without questioning where it came from, or imagining a kid from a poor town on a BMX bike. Nobody thought of Afghanistan, or Colombia, or trafficking or slavery or women in the cocaine supply chain. Still, here she was.

She stared at the powder a long time. It was in a small sandwich bag tied tightly with a cord. It looked like a lot. Paul told her to 'go easy', it was potent stuff – whatever that meant. She had never heard of PCP but he'd assured her it was just a painkiller. An anaesthetic. 'Snort a little bit at a time, and it will give you a buzz without getting you wasted.'

Laura wanted to get wasted. She wanted one day when she didn't think about her dad, or Dele, or Olivia. One day. She took her house key out of her handbag, and scooped up some of the powder, sticking it underneath her nostril before inhaling deeply. It took only a few moments before Laura felt it, a kind of whooshing through her body, a pulling away of her brain. Then, she floated.

She had no idea how they got there. Everything around her glowed orange and flashed. Laura could barely stand, but every now and then she felt Paul's arm holding her up, heard his voice from far away. 'It's good stuff, isn't it?' One moment they were in City Tavern, the next they were standing outside a large house opposite the park. The party was already out of control when Laura and Paul arrived. Teenage and young adult bodies were strewn across the grass clutching bottles and fags. The beat was heavy in the air, some sort of garage music that Laura could feel in her teeth. They weaved their way across the grass and tiptoed between the bodies. Most of the women were wearing tiny dresses held up with string, or crop tops, and tiny skirts. Laura wore her jeans and a jumper and for some reason, instead of feeling overdressed, that made her laugh, and then Paul laughed too.

Anjali's face was there in front of hers, like a moon, her eyes dancing around on it. 'Laura! What have you done?' She hugged Laura and turned to Paul. 'What have you given her?'

'If you can't beat 'em, join 'em,' Paul said. He put his hand on Anjali's back, and they were far away.

The garden became a bit blurry, and Laura's legs buckled. A man caught her. She leaned on him. A medical student from class. Dean something.

There were only flashes of memory after that.

Her and Dean in a toilet, scooping out powder with her house key. Then inside a bedroom, covered in glitter, and laughing. There was water on her head. Some shouting. They were dancing in the living room, and Laura stopped still, saw demons everywhere, the gnashing of teeth, maybe hers? She watched a dragon breathe fire until the room slid and melted away like a Salvador Dalí painting. A clock distorted on the wall, became oval then disappeared. The bass steadily increased inside her until she was the music, and her body lost its outline and melted into the air, and she looked down at the people, all mashed up, dancing in jerky movements and kissing and shouting and fighting.

Olivia was there. She was sure of it, but maybe she imagined it? Olivia never came to parties, but Laura heard Olivia's voice, though it sounded strange and underwater. Muffled and far away. Time was moving slow or fast and they were inside a black hole of drugs and drink and danger, but the drugs were gone, the bag inside her bra empty, and she was sick. Even being sick, vomiting chunks into the ashtray, felt weirdly normal, and almost pleasant. Purging and rushing and sweet sickly acid. Colours exploded in Laura's head, and her body fizzed with electricity, and fearlessness. But something was suddenly very wrong. Laura felt like she was at the funfair, and the ride was too fast, and she wanted to get off, and all around her there was shouting then screaming and Laura was screaming too, and Laura looked at Anjali's eyes and they were black and different and broken.

'Run,' Olivia was standing next to Laura, pulling her back into the corner of the room. She gripped her hand and squeezed.

Olivia stood in front of Laura, the room now bathed in blue flashing lights. Was it an ambulance? Police? She tried to focus her brain, but it was mashed potato, and she couldn't stop retching. Olivia shook her head, then turned to Anjali, who was standing in front of them both, and then she looked down. On the ground, on the floor next to the green sofa, was Dean. He lay head tipped back, grey and quiet, too quiet, and there was a doctor from nowhere, Laura recognised the doctor things. The doctor looked up at Laura and Anjali and Olivia, but then began working. Laura stared at Dean's face, becoming paler, losing colour.

Olivia pulled her back further and she stared straight at Laura again. Her face was hard and full of shadows. She looked at Laura, for a second, as if she hated her. But she didn't know. She didn't know about Dele.

'Run.'

Laura ran, her legs flying out to the sides. She ran as if her life depended on it.

THIRTY-ONE

Laura (2024)

Laura carried a feather. It was snow white, and seeing it reminded her of a dove that her cousin had let out of a basket during her wedding ceremony, and her dad, standing next to her, muttering, 'Bloody stupid.' The dove flew around the church and then pooped on the vicar's head, which made the bride cry.

Laura held the feather tightly as she walked through the hospital corridors. It felt so heavy in her hand.

It was the opposite of a gun, perhaps, light and soft and gentle, yet it could be considered a weapon in these circumstances. She carried it in front of her heart, walking through the atrium of the hospital, past the recently commissioned artwork, giant paintings of nature, trees that were likely meant to be calming but were depicted in a real way, tooth and claw, gnarled and battling elements, and close-ups of flowers, unfurling, organ-like, a painting of the sea and a wave so sharp and high it resembled the blade of a scalpel.

Brain stem testing wasn't usually a dangerous act. Most of the times that Laura had ever been involved in it, and that was rarely, it was conclusive, and the team had all been confident in that before they began. Still, it is a strange and mysterious process, and undertaken with respect and reverence as the implications of the results mean life or death, or something even more important than that. If a person whose heart is still beating is declared brain stem dead, the doctors are ethically obliged to discuss and plan for the withdrawal of life support. Brain stem dead means that a person is dead. But although clinically dead, they might still be breathing via a machine. A person would remain warm. They might look like themselves. They would have a heartbeat, and other organs that work – kidneys, liver and gut, for example – and appear alive to the family. But they are not. Brain stem dead people are dead by law. At least in the UK.

Joe was not brain stem dead, but still it was complicated. Laura needed the inconclusive tests to further confuse the prognosis. The entire team, including Laura, understood that Joe Duggard was in an unrecoverable state. He was devastatingly stable. In a continuing vegetative state, so termed as he had been this way for four weeks now. Laura understood that after six months a person like Joe could be diagnosed as in a persistent vegetative state, and a strong legal case be made to withdraw treatment. Joe was in this daily static place, not alive, not dead, a sleeping beauty of sorts, locked in a deep unconscious place, frozen in time. His brain had no signs of any awareness, the tests on his brain waves showed no spikes or peaks of activity that aligned with anything external. Brain stem testing was designed to show no arousal at all of brain stem function, and Laura knew that although Joe's brain was not functioning in any meaningful way, the testing would show partial arousal, prove that he was not brain stem dead, rather in this no man's land. This was not what brain stem testing was for. It was to show that a person was dead. Not to prove that they were half alive, a zombie, never going to recover but giving a glimmer of hope to desperate family members who read stories of miracles, and could not face this tragic, desperate reality.

Laura knew that vocal advocates in the legal system as well as the public, included those who believed people in Joe's state, a vegetative state, should be allowed to die. Others were equally determined that, if recovery was at all possible, care should continue. The law is absolute. Medicine is not. A handful of Joes around the world have made some sort of improvement in cognitive function, and because of this, no doctor in the world could say that Joe would never recover. Laura was relying on that.

When she started out as a doctor, her biggest fear had been a patient dying, accidentally killing someone. Now, often, it was accidentally keeping a patient alive. The weight of intentionally keeping a patient alive when they should be allowed to die. People's wishes can be manipulated, and often are, by doctors, Laura was realising.

Olivia was wrong about Rudy. Laura had confronted him, and he'd sworn till he was blue in the face that it was Freya who'd pushed Joe. Laura knew her own son. She knew he was not capable of lying. He was certainly not capable of pushing someone downstairs. Freya must have been terrified enough to make that up. No wonder. If Joe died, Freya would likely end up in a young offenders' institution. Laura heard Olivia's voice inside her. She always heard Olivia's voice inside her. She carried that voice for decades: *I will fix this. You need to be a doctor. This is the right thing to do. For you. For your parents. For Anjali too* . . . Olivia had always protected them, and now it was Laura's turn to protect Olivia. She knew what she had to do. And why.

Intensive care was quiet: they'd picked the quietest time between the morning doctors' rounds and the physios, the flurry of activity at lunchtime when family members wanted answers, and the night staff began to ring in sick. They had tried a 'quiet time' window on intensive care, but it was never really chaos anyway. She walked towards Joe and nodded at his parents, who sat next to the bed. It was encouraged that families were nearby to see the staff do all they could. Nobody was expecting good results by the time someone was brain stem death testing.

The process was to be carried out by two doctors to be conclusive, but as Laura had offered to go first, the second doctor wouldn't be needed. Because Joe Duggard was not brain stem dead. The test was unwarranted. The feather felt even heavier in her fingers, weighted. Heavy as a feather. A symbol of what she was about to do. When she had trained, they used feathers, medical quills, to perform brain stem testing. She remembered Mrs Steyn gently touching a patient's eye with a feather, and when it did not move, placing the feather on his unmoving chest, and using her hand to close his eyelids. Nowadays it was the corner of sterile gauze. Still, Laura held the feather in her scrubs to remind her what was at stake. The weight of the present and the weight of the past.

Sandra stood as Laura approached. This woman who wanted no more suffering for her only son. The bravest of women. Laura forced a smile and pressed her teeth together. 'Do you want to stay?' Laura was certain that the tests would show that Joe was not brain stem dead. Any discussions about withdrawing his treatment after that would be confusing for his family. She needed to cause that confusion, show them it wasn't cut and dried. Fuel false hope.

Sandra nodded. She wasn't wearing eye make-up, Laura noticed. She usually did. Winged eyeliner and thick, clumpy mascara. But today she was expecting to cry.

Joe would likely breathe without the ventilator after a while, as his basic reflexes were intact. Eventually, after a period of months of him doing nothing but perhaps yawning, or blinking, the team would discuss a peaceful death, and the withdrawal of nutritional support, the food going in as milk via a feeding tube. At that time if the family disagreed because they had hope, *hope that Laura would give them*, then the team would get a court order. Joe would be sentenced to starve to death. The doctors would tell his family that he would not feel a thing, or be aware in any way, but of course, they wouldn't believe that by then. False hope was perhaps the deadliest of all emotions. Doctors could not choose if a person lived or died, Laura had taken a lifetime to learn that, but they could decide when and how a person died. That was an uncomfortable power. Dark, rather than light.

'I'm going to do a few tests to see if Joe's brain is working,' she paused, 'or not. I know you've spoken to lots of people about how this might work, but do you have any questions before I start?'

Sandra looked down at Joe and reached out for his hand. She shook her head.

'I'll disconnect the ventilator first. If a brain is functioning at all, there is something called the gag reflex. The tube in Joe's throat, his breathing tube, is really irritating to anyone conscious on any level. So, if Joe's brain stem, the base of his brain is working, he should fight against it, cough, and try and pull it out. Coughing is a deep reflex. One we can't control even in a coma. That's why we had to give Joe the drugs to paralyse his muscles as well as sedate him, so he's unaware. The nurses stopped the drugs a long time ago to try and wake Joe up.'

Laura watched Sandra's face, still devoid of tears. There was a moment in every person when there was no more crying. It was like the time in a marriage when there was no more arguing. It signified the end. Her thoughts flicked to Owen sitting in the living room after another unexpected call-out with HEMS and cancelled dinner. They had been shouting and screaming and crying for what felt like months, but it was silent then. Eerily still. Owen's face was expressionless. She felt empty too, and questioned if she loved him. If she'd ever loved him. Was she capable of it? Laura felt most of her adult life that romantic love was a switch she'd turned off a long time ago, and once it was off, she had no idea how to switch it back on.

'Will it hurt him?' Sandra had lifted his hand up and was holding it near to her side.

Laura shook her head vigorously. 'Not at all.'

The intensive care around them was an angry, noisy place that day. Bright strip lights, loud voices, the slapping of nurses' clogs on the shiny floor, alarms, as ever, and the metal door and metal bins swinging open and closed, then slamming every now and then. A smell wafted in of feet and blood. A cleaner poked her head around the curtain, blinked at Laura standing solemn above Joe, then vanished. 'I'll change the bin later,' she said.

Laura first silenced the ventilator, then carefully disconnected the ventilator from the tubing. Joe's ET tube, his breathing tube, was cut appropriately, near to his mouth. The test should be null and void with a long ET tube, which would be like breathing through a straw, but of course, it happened regularly. Lots of things happened in medicine that shouldn't happen. She looked at Joe's eyelashes, covering his half-closed eyes, glistening with Vaseline. His skin was perfect. Not a hint of acne. Funny, the things we worry about, like teenagers suffering acne.

Sandra and Laura both looked at Joe's breathing tube, and held their own breath as long as possible, until Laura began to

243

see distant stars. Joe made no attempt to breathe, or cough, or move or fight against the tube. But Laura and Sandra eventually had to breathe, their reflexes intact, even though, Laura knew, Sandra would have given hers to Joe if she could.

A mother would do anything for her child. Anything. She may have struggled with romantic love, but Laura knew motherhood. She loved Rudy more than life itself. Any mother loved her child like that.

The minutes felt like longer. Laura heard ticking, but possibly it was internal. A knotted clock of anxiety. Then, there it was. A slight movement. A tiny rise of his chest as his carbon dioxide rose. She replaced the ventilator trunk onto the tubing and Joe's chest rose and fell, rose and fell, rhythmically, perfectly. 'Technology has developed at a rate of knots,' her old tutor told her at medical school, 'but ethics is slow science, a long conversation, late night, in a pub where everyone is a bit drunk, and nobody has any real answers.'

'Now I'm going to do this other test. These days it's usually done with gauze, but we used to use quills. Feathers.' Laura held the feather to the light. She wondered what bird it had once belonged to, and how all of life was intrinsically connected. She thought about the young men, boys, Joe's age, who were handed a feather if they were not off to fight in the First World War. How it symbolised cowardice. Only she was the coward here. Not Joe.

Sandra looked confused now. His respiratory effort was minuscule, but it was there. There were so many confusing things about intensive care. She shrugged a fraction, then stood perfectly still.

'It's about ophthalmic reflexes. Our eyes have nerves that go all the way through the brain. If there is a problem anywhere in the brain, or activity anywhere in the brain, we should be able to detect it with the eyes, with things like pupil reactions, and such. I'll touch the cornea of Joe's eyes with the corner of a piece of gauze, and if there's any connection his eyes will move a tiny bit.' She lay the feather on Joe's chest. It rose and fell as the ventilator pushed air into his lungs. Sandra concentrated on it rising and falling, at total odds with death.

Laura very gently and very softly opened Joe's eyes and lowered a piece of gauze to the sclera, the white part of his eyeball, that was red and bloodshot in his case. She touched it with the gauze and stroked the edge of it a millimetre. Joe's eyes moved a fraction. It was enough to plant doubt. But Laura knew what she had to do. She heard Olivia's voice inside her, a Jiminy Cricket gone wrong. Or maybe the voice was right. Or maybe there was no right or wrong at all, only a series of difficult decisions and complexities of character.

'Did you see that?' Laura turned to Sandra, and made her face open up.

Sandra looked at Laura's face, the light in her eyes, then back to the feather on his chest, and Joe's eyes. It was a moment, a few seconds, before the seed Laura had planted began to grow tall inside Sandra. A matter of seconds. A seed of hope in the darkness. 'His eye moved,' Sandra said. Asked. 'I think he tried to breathe? His eye moved.'

Laura nodded and nodded. 'I think so too.' She squeezed Sandra's arm, and with one movement, one insinuation, one *lie*, changed the course of history of this family, for Olivia's family, and for her own. 'He might recover.'

There was no going back now. Not on any of it. Laura put the feather into Sandra's hand and watched her holding it tightly. The opposite of a murder weapon. In the wrong hands, a feather was more dangerous than a gun. 'Hold on to that,' she whispered.

She watched Sandra fold over, and more tears arrive, and she sobbed on Joe's chest that was rising and falling and whooshing with the ventilator.

Medicine was about saving lives, after all.

Laura rested her hand on the small of Sandra's back for a few moments, and then left the bedspace, walking slowly and carefully towards the heavy exit doors. 'What are you doing? I saw you in there.' Donna stood in front of her, hands on her hips.

'Hi.' Laura shook her head a fraction, unable to place her a moment. An unexpected face in an unexpected place. She moved forward instinctively to hug her, but Donna stepped away. Almost lunged.

'I saw you,' she said. 'I saw you tampering with that patient's ventilator. Joe Duggard.'

Laura tried a half-smile and shrug, but her insides burned. She felt the accusation inside her bones, permanently calcifying. 'Donna, what are you doing here? I wasn't tampering with anything,' she laughed. A fake and tinny laugh that echoed in the ICU hallway. She lowered her voice and pulled Donna by the arm to the corner, and they stood next to a broken photocopier. 'I was performing brain stem tests,' she whispered. 'Anyway, what are you doing here? Tampering with a ventilator?' She laughed again.

Donna's face didn't move. She stared frozen and hard at Laura.

Something inside Laura broke open. She was sick of lying. This was her friend. Her friend who could clearly see something was wrong. 'I know Anjali told you about Paul,' she whispered. 'God, it's all so complicated.'

'What has that got to do with anything.' Donna was angry: the hairs at the base of her neck were standing out. 'What are you talking about?'

'I had to lie in court. I had to. I know what it looks like, that I was protecting myself, but it was the only way to save Anj. You have to believe me, Donna.'

Donna looked over to Joe, momentarily confused, then back at Laura. Her mouth opened and she snapped it closed before running towards the door.

THIRTY-TWO

Olivia (1999)

Lying was easier than she'd thought it would be. When so much was at stake it was possible to do anything. But Olivia wasn't thinking about Anjali, or the danger of Paul. She wasn't thinking of their careers as doctors either, the very thing that knotted them together, that they'd worked so very hard for. It wasn't anxiety that burned inside her, but anger, a heartbeat of rage. Liv was thinking, constantly, even during dreams, of Dele and Laura. They were impossible to separate in her head, like conjoined twins. She'd watched an operation once, to separate conjoined twins who had been flown over from rural India to be treated by an expert at City, known for his pioneering surgery. They were joined at the head, sharing a piece of skull, their brains fused together, making the operation critical and extremely unlikely to have what the surgeon called a 'positive outcome'. She sat in as the translator spoke his words in Urdu to the twins' parents, a too-thin couple who looked as if they'd eaten only fear, all the worry of the universe. 'The best we can hope,' he said, 'is that we can save one. In order to save either of them, we need to sacrifice one.'

Every time Liv closed her eyes, she pictured Laura and Dele, conjoined at the head, attached to each other in all senses, saying the same words in unison, both grinning. Happy. She imagined them shagging. She could no longer masturbate; every

248

time she touched herself her thoughts ran to Laura and Dele, their faces as they made love. Worse than that, she imagined them talking. Looking into each other's eyes. She wanted to scratch her own face off.

At mass she cleared her head and sang the hymns and nodded at friends. She drank the wine in a gulp, and stood in line for confession, before really deciding what she might and might not confess. The confession box smelled of Pledge polish and barrel-aged Chardonnay, the buttery kind that was out of fashion, but Dele liked anyway. 'Forgive me, Father, for I have sinned, and it's been over two weeks since my last confession. Well, I haven't sinned yet. I mean it's something I'm contemplating, and that in itself feels sinful.'

'I'm not sure confession works like that.' The priest, John, was a dear family friend and had known Olivia since she'd been born. He'd baptised her, and he would officiate at her wedding. He was close enough to her mother that her father said he would be worried about him if he wasn't a celibate man; 'cigarette-paper close', he called it, and her mother smiled. She liked being Queen Bee in church. It gave her purpose, to oversee the fete and the flowers.

'I told a lie that will protect people, do some good in fact, and save a marriage most likely. But it was a lie.'

Father John was silent. It was not the sort of silence where he was waiting for more information, a kind of pensive silence. 'If you've done something criminal, then I'd urge you to report your conduct to the appropriate authorities. I can't offer you absolution until then . . .'

Olivia sat upright. 'I've done nothing, Father. It's just a thought going through my mind . . .'

His head tilted a fraction. He then said, 'Five Hail Marys should cover it then,' and straightened his head up.

Olivia thought a lot about the clergy, and how, like doctors, they lived in the grey, and how abstract it was to translate the Bible when even the literal text had been written through the lens of men who also had agendas. There was no such thing as total objectivity in human beings. It simply didn't exist.

Lying came more easily than thinking about Dele and Laura conjoined at the head. Lying disconnected them from each other, and from Liv's thoughts. The lie was the blade, the surgeon's scalpel, the instrument that would save lives. Still, one had to be sacrificed. Laura hadn't stopped crying since the party. Her face was so puffy and distorted she looked totally different, rounder, like she'd put on ten stone or was heavily pregnant. 'I need to go to the police,' she repeated. The night of the party they all lay in Anjali's room. Laura couldn't sleep in her own bed. She needed mess and stink and distractions and piles of dirty clothes around her, she said, to tidy and clean and keep busy. The three of them had fallen asleep eventually, after watching Laura potter around Anjali's room attempting to clean away the mess they were in, in literal terms, and failing dramatically. She stopped scrubbing at around midnight, and began to weep, and lay down in between Liv and Anjali, who sardined close to her and rubbed her back.

'Someone is dead,' said Laura. It was still dark but nearly dawn, and they were completely sober by then, the horror of the events stark and bright. She was sitting propped up against the headboard. Anjali was lying next to her, and Olivia sat cross-legged at the foot of the bed.

Olivia watched Laura. Her head was dizzy with all that had happened in the last few days. It was Shakespearean: betrayal, sex, death, *tragedy*.

'It was an accident.' Anjali curled into a comma. Liv could see each vertebra of her back. She'd lost so much weight since meeting Paul.

'There was nothing accidental about it. He died of an overdose, and we let the police arrest Paul. What a mess.' Laura took each breath in sections, inhaling in parts, exhaling in parts. 'I mean, surely Paul won't be in trouble in any case? Dean took the drugs himself. He wasn't forced to . . . Nobody had a gun to his head.'

'You're right.' Olivia pressed her knees towards the mattress. 'But whoever gave him the drugs will go to prison. Absolutely. I know this for a fact. It happened to a friend of the family.' She held her breath a fraction. She did not know this for a fact. She did not know a friend of the family who went to prison. The idea was preposterous. But she had to speak with confidence. Her voice was steady and certain as ever, and Laura and Anjali looked at her with trusting eyes. As ever.

Laura shrugged, slowly. 'Well, I'm going to prison then, surely.' She put a piece of hair into her mouth and started chewing it. She looked ten years old.

'We can fix this,' Olivia said. 'It might work out for the best. A good thing coming out of a tragedy.' Perhaps nobody was going to prison. Sure, a young man had taken drugs. He overdosed. But he took the drugs himself. *Nobody had a gun to his head.* He wasn't spiked. Still, Laura was convinced she was responsible. She was easy to convince. Selfless Laura. Olivia knew her inside and out. She understood that Laura would confess. And although it was unlikely she would go to prison, or even lose her place at medical school, Laura would want everything out in the open. *Everything.* Olivia held her fist closed so tightly, digging her nails into her skin.

'Why did I take drugs? Why? How? How can we fix this?

Someone is dead. A medical student. Imagine that. We've killed someone. I have . . . It's me who was responsible. I'll go to the police and tell them everything.'

Olivia looked at Laura in anguish and something quietened inside her. There was no flash of her and Dele, just an image burning in her head of Laura, broken, grieving, guilty. But it was gone in seconds. Anjali's back curled a fraction more, and Olivia thought of anvils, the tools her dad had in the man shed that stabilised things before they were cut off. She looked at Laura, in her eyes, and forced herself to imagine those eyes looking at Dele. 'Laura, we can fix this.' She paused and watched Laura's eyes get wet and her pupils constrict with fear. 'We can do some good. Even with this.'

She told them everything then. Her idea that would solve this. How nobody ever needed to know anything. How Paul deserved to be in prison anyway. They couldn't bring Dean back now. 'They were Paul's drugs. He's got form. Intent to supply at least . . .'

Anjali sat up at the word 'Paul' and swung her legs underneath her. 'They were his drugs after all. The last time he was in court was for drugs. Surely he should go to prison.' Anjali was animated, alive, suddenly filled with the idea of freedom. Olivia was counting on that.

'But whoever gave Dean the drugs is the person responsible for his death? Which means a prison sentence, and even if I'm not struck off by the GMC, I won't be a doctor. I will not practise medicine. Everything I ever wanted and promised to my dad, and I'll never do it now.' Laura tipped her head back and rested it on the headboard. She was shaking enough that the headboard juddered.

'Paul is dangerous, and he'll be even more dangerous now.' Olivia knew how to convince Laura. She was the most protective person she'd ever met. Loyal to her bones. There was a simple way to control her, and that was to convince her that she was helping, or even better, *saving*. They had no idea where Laura's perfectionism and need to save people and help people came from, but it was as much Laura as her red hair. 'Paul will kill you now, Anj, unless we get him put away. We can't bring anyone back from the dead, but we can prevent another one. He'll get a custodial sentence for sure, if one of us saw him give the drugs to Dean . . .' Olivia had long suspected Paul was hitting Anjali. She had confronted Anjali about it but had been met with denial.

Laura took her hair out of her mouth. 'What do you mean?'

Anjali unfolded and sat up. She started talking then about Paul. About Paul hitting her and kicking her and strangling her. She spoke in a quiet voice that sounded as if it belonged to someone else. 'He kicked me so hard once, I was pissing blood.' She stopped talking and looked at them both. Her eyes shone with fear. 'I'm sorry I didn't tell you. I should have told you all of it.'

Laura's face criss-crossed with pain. 'I can't believe this. Anjali, why didn't you say? I'm so sorry. So sorry.' She frowned and Olivia watched the wheels in motion, her protective instinct kick in. 'I'll say I saw him give Dean the drugs. It was my fault, and I should be the one who solves this.'

Anjali put her hand on her chest, over her heart. 'I appreciate it, Laura, but it would kill you lying about something like this. I know you.'

Olivia shook her head. 'Laura's right. It's the only way. Loz, I will forget seeing you give Dean the drugs. I'll bury it always. It will stay secret between us forever. Let's put that pig behind bars. Where he belongs.' She watched Laura pull Anjali towards her and close her arm around her. Laura would do anything to protect the ones she loved. So would Olivia.

That night the three of them made a pact to never ever speak of it. Anjali asked Olivia about Dele. 'Surely you can't keep a secret like this from your fiancé? Not forever?'

Olivia looked straight at Anjali but could see Laura in her peripheral vision. She had closed her eyes. Two nights before, when eventually they had fallen asleep together, Dele had spoken a single word. He'd never sleep-talked before then, and Olivia had sat bolt upright, wide awake to the sound of his voice.

Laura.

'I'll never tell him. Ever. It would put his job at risk if he knew. I love him too much to ever tell him the truth. I could never put him in jeopardy.' Olivia turned around and looked at Laura and thought of all that Laura had taken from her. Her security. Her love. Her commitment. Her truth.

Olivia could not take those things. But she could take Laura's identity.

There wasn't even an investigation, at least not a real one. The university put out a statement about a 'tragic incident at a birthday party', and Anjali turned to Olivia and asked, 'Whose birthday?' to which Liv shrugged. Nobody knew. Maybe there wasn't a birthday. In any case the university clearly wanted the matter finished and closed and, aside from offering half-hearted counselling sessions for anyone affected by what they were quickly terming 'the overdose' and sending out suicide prevention leaflets to all new medical students, there was no noise. There were no suspicious circumstances. Another student who couldn't deal with the pressure of medical school. Nobody really knew Dean, the student who'd died, that well. He was a bit of a loner, from Manchester, a year younger than everyone else and fast-tracked through the system as super smart. He played chess. When Olivia found this out, her mouth filled up with metallic saliva. These small details about a person, that he played chess, humanised him in a way she was unprepared for, and she pictured him, just once, his face clear as day, playing chess with friends in a square on wooden tables, cups of coffee and mint tea dotted around and intense looks on their faces. She didn't wallow. She didn't allow herself the luxury. Liv pushed that thought away and replaced it with the image of her and Dele in wedding outfits, surrounded by confetti-like stars.

THIRTY-THREE

Anjali (2024)

'It's Laura.' Donna's voice was breaking up. 'Honestly, I feel so sick. God, Anjali. I saw her, in ICU . . .'

'What's wrong?' Anjali felt her skin heat up. The room got darker. 'What are you talking about?'

'I'm heading to Brixton police station. She's tampering with a patient, Anj. The eighteen-year-old with a brain injury, Joe Duggard, Miles told us about him and that party. I saw her. I've watched her. I didn't mean to, but I knew, I knew she was doing something . . . something was so off . . .'

Anjali pressed the phone so hard against her ear it burned. She pictured Laura, telling her she was being followed. She saw the three of them, Olivia with her head in her hands. 'Donna. I need to talk to you. Donna, listen. Listen.'

'I can't. Not now. I'll see you there, but I have to go. I'll call from the police station. I need to phone the hospital.' She breathed hard down the receiver.

'What are you talking about? Donna, you're scaring me.'

She hung up and leaned against the door frame to hold herself up. She heard a cracking noise, coming from her own mouth. It sounded like the entire world was breaking open.

'Donna, pick up, Donna,' she called repeatedly to a dead tone. She had to get there. She had to get there before Donna got to the police station and told them everything. Everything that was wrong. Laura filled her head and Olivia too and then she clearly saw Dean. The medical student who'd died at the party all those years ago. Dean who *Anjali* had given drugs to. Dean, who died. *Run. Run. Run.* She closed her eyes, and she couldn't see Olivia or Laura or even Donna. Instead, she saw little Khadija, but her face was blurred, and she was far away.

She wouldn't be there in time. Donna would walk to Brixton police station in eighteen minutes. They'd timed the walk into Brixton when they looked around the Loughborough Junction flat, working out that they could be eating ramen within a twenty-minute walk. 'The best ramen outside Tokyo,' Donna had said, and smiled.

Her head was thick with stark lightbulbs. Donna had known about Paul. She had seen Laura on intensive care with Joe, the boy Miles told them about. The patient they didn't confront Olivia and Laura about, not wanting to be anywhere near to controversy or trouble. They were weeks away from being parents. Khadija was almost theirs. Almost.

They didn't want to know. *But Donna did. Donna checked on Joe and found Laura there. Laura. She's put two and two together and come up with ten.*

'My God,' she whispered out loud. The Uber driver glanced at her in the rear-view mirror. 'Please hurry,' she said. 'Please.' Then she mumbled again, 'What a fucking mess. What a fucking mess.' She was thinking of Laura's face. What would happen to Laura if Donna told the police Laura had been responsible for Dean's death? That a man had been falsely accused and put in prison. That Laura was tampering with a patient on intensive care. What would happen to Laura? What would happen to all of them? She wrung her hands over and over, scratching at her skin, pulling hangnails off until the skin around her fingernails bled. Her hands had blood on them. So much blood.

'There you go. Now you take care.' The driver pulled over on a red line outside the police station, blocking the P4 bus. The driver beeped. Anjali ran. She ran up the stairs to the entrance, ignoring the teenagers fighting outside. The doors were so heavy she had to press her whole body into them, and they slammed open. Everyone looked. Donna was at the desk, talking and gesticulating to a police officer behind a protective screen. Anjali could hear the words from across the room.

'A doctor. No, you don't understand, it was twenty years ago but there's a person in danger now. Right now. A patient. She's tampering with his breathing tube. I saw her. A medical student died. I think she was involved. She lied. She lied about everything. And now she's a doctor and I think she's dangerous. She's tampering with a patient's life support . . . Please. It's urgent.'

A side door opened, and a man's head poked through. He beckoned Donna. 'You'd better come in.'

'Donna!' Anjali shouted. The man behind the door and the police officer behind the screen flicked their heads towards her. Donna turned but carried on walking to where she was being ushered into a room. A row of plastic chairs was filled with people all ignoring the scene. A woman was knitting.

'I'll see you in a minute,' Donna said. 'Anj, this is urgent.'

'Donna,' Anjali said. She ran towards her. 'Donna. Don't.'

Donna turned then, and Anjali saw the anger on her face. 'I'm sorry, Anj,' she said. 'We can't ignore this, we just can't . . .' She walked towards the doorway.

'It was me.'

You could hear the silence in the room. It bounced off the

walls. An eerie empty sound. A flash of memory and Anjali, Olivia and Laura were standing in an operating theatre, their whole lives ahead of them. Anjali was sobbing now. 'Laura isn't trying to kill a patient, she wouldn't. Not ever . . .'

'She lied under oath!' Donna never raised her voice. 'She's capable of anything.'

'I gave Dean the drugs. The student who overdosed. It was me . . .'

There was a look on Donna's face that was so full of horror and fear and disgust that it would stay with Anjali forever. A flash of Dean's face. 'Laura isn't responsible for killing *anyone*. I am.'

'You'd better both come with me then.' The detective behind the door opened it fully and widened his eyes at the other officer at the desk. 'Sounds like we've got a lot to unpick.'

They followed the officer out to the back and all the while, Anjali heard a child crying. It was coming from inside her chest.

THIRTY-FOUR

Laura (1999)

Laura watched the vascular surgeon, Mrs Steyn, grunting and huffing as she worked, a look of something animalistic in her eyes. She was a quiet woman, softly spoken and considered, and Laura had enjoyed this rotation with her teaching. But today she was someone else. Laura held the patient's necrotic leg as Mrs Steyn cut it off. It was like working with a serial killer, sawing off body parts to fit a torso in a suitcase. She held the leg at the calf muscle, and felt it twitch as the saw broke through flesh, layers of skin, cartilage, bone. Medicine could be brutal and bloody and violent. There was nothing gentle about it. She'd imagined it to be about knowledge and kindness in equal measure, but really it was about horror a lot of the time. She was living in a horror film. The leg finally came away from the man, who was twenty years old and had contracted meningococcal sepsis at a festival, the 'kissing disease', so nicknamed as the main demographics were toddlers and teens. Slobbering all over each other could be a dangerous sport. Especially with all the anti-vaxxers. Laura stood still a few seconds while Mrs Steyn went to work cleaning and closing the wound. She held the leg like a violin, the foot balanced under her chin, bloody end resembling an uprooted tree with roots hanging off it.

*

'You OK?' Mrs Steyn was back to her normal self, her eyes no longer wild. She passed her a cup of tea in a mug that looked as if it had never been washed.

Laura shrugged. 'I'll be fine.' But she could still feel the weight of the young man's leg. She added that fact to the list of things she was learning about medicine, that the books didn't teach you:

Limbs are heavy.
After a person dies they can exhale air, twitch, and even fart.
Most, if not all, doctors have mental health issues.
Meningococcal sepsis is treated with antibiotics. If not, the patient dies. But the antibiotics don't destroy the bacteria. They merely disperse it, and the bits of bacteria lodge in organs and then cause multi-organ failure. And the patient might die. But they might not.

'He was dying from the outside in.' Mrs Steyn sipped her coffee, then added two more spoonfuls of granules. 'That's the thing about sepsis. His lactate was 10.'

Laura gulped. 'Incompatible with life, surely?'

'Just because a couple are incompatible,' she smiled, 'doesn't mean they're not bedfellows.'

'Will he survive, do you think?'

'He'll have a few months in ICU. He's in renal and liver failure, will need haemofiltration, and his lungs are fucked. But you never know. Now he's not got the gangrenous leg, he has a better chance . . .' Her pager bleeped and she took it from her pocket, looked at the message and swigged the coffee. 'Got to go.'

Laura sat in the coffee room, drinking the disgusting tea, and thinking. She was learning medicine. And today, another lesson:

We can die from the outside in. If something is very, very bad for you – cut it off.

She heard another voice inside herself. *If you are very bad for it, cut it off.*

In the months leading up to the court case, Laura did nothing but work and run or lie in her bed completely numb. She avoided Dele entirely, and he avoided her. In the scheme of everything that had happened, it was no longer the huge event that threatened to ruin everyone's life. This was. Still, she couldn't stop thinking about him. Even now. Even today.

'I'll never hold you again,' she whispered to the air.

Laura had borrowed a skirt suit that was Olivia's and it hung loose on her, made her look shapeless. She tied a scarf around her neck on Liv's advice, and put her hair into a high ponytail, kept her jewellery simple and elegant, and wore flat shoes rather than heels. 'I feel like I'm on trial,' she said, before they left the flat.

Anjali was eating a bowl of Coco Pops and wearing pyjamas, having decided it would be better for them all not to be there en masse. She couldn't face Paul. But Olivia would be there, for moral support. 'He'll kill me,' said Anjali. 'He will literally kill me if he knows what we're doing.'

'Paul is going to prison for a long time.' Liv's voice had jagged edges. Laura flicked her eyes at Olivia. They were full of gratitude. For a moment Liv felt uneasy, as though the ground was moving underneath her.

Anjali scooped up more cereal and began crunching, but her spoon was shaking. It rattled against her teeth.

Laura reached across the sofa and put her hand on Anjali's knee. 'It'll be OK.'

'Remember what we agreed.' Liv looked up at Laura. 'Stick to the plan. We can make this all go away today. Paul would be going to prison anyway, with the amount of gear he had, intent to supply and all that jazz. So we're doing nothing wrong. Nothing.' She took a quiet, long breath, and smiled at Laura. 'You made one mistake. Today is the day we put it all behind us. You are not giving up your whole life for one mistake. You've worked too hard. We've all worked too hard.'

They sat together in silence, the truth and the lies dancing around in the air between them until it was impossible to clearly know what was what. The air itself looked thick and opaque. Anjali put her bowl down on the table and hugged them both close. 'Thank you,' she said. 'Thank you, thank you.' For a moment it felt like a good thing they were all doing, to save their friend, help Anjali.

The court was a square block with disabled access and a dozen or so people smoking outside. It wasn't a big case. A local drug dealer and an overdose. That Dean was a medical student created a tiny flurry of interest from the local press, though, and a journalist – cheap suit, harassed expression, was standing at the entrance holding a small Dictaphone. 'Did you know the deceased?' he asked everyone that entered. Nobody said yes, whether they knew him or not. Laura found that a bit odd. She looked around the courtroom as people took their seats, in rows like pews at church. Nobody seemed that bothered that a young man was dead. A promising young medical student. Their tutor was there, holding a hanky, despite having only met Dean a few times, during lectures when he'd have been one among many first-year students. Laura winced each time the barrister said his name. Olivia looked at Laura as she took the stand, shaking and sweating, and she gave a tiny nod of encouragement. The courtroom blurred, and as she stood in her too-big suit, trying to focus on the barrister at the front, Laura felt as if she was the one who was on trial for murder. After all, it should have been her.

Paul looked evil. He stared at her across the courtroom, creepy and sinister, as if he'd devour her given half a chance. Anjali had warned them that, if they did this, they'd better hope he got put away for a very long time, otherwise he'd likely kill them all. 'I mean it,' she'd said, wide-eyed, while they planned and plotted in whispers. 'He'll do anything. Anything.' She rubbed her face, her fingertips tracing the area around her eye where he'd last punched her. Laura wasn't sure if she was conscious of what she was doing, or simply had some sort of traumatic muscle memory. But in any case, it made her more determined. Olivia was right: this was their chance to put Paul in prison where he belonged. This wasn't about Laura saving herself; it was about rescuing Anjali.

She put her hand on the Bible and listened to the words from a film. That's what it felt like. Acting. Being inside a film. Smoke and mirrors. 'Do you promise to tell the truth, the whole truth and nothing but the truth, so help you God?'

She glanced up at Olivia. A fraction of a second. Her eyes couldn't help it, they moved independently of her brain telling them not to. Olivia gave her strength. Just the very sight of her. But every time Laura looked at her friend she thought of her betrayal.

'Please tell the court, in your own words, exactly what you saw the night of June sixteenth.' The barrister wore a standard wig, floaty gown, not unlike a theatre gown, and chunky gold earrings that weighed her earlobes down.

'I told you. I went to the party with everyone else. I was with Anjali all evening, and Olivia joined us later. We were having a good time until . . .' She looked at Paul but forced her eyes to look away.

'You say you saw the defendant dealing drugs?' The barrister's voice sounded bored. This was a clear-cut case, according to the police. Paul had been caught with drugs and charged with intent to supply, and a young man who'd taken those drugs was dead.

'Did you see the defendant selling or giving drugs to the victim at the party?'

A straightforward question, but the room became hot and sticky with the lie that was waiting to float away from her. Laura nodded.

'For the record, please.'

'Yes. Yes, I saw Paul sell Dean drugs. A bag of white powder. A large bag of white powder.'

'To your knowledge, had Dean ever taken drugs before this evening?'

'No. We were chatting – I mean, I didn't know him that well, but we were talking, and he said he was going to try crystal meth, PCP. He was drunk. Paul gave him the packet, took money and put it in his pocket, then followed Dean into the toilet. I saw Dean stagger out and that's when he collapsed.' Her voice was monotone and robotic. But nobody seemed to bat an eyelid in the court. The barrister sighed, the jury looked bored, Paul looked mad the whole way through, which clearly wasn't helping his case.

But Olivia stared at Laura as she spoke. As if she saw right through her.

THIRTY-FIVE

Anjali (2024)

Anjali pleaded and begged and howled and cried but there was no coming back from this, they both knew it. Eventually, after hours of crying, she lay curled up like a comma, next to Donna who was lying on her back, staring at one point of the ceiling, a patch of damp caused by an overflowing bath that they'd made love in, thrashing around with water sloshing over the sides. They would surely never make love again.

'I don't think you're clear. Are you sure?'

Anjali rolled onto her side. 'I was responsible for Dean's death and putting Paul in prison.' She waited for tears, but they didn't come. She felt entirely numb, her skin belonged to another person. 'I didn't know it then, I couldn't remember . . . But Olivia told me, in no uncertain terms . . . The only reason I let Laura take the stand was because I thought she'd done it. We pretty much had a choice between Paul going to prison, or Laura. That's what I thought anyway . . . All these years.'

'Paul hurt you . . . Dean was an accident. A total accident. It's not like you purposely drugged him.' She began to sob, crying enough tears for the both of them. 'But Olivia . . . I can't get over it. Why on earth would she let you and Laura believe it was Laura who gave Dean those drugs? And now

I feel like shit. Poor Laura. Fuck, what a mess.' She made a choking sound. 'Khadija. What about Khadija?'

Anjali looked away and didn't respond. She couldn't. Not yet.

'I had such a bad feeling about Laura. Thinking of her lying on the witness stand. I mean, I know she was protecting you. But something was off with her. And Olivia, come to think of it. I heard them both talking in whispers about a patient, and a party, and the police. Then when Miles mentioned Joe Duggard, the patient, I mean, I'd seen her hanging around ICU. One of my patients is there with neutropenic sepsis. I could tell she was lying. Something was off about her. Something.'

Anjali let Donna's words land on her skin and seep into her. It all made sense. Donna knew Laura had lied in court. Donna told Anjali how she'd agonised over disclosing that, but she also knew that Paul should be in prison. He needed to be in prison. So she was torn between the truth, and protecting Anjali. 'I had no idea at all that Laura thought it was *her* who'd caused Dean's death. What a thing to carry. *That's* why she was so strange, and skittish. I could smell the guilt on her. Eventually I decided to just live with it. Like Laura did, in the end, I guess . . . But the way her and Olivia were behaving, I kept thinking. It was almost an obsession. Do you remember the night we argued?'

Anjali nodded. Realisation filling her belly.

'I went for a run much earlier but found myself on a train to Beckenham. I ran to Laura's house. I wanted to confront her. To ask her what was going on. *Something* was clearly going on. Olivia and Laura, they've been slightly off for a month. Hiding something.'

Anjali groaned. 'Oh God.'

'I know. I'm so sorry. I couldn't do it in any case, and I just stared at her through the window. She and Rudy were arguing.

Rudy was sobbing, that kind of crying when something really terrible has happened. Wailing! It all sounded so dangerous, and it didn't make any sense. Then when I went back to ask her about it, Laura and Olivia were talking about ending a patient's life support . . . Laura was guilty of something. That's all I knew. She jumped whenever I saw her.'

Anjali sat upright. 'You *stalked* her? I mean, Donna . . .'

'I know. Well, it wasn't exactly stalking. I watched them and wanted to confront her but hid in the shed instead.'

'Well, you're a shit stalker,' said Anjali. But she didn't smile.

'She was twitchy. Jumpy. I could smell secrets and lies a mile off. I wanted to tell you then that Laura was hiding something about that patient. I felt it somehow linked to what you told me about Paul, and him going to prison, I just couldn't put my finger on it. And the adoption and everything happening. They'd sent Khadija's profile that day. So I just got Shar – you know we trained together? I asked Sharmaine to call if Laura turned up in intensive care. She was there a lot, Anj. A lot. By his bedside. I couldn't work out why. And after Miles asked us to check on him, that's when I saw her with my own eyes, next to Joe Duggard, at the hospital. Tampering . . .'

'It's a fucking mess.'

'I thought she was trying to kill a patient. Honestly. It was like a Netflix fucking series.' Donna was crying.

Anjali wanted to reach out and hold her. But her arms froze to her side.

'We were going to be a family,' Donna went on. 'I don't know who we are now. Who you are anymore. Who I am.'

Anjali held her. She stroked her hair and pressed Donna's face to her chest and kissed her forehead. 'I'm so sorry.'

'Someone died. It wasn't anyone's fault. He took the drugs himself. But an innocent man went to prison for ten fucking years, Anj. And maybe it is understandable, when Paul hurt you so badly. But that's not our call to make. And now it'll come out to the panel.' Donna was crying then. 'We won't get our baby girl now. She's not ours anymore.'

There were so many apologies, you could almost see them in the sky, in giant neon letters: SORRY. Anjali's mum always used the word differently, saying, 'Sorry' whenever a person tripped up or hurt themselves, often to be told: 'Don't worry, it's not your fault.' Invariably she would reply that where she grew up, sorry was not an admission of guilt, it meant *I am with you.* Anjali kept hearing herself saying the word sorry but she felt alone, totally at sea. It *was* her fault. Nobody was with her now. She'd carved out a life, a career, friendships and deep, deep love, and now it was all gone. Just like that, she was alone with nothing and nobody, and the ground beneath her had vanished.

The train to Beckenham Junction was thirteen minutes from Herne Hill, but it was another country entirely. The women of Herne Hill wore hand-knitted jumpers with holes in them and had serious money. The Beckenham women wore skyscraper heels and thick false eyelashes. Anjali hated Beckenham as much as Laura loved it. The porter questioned her at the gate, asking if she was expected, and Anjali felt the tiny hairs stand up on the back of her neck, alert to constant racism that was sometime so microaggressive it was barely detectable beyond a feeling. A creeping and crawling around in the pit of your stomach.

Laura answered the door before Anjali had rung the bell. The porter must have called ahead. She was thin, grey-eyed and dull-skinned. She looked as if she hadn't seen daylight for a long time. Anjali followed her in, and Laura closed the door behind her. They stood a foot apart before falling towards each other and hugging a long time. Neither of them cried, but they took big breaths and squeezed each other's backs, hands clamped on shoulders. Eventually Anjali pulled away and looked at Laura. 'I'm so sorry,' she said. 'I'm so sorry.'

They sat in the living room side by side on the giant sofa and were silent a few moments. Laura's face was expressionless, open and hard to read. Anjali didn't know where to start. It came out in a rush. The apology, the feelings she'd been having for so long that something wasn't quite right. 'It was the adoption process, I think. I started having flashbacks to the night of the party. Our party, I mean. Oh God, it could have been the history repeating itself thing . . . I don't know. What a fucking mess. I can't believe it.'

Laura put her head in her hands and opened her fingers around her eyes. She took bites of air. 'I thought Paul was following me. I've been so paranoid. I mean, seeing things, hearing things. Donna was in my shed? Why?'

'She knew something was off. She put two and two together and came up with ten and came to confront you, but when she got there you and Rudy were arguing, and that's when she overheard the name Joe Duggard. She thought you were tampering. Trying to kill him. I'm so fucking stupid I didn't put it together. I'm responsible for Dean's death. Me. I gave him the drugs and I let you take the blame. All these years you've carried the blame for my actions . . .' She pressed her teeth together.

'We don't know for sure. Olivia *saw* me,' said Laura. 'It wasn't you.' She shook her head so vigorously her earrings rattled. Small silver leaves. 'I was trying to keep Joe Duggard alive, not kill him. But I've done something even more terrible than accidentally killing someone, by keeping that poor kid alive. My patient is suffering because of me. Olivia just thought there was no other way, that we had to protect Freya and Rudy. I owed her so much, Anj, I didn't have a choice. We owe her . . .'

Anjali watched the silver of the earrings. Then she focused on Laura's eye. 'Olivia didn't see you.'

'We put a man in prison,' Laura said, not listening. 'I took the stand.'

They were silent a few minutes, as the weight of their actions thudded around the room. However you looked at it, they would likely lose their jobs. They both knew it. But couldn't speak it, Anjali suspected. Who would they be without medicine? Medicine was the spine that held them upright. It ran through their centre.

'Olivia said she didn't see you at all. I tried to tell you as soon as Olivia told me. I called and called. But Donna got to the police first. Anyway, I've told the police and I'll take the full rap for this. I'll go to prison if I have to. Honestly, I am taking this from you. It is my fault. Mine entirely.' Anjali shook her head. Slowly. A small sensation at the back of her brain became a dull ache. A heaviness inside her. She thought of Donna's face. 'But I don't know why Olivia would lie. It doesn't make sense. She said it was to protect me, by throwing you under the bus. But it doesn't add up. We wouldn't have even been in that much trouble if we'd told the truth. She got us – you – to lie. Why? It wasn't to put Paul away. That's not the whole truth.'

There was quiet a moment as the women stood looking at each other, an Olivia-shaped space next to them.

'Why would Olivia let me take the blame for something like that? To carry guilt of such a thing all these years? To make me think I was totally responsible for a man's death. To make me lie and put a man in prison. Why would she have me lie again now and cause such suffering for Joe Duggard. She keeps telling me it was Rudy, not Freya who pushed him. Surely she would never lie about that. No way. For what?'

Anjali shook her head. 'I don't know, it makes no sense. But I'm telling you, Olivia knew it was me at that party who gave Dean the drugs. She knew all along. Maybe she thought I'd get a long custodial sentence, or that Paul would kill me. Perhaps that was it. He was dangerous, Laura. Fucking dangerous. I explained everything at the police station. They'll open the investigation again. Back then . . .'

But Laura had closed her eyes and was whispering a single word. *Dele.*

THIRTY-SIX

Olivia (2000)

Olivia looked at herself in the long hallway mirror, piles of boxes already packed up behind her, lining the living-room walls. Graduation day. Moving day. This was their last day together, the three of them, though it felt like a beginning rather than an ending. Olivia couldn't wait to get the graduation gown off and replace it with a theatre gown, but it would be some time yet. She was a qualified doctor, but it would take many more years to become a surgeon, especially a cardiothoracic surgeon. She'd get there, though. She'd never felt more determined.

'We get to throw our hats in the air in precisely three hours.' Anjali's gown swamped her.

Olivia followed Anjali back into the living room, where Laura was biting slices of Sellotape and sticking them on the table edge in a neat row. 'I don't think we're allowed to,' Laura shouted. 'Apparently we're liable for hat damage.'

'You and the rule book . . .' Olivia tailed off, remembering that they'd broken the worst possible rules in life, all of them. Her, perhaps, the most. These moments of guilt kept sneaking up on her. Pressing down on her back, a heavy hand.

There was a small pause between them, thick air. They watched the dust dancing in the light. 'I love you,' said Laura. They laughed.

Olivia looked around their near-empty living room, a thousand memories sticking to the walls. The three of them moving in, the excitement of a blank page, the endless possibilities of their futures, as well as the traumas they'd lived through already. All of life they'd lived in just one year. She felt older and wiser but in a strange way, as though she'd been far away on a ship to a foreign place and was now coming home. Medicine was home. It would be home for them all. A place where they could live in the margins, in the in-between grey areas of life, where they embraced the line between life and death, right and wrong. She could see them twenty years from now, all having coffee and laughing, all accomplished in their chosen fields of medicine. It fascinated Olivia, the choices they were making for their careers and what drove those choices. Anjali had wanted to be a surgeon and was now planning a career in general practice, where she could help people who were suffering, ordinary people who had mental health problems and physical ailments and where the stakes were not too high, or scary. 'I want to help people who are falling apart, quietly. Like I had been. Until you both helped me.' It made sense. Anjali had a complete mental breakdown following Paul going to prison. It was as if her body had been bound together and was suddenly free and all the pain rushed through her. She was diagnosed with depression, but Olivia's money was on PTSD. Still, they all had a touch of that. What doctor didn't?

Laura was drawn to the emergency department and extremis, always needing to be busy and swallow up trauma. Perhaps working with other people's trauma helped them all forget about their own. Of course, that's what she needed to do. Altruism was a bullshit concept. The clue about the doctor was always contained in where they worked, what speciality they chose. Medicine was not only about the patients' needs; it was the doctor's need too. And of course, Olivia wanted to fix broken hearts.

The ceremony itself was long and arduous. The university had managed to get a semi-famous alumnus to give a speech, followed by a presentation from a Nobel Prize winner who had also attended City University Medical School. He advised the students to always go back to Hippocrates and Do No Harm. Never torture your patients, he said, and the recent graduates did not follow what he was saying. None of them had learned yet that medicine was knowing when to stop; it was not winning a race, but quitting a race at the right moment that mattered. Anjali, Laura and Olivia sat two rows back, and held hands all the way through the speeches. It felt so surreal that they had made it. At one point Olivia imagined they'd all lose this love of their life, the job, and couldn't comprehend what they'd do then. But somehow the days became weeks and weeks became months, and they got away with it. They escaped. Paul was where he belonged. Anjali was recovering. Laura paid penance for what she had done. Olivia was guilt-free. She steered the ship of their lives and friendship away from the icebergs that threatened to sink them. She had no regrets. She squeezed her best friends' hands tightly. 'Ouch,' said Anj, laughing.

'It's hard to know where you end, and I begin,' whispered Laura. 'My hand is entirely numb.'

Olivia knew where she began, though. She knew exactly who she was, and who she would be. Her future, now, was set in stone. Cardiothoracic surgeon. Safe, capable Olivia. She would save many lives. This was the beginning.

When it was their time to receive their handshakes from the faculty, and their MD certificates, which they'd no doubt frame and hang on the wall forever, they stood together and walked single file to the front, each footstep in time. Olivia went first, and she looked down at Dele in the family area, beaming from ear to ear, prouder than proud. It made her heart swell a fraction, and the ground felt steady and certain beneath her. She watched her parents, too. Her mum, straight-backed as ever, smiled as she clocked Dele beaming at Olivia. She gave Olivia a knowing nod, sharp enough to see from far away, and then lifted her dad's hand in hers. She waited in the wings as Anjali went next, taking a small bow to mild laughter. Nobody had thought she'd make it, least of all Anjali's poor parents who were standing at the side, each carrying a large camera, the pair of them crying giant tears visible from across the room.

Laura was last. Olivia watched her serious face as she walked across the stage. Her hat was too big for her. Her mother sat at the back of the hall, in a wheelchair, squinting in the distance. She was so relieved Laura had managed to graduate after losing her dad. Medicine was her family now too. At least she had that after the time she'd had. A lifelong love affair with saving lives. Olivia watched Laura earnestly shaking the hand of their tutor. She was the favourite, the most hard-working among them. She deserved this more than any of them. Olivia smiled at Laura and tried to catch her eye, to remind her they'd be friends forever, that Olivia and Anjali were her best friends always. They belonged to medicine. But they belonged to each other too.

But Laura's eyes were scanning the audience, and they settled on Dele's face. Dele beaming at Laura with a look of total pride. Olivia wanted to look away, but she couldn't.

They planned to celebrate afterwards with drinks in Gordon's Wine Bar, the main bar smelling of damp and mould and candlelight. All three of them had gone there on arrival at medical school and marvelled at how romantic and historic the place was, full of thick walls and nooks and crannies. They'd got so drunk there one night on a white wine that Olivia picked, a Riesling that was ten pounds a bottle and had thick legs that she'd shown them in the near darkness. 'Spidery thick legs on the side of the glass indicates a really good wine.' She held the glass up and looked at their faces through it. Anjali downed her wine like water, but Laura stared at the legs in her glass and squeezed Liv on the shoulder. Lovely Laura.

It was June and sunny. Gordon's had opened the outside area and put up marquee tents. On high tables balanced large buckets full of ice and white wine bottles. Family and friends of the medical school graduates were red-faced and flushed. Many of them had *a doctor in the family at last*. It was a journey for them too – not least a financial one, and any child with aspirations of medicine would bring their family along with them, listening to heartbreaking stories at 2 a.m. after a particularly difficult shift, coming home after first clinical rotation skinny and dead-eyed and causing parental worry about their mental health and ability to cope with such a job.

Olivia would not be that kind of doctor. She knew what the job was. It was part of her DNA, medicine. Before her dad, her grandad had been a surgeon, and his dad before him. Her earliest memories were hearing stories of a brutal time in medicine, pre-anaesthesia, when patients were encouraged to bite down on a piece of wood until they passed out from the pain. 'We did a pretty good job,' her grandad had told her. He was her favourite grandparent. Blunt-talking and stoic and no-nonsense. 'Medicine is a different country these days. Kindness, in my opinion, is overrated. What patients want is to be fixed by a doctor who knows their onions.'

Olivia's dad was possibly the proudest, certainly the loudest person at the bar. He wore a dark blue suit and jazzy tie and slapped everyone on the back while reciting Shakespeare. 'We know what we are but not what we may be.' He hugged Olivia so hard the breath was squeezed out of her. His nose was red from sun and alcohol, and she'd never seen his eyes look that glistening. Happy. Dele was chatting to some people he knew and floating around social butterfly style, champagne in hand. But her dad didn't leave her side. When Laura turned up late, he beamed at her. Olivia's mum was standing behind them in the shade, drinking a tonic water and complaining of a slight headache at the temples. She hated outdoor bars and said that Gordon's was tacky. 'Why don't we simply book Claridge's? I mean, if we can't have a decent vintage champagne at Claridge's on this occasion when can we?' But Olivia knew all her friends would be priced out, and even getting them to Gordon's had involved serious planning and a few hundred pounds behind the bar. 'Everyone is skint, Mum,' she said. Her mum tutted as though it was a sign of bad character to be poor.

Her dad picked Laura a few inches off the ground: 'Though she be but little, she is fierce.' Laura laughed and Olivia realised it was the first time she'd heard her laugh in a long time. Laura loved being around Olivia's dad. She became charming and girly whenever he was near, Liv noticed, as though it was as close to her own dad as she could get, and she needed to maximise the fatherly feeling. A pang of something twisted inside Olivia then, deep in her abdomen. She pushed it away.

'What kind of medicine is our Laura going to practise? I'll make a spot for you on the surgical head and neck team after your training years. You'd be a great asset. You don't want to be pilfering around with A&E. It's all human factors training these days. I'd get you on the difficult airway team, day one . . .'

Laura grinned. 'Ah, I know the training is really long. Which is a funny thing to say on graduation day! But I'd like to be a helicopter trauma doctor one day. I think I need some adrenaline . . .'

'Olivia never described you as an adrenaline junkie.' He swigged his wine. 'But there's nothing more satisfying than curing throat cancer. Reversing a temporary tracheostomy. Ripping a nasty cancer out of someone's face and giving it the heave-ho. Giving back someone's life but also their voice, and taste and ability to smile. Imagine that.'

Olivia closed her eyes a split second and thought about Laura's recent quiet voice, her loss of interest in all food, her lack of smile. She had done exactly the opposite of what her dad did. Instead of Do No Harm she had harmed.

'I don't think Laura has the aptitude for what you do.' Olivia's mum stepped off her stool and stood in front of Laura. For a fraction of a second Olivia wondered if she'd confront her about Dele. If she did that – if Laura ever knew that Olivia knew – she'd surely question the truth about Dean, and the party, and Paul being in prison. She'd question the lie upon lie upon lie. But she didn't confront her. She simply said, 'Good luck.'

THIRTY-SEVEN

Laura (2024)

Laura marched through the operating theatres, a labyrinth of corridors lined with equipment: autoclave machines, trays of surgical instruments, ventilators. The fire door was propped open with an oxygen cylinder, and her mind flashed back decades, to the first day she'd ever laid eyes on Olivia, during a fire safety lecture. Olivia had teased her about getting all the questions right and concentrating so hard when the instructor showed slides of dramatic hospital fires caused, often, he said, by fire doors being propped open with oxygen cylinders. Laura had been the sort of person who would have moved it back then. Conscientious. She carried on walking, no longer caring at all about danger. Her blood was so hot it felt like she was burning from the inside out. Lightbulbs flashed on in her head, one by one, electric revelations.

It was all Olivia. It always had been. Laura knew why. Everything made sense to her. Olivia had known about Dele all along. She had made Laura lie in court. Worse than all of that, though, was the present. Lying about Laura was one thing. Lying about Rudy, suggesting he had pushed Joe Duggard, was unforgivable. It was the cruellest thing she could ever imagine.

She glanced in the anaesthetic rooms and pushed open the doors to each theatre either side of the corridor. It was quiet.

It was Saturday and must be nearly midnight. Only the Olivias of this world would be at work. Laura knew she was on call; she had cancelled their Sunday lunch last minute as there was no cover. A few theatre nurses were checking kit and wiping down theatre trolleys with antiseptic wipes. That Olivia could manipulate her and lie to her was unforgivable, but she had loved Rudy like he was hers, she said. Like Laura loved Freya and Miles. Laura bit her tongue until she could taste metal. That she would lay Rudy out to dry, as well as Laura, tipped her over a psychological ledge.

Olivia was in theatre five, studying a scan with Frankie, her scrub nurse friend. The theatre was dark when she went in and Laura stood for a few moments, watching them chatting normally, Olivia excitedly pointing to the photograph of a person's insides. 'Totally unexpected,' she said, 'aortic mass.'

Laura switched on the overhead lights and the room was white and stark in seconds. 'You never can tell what is going on inside someone,' she said. Her voice was cold and metal, and her words bounced around the room.

Olivia turned slowly around and looked at Laura. She glanced at Frankie, who was already making his way to the door. 'I'll pop back later,' he said. He gently touched Laura's arm on the way out, and only then did she realise she was shaking.

They stood facing each other. It was clear from Olivia's silence that she knew something was very wrong. The light above them hummed. Laura watched Olivia's face and heard every word she'd ever said inside her head. *I saw you giving the drugs. You can save Anjali. You need to lie.*

'You fucking bitch.' Olivia stepped backwards.

Laura felt outside her own body, as if she was looking down on them both. Words flew through her that she had no control over. 'You sent a man to prison. You fucking ruined my life.

And Rudy? Blaming Rudy? How the fuck could you? That poor boy in ICU is suffering and you fucking know it – what, do you want the whole fucking world to suffer? Olivia, the safe pair of hands, the surgeon who fixes things? You have ruined my life. And almost destroyed Rudy's. You total and utter bitch.'

Olivia's face was red, and she sneered. She spoke in a quieter voice than usual, and slower. 'Oh you did a pretty good job of that yourself, Laura. You ruined your own life. I wasn't about to let you ruin Dele's too. You don't deserve him. You never did. You're at fault here, you. Sleeping with your best friend's fiancé? Despicable. Utterly despicable.'

Laura could barely see. Her eyes were blurred and gritty, and her fists clenched. She wanted to scream. The room melted away and it felt like they were in the middle of a fire, just her and Olivia, standing together burning. She had no control over her arms, her hands. They reached towards the theatre tray with equipment, and grabbed something, anything.

A scalpel.

Laura couldn't stop. Her head was full of Olivia's lies, and shock and sadness and grief. She ran at her and grabbed her by the scrub pocket, ripping it off, and with her other hand, Laura slid the scalpel straight into Olivia's abdomen.

There was a moment. A brief time where everything slowed down, and the room came into focus. Sharp focus. Olivia's eyes grew wider, and she and Laura both looked down, and Laura pulled the scalpel out of her, holding it, her hand and the blade soaked in blood.

THIRTY-EIGHT

Olivia (2024)

They had stood for so many moments, breathless and shocked, unable to move or talk. Olivia looked down at the blood. She felt no pain. Numb. Of course, she knew that meant nothing at all. In fact, the worst injuries or the deepest burns could sometimes mean damage to nerves. Pain was a language, telling you to do something. Its absence spoke volumes too.

Laura held her hands in front of her face and dropped the scalpel. It clattered on the floor. She looked at the blood, and her hands, and Olivia's face. Olivia expected her to cry. To scream and wail about how sorry she was. To rush her to A&E. But Laura stepped backwards, bent down, picked up the scalpel and walked over to the sink. She walked slowly and upright, like a different person.

Olivia pressed her stomach where she'd stabbed her. How bad was it? Everything flashed in front of her. Most of all Freya and Miles and Dele. Was it serious? 'Laura,' she managed. Her voice was clearer than she'd thought it would be. 'How could you?'

Laura dropped the scalpel into the yellow sharps bin at the side of the sink and started washing her hands. She said nothing. Olivia watched her shoulders, a fraction higher than usual, but she carried on calmly washing her hands, ignoring Olivia, ignoring the emergency in front of her.

'I'm fucking serious. Pull the red cord! You've stabbed me!' Liv looked down then and pulled her scrub top up, revealing a coin-sized cut above her hip bone, bleeding fairly heavily. 'You tried to kill me.' She staggered over to the operating table and sat on the trolley. 'Fuck.' Olivia scanned the room for the emergency cord, but everything was blurred. She felt sick and dizzy at once. Was she dying? 'You tried to kill me.'

Laura turned around. 'Don't be so dramatic,' she said. 'It's a surface wound.'

Olivia stared at her in disbelief. She tried to picture an anatomy class and work out how far the incision was from her spleen. She took her own pulse at her carotid artery. It was strong and steady. Still, no pain.

Laura started pulling things onto a silver tray with wheels: gloves, saline, Hibiscrub, suture kit, forceps. She pushed the trolley towards Olivia.

'You are fucking joking, right? Get me my phone. Oh, you'll go to prison for this. You'll go this time.' Olivia felt her temperature rise until her blood was surely bubbling inside her.

Laura calmly pulled up a chair and opened the sterile gloves, stretching them on one by one, then holding her hands in front of her as if she had indeed been arrested. 'Pull up your scrub top,' she said. Her voice was steady.

Olivia tried to sit up but almost fell backwards on the trolley. 'I'm going to report you. You'll lose your job. This time you'll lose your job. You're not fit to practise medicine.'

Laura simply stared and waited.

The pain arrived suddenly. A stabbing pain indeed. Olivia groaned and held her side. 'Owww.'

'Stop being so weak,' said Laura.

Olivia would have laughed if she could. Weak. Weak Laura, who was so easy to use and manipulate and mould into any shape was calling her weak? Olivia was the strongest of women, everyone knew it. They relied on it. But the pain was worse. The blood must be gushing. She lifted the scrub top. The cut looked deeper now, but it was not bleeding out. A thick groove. She knew enough about stab wounds to know it needed suturing and that she needed examining to see how bad the injury. Was it bad? Maybe it was a surface wound? 'Get my phone, you absolute snake.'

Laura lowered her hands. She took a breath. 'Olivia,' she said.

Olivia waited for her to call her a fucking bitch again. She waited for Laura to shout and uncharacteristically swear and scream that Olivia had taken her whole life from her. But Laura didn't say any of that.

'Liv, I'm sorry for what happened with Dele.'

The words moved between them. They almost echoed from the clinical operating theatre walls. Olivia closed her eyes. It was stinging. Sharp agony. But her head hurt too. She felt pain where Laura had stabbed her, but she felt pain everywhere. All her body seemed to be in pain.

'What you did all those years ago is totally unforgivable.' Her voice was eerily calm. 'But to lie that Rudy pushed that patient, to want to hurt my son all these years later? There is a special place in hell for you.'

Olivia had nothing to say. She had no control here. Not anymore. 'Lift your top up,' Laura said.

Olivia, shaking, slowly lifted the scrub top up, and held her breath as Laura leaned towards her, and slowly and carefully, she patched her up.

As she stitched her together, Laura looked straight at Olivia. 'I never loved Dele,' she said. 'It was a stupid, awful mistake. But I always loved you.'

'Laura . . .'

Laura shook her head. 'Don't ever come near me or Rudy again.'

THIRTY-NINE

Anjali (2024)

So much had happened since the visit to the police station. Paul was offered a retrial and compensation, but was nowhere to be found. Anjali wasn't surprised. When he'd first been released from prison the three of them had been on high alert, but that was well over a decade before, and he had never shown up, and if he was going to, surely he would have done by then. Olivia had wanted Anjali to get a restraining order against him when he'd been released, said that violent men were most dangerous when women regained their power. But after a few weeks of anxiety, and watching her back, Anjali began to relax. She *knew* Paul. If he was going after her he'd have done so immediately. He was the most impulsive person she'd ever met. She asked around and contacted the prison doctor, pretending to be his GP following up, and had been told Paul had addiction issues, developed in prison, and was likely 'not long for this earth'. Anjali had cried at that, tears of relief, but sadness too. He'd behaved like a monster. But he was human.

Still, Bola had kept her eyes peeled but said there was no sign of him at all. She phoned Anjali daily, telling her stories about the new GP, a locum with bad breath who drove a BMW. 'We miss you, Anj. Let the GMC investigate. It was so long ago.'

But Anjali took herself off the General Medical Council register. 'I'm not fit to practise,' she told the receptionist, who replied that there was a process, despite Anjali saying she was being investigated by the police for a historic case of death by misadventure and perverting the course of justice. It was impossible to get fired, it seemed, from medicine. But she had a call a week later from the practice manager to accept her resignation, and then it was done. She was no longer a GP. As easy as that. Her parents had not been as distraught or shocked as she'd imagined. Ever supportive, ever kind. Her mother had hugged Anjali so hard and didn't let go for an age. 'There's more to life than work. We always knew something terrible was happening around then. We always knew. It feels desperate now, I'm sure. But really, it's only a job. You'll be OK.' She let Anjali go and held her face between her hands. 'Daughter of mine,' she said, 'you never really enjoyed being a doctor. Dad thought it suited you, but I always had my doubts. It was not a good fit for you. Your character is not based on what you do, it is who you are.'

But for a few weeks Anjali didn't recognise herself. The foundations of her life: her friends, her work, the adoption, had crumbled away overnight. It was hard enough talking to her mum, and her employers. But there was an even more difficult conversation she had to have. Anjali didn't want Donna to have to suffer it. She waited until Donna was safely at work, then headed towards Lambeth Town Hall, where Emma and the rest of the Children and Families social workers were based.

'Emma Branken, please. Could you tell her it's urgent?' Anjali looked around at the waiting area. It was much like the one at the surgery, but on a bigger scale. Impoverished, stressed-out people were clock-watching. A man was vaping next to the *No Vaping* sign. The smells of urine and vomit competed.

The receptionist was more like a nightclub bouncer. She tapped on the computer without looking up. A security guard hovered by the entrance, watching a group of young, drunk men who were on the edge of kicking off.

'I'm afraid she doesn't have an appointment until . . .' she kept tapping, '. . . six weeks on Friday. Do you want me to book you in?' Finally, the receptionist glanced up. She had abnormally bulging eyes. Thyroid issue, most likely.

'Anjali, what are you doing here?' Emma walked past, carrying a tray of Krispy Kreme doughnuts. She turned to the receptionist. 'Elanor, I've got this, don't worry.'

Elanor shrugged then turned to the man waiting behind Anjali in the long queue.

'Want to follow me?' Emma handed Anjali her rucksack, and Anj followed her towards the lift. She pressed floor ten, and smiled at Anjali, chatting about how it was her manager's birthday and they always had cake, but Anjali barely heard a word. 'Wait, what's wrong?'

Anjali hadn't realised she was crying. It had already been a few weeks since the police station, and her quitting work, and the terrible truth getting out. But Emma didn't know any of this.

She reached out and held Anjali's hands in hers. 'Right, follow me and tell me everything.' Emma led Anjali out of the lift, shouting hellos at her team members, and Anjali followed her. They went into an office and Emma closed the door, put the doughnuts on the messy desk, then turned around and hugged Anjali. After a long hug, Anjali sat down opposite Emma, who had opened the box of doughnuts, gestured to them with her head, and reached for one herself, leaning back in her chair to listen.

Anjali ate two doughnuts in succession, then she told Emma everything.

*

Anjali was out in all weathers, but rainy days were her favourite. She let the wind and rain drench her until her skin goosebumped and her feet became wet through her shoes, and the air smelled different on different days, and the days they passed, one by one. Sometimes she worked alongside a group of late teen boys and tried not to imagine their faces as Dean, but it was difficult. They had the same eyes. Other days she was completely alone in her thoughts, listening to music and concentrating on nothing but picking rubbish off the ground, weeding, planting. She could breathe. There was no more confusion in her head. No more niggles at the base of her spine. Her body had been on high alert, she realised. Now it was fluid. She moved more easily. The knot inside her was gone. She felt light. Floaty. More like who she used to be before she met Paul. Before medicine. She felt young. After feeling old for such a long time, it was a curious backwards feeling. Like falling, but not unpleasant. Anjali was enjoying this part-time charity job more than she'd liked being a GP, so it seemed her mum had been right all along. Her wonderful, understanding, lovely mum who supported her even now, even when she had been a giant dickhead. The police also offered her support for domestic violence, despite it having happened all those years ago. 'We carry trauma,' the police officer said. 'I don't need to tell you that. Of course, there may be a retrial, but, unofficially, I doubt you're in any trouble here . . .'

Anjali couldn't believe it. The weight of what they had always carried. The horror of it. Everything seemed smaller out in the open.

'What's on the agenda today?' Donna was carrying two flasks and walking towards her in a thick coat. She handed Anjali one, and they sat down in the stairwell.

Anjali gestured to the side of the wall where someone had spray-painted *wanker* over the sign that said *No Ball Games*. It was a typical estate in Loughborough Junction. Half the building had incredible street art; a giant painting of Muhammad Ali dominated the building at the front. At the back was the murkier art, and some choice words. 'At least it's spelled correctly. We have a load of service users from the Maudsley coming to transform this space.' Anjali grinned. She was enjoying this job. A charity to help people with mental health struggles by social prescribing – in this instance, gardening. Anjali found herself able to help people in a different way to medicine. A different kind of medicine. A more effective kind, perhaps, for many people.

They sat side by side drinking hot chocolate that Donna had laced with cinnamon and chocolate sprinkles. Typical Donna. Small acts of love. That Donna had kept secrets from Anjali no longer felt enormous. She'd kept secrets too, even from herself. This new space they found themselves in was not giddy or at all passionate. It was a boring, hard, messy grind towards understanding. Yet it felt so real, so beautiful. This bad stuff was the good stuff. The forever layer. She leaned against Donna's coat and put her head on Donna's shoulder. 'You smell of chemotherapy.'

'Clinic today. There was this couple. A woman with breast cancer, palliative chemo, but still she wanted to cold cap. Her husband sat beside her and read to her. All day. A Danielle Steel book.'

Anjali laughed. 'During my final days, pick a better novel.'

'It was so perfect, Anj. They are facing this enormous thing together. He looked at her like she was the most beautiful woman in the world, despite the steroid bloat and wispy hair.' She leaned down and kissed Anjali softly on the lips.

A feather kiss. 'You're the most beautiful woman in the world, to me.'

'Even now?' Anjali sat up and looked at Donna's face, her freckles, the scrunch above her nose, her eyes.

'Weirdly,' she said, 'especially now.'

Her words made no sense at all. Her words made perfect sense.

It had taken a long time to get to where they were, since the truth all came out that had threatened to destroy them, since Anjali had left her job, and gone to see Emma to tell her that they could no longer be considered as parents for Khadija, and why. She had felt such shame. Emma had listened a long time, then asked Anjali a few questions. 'So, you took drugs decades ago, in your early twenties, with this young man Dean, and he reacted badly and overdosed? And a man who was abusing you also gave him drugs, and he was sent to prison?'

Anjali had nodded. She felt dreadful. She had never liked Emma that much, and yet found herself held by her. She had been wrong about Emma too.

'But the man sent to prison *was* involved, surely? I mean, as much as any of you . . . Sounds like he had it coming.'

Anjali closed her eyes and listened to Emma's words. She'd never thought about it in those terms. The words out loud did not sound as dreadful as they did in Anjali's heart. 'I accidentally killed a man,' she said.

Emma shook her head. 'No. No you didn't. You didn't spike his drink. He took the drugs himself, no?'

The matching panel was delayed a month while the social work team reassessed Anjali and Donna in light of all the new information. 'There is a lot of unresolved trauma,' Emma had warned them, 'which will be the biggest issue. Hiding things from your past is never a good look for the matching panel.'

Both Donna and Anjali had resigned themselves to rejection. They had hope, though, that in the future they could go through the process and start again. A glimmer of long-term hope. But of course, Khadija would go to another family.

'Shall we have teriyaki salmon for dinner? I've got a new green bean recipe. Green beans, oranges, hazelnuts. It's Ottolenghi. Delish.' Donna threaded her arm through Anjali's.

'Sounds amazing. One of these days you'll let me cook.'

They walked arm in arm towards Brixton, and the small nursery in St Jude's Church. The sound greeted them before they arrived, children playing and laughing. Trikes. Zooming sounds. A group of children in a hall singing 'Twinkle Twinkle'.

A few parents were standing outside, holding snacks and scooters. They greeted Donna and Anjali, chatting about the warm sunshine and terrible twos.

The doors opened and the nursery nurse stood with a clipboard, peering out at the families beyond the gate. One by one the children came out, holding lunch boxes and large paintings, talking excitedly as they walked towards whoever was collecting them.

Khadija appeared in the doorway carrying a large pink soft toy bunny rabbit and a certificate with a medal around her neck. She waved frantically at Donna and then noticed Anjali. She hadn't been expecting her. The nursery teacher didn't have time to do her mac up, she was off, running towards the gate, limbs flying outwards. 'Mummy, Mumma, I'm star of the week. I get Fraggle for the weekend, star of the week, look, look!'

Anjali's heart swelled up every time she saw Khadija. To their amazement the matching panel said yes, with a few stipulations. They said that, on reflection, having gone through trauma themselves and resolved it, Anjali and Donna would be all the better as parents for Khadija.

She squeezed Donna's hand as they watched her running out of the gate towards them. Theirs. Their daughter forever. A family. Anjali dropped to a crouch and hovered at Khadija's level as she hugged her, all the while talking excitedly.

Donna extricated the rabbit and held the certificate in the air. 'Oh my goodness, what a superstar you are. Look, Mummy, look at this.'

Anjali could see Donna waving the certificate around from the corner of her eye, but she looked straight at Khadija and kissed her face all over, then lifted her up in her arms. When she put her back on the ground, she noticed Khadija's shoes were on the wrong feet. Perfect.

FORTY

Laura (2024)

It was pouring with rain and Laura was about to deliver a DC shock, sending a fair whack of electricity into the man. One of her colleagues had received a significant head injury once, after being thrown across the room by a small explosion caused by mixing a defibrillator with high-flow oxygen. She stuck the pads firmly onto his chest, then nodded at Ravinder to carry on chest compressions. Rav was getting better, more of an asset less of a fainter these days.

'Get these people away.' A crowd was gathering at the roadside, a few people trying to film on phones. Juan pushed them back. Laura charged up the defib. 'Charging. Stand clear.'

Rav jumped up and away, and Laura pressed the button, hoping that the circuit wasn't wet. Water and electricity was as much of a bad mix as oxygen and electricity. The man, a slim man in his twenties, jolted a few inches off the road, then collapsed. 'Back on the chest.'

Rav started CPR again, leaning over with his arms straight, counting out loud. 'Want me to take over?'

He shook his head. 'I'm good.'

After two minutes, they did a three-point pulse check: two femoral and one carotid, pressing gently to assess for signs of life. 'He has a pulse.' Laura let go and looked up at Juan. 'Trolley.'

They strapped him onto the trolley and began the walk to the air ambulance. They'd landed in Hyde Park, a short distance from the road, but long enough that he might arrest again on the way there. Laura kept her fingers on his neck while they walked, to make sure his pulse remained. It was weak and thready, but present. Rav delivered a breath every six seconds, via an IGEL that he'd inserted into the man's trachea.

'He's young. What's your thinking?' He looked at Laura for answers. They all did. She was the most experienced doctor on the team. There had been a moment where she thought she would lose her job. It seemed inevitable. She'd gone to a panel at the GMC, and then an internal investigation into her conduct on the Ethics Committee meant all her colleagues were interviewed about the care of Joe Duggard. Laura expected Peter to spell out for them the near miss, the harm she'd caused with her manipulation of the decision-making process. But the team had unanimously backed her, highlighting that there was no right or wrong in discussions about treatment, and it was a whole team endeavour. There was no ongoing investigation into her conduct. The hospital concluded that Joe Duggard was treated appropriately and ethically, and in accordance with the hospital guidelines, and the GMC concluded that Laura giving false testimony decades before had no bearing on her current career. Even the police were uninterested in Laura. Anjali left medicine, willingly. That seemed to satisfy them. Joe Duggard remained stable on intensive care. Laura quit the Ethics Committee and withdrew from any decision-making about his care. She felt sick about her involvement in his case, and the possibility that she'd kept him alive when he should have died. She told the hospital managers, the GMC, the police that she had made the wrong decisions for Joe, and she'd made a terrible mistake. Laura's actions were disclosed to the family, and they were asked their wishes, but they didn't want Laura to be punished. If anything, Joe Duggard's family were grateful to her. Of course, she did not discuss the driver of her decision-making. The thing at the heart of medicine wasn't the diagnosis, or treatment. It was the decisions made by doctors, who got to make those decisions, and what influenced that. Freya and Rudy would have to live with a lie, and that was punishment enough. Laura knew it.

'Let's get the drugs in him.' Rav strapped the patient into the air ambulance and pulled out the small cardboard trays of pre-made drugs.

Laura put an IV line in, a miracle given his circulatory collapse, but she was a miracle worker with these things. She pushed the medications into his vein, putting him into a medical coma. It was a space where they had complete control over his body, giving him the most chance of survival.

Rav rooted around in his rucksack, as Laura rang ahead. 'He'll need ECMO, I think. Pre-warning.'

'Josh Claire. He's twenty-four.' Rav switched on his phone and opened one of Josh's eyes to hold the phone over. 'Thank God for tech.' He sat down and turned away, ready to make the worst phone calls they all dreaded.

Laura stood up, and then walked to the chair at the bottom of the trolley, strapping herself in. She glanced at the patient's monitors, all the numbers stable. They'd get him in, at least. There was very little history or information other than that he was riding a bike and collapsed in the road with a cardiac arrest. He'd probably have an undiagnosed congenital issue and end up in theatres. Maybe Olivia would be there, waiting?

Laura looked out the window as the helicopter rose higher and higher. Olivia. Her entire life had been controlled by Olivia. It was incredible how she could only see that now.

Perhaps she should have been with Dele? Who could say. Maybe Owen was a rebound, the polar opposite of Dele. But if she hadn't met Owen, she'd never have had Rudy. In any case, no man would put up with the hours she worked. She worked double what Olivia did, and that was saying something. She had married her work, like a medical nun. Laura didn't mind that. She listened to the chugging blades, the hum of the engine, smelled the metallic rubber. This was home. She was where she was meant to be. Olivia had not taken that from her, at least.

They sloped off to the hospital canteen after stabilising the patient and handing over. It was early morning and there was a queue of people, hungover doctors mostly, waiting for a fry-up. Rav and Laura jumped the queue and grabbed some toast. Rav pocketed a dozen miniature Marmite sachets and margarines, and they walked back to the staffroom, kicking their shoes off and sitting down at last. 'Knackered,' Rav said, handing Laura a cup of tea.

'Cheers, Maverick.' She took out her phone.

Rav started opening the Marmite and buttering some toast. 'Is that your son? How's he doing?'

Laura grinned. Swigged her crappy NHS tea. She thought of Rudy's face. He had thrown himself into school work and planning his future. He avoided Freya, and even Miles, which must have broken his heart, but he was looking ahead. 'I want to study medicine,' he said. Neither of them spoke of motivation, or the possibility of Rudy wanting to save patients like Joe Duggard. But Laura was coming to realise that for some doctors, medicine was a lifelong penance. It was not the worst solution to tragedy. 'Rudy's good. But actually . . .' She turned the phone around to show him. 'It's Flame.'

He laughed. 'When will you come on a date with me?'

'When hell freezes over.'

The bleep flashed in her scrub pocket, and she lifted it out. 'Look lively.'

Rav rolled his eyes and ate a huge bite of toast, then chucked the rest in the bin.

The bleep went again. 'Adult major trauma call. Adult major trauma.' She pushed the door open, and Rav followed her. They walked through the hospital corridors, past the chlorine smell of the hydrotherapy pool, the linen room where Magic FM belted out day and night. They weaved their way through the bowels of the hospital, the secret tunnels lined with rat traps and fag ends and broken pieces of kit. The quick way. Eventually they climbed the stairs by the psychiatry offices, and the ophthalmology unit, where Laura ran up two at a time. Rav couldn't keep up. She slowed down a bit outside the palliative radiotherapy unit, where patients leaned against the walls, unable to stand unsupported, waiting for their turn.

The bleep again. 'Adult major trauma call.' Laura responded again. 'Adult trauma en route.' She walked fast, almost running, but outside pharmacy, she suddenly stopped dead in her tracks.

Olivia.

She was coming in the other direction, also walking quickly. They stood at either end of the corridor staring. Laura glanced down to Olivia's waist, the place she'd stabbed her. Olivia never had reported her.

Laura took a breath, and walked ahead, and pushed past Liv as if she was a stranger. 'Laura,' she heard the desperation in Olivia's voice. It didn't sound like her at all. She walked on anyway, as if Olivia was totally invisible.

FORTY-ONE

Olivia (2024)

Olivia weaved her way through the dark corridors, her theatre cape billowing out behind her, as though she was a magician. The smell was reassuringly familiar, a mix of near-death and cleaning products, a warm safe smell that reminded her of the Milton tablets she'd used to clean Freya's baby bottles. She'd spent her life protecting Freya from harm, that's what all parents did, or should do, the primal protective response of a mother. The pull of that emotion overwhelmed her; as strong as love, it was animalistic. She'd kill for her children. That didn't make her a bad person. It made her a good mother.

She opened the doors to leave the cool dark theatre area and walked through recovery, always chaos, brightly lit and a hive of intense activity. The recently operated-on patients lined up, nurses by each bedspace fiddling with breathing tubes, and talking in loud voices. There was a sign over the nurses' station: *Speak in English*, which seemed redundant when all the patients were semi-conscious and unlikely to recall anything, other than perhaps a dream set in the Philippines, where pretty much every nurse originated from. Olivia loved working with nurses from the Philippines. They were the best nurses she ever worked with, hard-working and knowledgeable, but always kind. Not so some of the British scrub nurses she had come across, who tended to be either brilliant or total shit and nothing in between. She nodded at Gloria, who was shouting 'Mr Ransten' at an elderly man flailing his arms around trying to pull out his endotracheal tube. 'Mr Ransten,' she said. 'You are safe, and the operation went well . . .' Safe. That's what this job was. Safety. Keeping people safe. Her thinking had evolved again. Transparency and integrity were the real skills of surgery, as well as a sharp mind and nimble fingers, but a safe pair of hands trumped all of it.

At the end of recovery, a thin curtain then the hospital main corridor, the atrium, the walls lined with commissioned art that was designed to be cheerful and calming, and the lifts, always bursting full. The third floor was the paediatric intensive care unit, where her patient, at eighteen, was waiting. Louise was officially an adult but there was no bed, and there was a heart, which she so desperately needed. The atmosphere in the ward was different again, the hospital departments and wards each with their own subculture. Olivia breathed it all in, the smell of marzipan, the squeak of the floor, the feeling that landed on her skin of hope, and of desperation. There was an atmosphere that stayed in the air long after conversations had ended, as if the air itself remembered. As if words echoed forever and bounced off the walls, conversations families had with doctors about their loved ones. If theatres were a place of answers, then this ward was one of questions: *How long will the operation take? Will he wake up straight away? What are her chances?*

'It's me, Olivia. Can I come in?' She poked her head around the thick door, and walked towards Louise, who was lying frail and grey, with oxygen prongs in her nostrils. She held a large white teddy bear, and her room was covered in cards and balloons. It was the room of a much younger child. She sat carefully on the edge of Louise's bed. She was holding a salmon pink sponge to her dry, almost translucent lips. Nil by mouth. As she smiled, the small cracks disappeared. But there were tears dripping from her eyelashes as she smiled. 'I'm one of the surgeons who will be helping with the operation today and I thought I'd come say hello and see how you're doing.' Olivia touched the teddy bear. 'My daughter has a bear like this. She named it Slay.'

Louise grinned. 'Good name. This is Cuddles. I named her when I was around four.' She gulped. Terrified.

Olivia stood and rustled around for the notes at the end of Louise's bed, finding an X-ray and pulling it out. She went back to the bed and sat on the edge. Louise shuffled over a fraction. Even shuffling across a bed Olivia could see how weak she was, how slow her movements. She glanced at her coat-hanger collarbone, her twig-arms. Louise's head looked alien-sized, too big for the rest of her. Bodies died at different speeds. She thought of the man in intensive care who was dying in the opposite direction, brain dead and body functioning, kept alive of sorts until they could harvest what they needed. Corneas for an elderly man who was blind; kidneys in two different directions, one for a child on dialysis, another for a grandmother who had suffered a fall from a ladder onto concrete and smashed her insides up; his liver would end up in a recovering alcoholic, most likely, and his skin transplanted to a patient in the burns unit. His heart, though, would go to Louise. Olivia held up the X-ray. 'Cardiomyopathy means your heart is bigger than it should be. Can you see? It is taking up all the room inside your chest. Sometimes when hearts are this big, they don't work properly, which is why you've been so ill.'

Louise studied the image of her insides. 'My heart is too big.'

'Your heart is too big. Some people have hearts that are simply too big . . .' She blinked and Laura was there behind her eyelids.

'I don't feel like I have a big heart,' she said. 'I can be pretty annoying.'

Olivia laughed. 'Well, we have evidence.' She put the X-ray down and let her hand rest on top of Louise's hand. 'This will make you well again. But I know it's very scary.'

Louise nodded. She looked at Olivia as if she was trying to figure her out.

'Do you have any questions for me?' Olivia imagined what Louise might ask, but she never could predict what went on in people's heads. Once she was asked if she'd go on a date with the patient, after he'd recovered.

'I wondered if I'll change,' she whispered. 'Maybe if I have a different heart, I'll become a different person.'

'I doubt that. People don't really change. You'll still be you, but with much more energy.'

'I don't worry that he might be a murderer or anything like that – my brother was worried about that. But I'm guessing murderers' hearts are pretty rare! But what if he was a bad person. Someone who was not kind. A liar or, worse, a man who was evil. Would I become bad? If this man's heart is cruel and mean, then what happens to me?'

Olivia took a deep breath. She forced herself not to blink in case Laura lit up inside her. 'I honestly don't think it works like that. I've done a lot of heart operations, and nobody has ever changed personality afterwards.' She smiled, and Louise smiled back. It was an intense relationship, one built quickly yet profoundly, between surgeon and patient. Life and death danced between them.

'I don't want a cruel heart,' said Louise. 'I'd rather die than that.'

Olivia looked away.

*

It was brightly lit in the theatres, but one of the overhead lights was flickering. Olivia looked through the thick glass at her theatre. It was home. More familiar even than her bedroom. The nurses, perfusionists and junior doctors were pottering around, setting up kit, checking and double-checking. She watched them all in their pale blue scrubs, perfectly choreographed movements. It was better than watching Rambert at Sadler's Wells. Before scrubbing in, Olivia glanced at the clock and took out her phone. She first texted Freya who was home unwell. She was often sick these days, and spent much time alone scrolling on social media, her eyes baggy, dark and haunted. She'd be OK though. Olivia would boost her up. Get her through it. The important thing was to pull together, and bury anything unwanted underneath the floorboards where it belonged. *There's a cherry pie for you in the fridge. Filo pastry. I'll come say goodnight later, darling.*

Still, it was hard to bury everything. Joe Duggard remained a messy secret that the children would need to keep forever. Freya's response was appropriate. Rudy, on the other hand, had seemingly thrown himself into study and tutoring. 'He's going to study medicine,' Freya told Liv. 'To help people like Joe . . .' Olivia thought of her dad's pride the day she'd graduated. She looked at Dele watching Freya shrink and shrink. She thought of the drugs that Rudy had given their precious daughter. Rudy would not come out of this on top. Olivia wouldn't let him.

She couldn't take Laura's identity, after all. *But she could take Rudy's . . .*

Laura and Anjali had blocked her. It did not seem possible that their friendship would fall apart after decades. But she knew they'd never forgive her. Anjali's life had been ripped apart, and she'd lost her job, nearly lost Donna too. Thinking of them gave Olivia stomach cramps. Anjali hadn't been so angry about the job. She had never really liked it. Not for years, anyway. But once you're in medicine, it's incredibly difficult to leave, like the mafia. They needed someone to blame. Of course, Olivia knew that deep down it wasn't her fault. Laura was the one who had committed the crime.

She had slept with her best friend's fiancé. She made him fall in love with her, even if she insisted she'd never loved him. Everything that happened afterwards was a result of Laura's actions. Surely one day they would all see that. She put the phone away and took a deep breath. Dele would see that too. He would never leave them, could never leave their children. Olivia knew that in her centre. Dele was hers, forever, no matter what her friends thought or did. It would all be fine. Of course he knew now, that Laura had stabbed her. 'She was ready to kill me. Psychopath,' she whispered. She had spoken quietly and touched the small scar on her lower abdomen where Laura had pressed the blade deep enough to leave a silver line, but not deep enough to do serious damage. Laura was an expert in stabbings, she'd always said. Her *Mastermind* subject.

'She tried to kill me,' she told Dele. 'She had this look in her eyes, demented and dangerous.' Dele was more and more quiet and withdrawn. But he was still there. Their marriage was unbreakable.

He'd suggested the police or reporting her at least to the GMC. Olivia had shaken her head. 'Everyone in this world does bad things or stupid things that sometimes have catastrophic consequences,' she'd told Dele. 'These are the human factors. We are only human.' He listened carefully. Olivia could tell he thought that she was talking about Laura.

*

Heart surgery was incredibly noisy at first. It reminded Liv of the sound of road diggers where men wearing high-vis jackets stood around a thumping machine, wearing ear protectors. She was working with a team today: a transplant surgeon, another cardiothoracic surgeon and anaesthetists, as well as the scrub nurses. A transplant took a village. The saw made a piercing sound. Cracking a chest was like breaking tarmac open. Sternums were thick bone. To perform a sternotomy meant to cut through the thickest part of a human, the centre, to get to the core. Olivia pressed the electric saw down onto Louise's chest, as the screech filled the room. It sounded a bit like a faraway, long-ago scream, unnatural and shocking. Once the bone was cut into two, the spreading of ribs meant getting her hands dirty. She'd double-gloved as usual, but within seconds the white latex was bright red, the colour of the MAC Christmas lipstick range. The fiddling to disconnect vessels and arteries, the clamping and unclamping and careful cutting with a tiny scalpel the most delicate of all tasks. Olivia became dream-like with concentration. They all did. The surgeons were in a trance, all working together and listening to the instructions of the transplant surgeon who, in this case, was leading the operation. Time was nothing here. Hours shrank into minutes, into seconds. Once Louise was hooked up to bypass, and everything disconnected from her centre, the room changed colour. The quiet arrived. Reverence, of sorts, for the enormity of what her human hands were doing.

You could hear a pin drop. There was no music. The only sound Olivia could hear was the thump of her own heart as she heard the transplant surgeon say, 'Free to lift now,' and she lifted out Louise's heart, slowly and carefully. It was heavy and soggy and maroon, almost placenta like, and it was perfectly still. She stood a few moments, holding the weight of it, of all of it. Memories lit up in her own chest, firefly flashes. She thought of the first night she ever saw Dele, and watched him laughing with Laura, and reminded herself that two magnets placed side by side eventually pointed in opposite directions. She thought of the night they were engaged, when Dele told her that human heart cells beat in time if you left them long enough. Olivia's head was full of Dele memories, and flashes of confession, giving birth, her mother's voice, Laura and Anjali. She was a vessel for all of it, full of blood and bones and flesh and stories. Light, dark, cruelty and hope. The stuff we are made of. Deep breaths and focus. Faith. Her hands were steady and sure, her core was steel. Olivia lifted the young heart up to the light, until it was level with her own. She was a mum, a daughter, a friend. She was a wife to Dele. This was who she was. But most of all, she was a surgeon. A cardiothoracic surgeon. A human heart in her capable hands.

Acknowledgements

Heartfelt thanks to: My editor, Katie Espiner, and team at W&N and Orion. Alice Hoskyns and all at C&W, and Camilla Young at Curtis Brown. Gráinne Fox, United Talent Agency, and Millicent Bennett and Liz Velez and HarperCollins US.

My very first readers: Kate Bowler, John Sutherland, Nikki Smith, Elizabeth Day, Sarah Langford, Nathan Filer, Emma Jane Unsworth.

Finally, as ever, the biggest of thanks goes to my brilliant agent, Sophie Lambert. I feel so lucky to work with you, and even luckier to call you my friend. I am truly grateful.

Credits

Weidenfeld and Nicolson would like to thank everyone at Orion who worked on the publication of *Moral Injuries*.

Agent
Sophie Lambert

Editor
Katie Espiner

Editorial Management
Georgia Goodall
Sophie Nevrkla
Jane Hughes
Charlie Panayiotou
Lucy Bilton
Claire Boyle

Copy-editor
Anne O'Brien

Proofreader
Amber Burlinson

Audio
Paul Stark
Jake Alderson
Georgina Cutler

Contracts
Dan Herron
Ellie Bowker
Alyx Hurst

Design
Nick Shah
Steve Marking
Joanna Ridley
Helen Ewing

Photo Shoots & Image Research
Natalie Dawkins

Finance
Nick Gibson
Jasdip Nandra
Sue Baker
Tom Costello

Inventory
Jo Jacobs
Dan Stevens

Production
Francesca Sironi
Katie Horrocks

Marketing
Cait Davies
Lynsey Sutherland
Jen Hope

Publicity
Virginia Woolstencroft

Sales
Jen Wilson
Victoria Laws
Esther Waters
Tolu Ayo-Ajala
Group Sales teams
    across Digital, Field,
    International and
    Non-Trade

Operations
Group Sales Operations team

Rights
Rebecca Folland
Tara Hiatt
Ben Fowler
Alice Cottrell
Ruth Blakemore
Ayesha Kinley
Marie Henckel